THE BEST FROM

Fantasy &

Science Fiction

THE BEST FROM

Fantasy &
Science Fiction

THE FIFTIETH ANNIVERSARY ANTHOLOGY

Edited by EDWARD L. FERMAN
and GORDON VAN GELDER

TOR®

A TOM DOHERTY ASSOCIATES BOOK
NEW YORK

THE BEST FROM *FANTASY & SCIENCE FICTION:*
THE FIFTIETH ANNIVERSARY ANTHOLOGY

Copyright © 1999 by Mercury Press

This book is printed on acid-free paper.

Book design by Victoria Kuskowski

A Tor Book
Published by Tom Doherty Associates, LLC
175 Fifth Avenue
New York, NY 10010

www.tor.com

Fantasy & Science Fiction Web site: www.sfsite.com/fsf/

Tor® is a registered trademark of Tom Doherty Associates, LLC.

Library of Congress Cataloging-in-Publication Data

   The best from fantasy & science fiction : the fiftieth anniversary
anthology / edited by Edward L. Ferman and Gordon Van Gelder.
     p. cm.
   "A Tom Doherty Associates book"
   ISBN 0-312-86973-8 (hc)
   ISBN 0-312-86974-6 (pbk)
   1. Fantasy fiction, American. 2. Science fiction, American. I. Ferman,
Edward L. II. Van Gelder, Gordon. III. Title: Best from fantasy and
science fiction.
PS648.F3B475 1999
813'. 087608—dc21   99-40560
                                                                      CIP

First Hardcover Edition: October 1999
First Trade Paperback Edition: September 2000

Printed in the United States of America

0 9 8 7 6 5 4 3 2 1

Copyright Acknowledgments

FOR AUDREY FERMAN, AND IN MEMORY OF JUDITH MERRIL

Contents

THE BEST FROM

Fantasy &
Science Fiction

Introduction

FIFTY YEARS! GOSH, IT SEEMS LIKE ONLY LAST WEEK I WAS SITTING around with Tony and Mick, discussing various stories and deciding whether to add the words "Science Fiction" to the magazine's title.

Well . . . actually no. The truth of the matter is that my parents were college undergraduates when *F&SF* was founded and didn't even meet until thirteen years later. By the time I was born, *F&SF* had its sixth editor at the helm.

I became the magazine's eighth editor in the beginning of 1997. At the time, I likened the experience to becoming manager of the New York Yankees. There's such a strong sense of history, even dynasty, to this magazine that I still feel some days as if Anthony Boucher or Avram Davidson is sitting in my office, making suggestions for the month's lineup and whether to let one of the sluggers swing away or try a hit and run. (In this analogy, it should be noted that Boss Ed has nothing but longevity in common with Boss George.)

I tend to listen closely to any advice I can find from the past editors, be it in old issues of the magazine, in past volumes of this anthology series, or the suggestions Kristine Kathryn Rusch makes now and then. (Kris, it should be noted, originally acquired most of the stories in this collection, and I'm grateful to her for making my job of keeping this book to a manageable length so difficult.) It seems to me that the editor's fundamental role at *F&SF* has changed very little in the past half century: Each month we strive to bring readers the best examples of fantastic literature. The editor's job is to find those stories and make them as good as possible.

That prescription is deceptively simple. Time was (around fifty years ago) that the notion of publishing SF and fantasy in one magazine seemed radical—and then emphasizing literary quality probably sounded like a recipe for creating one more unsuccessful magazine.

But the formula (or rather, the lack of a formula) has proved to be farsighted on the part of those good folks at Mercury Press back then. Because while trends in popular fiction come and go with the seasons (this decade's serial killer craze, for instance, seems to have abated), the interest in a good fantasy story, told well, seems to have run steadily throughout the history of narrative fiction, starting with Homer and entering English with *Beowulf.*

This book, then, collects many of the best fantasies we've published in the past five years. They range from speculative SF stories to fairy tales, from alternate histories to supernatural horror tales, and we couldn't resist throwing in one of Paul Di Filippo's farcical "Plumage from Pegasus" columns for good measure. Very little links them all—just that they all have some element of the unreal and they're all very good reading in our opinions. We think that's enough.

We discussed assembling a big historical anthology representing the magazine's whole five-decade span, but ultimately we felt that (a) too many of the magazine's greatest stories are anthologized widely already and (b) there are too many excellent uncollected stories since the last "Best of" anthology five years ago. (As it is, of course, we had to omit many favorites for lack of space.) Personally, I think the stories here are as interesting and as entertaining as anything the magazine has published in the course of its history, and I believe things are only getting better. If you'll allow me one speculative fantasy, I like to think that when our Hundredth Anniversary anthology comes out in 2049, people will look back on this period in the magazine's history and say, "They were giants standing on the shoulders of giants back then."

—Gordon Van Gelder

Last Summer at Mars Hill

ELIZABETH HAND

*Liz Hand lives with her two children on the coast of Maine.
She is the author of six novels, including* Waking the Moon,
Glimmering *and, most recently,* Black Light. *Her
infrequent stories, like her novels, tend to be lyrical, character-
driven human dramas—which is just our sort of tale.*

EVEN BEFORE THEY LEFT HOME, MOONY KNEW HER MOTHER
wouldn't return from Mars Hill that year. Jason had called her
from his father's house in San Francisco—

"I had a dream about you last night," he'd said, his voice
cracking the way it did when he was excited. "We were at Mars
Hill, and my father was there, and my mother, too—I knew it was
a dream, like can you imagine my *mother* at Mars Hill?—and you
had on this sort of long black dress and you were sitting alone by
the pier. And you said, 'This is it, Jason. We'll never see this again.'
I felt like crying, I tried to hug you but my father pulled me back.
And then I woke up."

She didn't say anything. Finally Jason prodded her. "Weird,
huh, Moony? I mean, don't you think it's weird?"

She shrugged and rolled her eyes, then sighed loudly so that
he'd be able to tell she was upset. "Thanks, Jason. Like that's
supposed to cheer me up?"

A long silence, then Jason's breathless voice again. "Shit,
Moony, I'm sorry. I didn't—"

She laughed, a little nervously, and said, "Forget it. So when
you flying out to Maine?"

Nobody but Jason called her Moony, not at home at least, not in Kamensic Village. There she was Maggie Rheining, which was the name that appeared under her junior picture in the high school yearbook.

But the name that had been neatly typed on the birth certificate in San Francisco sixteen years ago, the name Jason and everyone at Mars Hill knew her by, was Shadowmoon Starlight Rising. Maggie would have shaved her head before she'd admit her real name to anyone at school. At Mars Hill it wasn't so weird: there was Adele Grose, known professionally as Madame Olaf; Shasta Daisy O'Hare and Rvis Capricorn; Martin Dionysos, who was Jason's father; and Ariel Rising, née Amanda Mae Rheining, who was Moony's mother. For most of the year Moony and Ariel lived in Kamensic Village, the affluent New York exurb where her mother ran Earthly Delights Catering and Moony attended high school, and everything was pretty much normal. It was only in June that they headed north to Maine, to the tiny spiritualist community where they had summered for as long as Moony could remember. And even though she could have stayed in Kamensic with Ariel's friends the Loomises, at the last minute (and due in large part to Jason's urging, and threats if she abandoned him there) she decided to go with her mother to Mars Hill. Later, whenever she thought how close she'd come to not going, it made her feel sick: as though she'd missed a flight and later found out the plane had crashed.

Because much as she loved it, Moony had always been a little ashamed of Mars Hill. It was such a dinky place, plopped in the middle of nowhere on the rocky Maine coast—tiny shingle-style Carpenter Gothic cottages, all tumbled into disrepair, their elaborate trim rotting and strung with spiderwebs; poppies and lupines and tiger lilies sprawling bravely atop clumps of chickweed and dandelions of truly monstrous size, even the sign by the pier so faded you almost couldn't read the earnest lettering:

MARS HILL
SPIRITUALIST COMMUNITY
FOUNDED 1883

"Why doesn't your father take somebody's violet aura and repaint the damn sign with it?" she'd exploded once to Jason.

Jason looked surprised. "I kind of like it like that," he said, shaking the hair from his face and tossing a sea urchin at the silvered board. "It looks like it was put up by our Founding Mothers." But for years Moony almost couldn't stand to even look at the sign, it embarrassed her so much.

It was Jason who helped her get over that. They'd met when they were both twelve. It was the summer that Ariel started the workshop in Creative Psychokinesis, the first summer that Jason and his father had stayed at Mars Hill.

"Hey," Jason had said, too loudly, when they found themselves left alone while the adults swapped wine coolers and introductions at the summer's first barbecue. They were the only kids in sight. There were no other families and few conventionally married couples at Mars Hill. The community had been the cause of more than one custody battle that had ended with wistful children sent to spend the summer with a more respectable parent in Boston or Manhattan or Bar Harbor. "That lady there with my father—"

He stuck his thumb out to indicate Ariel, her long black hair frizzed and bound with leather thongs, an old multicolored skirt flapping around her legs. She was talking to a slender man with close-cropped blond hair and goatee, wearing a sky-blue caftan and shabby Birkenstock sandals. "That your mom?"

"Yeah." Moony shrugged and glanced at the man in the caftan. He and Ariel both turned to look at their children. The man grinned and raised his wineglass. Ariel did a little pirouette and blew a kiss at Moony.

"Looks like she did too much of the brown acid at Woodstock," Jason announced, and flopped onto the grass. Moony glared down at him.

"She wasn't *at* Woodstock, asshole," she said, and had started to walk away when the boy called after her.

"Hey—it's a joke! My name's Jason—" He pointed at the man with Ariel. "That's my father. Martin Dionysos. But like that's not his real name, okay? His real name is Schuster but he changed it, but *I'm* Jason Schuster. He's a painter. We don't know anyone here. I mean, does it ever get above forty degrees?"

He scrambled to his feet and looked at her beseechingly. Smaller even than Moony herself, so slender he should have looked younger than her, except that his sharp face beneath floppy white-blond hair was always twisted into some ironic pronouncement, his blue eyes always flickering somewhere between derision and pleading.

"No," Moony said slowly. The part about Jason not changing his name got to her. She stared pointedly at his thin arms prickled with gooseflesh, the fashionable surfer-logo T-shirt that hung nearly to his knees. "You're gonna freeze your skinny ass off here in Maine, Jason Schuster." And she grinned.

He was from San Francisco. His father was a well-known artist and a member of the Raging Faery Queens, a gay pagan group that lived in the Bay Area and staged elaborately beautiful solstice gatherings and AIDS benefits. At Mars Hill, Martin Dionysos gave workshops on strengthening your aura and on clear nights led the community's men in chanting at the moon as it rose above Penobscot Bay. Jason was so diffident about his father and his father's work that Moony was surprised, the single time she visited him on the West Coast, to find her friend's room plastered with flyers advertising Faery gatherings and newspaper photos of Martin and Jason at various ACT-UP events. In the fall Jason would be staying in Maine, while she returned to high school. Ultimately it was the thought that she might not see him again that made Moony decide to spend this last summer at Mars Hill.

"That's what you're wearing to First Night?"

Moony started at her mother's voice, turned to see Ariel in the middle of the summer cottage's tiny living room. Wine rocked back and forth in her mother's glass, gold shot with tiny sunbursts from the crystals hung from every window. "What about your new dress?"

Moony shrugged. She couldn't tell her mother about Jason's dream, about the black dress he'd seen her wearing. Ariel set great store by dreams, especially these last few months. What she'd make of one in which Moony appeared in a black dress and Ariel didn't appear at all, Moony didn't want to know.

"Too hot," Moony said. She paused in front of the window and adjusted one of three silver crosses dangling from her right ear. "Plus I don't want to upstage you."

Ariel smiled. "Smart kid," she said, and took another sip of her wine.

Ariel wore what she wore to every First Night: an ankle-length patchwork skirt so worn and frayed it could only be taken out once a year, on this ceremonial occasion. Squares of velvet and thread-bare satin were emblazoned with suns and moons and astrological symbols, each one with a date neatly embroidered in crimson thread.

Sedona, Aug 15 1972. Mystery Hill, NH, 5/80. The Winter Garden 1969. Jajouka, Tangiers, Marrakech 1968.

Along the bottom, where many of the original squares had disintegrated into fine webs of denim and chambray, she had begun piecing a new section: squares that each held a pair of dates, a name, an embroidered flower. These were for friends who had died. Some of them were people lost two decades earlier, to the War, or drugs or misadventure, names that Moony knew only from stories told year after year at Mars Hill or in the kitchen at home.

But most of the names were those of people Moony herself had known. Friends of Ariel's who had gathered during the divorce, and again, later, when Moony's father died, and during the myriad affairs and breakups that followed. Men and women who had started out as Ariel's customers and ended as family. Uncle Bob and Uncle Raymond and Uncle Nigel. Laurie Salas. Tommy McElroy and Sean Jacobson. Chas Bowen and Martina Glass. And, on the very bottom edge of the skirt, a square still peacock-bright with its blood-colored rose, crimson letters spelling out John's name and a date the previous spring.

As a child Moony had loved that skirt. She loved to watch her mother sashay into the tiny gazebo at Mars Hill on First Night and see all the others laugh and run to her, their fingers plucking at the patchwork folds as though to read something there, tomorrow's weather perhaps, or the names of suitors yet unmet.

But now Moony hated the skirt. It was morbid, even Jason agreed with that.

"They've already got a fucking quilt," he said, bitterly. "We don't need your mom wearing a goddamn *skirt.*"

Moony nodded, miserable, and tried not to think of what they were most afraid of: Martin's name there beside John's, and a little rosebud done in flower-knots. Martin's name, or Ariel's.

There was a key to the skirt, Moony thought as she watched

her mother sip her wine, a way to decode all the arcane symbols
Ariel had stitched there over the last few months. It lay in a heavy
manila envelope somewhere in Ariel's room, an envelope that Ariel
had started carrying with her in February, and which grew heavier
and heavier as the weeks passed. Moony knew there was something
horrible in that envelope, something to do with the countless ap-
pointments Ariel had had since February, with the whispered
phone calls and macrobiotic diets and the resurgence of her
mother's belief in *devas* and earth spirits and plain old-fashioned
ghosts.

But Moony said nothing of this, only smiled and fidgeted with
her earrings. "Go ahead," she told Ariel, who had settled at the
edge of a wicker hassock and peered up at her daughter through
her wineglass. "I just got to get some stuff."

Ariel waited in silence, then drained her glass and set it on the
floor. "Okay. Jason and Martin are here. I saw them on the hill—"

"Yeah, I know, I talked to them, they went to Camden for
lunch, they can't wait to see you." Moony paced to the door to her
room, trying not to look impatient. Already her heart was pounding.

"Okay," Ariel said again. She sounded breathless and a little
drunk. She had ringed her aquamarine eyes with kohl, to hide how
tired she was. Over the last few months she'd grown so thin that
her cheekbones had emerged again, after years of hiding in her
round peasant's face. Her voice was hoarse as she asked, "So you'll
be there soon?"

Moony nodded. She curled a long tendril of hair, dark as her
mother's but finer, and brushed her cheek with it. "I'm just gonna
pull my hair back. Jason'll give me shit if I don't."

Ariel laughed. Jason thought that they were all a bunch of
hippies. "Okay." She crossed the room unsteadily, touching the
backs of chairs, a windowsill, the edge of a buoy hanging from the
wall. When the screen door banged shut behind her Moony sighed
with relief.

For a few minutes she waited, to make sure her mother hadn't
forgotten something, like maybe a joint or another glass of wine.
She could see out the window to where people were starting downhill toward the gazebo. If you didn't look too closely, they might
have been any group of summer people gathering for a party in
the long northern afternoon.

But after a minute or two their oddities started to show. You saw them for what they really were: men and women just getting used to a peculiar middle age. They all had hair a little too long or too short, a little too gray or garishly colored. The women, like Ariel, wrapped in clothes like banners from a triumphant campaign now forgotten. Velvet tunics threaded with silver, miniskirts crossing pale bare blue-veined thighs, Pucci blouses back in vogue again. The men more subdued, in chinos some of them, or old jeans that were a little too bright and neatly pressed. She could see Martin beneath the lilacs by the gazebo, in baggy psychedelic shorts and T-shirt, his gray-blond hair longer than it had been and pulled back into a wispy ponytail. Beside him Jason leaned against a tree, self-consciously casual, smoking a cigarette as he watched the First Night promenade. At sight of Ariel he raised one hand in a lazy wave.

And now the last two stragglers reached the bottom of the hill. Mrs. Grose carrying her familiar, an arthritic wheezing pug named Milton: ancient Mrs. Grose, who smelled of Sen-Sen and whiskey, and prided herself on being one of the spiritualists exposed as a fraud by Houdini. And Gary Bonetti, who (the story went) five years ago had seen a vision of his own death in the City, a knife wielded by a crack-crazed kid in Washington Heights. Since then he had stayed on at Mars Hill with Mrs. Grose, the community's only other year-round resident.

Moony ducked back from the window as her mother turned to stare up at the cottage. She waited until Ariel looked away again, as Martin and Jason beckoned her toward the gazebo.

"Okay," Moony whispered. She took a step across the room and stopped. An overwhelming smell of cigarette smoke suddenly filled the air, though there was no smoke to be seen. She coughed, waving her hand in front of her face.

"Damn it, Jason," she hissed beneath her breath. The smell was gone as abruptly as it had appeared. "I'll be *right there—*"

She slipped through the narrow hallway with its old silver-touched mirrors and faded Maxfield Parrish prints, and went into Ariel's room. It still had its beginning-of-summer smell, mothballs and the salt sweetness of rugosa roses blooming at the beach's edge. The old chenille bedspread was rumpled where Ariel had

lain upon it, exhausted by the flight from LaGuardia to Boston,
from Boston via puddlejumper to the tiny airport at Green Turtle
Reach. Moony pressed her hand upon the spread and closed her
eyes. She tried to focus as Jason had taught her, tried to dredge
up the image of her mother stretched upon the bed. And suddenly
there it was, a faint sharp stab of pain in her left breast, like a
stitch in her side from running. She opened her eyes quickly, fighting the dizziness and panicky feeling. Then she went to the bureau.

At home she had never been able to find the envelope. It was
always hidden away, just as the mail was always carefully sorted,
the messages on the answering machine erased before she could
get to them. But now it was as if Ariel had finally given up on
hiding. The envelope was in the middle drawer, a worn cotton
camisole draped halfheartedly across it. Moony took it carefully
from the drawer and went to the bed, sat and slowly fanned the
papers out.

They were hospital bills. Hospital bills and Blue Cross forms,
cash register receipts for vitamins from the Waverly Drugstore
with Ariel's crabbed script across the top. The bills were for tests
only, tests and consultations. Nothing for treatments; no receipts
for medication other than vitamins. At the bottom of the envelope,
rolled into a blue cylinder and tightened with a rubber band, she
found the test results. Stray words floated in the air in front of her
as Moony drew in a long shuddering breath.

*Mammography results. Sectional biopsy. Fourth-stage malignancy.
Metastasized.*

Cancer. Her mother had breast cancer.

"Shit," she said. Her hands after she replaced the papers were
shaking. From outside echoed summer music, and she could hear
voices—her mother's, Diana's, Gary Bonetti's deep bass—shouting above the tinny sound of a cassette player—

> *Wouldn't it be nice if we could wake up
> In the kind of world where we belong?*

"YOU BITCH," MOONY whispered. She stood at the front window
and stared down the hill at the gazebo, her hands clamped beneath

her armpits to keep them still. Her face was streaked with tears. "When were you going to *tell* me, when were you going to fucking *tell me?*"

At the foot of Mars Hill, alone by a patch of daylilies stood Jason, staring back up at the cottage. A cigarette burned between his fingers, its scent miraculously filling the little room. Even from here Moony could tell that somehow and of course, he already knew.

EVERYONE HAD A hangover the next morning, not excluding Moony and Jason. In spite of that the two met in the community chapel. Jason brought a thermos of coffee, bright red and yellow dinosaurs stenciled on its sides, and blew ashes from the bench so she could sit down.

"You shouldn't smoke in here." Moony coughed and slumped beside him. Jason shrugged and stubbed out his cigarette, fished in his pocket and held out his open palm.

"Here. Ibuprofen and valerian capsules. And there's bourbon in the coffee."

Moony snorted but took the pills, shooting back a mouthful of tepid coffee and grimacing.

"Hair of the iguana," Jason said. "So really, Moony, you didn't know?"

"How the hell would I know?" Moony said wearily. "I mean, I knew it was *something*—"

She glanced sideways at her friend. His slender legs were crossed at the ankles and he was barefoot. Already dozens of mosquito bites pied his arms and legs. He was staring at the little altar in the center of the room. He looked paler than usual, more tired, but that was probably just the hangover.

From outside, the chapel looked like all the other buildings at Mars Hill, faded gray shingles and white trim. Inside there was one large open room, with benches arranged in a circle around the walls, facing in to the plain altar. The altar was heaped with wilting daylilies and lilacs, an empty bottle of chardonnay and a crumpled pack of Kents—Jason's brand—and a black velvet hair ribbon that Moony recognized as her mother's. Beneath the ribbon was an old snapshot, curled at the edges. Moony knew the pose from years

back. It showed her and Jason and Ariel and Martin, standing at
the edge of the pier with their faces raised skyward, smiling and
waving at Diana behind her camera. Moony made a face when she
saw it and took another swallow of coffee.

"I thought maybe she had AIDS," Moony said at last. "I knew
she went to the Walker Clinic once, I heard her on the phone to
Diana about it."

Jason nodded, his mouth set in a tight smile. "So you should
be happy she doesn't. Hip hip hooray." Two years before Jason's
father had tested HIV positive. Martin's lover, John, had died that
spring.

Moony turned so that he couldn't see her face. "She has breast
cancer. It's metastasized. She won't see a doctor. This morning
she let me feel it . . ."

Like a gnarled tree branch shoved beneath her mother's flesh,
huge and hard and lumpy. Ariel thought she'd cry or faint or something but all Moony could do was wonder how she had never felt
it before. Had she never noticed, or had it just been that long since
she'd hugged her mother?

She started crying, and Jason drew closer to her.

"Hey," he whispered, his thin arm edging around her shoulders. "It's okay, Moony, don't cry, it's all right—"

How can you say that? she felt like screaming, sobs constricting
her throat so she couldn't speak. When she did talk the words
came out in anguished grunts.

"They're dying—how can they—*Jason*—"

"Shh—" he murmured. "Don't cry, Moony, don't cry . . ."

Beside her, Jason sighed and fought the urge for another cigarette. He wished he'd thought about this earlier, come up with
something to say that would make Moony feel better. Something
like, *Hey! Get used to it! Everybody dies!* He tried to smile, but he
felt only sorrow and a headache prodding at the corners of his
eyes. Moony's head felt heavy on his shoulder. He shifted on the
bench, stroking her hair and whispering until she grew quiet. Then
they sat in silence.

He stared across the room, to the altar and the wall beyond,
where a stained glass window would have been in another kind of
chapel. Here, a single great picture window looked out onto the
bay. In the distance he could see the Starry Islands glittering in

the sunlight, and beyond them the emerald bulk of Blue Hill and
Cadillac Mountain rising above the indigo water.

And, if he squinted, he could see Them. The Others, like tears
or blots of light floating across his retina. The Golden Ones. The
Greeters.

The Light Children.

"Hey!" he whispered. Moony sniffed and burrowed closer into
his shoulder, but he wasn't talking to her. He was welcoming
Them.

They were the real reason people had settled here, over a
century ago. They were the reason Jason and Moony and their
parents and all the others came here now; although not everyone
could see Them. Moony never had, nor Ariel's friend Diana, although Diana believed in Them, and Moony did not. You never
spoke of Them, and if you did, it was always parenthetically and
with a capital T—"Rvis and I were looking at the moon last night
(They were there) and we thought we saw a whale." Or, "Martin
came over at midnight (he saw Them on the way) and we played
Scrabble . . ."

A few years earlier a movement was afoot, to change the way
of referring to Them. In a single slender volume that was a history
of the Mars Hill spiritualist community, They were referred to as
the Light Children, but no one ever really called Them that.
Everyone just called them Them. It seemed the most polite thing
to do, really, since no one knew what They called Themselves.

"And we'd hate to offend Them," as Ariel said.

That was always a fear at Mars Hill. That, despite the gentle
nature of the community's adherents, They inadvertently would
be offended one day (a too-noisy volleyball game on the rocky
beach; a beer-fueled Solstice celebration irrupting into the dawn),
and leave.

But They never did. Year after year the Light Children remained. They were a magical commonplace, like the loons that
nested on a nearby pond and made the night an offertory with
their cries, or the rainbows that inexplicably appeared over the Bay
almost daily, even when there was no rain in sight. It was the same
with Them. Jason would be walking down to call his father in from
sailing, or knocking at Moony's window to awaken her for a three
A.M. stroll, and suddenly there They'd be. A trick of the light, like

a sundog or the aurora borealis: golden patches swimming through the cool air. They appeared as suddenly as a cormorant's head slicing up through the water, lingering sometimes for ten minutes or so. Then They would be gone.

Jason saw Them a lot. The chapel was one of the places They seemed to like, and so he hung out there whenever he could. Sometimes he could sense Them moments before They appeared. A shivering in the air would make the tips of his fingers go numb, and once there had been a wonderful smell, like warm buttered bread. But usually there was no warning. If he closed his eyes while looking at Them, Their image still appeared on the cloudy scrim of his inner eye, like gilded tears. But that was all. No voices, no scent of rose petals, no rapping at the door. You felt better after seeing Them, the way you felt better after seeing a rainbow or an eagle above the Bay. But there was nothing really magical about Them, except the fact that They existed at all. They never spoke, or did anything special, at least nothing you could sense. They were just *there;* but Their presence meant everything at Mars Hill.

They were there now: flickering above the altar, sending blots of gold dancing across the limp flowers and faded photograph. He wanted to point Them out to Moony, but he'd tried before and she'd gotten mad at him.

"You think I'm some kind of an idiot like my mother?" she'd stormed, sweeping that day's offering of irises from the altar onto the floor. "Give me a break, Jason!"

Okay, I gave you a break, he thought now. Now *I'll give you another.*

Look, Moony, there They are! he thought; then said, "Moony. Look—"

He pointed, shrugging his shoulder so she'd have to move. But already They were gone.

"What?" Moony murmured. He shook his head, sighing.

"That picture," he said, and fumbled at his pocket for his cigarettes. "That stupid old picture that Diana took. Can you believe it's still here?"

Moony lifted her head and rubbed her eyes, red and swollen. "Oh, I can believe anything," she said bitterly, and filled her mug with more coffee.

. . .

IN MARTIN DIONYSOS'S kitchen, Ariel drank a cup of nettle tea and watched avidly as her friend ate a bowl of mung bean sprouts and nutritional yeast. *Just like in* Annie Hall, she thought. *Amazing.*

"So now she knows and you're surprised she's pissed at you." Martin raised another forkful of sprouts to his mouth, angling delicately to keep any from falling to the floor. He raised one blond eyebrow as he chewed, looking like some hardscrabble New Englander's idea of Satan, California surfer boy gone to seed. Long gray-blond hair that was thinner than it had been a year ago, skin that wasn't so much tanned as an even pale bronze, with that little goatee and those piercing blue eyes, the same color as the Bay stretching outside the window behind him. Oh yes: and a gold hoop earring and a heart tattoo that enclosed the name JOHN and a T-shirt with the pink triangle and SILENCE=DEATH printed in stern block letters. Satan on vacation.

"I'm not *surprised*," Ariel said, a little crossly. "I'm just, mmm, disappointed. That she got so upset."

Martin's other eyebrow arched. "*Disappointed?* As in, 'Moony, darling, I have breast cancer (which I kept a secret from you for seven months) and I am very *disappointed* that you are not self-actualized enough to deal with this without falling to pieces'?"

"She didn't fall to pieces." Ariel's crossness went over the line into full-blown annoyance. She frowned and jabbed a spoon into her tea. "I *wish* she'd fall to pieces, she's always so—" She waved the hand holding the spoon, sending green droplets raining onto Martin's knee. "—so *something.*"

"Self-assured?"

"I guess. Self-assured and smug, you know? Why is it teenagers are always so fucking smug?"

"Because they share a great secret," Martin said mildly, and took another bite of sprouts.

"Oh yeah? What's that?"

"Their parents are all assholes."

Ariel snorted with laughter, leaned forward to get her teacup out of the danger zone and onto the table. "Oh, Martin," she said. Suddenly her eyes were filled with tears. "Damn it all to *hell* . . ."

Martin put his bowl on the table and stepped over to take her in his arms. He didn't say anything, and for a moment Ariel flashed back to the previous spring, the same tableau only in reverse, with her holding Martin while he sobbed uncontrollably in the kitchen of his San Francisco townhouse. It was two days after John's funeral, and she was on her way to the airport. She knew then about the breast cancer but she hadn't told Martin yet; didn't want to dim any of the dark luster of his grief.

Now it was her grief, but in a strange way she knew it was his, too. There was this awful thing that they held in common, a great unbroken chain of grief that wound from one coast to the other. She hadn't wanted to share it with Moony, hadn't wanted her to feel its weight and breadth. But it was too late now. Moony knew and besides, what did it matter? She was dying, Martin was dying, and there wasn't a fucking thing anyone could do about it.

"Hey," he said at last. His hand stroked her mass of dark hair, got itself tangled near her shoulder, snagging one of the long silver-and-quartz-crystal earrings she had put on that morning, for luck. "Ouch."

Ariel snorted again, laughing in spite of, or maybe because of, it all. Martin extricated his hand, held up two fingers with a long curling strand of hair caught between them: a question mark, a wise serpent waiting to strike. She had seen him after the cremation take the lock of John's hair that he had saved and hold it so, until suddenly it burst into flames, and then watched as the fizz of ash flared out in a dark penumbra around Martin's fingers. No such thing happened now, no Faery Pagan pyrotechnics. She wasn't dead yet, there was no sharp cold wind of grief to fan Martin's peculiar gift. He let the twirl of hair fall away and looked at her and said, "You know, I talked to Adele."

Adele was Mrs. Grose, she of the pug dog and suspiciously advanced years. Ariel retrieved her cup and her equanimity, sipping at the nettle tea as Martin went on. "She said she thought we had a good chance. You especially. She said for you it might happen. They might come." He finished and leaned back in his chair, spearing the last forkful of sprouts.

Ariel said, "Oh yes?" Hardly daring to think of it; no, don't think of it at all.

Martin shrugged, twisted to look over his shoulder at the endless sweep of Penobscot Bay. His eyes were bright, so bright she wondered if he was fighting tears or perhaps something else, something only Martin would allow himself to feel here and now. Joy, perhaps. Hope.

"Maybe," he said. At his words her heart beat a little faster in her breast, buried beneath the mass that was doing its best to crowd it out. "That's all. Maybe. It might. Happen."

And his hand snaked across the table to hers and held it, clutched it like it was a link in that chain that ran between them, until her fingers went cold and numb.

ON WEDNESDAY EVENINGS the people at Mars Hill gave readings for the public. Tarot, palms, auras, dreams—five dollars a pop, nothing guaranteed. The chapel was cleaned, the altar swept of offerings and covered with a frayed red-and-white checked tablecloth from Diana's kitchen and a few candles in empty Chianti bottles.

"It's not very atmospheric," Gary Bonetti said, as someone always did. Mrs. Grose nodded from her bench and fiddled with her rosary beads.

"Au contraire," protested Martin. "It's *very* atmospheric, if you're in the mood for spaghetti carbonara at Luigi's."

"May I recommend the primavera?" said Jason. In honor of the occasion he had put on white duck pants and white shirt and red bow tie. He waved at Moony, who stood at the door taking five-dollar bills from nervous, giggly tourists and the more solemn-faced locals, who made this pilgrimage every summer. Some regulars came week after week, year after year. Sad Brenda, hoping for the Tarot card that would bring news from her drowned child. Mr. Spruce, a ruddy-faced lobsterman who always tipped Mrs. Grose ten dollars. The Hamptonites Jason had dubbed Mr. and Mrs. Pissant, who were anxious about their auras. Tonight the lobsterman was there, with an ancient woman who could only be his mother, and the Pissants, and two teenage couples, long blond hair and sunburned, reeking of marijuana and summer money.

The teenagers went to Martin, lured perhaps by his tie-dyed caftan, neatly pressed and swirling down to his Birkenstock-clad feet.

"Boat trash," hissed Jason, arching a nearly invisible white-blond eyebrow as they passed. "I saw them in Camden, getting off a yacht the size of the fire station. God, they make me sick."

Moony tightened her smile. Catch *her* admitting to envy of people like that. She swiveled on her chair, looking outside to see if there were any newcomers making their way to the chapel through the cool summer night. "I think this is gonna be it," she said. She glanced wistfully at the few crumpled bills nesting in an old oatmeal tin. "Maybe we should, like, advertise or something. It's been so slow this summer."

Jason only grunted, adjusting his bow tie and glaring at the rich kids, now deep in conference with his father. The Pissants had fallen to Diana, who with her chignon of blond hair and gold-buttoned little black dress could have been one of their neighbors. That left the lobsterman and his aged mother.

They stood in the middle of the big room, looking not exactly uneasy or lost, but as though they were waiting for someone to usher them to their proper seats. And as though she read their minds (but wasn't that her job?), Mrs. Grose swept up suddenly from her corner of the chapel, a warm South Wind composed of yards of very old rayon fabric, Jean Naté After-Bath, and arms large and round and powdered as wheaten loaves.

"Mr. *Spruce*," she cried, extravagantly trilling her *rrr*s and opening those arms like a stage gypsy. "You have come—"

"Why, yes," the lobsterman answered, embarrassed but also grateful. "I uh—I brought my mother, Mrs. Grose. She says she remembers you—"

"I do," said Mrs. Spruce. Moony twisted to watch, curious. She had always wondered about Mrs. Grose. She claimed to be a true clairvoyant. She *had* predicted things—nothing very useful, though. What the weather would be like the weekend of Moony's Junior Prom (rainy), but not whether she would be asked to go, or by whom. The day Jason would receive a letter from Harvard (Tuesday, the fifth of April), but not whether he'd be accepted there (he was not). It aggravated Moony, like so much at Mars Hill. What was the use of being a psychic if you could never come up with anything really useful?

But then there was the story about Harry Houdini. Mrs. Grose loved to tell it, how when she was still living in Chicago this short guy came one day and she gave him a message from his mother and he tried to make her out to be a fraud. It was a stupid story, except for one thing. If it really had happened, it would make Mrs. Grose about ninety or a hundred years old. And she didn't look a day over sixty.

Now Mrs. Grose was cooing over a woman who really *did* look to be about ninety. Mrs. Spruce peered up at her through rheumy eyes, shaking her head and saying in a whispery voice, "I can't believe it's you. I was just a girl, but you don't look any different at all . . ."

"Oh, flattery, flattery!" Mrs. Grose laughed and rubbed her nose with a Kleenex. "What can we tell you tonight, Mrs. Spruce?"

Moony turned away. It was too weird. She watched Martin entertaining the four golden children, then felt Jason coming up behind her: the way some people claim they can tell a cat is in the room, by some subtle disturbance of air and dust. A cat is there. Jason is there.

"They're *all* going to Harvard. I can't *believe* it," he said, mere disgust curdled into utter loathing. "And that one, the blond on the end—"

"They're all blond, Jason," said Moony. "*You're* blond."

"I am an *albino*," Jason said with dignity. "Check him out, the Nazi Youth with the Pearl Jam T-shirt. He's a legacy, absolutely. SAT scores of 1060, tops. I *know*." He closed his eyes and wiggled his fingers and made a *whoo-whoo* noise, beckoning spirits to come closer. Moony laughed and covered her mouth. From where he sat Martin raised an eyebrow, requesting silence. Moony and Jason turned and walked outside.

"How old do you think she is?" Moony asked, after they had gone a safe distance from the chapel.

"Who?"

"Mrs. Grose."

"Adele?" Jason frowned into the twilit distance, thinking of the murky shores and shoals of old age. "Jeez, I dunno. Sixty? Fifty?"

Moony shook her head. "She's got to be older than that. I mean, that story about Houdini, you know?"

"Huh! Houdini. The closest she ever got to Houdini is seeing some Siegfried and Roy show out in Las Vegas."

"I don't think she's ever left here. At least not since I can remember."

Jason nodded absently, then squatted in the untidy drive, squinting as he stared out into the darkness occluding the Bay. Fireflies formed mobile constellations within the birch trees. As a kid he had always loved fireflies, until he had seen Them. Now he thought of the Light Children as a sort of evolutionary step, somewhere between lightning bugs and angels.

Though you hardly ever see Them at night, he thought. *Now why is that?* He rocked back on his heels, looking like some slender pale gargoyle toppled from a modernist cathedral, the cuffs of his white oxford-cloth shirt rolled up to show large bony wrists and surprisingly strong square hands, his bow tie unraveled and hanging rakishly around his neck. Of a sudden he recalled being in this same spot two years ago, grinding out a cigarette as Martin and John approached. The smoke bothered John, sent him into paroxysms of coughing so prolonged and intense that more than once they had set Jason's heart pounding, certain that This Was It, John was going to die right here, right now, and it would be all Jason's fault for smoking. Only of course it didn't happen that way.

"The longest death since Little Nell's," John used to say, laughing hoarsely. That was when he could still laugh, still talk. At the end it had been others softly talking, Martin and Jason and their friends gathered around John's bed at home, taking turns, spelling each other. After a while Jason couldn't stand to be with them. It was too much like John was already dead. The body in the bed so wasted, bones cleaving to skin so thin and mottled it was like damp newsprint.

By the end, Jason refused to accompany Martin to the therapist they were supposed to see. He refused to go with him to the meetings where men and women talked about dying, about watching loved ones go so horribly slowly. Jason just couldn't take it. Grief he had always thought of as an emotion, a mood, something that possessed you but that you eventually escaped. Now he knew it was different. Grief was a country, a place you entered hesitantly, or were thrown into without warning. But once you were there, amid the roiling formless blackness and stench of despair, you could not leave. Even if you wanted to: you could only walk and walk and walk, traveling on through the black reaches with the sound of screaming in your ears, and hope that someday you might glimpse far off another country, another place where you might someday rest.

Jason had followed John a long ways into that black land. And now his own father would be going there. Maybe not for good, not yet, but Jason knew. An HIV-positive diagnosis might mean that Death was a long way off, but Jason knew his father had already started walking.

". . . you think they don't leave?"

Jason started. "Huh?" He looked up into Moony's wide gray eyes. "I'm sorry, what?"

"Why do you think they don't leave? Mrs. Grose and Gary. You know, the ones who stay here all year." Moony's voice was exasperated. He wondered how many times she'd asked him the same thing.

"I dunno. I mean, they *have* to leave sometimes. How do they get groceries and stuff?" He sighed and scrambled to his feet. "There's only two of them, maybe they pay someone to bring stuff in. I know Gary goes to the Beach Store sometimes. It's not like they're under house arrest. Why?"

Moony shrugged. In the twilight she looked spooky, more like a witch than her mother or Diana or any of those other wannabes. Long dark hair and those enormous pale gray eyes, face like the face of the cat who'd been turned into a woman in a fairy tale his father had read him once. Jason grinned, thinking of Moony jumping on a mouse. No way. But hey, even if she did, it would take more than *that* to turn him off.

"You thinking of staying here?" he asked slyly. He slipped an arm around her shoulders. " 'Cause, like, I could keep you company or something. I hear Maine gets cold in the winter."

"No." Moony shrugged off his arm and started walking toward the water: no longer exasperated, more like she was distracted. "My mother is."

"Your *mother*?"

He followed her until she stopped at the edge of a gravel beach. The evening sky was clear. On the opposite shore, a few lights glimmered in Dark Harbor, reflections of the first stars overhead. From somewhere up along the coast, Bayside or Nagaseek or one of the other summer colonies, the sounds of laughter and skirling music echoed very faintly over the water, like a song heard on some distant station very late at night. But it wasn't late, not yet even nine o'clock. In summers past, that had been early for Moony and Jason, who would often stay up with the adults talking and poring over cards and runes until the night grew cold and spent.

But tonight for some reason the night already felt old. Jason shivered and kicked at the pebbly beach. The last pale light of sunset cast an antique glow upon stones and touched the edge of the water with gold. As he watched, the light withdrew, a gauzy veil drawn back teasingly until the shore shimmered with afterglow, like blue glass.

"I heard her talking with Diana," Moony said. Her voice was unsettlingly loud and clear in the still air. "She was saying she might stay on, after I go off to school. I mean, she was talking like she wasn't going back at all, I mean not back to Kamensic. Like she might just stay here and never leave again." Her voice cracked on the words *never leave again* and she shuddered, hugging herself.

"Hey," said Jason. He walked over and put his arms around her, her dark hair a perfumed net that drew him in until he felt dizzy and had to draw back, gasping a little, the smell of her nearly overwhelming that of rugosa roses and the sea. "Hey, it's okay, Moony, really it's okay."

Moony's voice sounded explosive, as though she had been holding her breath. "I just can't believe she's giving *up* like this. I mean, no doctors, nothing. She's just going to stay here and die."

"She might not die," said Jason, his own voice a little desperate. "I mean, look at Adele. A century and counting. The best is yet to come."

Moony laughed brokenly. She leaned forward so that her hair once again spilled over him, her wet cheek resting on his shoulder. "Oh, Jason. If it weren't for you I'd go crazy, you know that? I'd just go fucking nuts."

Nuts, thought Jason. His arms tightened around her, the cool air and faraway music nearly drowning him as he stroked her head and breathed her in. *Crazy, oh yes.* And they stood there until the moon showed over Dark Harbor, and all that far-off music turned to silvery light above the Bay.

TWO DAYS LATER Ariel and Moony went to see the doctor in Bangor. Moony drove, an hour's trip inland, up along the old road that ran beside the Penobscot River, through failed stonebound farms and past trailer encampments like sad rusted toys, until finally they reached the sprawl around the city, the kingdom of car lots and franchises and shopping plazas.

The hospital was an old brick building with a shiny new white wing grafted on. Ariel and Moony walked through a gleaming steel-and-glass door set in the expanse of glittering concrete. But they ended up in a tired office on the far end of the old wing, where the squeak of rubber wheels on worn linoleum played counterpoint to a loudly echoing, ominous *drip-drip* that never ceased the whole time they were there.

"Ms. Rising. Please, come in."

Ariel squeezed her daughter's hand, then followed the doctor into her office. It was a small bright room, a hearty wreath of living ivy trained around its single grimy window in defiance of the lack of sunlight and, perhaps, the black weight of despair that Ariel felt everywhere, chairs, desk, floor, walls.

"I received your records from New York," the doctor said. She was a slight fine-boned young woman with sleek straight hair and a silk dress more expensive than what you usually saw in Maine. The little metal name-tag on her breast might have been an odd bit of heirloom jewelry. "You realize that even as of three weeks ago, the cancer had spread to the point where our treatment options are now quite limited."

Ariel nodded, her arms crossed protectively across her chest. She felt strange, light-headed. She hadn't been able to eat much the last day or two; that morning had swallowed a mouthful of coffee and a stale muffin to satisfy Moony but that was all. "I know," she said heavily. "I don't know why I'm here."

"Frankly, I don't know either," the doctor replied. "If you had optioned for some kind of intervention oh, even two months ago; but now . . ."

Ariel tilted her head, surprised at how sharp the other woman's tone was. The doctor went on, "It's a great burden to put on your daughter—" She looked in the direction of the office door, then glanced down at the charts in her hand. "Other children?"

Ariel shook her head. "No."

The doctor paused, gently slapping the sheaf of charts and records against her open palm. Finally she said, "Well. Let's examine you, then."

An hour later Ariel slipped back into the waiting room. Moony looked up from a magazine. Her gray eyes were bleary and her tired expression hastily congealed into the mask of affronted resentment with which she faced Ariel these days.

"So?" she asked as they retraced their steps back through cinder-block corridors to the hospital exit. "What'd she say?"

Ariel stared straight ahead, through the glass doors to where the summer afternoon waited to pounce on them. Exhaustion had seeped into her like heat; like the drugs the doctor had offered and Ariel had refused, the contents of crystal vials that could buy a few more weeks, maybe even months if she was lucky, enough time to make a graceful farewell to the world. But Ariel didn't want weeks or months, and she sure as hell didn't want graceful good-byes. She wanted years, decades. A cantankerous or dreamy old age, aggravating the shit out of her grandchildren with her talk about her own sunflower youth. Failing that, she wanted screaming and gnashing of teeth, her friends tearing their hair out over her death, and Moony . . .

And Moony. Ariel stopped in front of a window, one hand out to press against the smooth cool glass. Grief and horror hit her like a stone, struck her between the eyes so that she gasped and drew her hands to her face.

"Mom!" Moony cried, shocked. "Mom, what *is* it, are you all right?"

Ariel nodded, tears burning down her cheeks. "I'm fine," she said, and gave a twisted smile. "Really, I'm—"

"What did she *say?*" demanded Moony. "The doctor, what did she tell you, *what is it?*"

Ariel wiped her eyes, a black line of mascara smeared across her finger. "Nothing. Really, Moony, nothing's changed. It's just— it's just hard. Being this sick. It's hard, that's all."

She could see in her daughter's face confusion, despair, but also relief. Ariel hadn't said *death*, she hadn't said *dying*, she hadn't since that first day said *cancer*. She'd left those words with the doctor, along with the scrips for morphine and Fiorinal, all that could be offered to her now. "Come on," she said, and walked through the sliding doors. "I'm supposed to have lunch with Mrs. Grose and Diana, and it's already late."

Moony stared at her in disbelief: was her mother being stoic or just crazy? But Ariel didn't say anything else, and after a moment her daughter followed her to the car.

IN MARS HILL'S little chapel Jason sat and smoked. On the altar in front of him were several weeks' accumulated offerings from the denizens of Mars Hill. An old-fashioned envelope with a glassine window, through which he could glimpse the face of a twenty-dollar bill—that was from Mrs. Grose, who always gave the money she'd earned from readings (and then retrieved it at the end of the summer). A small square of brilliantly woven cloth from Diana, whose looms punctuated the soft morning with their steady racketing. A set of blueprints from Rvis Capricorn. Shasta Daisy's battered *Ephemera*. The copy of Paul Bowles's autobiography that Jason's father had been reading on the flight out from the West Coast. In other words, the usual flotsam of love and whimsy that washed up here every summer. From where Jason sat, he could see his own benefaction, a heap of small white roses, already limp but still giving out their heady sweet scent, and a handful of blackberries he'd picked from the thicket down by the pier. Not much of an offering, but you never knew.

From beneath his roses peeked the single gift that puzzled him, a lacy silk camisole patterned with pale pink-and-yellow blossoms. An odd choice of offering, Jason thought. Because for all the unattached adults sipping chardonnay and Bellinis of a summer evening, the atmosphere at Mars Hill was more like that of summer camp. A chaste sort of giddiness ruled here, compounded of equal parts of joy and longing, that always made Jason think of the garlanded jackass and wistful fairies in *A Midsummer Night's Dream*. His father and Ariel and all the rest stumbling around in the dark, hoping for a glimpse of Them, and settling for fireflies and the lights from Dark Harbor. Mars Hill held surprisingly little in the way of unapologetic lust—except for himself and Moony, of course. And Jason knew that camisole didn't belong to Moony.

At the thought of Moony he sighed and tapped his ashes onto the dusty floor. It was a beautiful morning, gin-clear and with a stiff warm breeze from the west. Perfect sailing weather. He should be out with his father on the *Wendameen*. Instead he'd stayed behind, to write and think. Earlier he'd tried to get through to Moony somewhere in Bangor, but Jason couldn't send his thoughts any farther than from one end of Mars Hill to the other. For some reason, smoking cigarettes seemed to help. He had killed half a pack already this morning, but gotten nothing more than a headache and raw throat. Now he had given up. It never seemed to work with anyone except Moony, anyhow, and then only if she was nearby.

He had wanted to give her some comfort. He wanted her to know how much he loved her, how she meant more to him than anyone or anything in the world, except perhaps his father. Was it allowed, to feel this much for a person when your father was HIV-positive? Jason frowned and stubbed out his cigarette in a lobster-shaped ashtray, already overflowing with the morning's telepathic aids. He picked up his notebook and Rapidograph pen and, still frowning, stared at the letter he'd begun last night.

DEAREST MOONY,

(he crossed out *est*, it sounded too fussy)

I just want you to know that I understand how you feel. When John died it was the most horrible thing in the world, even worse than the divorce because I was just a kid then. I just want you to know how much I love you, you mean more than anyone or anything in the world, and

And what? Did he really know how she felt? His mother wasn't dying, his mother was in the Napa Valley running her vineyard, and while it was true enough that John's death had been the most horrible thing he'd ever lived through, could that be the same as having your mother die? He thought maybe it could. And then of course there was the whole thing with his father. Was that worse? His father wasn't sick, of course, at least he didn't have any symptoms yet; but was it worse for someone you loved to have the AIDS virus, to watch and wait for months or years, rather than have it happen quickly like with Ariel? Last night he'd sat in the living room while his father and Gary Bonetti were on the porch talking about her.

"I give her only a couple of weeks," Martin had said, with that dry strained calm voice he'd developed over the last few years of watching his friends die. "The thing is, if she'd gone for treatment right away she could be fine now. She could be *fine*." The last word came out in an uncharacteristic burst of vehemence, and Jason grew cold to hear it. Because of course even with treatment his father probably wouldn't be all right, not now, not ever. He'd never be fine again. Ariel had thrown all that away.

"She should talk to Adele," Gary said softly. Jason heard the clink of ice as he poured himself another daiquiri. "When I had those visions five years ago, that's when I saw Adele. You should too, Martin. You really should."

"I don't know as Adele can help me," Martin said somewhat coolly. "She's just a guest here, like you or any of the rest of us. And *you* know that you can't make Them . . ."

His voice trailed off. Jason sat bolt upright on the sofa, suddenly feeling his father there, like a cold finger stabbing at his brain.

"Jason?" Martin called, his voice tinged with annoyance. "If you want to listen, come in *here*, please."

Jason had sworn under his breath and stormed out through the back door. It was impossible, sometimes, living with his father. Better to have a psychic wannabe like Ariel for a parent, and not have to worry about being spied on all the time.

Now, from outside the chapel came frenzied barking. Jason started, his thoughts broken. He glanced through the open door to see Gary and his black labrador retriever heading down to the water. Gary was grinning, arms raised as he waved at someone out of sight. And suddenly Jason had an image of his father in the *Wendameen*, the fast little sloop skirting the shore as Martin stood at the mast waving back, his long hair tangled by the wind. The vision left Jason nearly breathless. He laughed, shaking his head,

and at once decided to follow Gary to the landing and meet his
father there. He picked up his pen and notebook and turned to
go. Then stopped, his neck prickling. Very slowly he turned, until
he stood facing the altar once more.

They were there. A shimmering haze above the fading roses,
like Zeus's golden rain falling upon imprisoned Danaë. Jason's
breath caught in his throat as he watched Them—They were so
beautiful, so *strange*. Flickering in the chapel's dusty air, like so
many scintillant coins. He could sense rather than hear a faint
chiming as They darted quick as hummingbirds from his roses to
Mrs. Grose's envelope, alighting for a moment upon Diana's weav-
ing and Rvis's prize tomatoes before settling upon two things: his
father's book and the unknown camisole.

And then with a sharp chill Jason knew whose it was. Ariel's,
of course—who else would own something so unabashedly romantic but also slightly tacky? Maybe it was meant to be a bad
joke, or perhaps it was a real offering, heartfelt, heartbreaking. He
stared at Them, a glittering carpet tossed over those two pathetic
objects, and had to shield his eyes with his hand. It was too bright,
They seemed to be growing more and more brilliant as he
watched. Like a swarm of butterflies he had once seen, mourning
cloaks resting in a snow-covered field one warm March afternoon,
their wings slowly fanning the air as though They had been
stunned by the thought of spring. But what could ever surprise
Them, the Light Children, the summer's secret?

Then as he watched They began to fade. The glowing golden
edge of the swarm grew dim and disappeared. One by one all the
other gilded coins blinked into nothing, until the altar stood as it
had minutes before, a dusty collection of things, odd and somewhat
ridiculous. Jason's head pounded and he felt faint, then realized
he'd been holding his breath. He let it out, shuddering, put his
pen and notebook on the floor and walked to the altar.

Everything was as it had been, roses, cloth, paper, tomatoes;
excepting only his father's offering, and Ariel's. Hesitantly he
reached to touch the book Martin had left, then recoiled.

The cover of the book had been damaged. When he leaned
over to stare at it more closely, he saw that myriad tiny holes had
been burned in the paper, in what at first seemed to be a random
pattern. But when he picked it up—gingerly, as though it might

yet release an electrical jolt or some other hidden energy—he saw that the tiny perforations formed an image, blurred but unmistakable. The shadow of a hand, four fingers splayed across the cover as though gripping it.

Jason went cold. He couldn't have explained how, but he knew that it was a likeness of his father's hand that he saw there, eerie and chilling as those monstrous shadows left by victims of the bombings at Hiroshima and Nagasaki. With a frightened gasp he tossed the book back onto the altar. For a moment he stood beside the wooden table, half poised to flee; but finally reached over and tentatively pushed aside his roses to fully reveal the camisole.

It was just like the book. Thousands of tiny burn holes made a ruined lace of the pastel silk, most of them clustered around one side of the bodice. He picked it up, catching a faint fragrance, lavender and marijuana, and held it out by its pink satin straps. He raised it, turning toward the light streaming through the chapel's picture window, and saw that the pinholes formed a pattern, elegant as the tracery of veins and capillaries on a leaf. A shadowy bull's-eye—breast, aureole, nipple drawn on the silken cloth.

With a small cry Jason dropped the camisole. Without looking back he ran from the chapel. Such was his hurry that he forgot his pen and notebook and the half-written letter to Moony, piled carefully on the dusty floor. And so he did not see the shining constellation that momentarily appeared above the pages, a curious cloud that hovered there like a child's dream of weather before flowering into a golden rain.

MOONY SAT HUNCHED on the front stoop, waiting for her mother to leave. Ariel had been in her room for almost half an hour, her luncheon date with Diana and Mrs. Grose notwithstanding. When finally she emerged, Moony could hear the soft uneven tread of her flip-flops, padding from bedroom to bedroom to kitchen. There was the sigh of the refrigerator opening and closing, the muted pop of a cork being pulled from a bottle, the long grateful gurgle of wine being poured into a glass. Then Ariel herself in the doorway behind her. Without looking Moony could tell that she'd put on The Skirt. She could smell it, the musty scents of patchouli and cannabis resin and the honeysuckle smell of the expensive detergent Ariel used to wash it by hand, as though it were some precious winding sheet.

"I'm going to Adele's for lunch."

Moony nodded silently.

"I'll be back in a few hours."

More silence.

"You know where to find me if anyone comes by." Ariel nudged her daughter gently with her toe. "Okay?"

Moony sighed. "Yeah, okay."

She watched her mother walk out the door, sun bouncing off her hair in glossy waves. When Ariel was out of sight she hurried down the hall.

In her mother's room, piles of clothes and papers covered the worn Double Wedding Ring quilt, as though tossed helter-skelter from her bureau.

"Jeez, what a mess," said Moony. She slowly crossed to the bed. It was covered with scarves and tangled skeins of pantyhose; drifts of old catering receipts, bills, canceled checks. A few paperbacks with yellowed pages that had been summer reading in years past. A back issue of *Gourmet* magazine and the *Maine Progressive*. A Broadway ticket stub from *Prelude to a Kiss*. Grimacing, Moony prodded the edge of last year's calendar from the Beach Store & Pizza to Go.

What had her mother been looking for?

Then, as if by magic, Moony saw it. Its marbled cover suddenly glimpsed beneath a dusty strata of Tarot cards and Advil coupons, like some rare bit of fossil, lemur vertebrae or primate jaw hidden within papery shale. She drew it out carefully, tilting it so the light slid across the title.

MARS HILL: ITS HISTORY AND LORE
BY
ABIGAIL MERITHEW COX,
A LOVER OF ITS MYSTERIES

With careful fingers Moony riffled the pages. Dried rose petals fell out, releasing the sad smell of summers past, and then a longer plume of liatris dropped to the floor, fresh enough to have left a faint purplish stain upon the page. Moony drew the book up curiously, marking the page where the liatris had fallen, and read:

> *Perhaps strangest of all the Mysteries of our Colony at Mars Hill is the presence of those Enchanted Visitors who make their appearance now and then, to the eternal Delight of those of us fortunate enough to receive the benison of their presence. I say Delight, though many of us who have conjured with them say that the Experience resembles Rapture more than mere Delight, and even that Surpassing Ecstasy of which the Ancients wrote and which is at the heart of all our Mysteries; though we are not alone in enjoying the favor of our Visitors. It is said by my Aunt, Sister Rosemary Merithew, that the Pasamaquoddie Indians who lived here long before the civilizing influence of the White Man, also entertained these Ethereal Creatures, which are in appearance like to those fairy lights called Foxfire or Will o' the Wisp, and which may indeed be the inspiration for such spectral rumors. The Pasamaquoddie named them Akiniki, which in their language means The Greeters; and this I think is a most appropriate title for our Joyous Guests, who bring only Good News from the Other Side, and who feast upon our mortality as a man sups upon rare meats . . .*

Moony stared at the page in horror and disgust. *Feasting* upon mortality? She recalled her mother and Jason talking about the things they called the Light Children, Jason's disappointment that They had never appeared to Moony. As though there was something wrong with her, as though she wasn't worthy of seeing Them. But she had never felt that way. She had always suspected that Jason and her mother and the rest were mistaken about the Light Children. When she was younger, she had even accused her mother of lying about seeing Them. But the other people at Mars Hill spoke of Them, and Jason, at least, would never lie to Moony. So she had decided there must be something slightly delusional about the whole thing. Like a mass hypnosis, or maybe some kind of mass drug flashback, which seemed more likely considering the histories of some of her mother's friends.

Still, that left Mrs. Grose, who never even took an aspirin.

Who, as far as Moony knew, had never been sick in her life, and who certainly seemed immune to most of the commonplace ailments of what must be, despite appearances, an advanced age. Mrs. Grose claimed to speak with the Light Children, to have a sort of understanding of Them that Ariel and the others lacked. And Moony had always held Mrs. Grose in awe. Maybe because her own grandparents were all dead, maybe just because of that story about Houdini—it was too fucking weird, no one could have made it up.

And so maybe no one had made up the Light Children, either. Moony tapped the book's cover, frowning. Why couldn't she see Them? Was it because she didn't believe? The thought annoyed her. As though she were a kid who'd found out about Santa Claus and was being punished for learning the truth. She stared at the book's cover, the gold lettering flecked with dust, the peppering of black and green where salt air and mildew had eaten away at the cloth. The edge of one page crumbled as she opened it once more.

> *Many of my brothers and sisters can attest to the virtues of Our Visitors, particularly Their care for the dying and afflicted . . .*

"Fucking *bullshit*," yelled Moony. She threw the book across the room, hard, so that it slammed into the wall beside her mother's bureau. With a soft *crack* the spine broke. She watched stonily as yellow pages and dried blossoms fluttered from between the split covers, a soft explosion of antique dreams. She left the room without picking up the mess, the door slamming shut behind her.

"I WAS CONSUMPTIVE," Mrs. Grose was saying, nodding as she looked in turn from Ariel to Diana to the pug sprawled panting on the worn chintz sofa beside them. "Tuberculosis, you know. Coming here saved me."

"You mean, like taking the waters?" asked Ariel. She shook back her hair and took another sip of her gin and tonic. "Like they used to do at Saratoga Springs and places like that?"

"Not like that *at all*," replied Mrs. Grose firmly. She raised one white eyebrow and frowned. "I mean, Mars Hill saved me."

Saved you for what? thought Ariel, choking back another mouthful of gin. She shuddered. She knew she shouldn't drink, these days she could feel it seeping into her, like that horrible barium they injected into you to do tests. But she couldn't stop. And what was the point, anyway?

"But you think it might help her, if she stayed here?" Diana broke in, oblivious of Mrs. Grose's imperious gaze. "And Martin, do you think it could help him too?"

"I don't think *anything*," said Mrs. Grose, and she reached over to envelope the wheezing pug with one large fat white hand. "It is absolutely not up to me at all. I am simply *telling* you the *facts*."

"Of course," Ariel said, but she could tell from Diana's expression that her words had come out slurred. "Of *course*," she repeated with dignity, sitting up and smoothing the folds of her patchwork skirt.

"As long as you understand," Mrs. Grose said in a gentler tone. "We are guests here, and guests do not ask favors of their hosts."

The other two women nodded. Ariel carefully put her glass on the coffee table and stood, wiping her sweating hands on her skirt. "I better go now," she said. Her head pounded and she felt nauseated, for all that she'd barely nibbled at the ham sandwiches and macaroni salad Mrs. Grose had set out for lunch. "Home. I think I'd better go home."

"I'll go with you," said Diana. She stood and cast a quick look at their hostess. "I wanted to borrow that book . . ."

Mrs. Grose saw them to the door, holding open the screen and swatting threateningly at mosquitoes as they walked outside. "Remember what I told you," she called as they started down the narrow road, Diana with one arm around Ariel's shoulder. "Meditation and nettle tea. And patience."

"Patience," Ariel murmured; but nobody heard.

THE WEEKS PASSED. The weather was unusually clear and warm, Mars Hill bereft of the cloak of mist and fog that usually covered it in August. Martin Dionysos took the *Wendameen* out nearly every afternoon, savoring the time alone, the hours spent fighting wind and waves—antagonists he felt he could win against.

"It's the most perfect summer we've ever had," Gary Bonetti said often to his friend. Too often, Martin thought bitterly. Recently, Martin was having what Jason called Millennial Thoughts, seeing ominous portents in everything from the Tarot cards he dealt out to stricken tourists on Wednesday nights to the pattern of kelp and maidenhair left on the gravel beach after one of the summer's few storms. He had taken to avoiding Ariel, a move that filled him with self-loathing, for all that he told himself that he still needed time to grieve for John before giving himself over to another death. But it wasn't that, of course. Or at least it wasn't *only* that. It was fear, *The* Fear. It was listening to his own heart pounding as he lay alone in bed at night, counting the beats, wondering at what point it all began to break down, at what point It would come to take him.

So he kept to himself. He begged off going on the colony's weekly outing to the little Mexican restaurant up the road. He even stopped attending the weekly readings in the chapel. Instead, he spent his evenings alone, writing to friends back in the Bay Area. After drinking coffee with Jason every morning he'd turn away.

"I'm going to work now," he'd announce, and Jason would nod and leave to find Moony, grateful, his father thought, for the opportunity to escape.

Millennial Thoughts.

Martin Dionysos had given over a corner of his cottage's living room to a studio. There was a tiny drafting table, his portable computer, an easel, stacks of books; the week's forwarded offerings of *Out!* and *The Advocate* and *Q* and *The Bay Weekly*, and, heaped on an ancient stained Windsor chair, the usual pungent mess of oils and herbal decoctions that he used in his work. Golden morning light streamed through the wide mullioned windows, smelling of salt and the diesel fumes from Diana's ancient Volvo. On the easel a large unprimed canvas rested, somewhat unevenly due to the cant of a floor slanted enough that you could drop a marble in the kitchen and watch it roll slowly but inexorably to settle in the left-hand corner of the living room. Gary Bonetti claimed that it wasn't that all of the cottages on Mars Hill were built by incompetent architects. It was the magnetic pull of the ocean just meters away; it was the imperious reins of the East, of the Moon, of the magic charters of the Otherworld, that made it impossible to find any two corners that were plumb. Martin and the others laughed at Gary's pronouncement, but John had believed it.

John. Martin sighed, stirred desultorily at a coffee can filled with linseed oil and turpentine, then rested the can on the windowsill. For a long time he had been so caught up with the sad and harrowing and noble and disgusting details of John's dying that he had been able to forestall thinking about his own diagnosis. He had been grateful, in an awful way, that there had been something so horrible, so unavoidably and demandingly *real*, to keep him from succumbing to his own despair.

But all that was gone now. John was gone. Before John's death, Martin had always had a sort of unspoken, formless belief in an afterlife. The long shadow cast by a 1950s Catholic boyhood, he guessed. But when John died, that small hidden solace had died, too. There was nothing there. No vision of a beloved waiting for him on the other side. Not even a body moldering within a polished mahogany casket. Only ashes, ashes; and his own death waiting like a small patient vicious animal in the shadows.

"Shit," he said. He gritted his teeth. This was how it happened to Ariel. She gave in to despair, or dreams, or maybe she just pretended it would go away. She'd be lucky now to last out the summer. At the thought a new wave of grief washed over him, and he groaned.

"Oh, shit, shit, shit," he whispered. With watering eyes he reached for the can full of primer on the sill. As he did so, he felt a faint prickling go through his fingers, a sensation of warmth that was almost painful. He swore under his breath and frowned. A tiny stab of fear lanced through him. Inexplicable and sudden pain, wasn't that the first sign of some sort of degeneration? As his fingers tightened around the coffee can, he looked up. The breath froze in his throat and he cried aloud, snatching his hand back as though he'd been stung.

They were there. Dozens of Them, a horde of flickering golden spots so dense They obliterated the wall behind Them. Martin had seen Them before, but never so close, never so many. He gasped and staggered back, until he struck the edge of the easel and sent the canvas clattering to the floor. They took no notice, instead followed him like a swarm of silent hornets. And as though

They were hornets, Martin shouted and turned to run.

Only he could not. He was blinded, his face seared by a terrible heat. They were everywhere, enveloping him in a shimmering cocoon of light and warmth, Their fierce radiance burning his flesh, his eyes, his throat, as though he breathed in liquid flame. He shrieked, batting at the air, and then babbling fell back against the wall. As They swarmed over him he felt Them, not as you feel the sun but as you feel a drug or love or anguish, filling him until he moaned and sank to the floor. He could feel his skin burning and erupting, his bones turning to ash inside him. His insides knotted, cramping until he thought he would faint. He doubled over, retching, but only a thin stream of spittle ran down his chin. An explosive burst of pain raced through him. He opened his mouth to scream, the sound so thin it might have been an insect whining. Then there was nothing but light, nothing but flame; and Martin's body unmoving on the floor.

MOONY WAITED UNTIL late afternoon, but Jason never came. Hours earlier, Moony had glanced out the window of her cottage and seen Gary Bonetti running up the hill to Martin's house, followed minutes later by the panting figure of Mrs. Grose. Jason she didn't see at all. He must have never left his cottage that morning, or else left and returned by the back door.

Something had happened to Martin. She knew that as soon as she saw Gary's stricken face. Moony thought of calling Jason, but did not. She did nothing, only paced and stared out the window at Jason's house, hoping vainly to see someone else enter or leave. No one did.

Ariel had been sleeping all day. Moony avoided even walking past her mother's bedroom, lest her own terror wake her. She was afraid to leave the cottage, afraid to find out the truth. Cold dread stalked her all afternoon as she waited for something—an ambulance, a phone call, *anything*—but nothing happened. Nobody called, nobody came. Although once, her nostrils filled with the acrid smell of cigarette smoke, and she felt Jason there. Not Jason himself, but an overwhelming sense of terror that she knew came from him, a fear so intense that she drew her breath in sharply, her hand shooting out to steady herself against the door. Then the smell of smoke was gone.

"Jason?" she whispered, but she knew he was no longer thinking of her. She stood with her hand pressed against the worn silvery frame of the screen door. She kept expecting Jason to appear, to explain things. But there was nothing. For the first time all summer, Jason seemed to have forgotten her. Everyone seemed to have forgotten her.

That had been hours ago. Now it was nearly sunset. Moony lay on her towel on the gravel beach, swiping at a mosquito and staring up at the cloudless sky, blue skimmed to silver as the sun melted away behind Mars Hill. What a crazy place this was. Someone gets sick, and instead of dialing 911 you send for an obese old fortune-teller. The thought made her stomach churn, because of course that's what her mother had done. Put her faith in fairydust and crystals instead of physicians and chemo. Abruptly Moony sat up, hugging her knees.

"Damn," she said miserably.

She'd put off going home, half hoping, half dreading that someone would find her and tell her what the hell was going on. Now it was obvious that she'd have to find out for herself. She threw her towel into her bag, tugged on a hooded pullover, and began to trudge back up the hill.

On the porches of the other cottages she could see people stirring. Whatever had happened, obviously none of *them* had heard yet. The new lesbian couple from Burlington sat facing each other in matching wicker armchairs, eyes closed and hands extended. A few houses on, Shasta Daisy sat on the stoop of her tiny Queen Anne Victorian, sipping a wine cooler, curled sheets of graph paper littering the table in front of her.

"Where's your mom?" Shasta called.

Moony shrugged and wiped a line of sweat from her cheek. "Resting, I guess."

"Come have a drink." Shasta raised her bottle. "I'll do your chart."

Moony shook her head. "Later. I got to get dinner."

"Don't forget there's a moon circle tonight," said Shasta. "Nine thirty at the gazebo."

"Right." Moony nodded, smiling glumly as she passed. What a bunch of kooks. At least her mother would be sleeping and not wasting her time conjuring up someone's aura between wine coolers.

But when she got home, no one was there. She called her mother's name as the screen door banged shut behind her, waited for a reply, but there was none. For an instant a terrifying surge raced through her: something else had happened, her mother lay dead in the bedroom . . .

But the bedroom was empty, as were the living room and bathroom and anyplace else where Ariel might have chosen to die. The heady scent of basil filled the cottage, with a fainter hint of marijuana. When Moony finally went into the kitchen, she found the sink full of sand and half-rinsed basil leaves. Propped up on the drainboard was a damp piece of paper towel with a message spelled out in runny Magic Marker.

> Moony: Went to Chapel
> Moon circle at 9:30
> Love love love Mom

"Right," Moony said, disgusted. She crumpled the note and threw it on the floor. "Way to go, Mom."

Marijuana, moon circle, astrological charts. Fucking *idiots*. Of a sudden she was filled with rage, at her mother and Jason and Martin and all the rest. Why weren't there any *doctors* here? Or lawyers, or secretaries, or anyone with half a brain, enough at least to take some responsibility for the fact that there were sick people here, people who were *dying* for Christ's sake and what was anyone doing about it? What was *she* doing about it?

"I've had it," she said aloud. "I have *had* it." She spun around and headed for the front door, her long hair an angry black blur around her grim face. "Amanda Rheining, you are going to the hospital. *Now*."

She strode down the hill, ignoring Shasta's questioning cries. The gravel bit into her bare feet as she rounded the turn leading to the chapel. From here she could glimpse the back door of Jason and Martin's cottage. As Moony hurried past a stand of birches, she glimpsed Diana standing by the door, one hand resting on its crooked wooden frame. She was gazing out at the Bay with a rapt expression that might have been joy or exhausted grief, her hair gilded with the dying light.

For a moment Moony stopped, biting her lip. Diana at least might understand. She could ask Diana to come and help her force Ariel to go to the hospital. It would be like the intervention they'd done with Diana's ex-husband. But that would mean going to Martin's cottage and confronting whatever it was that waited inside. Besides, Moony knew that no one at Mars Hill would ever force Ariel to do something she didn't want to do; even live. No. It was up to her to save her mother: herself, Maggie Rheining. Abruptly she turned away.

Westering light fell through the leaves of the ancient oak that shadowed the weathered gray chapel. The lupines and tiger lilies had faded with the dying summer. Now violet plumes of liatris sprang up around the chapel door beside unruly masses of sweet-smelling phlox and glowing clouds of asters. Of course no one ever weeded or thinned out the garden. The flowers choked the path leading to the door, so that Moony had to beat away a net of bees and lacewings and pale pink moths like rose petals, all of them rising from the riot of blossoms and then falling in a softly moving skein about the girl's shoulders as she walked. Moony cursed and slashed at the air, heedless of a luna moth's drunken somersault above her head, the glimmering wave of fireflies that followed her through the twilight.

At the chapel doorway Moony stopped. Her heart was beating hard, and she spat and brushed a liatris frond from her mouth. From inside she could hear a low voice; her mother's voice. She was reciting the verse that, over the years, had become a sort of blessing for her, a little mantra she chanted and whispered summer after summer, always in hopes of summoning Them—

> *"With this field-dew consecrate*
> *Every fairy take his gait*
> *And each several chamber bless,*
> *through this palace, with sweet peace;*
> *Ever shall in safety rest,*
> *and the owner of it blest."*

At the sound, Moony felt her heart clench inside her. She moved until her face pressed against the ancient gray screen sagging within its door frame. The screen smelled heavily of dust; she pinched her nose to keep from sneezing. She gazed through the fine moth-pocked web as though through a silken scrim or the Bay's accustomed fog.

Her mother was inside. She stood before the wooden altar, pathetic with its faded burden of wilting flowers and empty bottles and Jason's cigarette butts scattered across the floor. From the window facing the Bay, lilac-colored light flowed into the room, mingling with the shafts of dusty gold falling from the casements set high within the opposing wall. Where the light struck the floor a small bright pool had formed. Ariel was dancing slowly in and out of this, her thin arms raised, the long heavy sweep of her patchwork skirt sliding back and forth to reveal her slender legs and bare feet, shod with a velvety coat of dust. Moony could hear her reciting, Shakespeare's fairies' song again, and a line from Julian of Norwich that Diana had taught her:

All will be well, and all will be well, and all manner of things will be well.

And suddenly the useless purity of Ariel's belief overwhelmed Moony. A stoned forty-three-year-old woman with breast cancer and a few weeks left to live, dancing inside a ruined chapel and singing to herself. Tears filled Moony's eyes, fell and left a dirty streak against the screen. She drew a deep breath, fighting the wave of grief and despair, and pushed against the screen to enter. When she raised her head again, Ariel had stopped.

At first Moony thought her mother had seen her. But no. Ariel was staring straight ahead at the altar, her head cocked to one side as though listening. So intent was she that Moony stiffened as well, inexplicably frightened. She glanced over her shoulder, but of course there was no one there. But it was too late to keep her heart from pounding. She closed her eyes, took a deep breath and turned, stepping over the sill toward Ariel.

"Mom," Moony called softly. "Mom, I'm—"

Moony froze. In the center of the chapel her mother stood, arms writhing as she held them above her head, long hair whipping across her face. She was on fire. Flickers of gold and crimson ran along her arms and chest, lapped at her throat and face, and set runnels of light flaming across her clothes. Moony could hear her shrieking, could see her tearing at her breast as she tried to rip away the burning fabric. With a howl Moony stumbled across the room—not thinking, hardly even seeing her as she lunged to grab Ariel and pull her down.

"*Mom!*"

But before she could reach Ariel she tripped, smashed onto the uneven floor. Groaning she rolled over and tried to get back up. An arm's-length away, her mother flailed, her voice given over now to a high shrill keening, her flapping arms still raised above her head. And for the first time Moony realized that there was no real heat, no flames. No smoke filled the little room. The light that streamed through the picture window was clear and bright as dawn.

Her mother was not on fire. She was with Them.

They were everywhere, like bees swarming across a bank of flowers. Radiant beads of gold and argent covered Ariel until Moony no longer saw her mother, but only the blazing silhouette of a woman, a numinous figure that sent a prismatic aurora rippling across the ceiling. Moony fell back, horrified, awestruck. The figure continued its bizarre dance, hands lifting and falling as though reaching for something that was being pulled just out of reach. She could hear her mother's voice, muted now to a soft repetitive cry—*uh, uh!*—and a very faint clear tone, like the sustained note of a glass harmonica.

"Jesus," Moony whispered; then yelled, "*Jesus!* Stop it, *stop*—"

But They didn't stop; only moved faster and faster across Ariel's body until her mother was nothing but a blur, a chrysalis encased in glittering pollen, a burning ghost. Moony's breath scraped against her throat. Her hands clawed at her knees, the floor, her own breasts, as her mother kept on with that soft moaning and the sound of the Light Children filled the chapel the way wine fills a glass.

And then gradually it all began to subside. Gradually the glowing sheath fell from her mother, not fading so much as *thinning*, the way Moony had once read the entrance to a woman's womb will thin as its burden wakes to be born. The chiming noise died away. There was only a faint high echo in Moony's ears. Violet light spilled from the high windows, a darker if weaker wine. Ariel sprawled on the dusty floor, her arms curled up against her chest like the dried hollow limbs of an insect, scarab or patient mantis. Her mouth was slack, and the folds of tired skin around her eyes. She looked inutterably exhausted, but also somehow at peace. With a cold stab like a spike driven into her breast, Moony knew that this was how Ariel would look in death; knew that this was how she looked, now; knew that she was dead.

But she wasn't. As Moony watched, her mother's mouth twitched. Then Ariel sneezed, squeezing her eyes tightly. Finally she opened them to gaze at the ceiling. Moony stared at her, uncomprehending. She began to cry, sobbing so loudly that she didn't hear what her mother was saying, didn't hear Ariel's hoarse voice whispering the same words over and over and over again—

"Thank you, thank you, thank you!"

But Moony wasn't listening. And only in her mother's own mind did Ariel herself ever again hear Their voices. Like an unending stream of golden coins being poured into a well, the eternal and incomprehensible echo of Their reply—

"You are Welcome."

THERE MUST HAVE been a lot of noise. Because before Moony could pull herself together and go to her mother, Diana was there, her face white but her eyes set and in control, as though she were an ambulance driver inured to all kinds of terrible things. She took Ariel in her arms and got her to her feet. Ariel's head flopped to one side, and for a moment Moony thought she'd slide to the floor again. But then she seemed to rally. She blinked, smiled fuzzily at her daughter and Diana. After a few minutes, she let Diana walk her to the door. She shook her head gently but persistently when her daughter tried to help.

"You can follow us, darling," Diana called back apologetically as they headed down the path to Martin's cottage. But Moony made no move to follow. She only watched in disbelief—*I can follow you? Of* course *I can, asshole!*—and then relief, as the two women lurched safely through the house's crooked door.

Let someone *else* take care of her for a while, Moony thought bitterly. She shoved her hands into her pockets. Her terror had turned to anger. Now, perversely, she needed to yell at someone.

She thought briefly of following her mother; then of finding Jason. But really, she knew all along where she had to go.

MRS. GROSE SEEMED surprised to see her (*Ha!* thought Moony triumphantly; what kind of psychic would be *surprised?*). But maybe there was something about her after all. Because she had just made a big pot of chamomile tea, heavily spiked with brandy, and set out a large white plate patterned with alarmingly lifelike butterflies and bees, the insects seeming to hover intently beside several slabs of cinnamon-fragrant zucchini bread.

"They just keep *mul*tiplying." Mrs. Grose sighed so dramatically that Moony thought she must be referring to the bees, and peered at them again to make sure they weren't real. "Patricia— you know, that nice lady with the lady friend?—she says, *pick* the flowers, so I pick them but I still have too many squashes. Remind me to give you some for your mother."

At mention of her mother, Moony's anger melted away. She started to cry again.

"My darling, what is it?" cried Mrs. Grose. She moved so quickly to embrace Moony that a soft-smelling pinkish cloud of face powder wafted from her cheeks onto the girl's. "Tell us, darling, tell us—"

Moony sobbed luxuriously for several minutes, letting Mrs. Grose stroke her hair and feed her healthy sips of tepid brandy-laced tea. Mrs. Grose's pug wheezed anxiously at his mistress's feet and struggled to climb into Moony's lap. Eventually he succeeded. By then Moony had calmed down enough to tell the aged woman what had happened, her rambling narrative punctuated by hiccuping sobs and small gasps of laughter when the dog lapped excitedly at her teacup.

"Ah *so*," said Mrs. Grose, when she first understood that Moony was talking about the Light Children. She pressed her plump hands together and raised her tortoiseshell eyes to the ceiling. "They are having a busy day."

Moony frowned, wiping her cheeks. As though They were like the people who collected the trash or turned the water supply off at the end of the summer. But then Moony went on talking, her voice growing less tremulous as the brandy kicked in. When she finished, she sat in somewhat abashed silence and stared at the teacup she held in her damp hand. Its border of roses and cabbage butterflies took on a flushed glow from Mrs. Grose's paisley-draped Tiffany lamps. Moony looked uneasily at the door. Having confessed her story, she suddenly wanted to flee, to check on her mother; to forget the whole thing. But she couldn't just take off. She cleared her throat, and the pug growled sympathetically.

"*Well*," Mrs. Grose said at last. "I see I will be having lots of *company* this winter."

Moony stared at her uncomprehending. "I mean, your mother and Martin will be staying on," Mrs. Grose explained, and sipped her tea. Her cheeks like the patterned porcelain had a febrile glow, and her eyes were so bright that Moony wondered if she was very drunk. "So, at last! there will be enough of us here to really talk about it, to *learn*—"

"Learn what?" demanded Moony. Confusion and brandy made her peevish. She put her cup down and gently shoved the pug from her lap. "I mean, what happened? *What is going on?*"

"Why, it's Them, of course," Mrs. Grose said grandly, then ducked her head, as though afraid she might be overheard and deemed insolent. "We are so *fortunate—you* are so fortunate, my dear, and your darling mother! And Martin, of course—this is a wonderful time for us, a blessed, blessed time!" At Moony's glare of disbelief she went on, "You understand, my darling—They have come, They have *greeted* your mother and Martin, it is a very exciting thing, very rare—only a very few of us—"

Mrs. Grose preened a little before going on, "—and it is always so wonderful, so miraculous, when another joins us—and now suddenly we have *two!*"

Moony stared at her, her hands opening and closing in her lap. "But what *happened?*" she cried desperately. "What *are* They?"

Mrs. Grose shrugged and coughed delicately. "What are They," she repeated. "Well, Moony, that is a very good question." She heaved back onto the couch and sighed. "What are They? I do not know."

At Moony's rebellious glare she added hastily, "Well, many things, of course, we have thought They were many things, and They might be any of these or all of them or—well, none, I suppose. Fairies, or little angels of Jesus, or tree spirits—that is what a dear friend of mine believed. And some sailors thought They were Will-o-the-Wisps, and let's see, Miriam Hopewell, whom you don't remember but was *another* very dear friend of mine, God rest her soul, Miriam thought They came from flying saucers."

At this Moony's belligerence crumpled into defeat. She recalled the things she had seen on her mother—*devouring* her it seemed, setting her aflame—and gave a small involuntary gasp.

"But why?" she wailed. "I mean, *why?* Why should They care? What can They possibly get from us?"

Mrs. Grose enfolded Moony's hand in hers. She ran her fingers along Moony's palm as though preparing for a reading, and said, "Maybe They get something They don't have. Maybe we *give* Them something."

"But what?" Moony's voice rose, almost a shriek. "*What?*"

"Something They don't have," Mrs. Grose repeated softly. "Something everybody else has, but They don't—

"Our deaths."

Moony yanked her hand away. "Our *deaths?* My mother, like, sold her *soul,* to—to—"

"You don't understand, darling." Mrs. Grose looked at her with mild, whiskey-colored eyes. "They don't want us to *die.* They want our *deaths.* That's why we're still at Mars Hill, me and Gary and your mother and Martin. As long as we stay here, They will keep them for us—our sicknesses, our destinies. It's something They don't have." Mrs. Grose sighed, shaking her head. "I guess They just get lonely, or bored of being immortal. Or whatever it is They are."

That's right! Moony wanted to scream. *What the hell* are They? But she only said, "So as long as you stay here you don't die? But that doesn't make any sense—I mean, John died, *he* was here—"

Mrs. Grose shrugged. "He left. And They didn't come to him, They never greeted him . . .

"Maybe he didn't know—or maybe he didn't want to stay. Maybe he didn't want to live. Not everybody does, you know. *I* don't want to live forever—" She sighed melodramatically, her bosom heaving. "But I just can't seem to tear myself away."

She leaned over to hug Moony. "But don't worry now, darling. Your mother is going to be *okay.* And so is Martin. And so are you, and all of us. We're safe—"

Moony shuddered. "But I can't stay here! I have to go back to school, I have a *life*—"

"Of course you do, darling! We all do! Your life is out there—" Mrs. Grose gestured out the window, wiggling her fingers toward where the cold blue waters of the Bay lapped at the gravel. "And *ours* is *here*." She smiled, bent her head to kiss Moony so that the girl caught a heavy breath of chamomile and brandy. "Now you better go, before your mother starts to worry."

Like I was a goddamn kid, Moony thought, but she felt too exhausted to argue. She stood, bumping against the pug. It gave a muffled bark, then looked up at her and drooled apologetically. Moony leaned down to pat it and took a step toward the door. Abruptly she turned back.

"Okay," she said. "Okay. Like, I'm going. I understand, you don't know about these—about all this—I mean, I know you've told me everything you can. But I just want to ask you one thing—"

Mrs. Grose placed her teacup on the edge of the coffee table and waved her fingers, smiling absently. "Of course, of course, darling. Ask away."

"How old are you?"

Mrs. Grose's penciled eyebrows lifted above mild surprised eyes. "How old am I? One doesn't *ask* a lady such things, darling. But—"

She smiled slyly, leaning back and folding her hands upon her soft bulging stomach. "If I'd been a man and had the vote, it would have gone to Mr. Lincoln."

Moony nodded, just once, her breath stuck in her throat. Then she fled the cottage.

IN BANGOR, THE doctor confirmed that the cancer was in remission.

"It's incredible." She shook her head, staring at Ariel's test results before tossing them ceremonially into a wastebasket. "I would say the phrase 'A living miracle' is not inappropriate here. Or voodoo, or whatever it is you do there at Mars Hill."

She waved dismissively at the open window, then bent to retrieve the tests. "You're welcome to get another opinion. I would advise it, as a matter of fact."

"Of course," Ariel said. But of course she wouldn't, then or ever. She already knew what the doctors would tell her.

There was some more paperwork, a few awkward efforts by the doctor to get Ariel to confess to some secret healing cure, some herbal remedy or therapy practiced by the kooks at the spiritualist community. But finally they were done. There was nothing left to discuss, and only a Blue Cross number to be given to the receptionist. When the doctor stood to walk with Ariel to the door, her eyes were too bright, her voice earnest and a little shaky as she said, "And look: whatever you were doing, Ms. Rising—howling at the moon, whatever—you just keep on doing it. Okay?"

"Okay." Ariel smiled, and left.

"YOU REALLY CAN'T leave, now," Mrs. Grose told Martin and Ariel that night. They were all sitting around a bonfire on the rocky beach, Diana and Gary singing "Sloop John B" in off-key harmony, Rvis and Shasta Daisy and the others disemboweling leftover lobster bodies with the remorseless patience of raccoons. Mrs. Grose spread out the fingers of her right hand and twisted a heavy filigreed ring on her pinkie, her lips pursed as she regarded Ariel. "You shouldn't have gone to Bangor, that was *very foolish*," she said, frowning. "In a few months, maybe you can go with Gary to the Beach Store. *Maybe*. But no further than that."

Moony looked sideways at her mother, but Ariel only shook her head. Her eyes were luminous, the same color as the evening sky above the Bay.

"Who would want to leave?" Ariel said softly. Her hand crept across the pebbles to touch Martin's. As Moony watched them she felt again that sharp pain in her heart, like a needle jabbing her. She would never know exactly what had happened to her mother, or to Martin. Jason would tell her nothing. Nor would Ariel or anyone else. But there they were, Ariel and Martin sitting crosslegged on the gravel strand, while all around them the others ate and drank and sang as though nothing had happened at all; or as though whatever *had* occurred had been decided on long ago.

Without looking at each other, Martin and her mother smiled, Martin somewhat wryly. Mrs. Grose nodded.

"That's right," the old woman said. When she tossed a stone into the bonfire an eddy of sparks flared up. Moony jumped, startled, and looked up into the sky. For an instant she held her breath, thinking *At last!*—it was Them and all would be explained. The Fairy King would offer his benediction to the united and loving couples; the dour Puritan would be avenged; the Fool would sing his sad sweet song and everyone would wipe away happy tears.

But no. The sparks blew off into ashes, filling the air with a faint smell of incense. When she turned back to the bonfire, Jason was holding out a flaming marshmallow on a stick, laughing, and the others had segued into a drunken rendition of "Leaving on a Jet Plane."

"Take it, Moony," he urged her, the charred mess slipping from the stick. "Eat it quick, for luck."

She leaned over until it slid onto her tongue, a glowing coal of sweetness and earth and fire; and ate it quick, for luck.

LONG AFTER MIDNIGHT they returned to their separate bungalows. Jason lingered with Moony by the dying bonfire, stroking her hair and staring at the lights of Dark Harbor. There was the crunch of gravel behind them. He turned to see his father, standing silhouetted in the soft glow of the embers.

"Jason," he called softly. "Would you mind coming back with me? I—there's something we need to talk about."

Jason gazed down at Moony. Her eyes were heavy with sleep, and he lowered his head to kiss her, her mouth still redolent of burnt sugar. "Yeah, okay," he said, and stood. "You be okay, Moony?"

Moony nodded, yawning. "Sure." As he walked away, Jason looked back and saw her stretched out on the gravel beach, arms outspread as she stared up at the three-quarter moon riding close to the edge of Mars Hill.

"So what's going on?" he asked his father when they reached the cottage. Martin stood at the dining room table, his back to Jason. He picked up a small stack of envelopes and tapped them against the table, then turned to his son.

"I'm going back," he said. "Home. I got a letter from Brandon today"—Brandon was his agent—"there's going to be a show at the Frick Gallery, and a symposium. They want me to speak."

Jason stared at him, uncomprehending. His long pale hair fell into his face, and he pushed it impatiently from his eyes. "But— you can't," he said at last. "You'll die. You can't leave here. That's what Adele said. You'll *die*."

Martin remained silent, before replacing the envelopes and shaking his head. "We don't know that. Even before, we—*I*— didn't know that. Nobody knows that, ever."

Jason stared at him in disbelief. His face grew flushed as he said, "But you can't! You're sick—shit, Dad, look at John, you can't just—"

His father pursed his lips, tugged at his ponytail. "No, Jason, I *can*." Suddenly he looked surprised, a little sheepish even, and said more softly. "I mean, I *will*. There's too much for me to give up, Jason. Maybe it sounds stupid, but I think it's important that I go back. Not right away. I think I'll stay on for a few weeks, maybe until the end of October. You know, see autumn in New England and all. But after that—well, there's work for me to do at home, and—"

Jason's voice cracked as he shook his head furiously. "Dad. No. You'll—you'll die."

Martin shrugged. "I might. I mean, I guess I will, sometime. But—well, everybody dies." His mouth twisted into a smile as he stared at the floor. "Except Mrs. Grose."

Jason continued to shake his head. "But—you *saw* Them— They came, They must've done *something*—"

Martin looked up, his eyes feverishly bright. "They did. That's why I'm leaving. Look, Jason, I can't explain, all right? But what if you had to stay here, instead of going on to Bowdoin? What if Moony left, and everyone else—would you stay at Mars Hill? *Forever?*"

Jason was silent. Finally, "I think you should stay," he said, a little desperately. "Otherwise whatever They did was wasted."

Martin shook his head. His hand closed around a tube of viridian on the table and he raised it, held it in front of him like a weapon. His eyes glittered as he said, "Oh no, Jason. Not wasted. Nothing is wasted, not ever." And tilting his head he smiled, held out his arm until his son came to him and Martin embraced him, held him there until Jason's sobs quieted, and the moon began to slide behind Mars Hill.

JASON DROVE MOONY to the airport on Friday. Most of his things already had been shipped from San Francisco to Bowdoin College, but Moony had to return to Kamensic Village and the Loomises, to gather her clothes and books for school and make all the awkward explanations and arrangements on her own. Friends and relations in New York had been told that Ariel was undergoing some kind of experimental therapy, an excuse they bought as easily as they'd bought most of Ariel's other strange ideas. Now Moony didn't want to talk to anyone else on the phone. She didn't want to talk to anyone at all, except for Jason.

"It's kind of on the way to Brunswick," he explained when Diana protested his driving Moony. "Besides, Diana, if you took her she'd end up crying the whole way. This way I can keep her intact at least until the airport."

Diana gave in, finally. No one suggested that Ariel drive.

"Look down when the plane flies over Mars Hill," Ariel said, hugging her daughter by the car. "We'll be looking for you."

Moony nodded, her mouth tight, and kissed her mother. "You be okay," she whispered, the words lost in Ariel's tangled hair.

"I'll be okay," Ariel said, smiling.

Behind them Jason and Martin embraced. "If you're still here I'll be up Columbus Weekend," said Jason. "Maybe sooner if I run out of money."

Martin shook his head. "If you run out of money you better go see your mother."

It was only twenty minutes to the airport. "Don't wait," Moony said to Jason, as the same woman who had taken her ticket loaded her bags onto the little Beechcraft. "I mean it. If you do I'll cry and I'll kill you."

Jason nodded. "Righto. We don't want any bad publicity. *'Noted Queer Activist's Son Slain by Girlfriend at Local Airport. Wind Shear Is Blamed.'* "

Moony hugged him, drew away to study his face. "I'll call you in the morning."

He shook his head. "Tonight. When you get home. So I'll know you got in safely. 'Cause it's dangerous out there." He made an awful face, then leaned over to kiss her. "Ciao, Moony."

"Ciao, Jason."

She could feel him watching her as she clambered into the little plane, but she didn't look back. Instead she smiled tentatively at the few other passengers—a businessman with a tie loose around his neck, two middle-aged women with L. L. Bean shopping bags—and settled into a seat by the window.

During take-off she leaned over to see if she could spot Jason. For an instant she had a flash of his car, like a crimson leaf blowing south through the darkening green of pines and maples. Then it was gone.

Trailers of mist whipped across the little window. Moony shivered, drew her sweatshirt tight around her chest. She felt that beneath her everything she had ever known was shrinking, disappearing, swallowed by golden light; but somehow it was okay. As the Beechcraft banked over Penobscot Bay she pressed her face close against the glass, waiting for the gap in the clouds that would give her a last glimpse of the gray and white cottages tumbling down Mars Hill, the wind-riven pier where her mother and Martin and all the rest stood staring up into the early autumn sky, tiny as fairy people in a child's book. For an instant it seemed that something hung over them, a golden cloud like a September haze. But then the blinding sun made her glance away. When she looked down again the golden haze was gone. But the others were still there, waving and calling out soundlessly until the plane finally turned south and bore her away, away from summer and its silent visitors—her mother's cancer, Martin's virus, the Light Children and Their hoard of stolen sufferings—away, away, away from them all, and back to the welcoming world.

Maneki Neko

BRUCE STERLING

For the past two decades, Bruce Sterling has been looking into the future with remarkable clarity. His novels (seven to date, the most recent of which is Distraction*) and stories have anticipated many of the biggest changes we've seen in society . . . and they've also been ripping good reads. "Maneki Neko" was first published in* Hayakawa S-F *magazine in Japan and then this English-language version followed. Like much of Sterling's work, it seeks out the place of the human soul in the midst of a technological society.*

"I CAN'T GO ON," HIS BROTHER SAID.

Tsuyoshi Shimizu looked thoughtfully into the screen of his pasokon. His older brother's face was shiny with sweat from a late-night drinking bout. "It's only a career," said Tsuyoshi, sitting up on his futon and adjusting his pajamas. "You worry too much."

"All that overtime!" his brother whined. He was making the call from a bar somewhere in Shibuya. In the background, a middle-aged office lady was singing karaoke, badly. "And the examination hells. The manager training programs. The proficiency tests. I never have time to live!"

Tsuyoshi grunted sympathetically. He didn't like these late-night videophone calls, but he felt obliged to listen. His big brother had always been a decent sort, before he had gone through the elite courses at Waseda University, joined a big corporation, and gotten professionally ambitious.

"My back hurts," his brother groused. "I have an ulcer. My hair is going gray. And I know they'll fire me. No matter how loyal you are to the big companies, they have no loyalty to their employees anymore. It's no wonder that I drink."

"You should get married," Tsuyoshi offered.

"I can't find the right girl. Women never understand me." He shuddered. "Tsuyoshi, I'm truly desperate. The market pressures are crushing me. I can't breathe. My life has got to change. I'm thinking of taking the vows. I'm serious! I want to renounce this whole modern world."

Tsuyoshi was alarmed. "You're very drunk, right?"

His brother leaned closer to the screen. "Life in a monastery sounds truly good to me. It's so quiet there. You recite the sutras. You consider your existence. There are rules to follow, and rewards that make sense. It's just the way that Japanese business used to be, back in the good old days."

Tsuyoshi grunted skeptically.

"Last week I went out to a special place in the mountains . . . Mount Aso," his brother confided. "The monks there, they know about people in trouble, people who are burned out by modern life. The monks protect you from the world. No computers, no phones, no faxes, no e-mail, no overtime, no commuting, nothing at all. It's beautiful, and it's peaceful, and nothing ever happens there. Really, it's like a paradise."

"Listen, older brother," Tsuyoshi said, "you're not a religious man by nature. You're a section chief for a big import-export company."

"Well . . . maybe religion won't work for me. I did think of running away to America. Nothing much ever happens there, either."

Tsuyoshi smiled. "That sounds much better! America is a good vacation spot. A long vacation is just what you need! Besides, the Americans are real friendly since they gave up their handguns."

"But I can't go through with it," his brother wailed. "I just don't dare. I can't just wander away from everything that I know and trust to the kindness of strangers."

"That always works for me," Tsuyoshi said. "Maybe you should try it."

Tsuyoshi's wife stirred uneasily on the futon. Tsuyoshi lowered his voice. "Sorry, but I have to hang up now. Call me before you do anything rash."

"Don't tell Dad," Tsuyoshi's brother said. "He worries so."

"I won't tell Dad." Tsuyoshi cut the connection and the screen went dark.

Tsuyoshi's wife rolled over heavily. She was seven months pregnant. She stared at the ceiling, puffing for breath. "Was that another call from your brother?" she said.

"Yeah. The company just gave him another promotion. More responsibilities. He's celebrating."

"That sounds nice," his wife said tactfully.

NEXT MORNING, TSUYOSHI slept late. He was self-employed, so he kept his own hours. Tsuyoshi was a video format upgrader by trade. He transferred old videos from obsolete formats into the new high-grade storage media. Doing this properly took a craftsman's eye. Word of Tsuyoshi's skills had gotten out on the network, so he had as much work as he could handle.

At ten A.M., the mailman arrived. Tsuyoshi abandoned his breakfast of raw egg and miso soup and signed for a shipment of flaking, twentieth-century analog television tapes. The mail also brought a fresh overnight shipment of strawberries and a home-made jar of pickles.

"Pickles!" his wife enthused. "People are so nice to you when you're pregnant."

"Any idea who sent us that?"

"Just someone on the network."

"Great."

Tsuyoshi booted his mediator, cleaned his superconducting heads, and examined the old tapes. Home videos from the 1980s. Someone's grandmother as a child, presumably. There had been a lot of flaking and loss of polarity in the old recording medium.

Tsuyoshi got to work with his desktop fractal detail generator, the image stabilizer, and the interlace algorithms. When he was done, Tsuyoshi's new digital copies would look much sharper, cleaner, and better composed than the original primitive videotape.

Tsuyoshi enjoyed his work. Quite often he came across bits and pieces of videotape that were of archival interest. He would pass the images on to the net. The really big network databases, with their armies of search engines, indexers, and catalogs, had some very arcane interests. The net machines would never pay for data, because the global information networks were noncommercial. But the net machines were very polite and had excellent net etiquette. They returned a favor for a favor, and since they were machines with excellent, enormous memories, they never forgot a good deed.

Tsuyoshi and his wife had a lunch of ramen with naruto, and she left to go shopping. A shipment arrived by overseas package service. Cute baby clothes from Darwin, Australia. They were in his wife's favorite color, sunshine yellow.

Tsuyoshi finished transferring the first tape to a new crystal disk. Time for a break. He left his apartment, took the elevator, and went out to the corner coffeeshop. He ordered a double iced mocha cappuccino and paid with a chargecard.

His pokkecon rang. Tsuyoshi took it from his belt and answered it. "Get one to go," the machine told him.

"Okay," said Tsuyoshi, and hung up. He bought a second coffee, put a lid on it, and left the shop.

A man in a business suit was sitting on a park bench near the entrance of Tsuyoshi's building. The man's suit was good, but it looked as if he'd slept in it. He was holding his head in his hands and rocking gently back and forth. He was unshaven and his eyes were red-rimmed.

The pokkecon rang again. "The coffee's for him?" Tsuyoshi said.

"Yes," said the pokkecon. "He needs it."

Tsuyoshi walked up to the lost businessman. The man looked up, flinching warily, as if he were about to be kicked. "What is it?" he said.

"Here," Tsuyoshi said, handing him the cup. "Double iced mocha cappuccino."

The man opened the cup and smelled it. He looked up in disbelief. "This is my favorite kind of coffee . . . Who are you?"

Tsuyoshi lifted his arm and offered a hand signal, his fingers clenched like a cat's paw. The man showed no recognition of the gesture. Tsuyoshi shrugged, and smiled. "It doesn't matter. Sometimes a man really needs a coffee. Now you have a coffee. That's all."

"Well . . ." The man cautiously sipped his cup, and suddenly smiled. "It's really great. Thanks!"

"You're welcome." Tsuyoshi went home.

His wife arrived from shopping. She had bought new shoes. The pregnancy was making her feet swell. She sat carefully on the couch and sighed.

"Orthopedic shoes are expensive," she said, looking at the yellow pumps. "I hope you don't think they look ugly."

"On you, they look really cute," Tsuyoshi said wisely. He had first met his wife at a video store. She had just used her credit card to buy a disk of primitive black-and-white American anime of the 1950s. The pokkecon had urged him to go up and speak to her on the subject of Felix the Cat. Felix was an early television cartoon star and one of Tsuyoshi's personal favorites.

Tsuyoshi would have been too shy to approach an attractive woman on his own, but no one was a stranger to the net. This fact gave him the confidence to speak to her. Tsuyoshi had soon discovered that the girl was delighted to discuss her deep fondness for cute, antique, animated cats. They'd had lunch together. They'd had a date the next week. They had spent Christmas Eve together in a love hotel. They had a lot in common.

She had come into his life through a little act of grace, a little gift from Felix the Cat's magic bag of tricks. Tsuyoshi had never gotten over feeling grateful for this. Now that he was married and becoming a father, Tsuyoshi Shimizu could feel himself becoming solidly fixed in life. He had a man's role to play now. He knew who he was, and he knew where he stood. Life was good to him.

"You need a haircut, dear," his wife told him.

"Sure."

His wife pulled a gift box out of her shopping bag. "Can you go to the Hotel Daruma, and get your hair cut, and deliver this box for me?"

"What is it?" Tsuyoshi said.

Tsuyoshi's wife opened the little wooden gift box. A maneki neko was nestled inside white foam padding. The smiling ceramic cat held one paw upraised, beckoning for good fortune.

"Don't you have enough of those yet?" he said. "You even have maneki neko underwear."

"It's not for my collection. It's a gift for someone at the Hotel Daruma."

"Oh."

"Some foreign woman gave me this box at the shoestore. She looked American. She couldn't speak Japanese. She had really nice shoes, though . . ."

"If the network gave you that little cat, then you're the one who should take care of that obligation, dear."

"But dear"—she sighed—"my feet hurt so much, and you could do with a haircut anyway, and I have to cook supper, and besides, it's not really a nice maneki neko, it's just cheap tourist souvenir junk. Can't you do it?"

"Oh, all right," Tsuyoshi told her. "Just forward your pokkecon prompts onto my machine, and I'll see what I can do for us."

She smiled. "I knew you would do it. You're really so good to me."

Tsuyoshi left with the little box. He wasn't unhappy to do the errand, as it wasn't always easy to manage his pregnant wife's volatile moods in their small six-tatami apartment. The local neighborhood was good, but he was hoping to find bigger accommodations before the child was born. Maybe a place with a little studio, where he could expand the scope of his work. It was very hard to find decent housing in Tokyo, but word was out on the net. Friends he didn't even know were working every day to help him. If he kept up with the net's obligations, he had every confidence that some day something nice would turn up.

Tsuyoshi went into the local pachinko parlor, where he won half a liter of beer and a train chargecard. He drank the beer, took the new train card, and wedged himself into the train. He got out at the Ebisu station and turned on his pokkecon Tokyo street map to guide his steps. He walked past places called Chocolate Soup, and Freshness Physique, and The Aladdin Mai-Tai Panico Trattoria.

He entered the Hotel Daruma and went to the hotel barbershop, which was called the Daruma Planet Look. "May I help you?" said the receptionist.

"I'm thinking, a shave and a trim," Tsuyoshi said.

"Do you have an appointment with us?"

"Sorry, no." Tsuyoshi offered a hand gesture.

The woman gestured back, a jerky series of cryptic finger movements. Tsuyoshi didn't recognize any of the gestures. She wasn't from his part of the network.

"Oh well, never mind," the receptionist said kindly. "I'll get Nahoko to look after you."

Nahoko was carefully shaving the fine hair from Tsuyoshi's forehead when the pokkecon rang. Tsuyoshi answered it.

"Go to the ladies' room on the fourth floor," the pokkecon told him.

"Sorry, I can't do that. This is Tsuyoshi Shimizu, not Ai Shimizu. Besides, I'm having my hair cut right now."

"Oh, I see," said the machine. "Recalibrating." It hung up.

Nahoko finished his hair. She had done a good job. He looked much better. A man who worked at home had to take special trouble to keep up appearances. The pokkecon rang again.

"Yes?" said Tsuyoshi.

"Buy bay rum aftershave. Take it outside."

"Right." He hung up. "Nahoko, do you have bay rum?"

"Odd you should ask that," said Nahoko. "Hardly anyone asks for bay rum anymore, but our shop happens to keep it in stock."

Tsuyoshi bought the aftershave, then stepped outside the barbershop. Nothing happened, so he bought a manga comic and waited. Finally a hairy, blond stranger in shorts, a tropical shirt, and sandals approached him. The foreigner was carrying a camera bag and an old-fashioned pokkecon. He looked about sixty years old, and he was very tall.

The man spoke to his pokkecon in English. "Excuse me," said the pokkecon, translating the man's speech into Japanese. "Do you have a bottle of bay rum aftershave?"

"Yes I do." Tsuyoshi handed the bottle over. "Here."

"Thank goodness!" said the man, his words relayed through his machine. "I've asked everyone else in the lobby. Sorry I was late."

"No problem," said Tsuyoshi. "That's a nice pokkecon you have there."

"Well," the man said, "I know it's old and out of style. But I plan to buy a new pokkecon here in Tokyo. I'm told that they sell pokkecons by the basketful in Akihabara electronics market."

"That's right. What kind of translator program are you running? Your translator talks like someone from Osaka."

"Does it sound funny?" the tourist asked anxiously.

"Well, I don't want to complain, but . . ." Tsuyoshi smiled. "Here, let's trade meishi. I can give you a copy of a brand-new freeware translator."

"That would be wonderful." They pressed buttons and squirted copies of their business cards across the network link.

Tsuyoshi examined his copy of the man's electronic card and saw that his name was Zimmerman. Mr. Zimmerman was from New Zealand. Tsuyoshi activated a transfer program. His modern pokkecon began transferring a new translator onto Zimmerman's machine.

A large American man in a padded suit entered the lobby of the Daruma. The man wore sunglasses and was sweating visibly in the summer heat. The American looked huge, as if he lifted a lot of weights. Then a Japanese woman followed him. The woman was sharply dressed, with a dark blue dress suit, hat, sunglasses, and an attaché case. She had a haunted look.

Her escort turned and carefully watched the bellhops, who were bringing in a series of bags. The woman walked crisply to the reception desk and began making anxious demands of the clerk.

"I'm a great believer in machine translation," Tsuyoshi said to the tall man from New Zealand. "I really believe that computers help human beings to relate in a much more human way."

"I couldn't agree with you more," said Mr. Zimmerman, through his machine. "I can remember the first time I came to your country, many years ago. I had no portable translator. In fact, I had nothing but a printed phrasebook. I happened to go into a bar, and . . ."

Zimmerman stopped and gazed alertly at his pokkecon. "Oh dear, I'm getting a screen prompt. I have to go up to my room right away."

"Then I'll come along with you till this software transfer is done," Tsuyoshi said.

"That's very kind of you." They got into the elevator together. Zimmerman punched for the fourth floor. "Anyway, as I was saying, I went into this bar in Roppongi late at night, because I was jetlagged and hoping for something to eat . . ."

"Yes?"

"And this woman . . . well, let's just say this woman was hanging out in a foreigner's bar in Roppongi late at night, and she wasn't wearing a whole lot of clothes, and she didn't look like she was any better than she ought to be . . ."

"Yes, I think I understand you."

"Anyway, this menu they gave me was full of kanji, or katakana, or romanji, or whatever they call those, so I had my phrasebook out, and I was trying very hard to puzzle out these pesky ideograms . . ." The elevator opened and they stepped into the carpeted hall of the hotel's fourth floor. "So I opened the menu and I pointed to an entree, and I told this girl . . ." Zimmerman stopped suddenly and stared at his screen. "Oh dear, something's happening. Just a moment."

Zimmerman carefully studied the instructions on his pokkecon. Then he pulled the bottle of bay rum from the baggy pocket of his shorts and unscrewed the cap. He stood on tiptoe, stretching to his full height, and carefully poured the contents of the bottle through the iron louvers of a ventilation grate, set high in the top of the wall.

ZIMMERMAN SCREWED THE cap back on neatly and slipped the empty bottle back in his pocket. Then he examined his pokkecon again. He frowned, and shook it. The screen had frozen. Apparently Tsuyoshi's new translation program had overloaded Zimmerman's old-fashioned operating system. His pokkecon had crashed.

Zimmerman spoke a few defeated sentences in English. Then he smiled and spread his hands apologetically. He bowed, and went into his room, and shut the door.

The Japanese woman and her burly American escort entered the hall. The man gave Tsuyoshi a hard stare. The woman opened the door with a passcard. Her hands were shaking.

Tsuyoshi's pokkecon rang. "Leave the hall," it told him. "Go downstairs. Get into the elevator with the bellboy."

Tsuyoshi followed instructions.

The bellboy was just entering the elevator with a cart full of the woman's baggage. Tsuyoshi got into the elevator, stepping carefully behind the wheeled metal cart. "What floor, sir?" said the bellboy.

"Eight," Tsuyoshi said, ad-libbing. The bellboy turned and pushed the buttons. He faced forward attentively, his gloved hands folded.

The pokkecon flashed a silent line of text to the screen. "Put the gift box inside her flight bag," it read.

Tsuyoshi located the zippered blue bag at the back of the cart. It was a matter of instants to zip it open, put in the box with the maneki neko, and zip the bag shut again. The bellboy noticed nothing. He left, tugging his cart.

Tsuyoshi got out on the eighth floor, feeling slightly foolish. He wandered down the hall, found a quiet nook by an ice machine, and called his wife. "What's going on?" he said.

"Oh, nothing." She smiled. "Your haircut looks nice! Show me the back of your head."

Tsuyoshi held the pokkecon screen behind the nape of his neck.

"They do good work," his wife said with satisfaction. "I hope it didn't cost too much. Are you coming home now?"

"Things are getting a little odd here at the hotel," Tsuyoshi told her. "I may be some time."

His wife frowned. "Well, don't miss supper. We're having bonito."

Tsuyoshi took the elevator back down. It stopped at the fourth floor. The woman's American companion stepped onto the elevator. His nose was running and his eyes were streaming with tears.

"Are you all right?" Tsuyoshi said.

"I don't understand Japanese," the man growled. The elevator doors shut.

The man's cellular phone crackled into life. It emitted a scream of anguish and a burst of agitated female English. The man swore and slammed his hairy fist against the elevator's emergency button. The elevator stopped with a lurch. An alarm bell began ringing.

The man pried the doors open with his large hairy fingers and

clambered out into the fourth floor. He then ran headlong down
the hall.

The elevator began buzzing in protest, its doors shuddering
as if broken. Tsuyoshi climbed hastily from the damaged elevator
and stood there in the hallway. He hesitated a moment. Then he
produced his pokkecon and loaded his Japanese-to-English translator. He walked cautiously after the American man.

THE DOOR TO their suite was open. Tsuyoshi spoke aloud into his
pokkecon. "Hello?" he said experimentally. "May I be of help?"

The woman was sitting on the bed. She had just discovered
the maneki neko box in her flight bag. She was staring at the little
cat in horror.

"Who are you?" she said, in bad Japanese.

Tsuyoshi realized suddenly that she was a Japanese American.
Tsuyoshi had met a few Japanese Americans before. They always
troubled him. They looked fairly normal from the outside, but
their behavior was always bizarre. "I'm just a passing friend," he
said. "Something I can do?"

"Grab him, Mitch!" said the woman in English. The American man rushed into the hall and grabbed Tsuyoshi by the arm.
His hands were like steel bands.

Tsuyoshi pressed the distress button on his pokkecon.

"Take that computer away from him," the woman ordered in
English. Mitch quickly took Tsuyoshi's pokkecon away and threw
it on the bed. He deftly patted Tsuyoshi's clothing, searching for
weapons. Then he shoved Tsuyoshi into a chair.

The woman switched back to Japanese. "Sit right there, you.
Don't you dare move." She began examining the contents of Tsuyoshi's wallet.

"I beg your pardon?" Tsuyoshi said. His pokkecon was lying
on the bed. Lines of red text scrolled up its little screen as it
silently issued a series of emergency net alerts.

The woman spoke to her companion in English. Tsuyoshi's
pokkecon was still translating faithfully. "Mitch, go call the local
police."

Mitch sneezed uncontrollably. Tsuyoshi noticed that the room smelled strongly of bay rum. "I can't talk to the local cops. I can't speak Japanese." Mitch sneezed again.

"Okay, then I'll call the cops. You handcuff this guy. Then go down to the infirmary and get yourself some antihistamines, for Christ's sake."

Mitch pulled a length of plastic whipcord cuff from his coat pocket and attached Tsuyoshi's right wrist to the head of the bed. He mopped his streaming eyes with a tissue. "I'd better stay with you. If there's a cat in your luggage, then the criminal network already knows we're in Japan. You're in danger."

"Mitch, you may be my bodyguard, but you're breaking out in hives."

"This just isn't supposed to happen," Mitch complained, scratching his neck. "My allergies never interfered with my job before."

"Just leave me here and lock the door," the woman told him. "I'll put a chair against the knob. I'll be all right. You need to look after yourself."

Mitch left the room.

The woman barricaded the door with a chair. Then she called the front desk on the hotel's bedside pasokon. "This is Louise Hashimoto in room 434. I have a gangster in my room. He's an information criminal. Would you call the Tokyo police, please? Tell them to send the organized crime unit. Yes, that's right. Do it. And you should put your hotel security people on full alert. There may be big trouble here. You'd better hurry." She hung up.

Tsuyoshi stared at her in astonishment. "Why are you doing this? What's all this about?"

"So you call yourself Tsuyoshi Shimizu," said the woman, examining his credit cards. She sat on the foot of the bed and stared at him. "You're yakuza of some kind, right?"

"I think you've made a big mistake," Tsuyoshi said.

Louise scowled. "Look, Mr. Shimizu, you're not dealing with some Yankee tourist here. My name is Louise Hashimoto and I'm an assistant federal prosecutor from Providence, Rhode Island, USA." She showed him a magnetic ID card with a gold official seal.

"It's nice to meet someone from the American government,"

said Tsuyoshi, bowing a bit in his chair. "I'd shake your hand, but it's tied to the bed."

"You can stop with the innocent act right now. I spotted you out in the hall earlier, and in the lobby, too, casing the hotel. How did you know my bodyguard is violently allergic to bay rum? You must have read his medical records."

"Who, me? Never!"

"Ever since I discovered you network people, it's been one big pattern," said Louise. "It's the biggest criminal conspiracy I ever saw. I busted this software pirate in Providence. He had a massive network server and a whole bunch of AI freeware search engines. We took him in custody, we bagged all his search engines, and catalogs, and indexers . . . Later that very same day, these *cats* start showing up."

"Cats?"

Louise lifted the maneki neko, handling it as if it were a live eel. "These little Japanese voodoo cats. Maneki neko, right? They started showing up everywhere I went. There's a china cat in my handbag. There's three china cats at the office. Suddenly they're on display in the windows of every antique store in Providence. My car radio starts making meowing noises at me."

"You *broke* part of the network?" Tsuyoshi said, scandalized. "You took someone's machines away? That's terrible! How could you do such an inhuman thing?"

"You've got a real nerve complaining about that. What about *my* machinery?" Louise held up her fat, eerie-looking American pokkecon. "As soon as I stepped off the airplane at Narita, my PDA was attacked. Thousands and thousands of e-mail messages. All of them pictures of cats. A denial-of-service attack! I can't even communicate with the home office! My PDA's useless!"

"What's a PDA?"

"It's a PDA, my Personal Digital Assistant! Manufactured in Silicon Valley!"

"Well, with a goofy name like that, no wonder our pokkecons won't talk to it."

Louise frowned grimly. "That's right, wise guy. Make jokes about it. You're involved in a malicious software attack on a legal officer of the United States Government. You'll see." She paused, looking him over. "You know, Shimizu, you don't look much like the Italian mafia gangsters I have to deal with, back in Providence."

"I'm not a gangster at all. I never do anyone any harm."

"Oh no?" Louise glowered at him. "Listen, pal, I know a lot more about your setup, and your kind of people, than you think I do. I've been studying your outfit for a long time now. We computer cops have names for your kind of people. Digital panarchies. Segmented, polycephalous, integrated influence networks. What about all these *free goods and services* you're getting all this time?"

She pointed a finger at him. "Ha! Do you ever pay *taxes* on those? Do you ever *declare* that income and those benefits? All the free shipments from other countries! The little homemade cookies, and the free pens and pencils and bumper stickers, and the used bicycles, and the helpful news about fire sales . . . You're a tax evader! You're living through kickbacks! And bribes! And influence peddling! And all kinds of corrupt off-the-books transactions!"

Tsuyoshi blinked. "Look, I don't know anything about all that. I'm just living my life."

"Well, your network gift economy is undermining the lawful, government-approved, regulated economy!"

"Well," Tsuyoshi said gently, "maybe my economy is better than your economy."

"Says who?" she scoffed. "Why would anyone think that?"

"It's better because we're *happier* than you are. What's wrong with acts of kindness? Everyone likes gifts. Midsummer gifts. New Year's Day gifts. Year-end presents. Wedding presents. Everybody likes those."

"Not the way you Japanese like them. You're totally crazy for gifts."

"What kind of society has no gifts? It's a barbaric to have no regard for common human feelings."

Louise bristled. "You're saying I'm barbaric?"

"I don't mean to complain," Tsuyoshi said politely, "but you do have me tied up to your bed."

Louise crossed her arms. "You might as well stop complaining. You'll be in much worse trouble when the local police arrive."

"Then we'll probably be waiting here for quite a while," Tsuyoshi said. "The police move rather slowly here in Japan. I'm sorry, but we don't have as much crime as you Americans, so our police are not very alert."

The pasokon rang at the side of the bed. Louise answered it. It was Tsuyoshi's wife.

"Could I speak to Tsuyoshi Shimizu please?"

"I'm over here, dear," Tsuyoshi called quickly. "She's kidnapped me! She tied me to the bed!"

"Tied to her *bed?*" His wife's eyes grew wide. "That does it! I'm calling the police!"

Louise quickly hung up the pasokon. "I haven't kidnapped you! I'm only detaining you here until the local authorities can come and arrest you."

"Arrest me for what, exactly?"

Louise thought quickly. "Well, for poisoning my bodyguard by pouring bay rum into the ventilator."

"But I never did that. Anyway, that's not illegal, is it?"

The pasokon rang again. A shining white cat appeared on the screen. It had large, staring, unearthly eyes.

"Let him go," the cat commanded in English.

Louise shrieked and yanked the pasokon's plug from the wall.

Suddenly the lights went out. "Infrastructure attack!" Louise squealed. She rolled quickly under the bed.

The room went gloomy and quiet. The air conditioner had shut off. "I think you can come out," Tsuyoshi said at last, his voice loud in the still room. "It's just a power failure."

"No it isn't," Louise said. She crawled slowly from beneath the bed and sat on the mattress. Somehow, the darkness had made them more intimate. "I know very well what this is. I'm under attack. I haven't had a moment's peace since I broke that network. Stuff just happens to me now. Bad stuff. Swarms of it. It's never anything you can touch, though. Nothing you can prove in a court of law."

She sighed. "I sit in chairs, and somebody's left a piece of gum there. I get free pizzas, but they're not the kind of pizzas I like. Little kids spit on my sidewalk. Old women in walkers get in front of me whenever I need to hurry."

The shower came on, all by itself. Louise shuddered, but said nothing. Slowly, the darkened, stuffy room began to fill with hot steam.

"My toilets don't flush," Louise said. "My letters get lost in the mail. When I walk by cars, their theft alarms go off. And strangers stare at me. It's always little things. Lots of little tiny things, but they never, ever stop. I'm up against something that is very very big, and very very patient. And it knows all about me. And it's got a million arms and legs. And all those arms and legs are people."

There was the noise of scuffling in the hall. Distant voices, confused shouting.

Suddenly the chair broke under the doorknob. The door burst open violently. Mitch tumbled through, the sunglasses flying from his head. Two hotel security guards were trying to grab him. Shouting incoherently in English, Mitch fell headlong to the floor, kicking and thrashing. The guards lost their hats in the struggle. One tackled Mitch's legs with both his arms, and the other whacked and jabbed him with a baton.

Puffing and grunting with effort, they hauled Mitch out of the room. The darkened room was so full of steam that the harried guards hadn't even noticed Tsuyoshi and Louise.

Louise stared at the broken door. "Why did they do that to him?"

Tsuyoshi scratched his head in embarrassment. "Probably a failure of communication."

"Poor Mitch! They took his gun away at the airport. He had all kinds of technical problems with his passport . . . Poor guy, he's never had any luck since he met me."

There was a loud tapping at the window. Louise shrank back in fear. Finally she gathered her courage and opened the curtains. Daylight flooded the room.

A window-washing rig had been lowered from the roof of the hotel, on cables and pulleys. There were two window-washers in crisp gray uniforms. They waved cheerfully, making little catpaw gestures.

There was a third man with them. It was Tsuyoshi's brother.

One of the washers opened the window with a utility key. Tsuyoshi's brother squirmed into the room. He stood up and carefully adjusted his coat and tie.

"This is my brother," Tsuyoshi explained.

"What are you doing here?" Louise said.

"They always bring in the relatives when there's a hostage situation," Tsuyoshi's brother said. "The police just flew me in by helicopter and landed me on the roof." He looked Louise up and down. "Miss Hashimoto, you just have time to escape."

"What?" she said.

"Look down at the streets," he told her. "See that? You hear them? Crowds are pouring in from all over the city. All kinds of people, everyone with wheels. Street noodle salesmen. Bicycle messengers. Skateboard kids. Takeout delivery guys."

Louise gazed out the window into the streets, and shrieked aloud. "Oh no! A giant swarming mob! They're surrounding me! I'm doomed!"

"You are not doomed," Tsuyoshi's brother told her intently. "Come out the window. Get onto the platform with us. You've got one chance, Louise. It's a place I know, a sacred place in the mountains. No computers there, no phones, nothing." He paused. "It's a sanctuary for people like us. And I know the way."

She gripped his suited arm. "Can I trust you?"

"Look in my eyes," he told her. "Don't you see? Yes, of course you can trust me. We have everything in common."

Louise stepped out the window. She clutched his arm, the wind whipping at her hair. The platform creaked rapidly up and out of sight.

Tsuyoshi stood up from the chair. When he stretched out, tugging at his handcuffed wrist, he was just able to reach his pok-kecon with his fingertips. He drew it in and clutched it to his chest. Then he sat down again and waited patiently for someone to come and give him freedom.

No Planets Strike

GENE WOLFE

Over the course of his thirty-plus-year career, Gene Wolfe has written a wide variety of fantasy, SF, and science-fantasy stories. Among his many novels are Peace, The Devil in a Forest, Castleview, *and the classic* Book of the Long Sun *tetralogy. He notes that this story "began with a reference to that speech at the beginning of* Hamlet *in a book on clowns. I dug out the play and read the speech, and was struck by Shakespeare's idea that aliens could not attack on Christmas Eve. A couple months passed, and I unconsciously mixed in the legend that animals can talk at midnight, when Christmas Eve becomes Christmas Day."*

> *Some say that ever 'gainst that season comes.*
> *Wherein our Saviour's birth is celebrated,*
> *This bird of dawning singeth all night long,*
> *And then, they say, no spirit dare stir abroad;*
> *The nights are wholesome; then no planets strike,*
> *No fairy takes, nor witch hath power to charm,*
> *So hallow'd and so gracious is that time.*
> *—Hamlet* I.i.

YOU SURE YOU REALLY WANT TO HEAR ABOUT ALL THIS? I MEAN, me and Bully weren't really the main ones.

Okay. Is that thing on?

Hi. My name's Donnie, and I'm a donkey. My friend's name is Bully, only he's not really a bull, you know what I mean? They

cut off his—you know. So he wouldn't get mad. That's something
lots of people don't understand, they think he can't. He can, only
he hardly ever does. But if he does, watch out, because he's big
and real strong. I'm not big, but I'm strong anyhow. You'd be
surprised how much I can carry or how hard I can kick, and I can
run a lot faster than you think, too.

As well as I can figure, we were born on Earth, only they didn't
call it that back there, they called it Texas. There was a big school
that had farms and ranches all over for trying out new seeds and
new ways of growing silage and all that. And before we were ever
born they did stuff to us to make us as smart as most people, and
worked on our tongues and mouths some, too. Not enough to
make us sound like you—we know we don't—but enough so you
could understand us.

The idea was that there's still a lot of places like this one,
where people are poor and use animals where rich people'd use
machines. Like carrying firewood. If they're rich enough to have
a donkey, they use him for that, or somebody like Bully to plow
or pull a cart that's too big for me. They do all that here, probably
you've seen it. And they thought if we could talk to those people
and understand what they told us, it might be better.

I guess it didn't work out too good though, because after a
few years they dropped the whole thing and sold us off. I really
didn't know Bully up till then. I guess I'd seen him, but there were
a lot around, cows mostly. If I did, I didn't pay attention. Maybe
you've talked to him already?

He's mostly red and white, because there's Hereford in him,
and black because of other stuff. His hump's from Santa Gertrudis,
which is what his mom was, so there's Indian cattle and longhorns
back there. I'm little, and gray like you see except for this mark
on my back.

The way we got together was, the same man bought us both.
His name was Mango. Mango the Clown. He taught us a lot of
stuff we'd never known about back on the ranch, like various acts
and Bully to let people ride on his back. We went to so many
foreign worlds with Mango that I lost count after a while. I can
count up to ten, usually. It was more than that, so I started counting tens. I know you'd do it different, but that was the only thing
I could think of that would work for me, or Bully either. But after

a while I sort of forgot, because what difference did it make? Besides, sometimes we went back to one where we'd been before if the tip had been good.

We're clowns, too, and we're pretty famous now. I guess you've seen us.

We'd get painted up and put on ruffs. That's what you call the big collars, they're ruffs. Mango'd beat his drum to get us a crowd, and we'd put on one of our clown acts.

Like, Mango would be trying to lead me, only Bully would be lying down and Mango not see him, and he'd back into one of Bully's horns and jump, and Bully'd beller. We didn't any of us talk when we did our acts, and that sure was a swell idea of Mango's, I mean nobody talking, because it would've got us killed here on Sidhe. Quick, too. There's witches here, and the Beautiful Ones don't like them one little bit.

Then Mango'd put his finger up to his head and have an idea, and wink at everybody. He'd tie me to Bully so Bully'd pull me along, and that way I'd have to go. He'd do it, and Bully wouldn't get up. Mango'd kick him and poke him and holler at him, but Bully'd just yawn. Finally Mango'd back off and talk to both of us, only without talking, if you know what I mean. Talk with his eyes and face and hands, and his whole body. He'd show how he got us when we were little, and what good care he'd taken of us—we'd shake our heads at that—how he'd fed us and nursed us when we were sick. Then he'd say how all that was over now. He was going to sell us to the butcher—pointing to a butcher's shop, if there was one on that street—and the butcher'd cut our throats and skin us, and chop us up to sell. He'd say that I was pork, Mango'd say, and he'd say Bully was donkey meat.

That'd get Bully mad. He'd jump up and paw the ground and snort, and then he'd chase Mango around and around in a big circle, with me still tied to him standing in the middle and turning around to watch them. Pretty soon he'd get tired and Mango'd get tired, and they wouldn't run anymore, just walk. Then Bully'd lie down where he'd been lying down before, with Mango panting and mopping up sweat.

That's when I'd come up behind him and stand on my hind legs, and tap him on the shoulder with one of my front hoofs— that usually got the biggest laugh in the whole act. He'd turn around the wrong way, and I'd be down again. I'd try to get him to get on my back, pulling on his clown coat with my teeth and pushing him with my head, and making regular donkey noises, but he never would get the idea. After a lot of that—as long as it was getting good laughs—I'd get him to standing straddle-legged and then run between his legs and sort of scoop him up. Mango was one of those tall, skinny birds, and he'd have to pull his legs way up to keep his feet from dragging. Then I'd climb up on Bully's back, and he'd stand up, and the three of us would go 'round in a circle, me on Bully and Mango on me. And after that we'd pass the hat.

That was just one act, you understand. We had a lot of others, and if the money was good in a certain part of town, we'd go back there again next day and put on a different act. When we'd played out a city, we'd go on to another one, and when we'd played all the cities or Mango could find a way to get to some other world cheap, away we'd go. There were places where we could've stayed on and on, if you ask me, just going around five or six towns. But that wasn't Mango. If he'd wanted to live like that, he'd never have become a clown at all, he said. He told me once he wanted to see new smiles, and maybe that was it.

We'd loop back sometimes, and loop around. But somehow we were always outward bound, out toward the rim and farther every year. He'd meet somebody, some sailor usually, and he'd talk about someplace he'd just been to, what a hellhole it was. And after that, Mango'd always be itching to go there. He'd talk about it and me and Bully'd say it sounded pretty bad, all the killing and storms, bad air, nothing but trouble. And Mango'd say think how much they'd love us there, how they need somebody like us. When Mango looked in a mirror, I don't think he saw what other people saw, but something a whole lot bigger and nicer. And the longer he's gone, the more I get to thinking he was right, that was what was there, and not the long skinny bird with the long skinny face that I always saw when I looked at him. Now I like to think he's gone someplace better, that he's played out this universe and caught a ship up to a new one where there's sweet grass and clean water all over. Only Mango'd go down below, if he could. He'd think about how bad it was and how they needed us, and he'd say it was just for a couple weeks and go.

That's how it was going to be when we came here. Just a couple weeks. We've been here close to ten years, I think, me and Bully have now.

There aren't a lot of worlds with their own intelligent native races, I guess everybody knows that. And the ones that have them, that world's theirs, and generally they won't let humans settle on it at all. Sidhe's different, because the intelligent race here is the Beautiful Ones and there's nothing else in the galaxy like them. That's what I hear, and it's probably a real good thing too. The Beautiful Ones will let people come, only they can't have children here. Probably you've heard about that already.

People need a lot of high-class science to change genes and make something better. You take Bully and me. It was one of the smartest women on Earth that did us, and all the others there that could have done it too could've sat down in her living room. The Beautiful Ones don't have any science and don't want it, but they've got that built in, just like Bully's got all his stomachs. Whenever one's fixing to have a child, that child's going to look a lot like she wanted it to. She doesn't have to do anything but want, and the more she wants it the closer she gets.

So when the first humans got here, and they had ships and crawlers and all that, the Beautiful Ones thought that stuff was really swell, and every generation got to looking more and more like people until pretty soon it was like it is now, and the Beautiful Ones look a whole lot better than real people do, taller than Mango, most of them, and faces so pretty it sort of hurts to look at them, especially when you know they're not people at all. You've seen some, right?

Well, maybe I do, but I can't say it very good. I haven't got all the words. They move around like they're dancing all the time. And as soon as you see one, you know she's the best dancer in the whole universe. Or he is. Their hair's like the gold stuff you see in a jewelry store, and their skin's the color of bread baking, just starting to get brown. Their teeth are just so, and their eyes are all kinds of funny colors, and change while you're looking at them. That's what Mango said. I can't see most colors very good, but he knew a lot about them. I can't dance, either, not a lick, but I sing a little. Is that enough about the Beautiful Ones?

Okay. They wanted people to settle here, and they still do.

Most won't, because word's gotten around. You were pretty brave to come, is what I think.

Well, I sure hope they don't. They're not very good at keeping promises. I don't think it's forgetting or even badness as much as it's just that the promising idea doesn't make much sense to them. They don't really understand it. If I were you I'd get out quick and not tell anybody I was going till I'd gone.

People still come, though, mostly the ones that are too poor to go anyplace else. You know how it is. If a world thinks you're probably going to need a lot of help, they won't let you come. Not even just to stop over. But Sidhe will take all those, and the more kids they've got before they get here the better, so they'll grow up right here. Because on Sidhe nobody's going to look out for you except maybe your relatives and the folks next door.

We didn't have any relatives here, and we weren't living next door to anybody, really. We were going all around the way we always did, so there was just us. People kept telling us the Beautiful Ones wouldn't ever let us leave, so pretty soon Mango wanted to go and we came here and asked around at the spaceport. That's when we found out the people had been right. The Beautiful Ones weren't letting anybody go offworld unless there was somebody that had gotten away already that was asking about them, and nobody was asking about us. The sailors were afraid to get off their ships, even, because they figured the Beautiful Ones wouldn't let them back on. Some Beautiful Ones would go out to the port at night, or when it was dark weather or raining, and dance for them, dance around the ship, mostly, or make a figure-of-eight around two ships, when there was two ships, and sometimes a sailor would come out.

Then a female or male would hook up with him, depending on what he wanted, and show him how to dance. Or her, if the sailor was a woman, and they'd all dance some more. And finally they'd go off together, with the sailor grinning and waving to his friends on the ship. That sailor'd hardly ever come back, though.

We tried and tried, Mango talking to various ones, only nothing ever came of it. There were days—I remember two—when we went out to the port, Mango thinking we were going to get on a ship sure, only we never quite would. Then one day he said he thought he had a way to do it, but it would only work for him, not for us, so he was going to take it, and when he got offworld he'd start in on anybody from Earth that he could find, viewing the ambassador, and letters, and all that, and get us off, too. We said fine, because I didn't believe he'd really get off himself and neither did Bully.

This is something I'd rather I didn't have to tell about, but I guess I do. The way Mango'd found, or thought he had, was to hide in a cargo canister. The one he picked was full of furs, and the captain wanted it fumigated before he'd take it on board for fear there was fleas in them or something. So they opened it up and sprayed stuff in and Mango coughed, and that was how they found him.

And they killed him. There was two Beautiful Ones there to see nobody got away on that ship, is what we heard, and they chopped him up with their swords.

No, they can't make swords or much of anything. But they make people make the things for them, swords and lots of other stuff. That's why they want people here, to make stuff for them and make stuff to trade. Like those furs. It was people who caught the animals and skinned them, and the Beautiful Ones were going to trade them offworld and buy stuff they wanted, flitters and blasters and ships of their own. So they want a ton of people to do that.

Sure they want kids. There's Beautiful Ones on the other worlds around here now to get more people to come, and if it's a big family they'll pay passage. But they don't want any kids born here, because they're scared of them. They're afraid that what their mothers will want is somebody that can beat up the Beautiful Ones. The mothers would want it, too, I guess, only wanting doesn't work for people . . .

All right, if you'd really like to hear. I don't know anything about anything except clowning, I know that, and maybe it's just being here too long. But sometimes I wonder if the Beautiful Ones aren't right and the people wrong. Maybe people do get what they want a little, sometimes, or even animals like me and Bully do. Because everybody here kept talking about it. How if ever it happened and the Beautiful Ones didn't kill it, that'd be one that'd put people on top and the Beautiful Ones on the bottom, or anyhow make them treat people better. That kid would be, when he grew up.

Oh, sure. It happens. It happens a lot. Some woman and her husband get careless, or maybe just a boy and a girl. But the Beautiful Ones always hear. And pretty soon after the baby comes, they come too. What happened this time—

Right. I'm starting off before I'm hitched up, I guess.

With Mango gone, Bully and me figured to go on clowning by ourselves. We worked up a couple of acts for just the two of us, and we could pass the hat like we had before, holding it in our teeth. Only the first time we did it I could see it wasn't going to work. For one thing, we couldn't paint our faces the way Mango had, and without paint it didn't feel right. Another one was somebody was always grabbing us and saying we belonged to him. We had to hurt a couple of those birds pretty bad, and we didn't like that.

So pretty soon even Bully could see we needed somebody, and we found this boy, Ezry, that hadn't ever had a father and his mother was gone. We pay him to own us, only he has to do what we say. There's been some bad times besides the good ones, but it's worked out pretty well. We're satisfied, and so's he. He paints our faces and buttons our ruffs, and beats Mango's drum to get us a crowd just like Mango used to. Did you catch our act?

It's really pretty simple. I'm carrying a basket of corn on each side of me, and I come out and try to eat it myself. I circle around this way, only I can't get it. Then I try it the other way, going faster and faster, and get out of breath and walk around funny like I'm dizzy, and finally I fall down. It gets a big laugh.

Then Bully comes out, and he's got a basket on each side, too, only his are bigger and full of hay. He reaches around as far as he can and gets a few straws, then he reaches around the other way and gets a few more. He's got this thing where he tries to hook a basket with his horn, and he almost gets it. Maybe he does get it a little, but then it slips off. Then he starts trying to untie the rope around his belly with his back hoofs, first the left one, then the right. Finally he puts his head down and looks between his front legs at his back ones, left then right. And he tries to use them both at the same time, and naturally sits down. About then I get up and try reaching my mouth straight over my back, and that doesn't work either.

Then Ezry comes out and whispers in our ears, and after that I eat hay out of Bully's baskets and he eats corn out of mine, and then we pass the hat.

That act gets some good laughs and brings in the cash, but there's more to it. See, we're saying to everybody that we've got to pull together and look out for each other, and that goes right along with this family you want to know about.

They were just country people from some village upriver. He lumbered up there, he said, and had a little sawmill and so on. Well, she was about to have the kid, and where they lived there wasn't anybody to help her, and you know somebody's going to tell the Beautiful Ones next time some come through. It's bound to happen. So they'd come down here trying to get a ship out, and you know how that is. You know what happened to Mango. Then she goes into labor.

It was Ezry that found out about them when the place where they'd been staying wouldn't let them back in, and I guess if he'd told her husband about Bully and me maybe they wouldn't have come at all. But maybe they would, because they didn't have any time to fool around. We bedded her down on clean hay that Bully forked out of our loft, and it could've been worse. People found out, naturally. You can't hide a thing like that very long here in the city where people are poor and got to live so close together. So they came and stood around and gawked, because most of them hadn't ever seen a real newborn for years and years, and some that came here as kids never had.

We got witches here. I guess you've heard. A lot of the worlds I've been on, they don't think there are any, but we've got plenty. If you ask me it's because somebody has to store up all the stuff people know. On most worlds it's computers and maybe teachers, and some in books. But on a world like Sidhe, well, they got a little school started here. It's the first one on Sidhe.

Anyway, this witch comes and tells everybody that this new kid the woman had, he's going to be the one. When he gets big he's going to kick the Beautiful Ones' teeth out and black their eyes, and after that people here are going to get a better shake.

They'll be able to have kids of their own if they want them, and have a say in the way their taxes get spent and all that.

Then somebody laughed, a little skinny bird it was that'd worked his way to the front. This witch starts screeching at him, and he starts hollering back at her, so Bully shuts him up. Bully's got this big deep voice, you know? He says it's all true, and if the little bird don't believe it, he'll put a horn right through him, and anybody that runs off and tells Beautiful Ones about the new kid is in for a dose of the same.

Well, Bully's the best friend I've got, right? So I chime in. My voice isn't deep like his, but I can be pretty loud when I want to. The little bird shuts up and sort of stares at us, and after a minute I see they all are. Then he says, like he can't hardly get it out, he thought we didn't talk. So I say tonight we do, and Bully chimes in for me and says only tonight, but they better not talk themselves if they know what he means. So that's how we got to be sort of famous.

Right there's where we got lucky, too, because it's when the sheepherders came. There's a couple horses right beside this place Bully and me rent, and I guess somebody'd come in and got a horse, and when he got out into the country he told everybody. Anyway there was eight or ten sheepherders, and there's some real bad animals here on Sidhe, so if you're going to keep sheep you'd better be a real tough bird with some real tough dogs. They all had those big sticks, too, and when they talked folks listened.

So it was quiet, pretty quiet anyhow, for a week or so, and the Beautiful Ones never did catch on. Then three teachers from the new school came by—I guess three was all they had back then. They'd been passing the hat for this country family, and they'd gotten up quite a nice chunk of change.

Oh, sure, me and Bully put in some too, for Mango.

And with that much they were able to get a ship, just like they'd wanted when they came here. Folks say they went to some world called Biladmaser. Only some say Barrmaser, so I guess nobody really knows, or somebody heard somebody else wrong, you know how that is. But I know they really did get on a ship, because I took her and her new kid out to the port and watched her and her husband climb in it, him carrying the kid. Then I watched— we all did, that's Bully and me and Ezry—till it took off. I don't know if she waved or anything, except for when she was about to go in, because I couldn't see for sure. Ezry says she did, and he's got real good eyes. But I was the one she sat on, her nursing her new kid, all the way out there. Every time Bully reminds me he was the first one to talk to the people the night the new kid was born, I remind him about that.

Really? You think they're back here? You don't say! Out in the boondocks somewhere, I guess. It'd have to be. Only I don't know anything about it. I never heard a thing about them coming back till you said so, and probably I'll forget, too, as soon as you're out of here.

You ever think about how the Beautiful Ones are going to stick your feet in the fire if they hear you know something like that? You better know exactly where they are, and no mistakes, and who's hiding them and the rest of it. Because they're going to keep on doing this and that till you tell them all that stuff. You ever see them when they throw them into the street after a little conversation like that? Fingernails torn off, and they can't stand up or anything. They holler for their friends and relatives, but their friends and relatives know there's Beautiful Ones watching to see who tries to help. Pretty soon the street dogs come. The ones that got thrown out can generally keep them off at first, but when there gets to be too many to count, it's all over.

Yeah, I figured you didn't really know anything about her and her husband and the kid coming back. I figured you were just blowing off, because I do it too, sometimes—smartass is what Bully says. You have a real nice trip back to Earth, and when you get there you tell them I really don't know much of anything about whatever might be going on out here.

How could I? I'm just a donkey.

Sins of the Mothers

S. N. DYER

*S. N. Dyer has published stories in most of the leading SF
and fantasy magazines, including* Asimov's, SF Age, *and*
Realms of Fantasy. *Her stories tend to be very smart and
pointed. "Sins of the Mothers" is a particularly sharp look at
some tough decisions that might not be the province of
speculative fiction for much longer.*

I WAS ON THE FRONT PORCH, DRINKING ESPRESSO AND WATCHING
birds squabble at the feeder. It was late autumn; the apple and
cherry trees had dutifully dropped their leaves and stood naked
beside the evergreens. Otherwise, the only way to tell the closeness
of winter on my two acres of California was by the incredible
fruitfulness of the garden. I looked forward to the first good frost,
which would relieve me of the need to go out every day and find
homes for tomatoes and zucchini with friends who already had too
many of their own. Compared to that, giving away the last litter
of kittens had been a snap. I've considered imitating a desperate
friend, who abandons baskets of produce on the doorsteps of
strangers.

A limousine pulled up to the gate. One of those rented jobs,
a chauffeur in front. Two biker goons got out. Leather and chain
berserkers in a stretch Cadillac. Probably lost and needing direc-
tions to one of the illegal dope farms for which our county is
famous.

Then another man emerged. Slim, dissipated, a light Italian
suit with no shirt. Long hair limp and dirty. *Evan* something or
other. I recognized him from channel surfing past MTV. He was
evidently big with Beavis and Butt-Head.

He slipped inside the gate and walked up to the house. The dogs paced beside him, neither friendly nor unfriendly, like cops at a peaceful demonstration.

He stopped and looked up at me. "Hello. You're Arwen Wild-flower?"

Okay, the name seemed cool when I was a sixteen-year-old runaway with flowers in my hair. And now I'm stuck with it.

"The former Shirley O'Malley?"

I hadn't heard that name since 1969. A little knot of paranoia began to form somewhere under my cotton and lace peasant shirt. "Maybe. What's it to you?"

The rock star tried to smile with a face accustomed to leers and smirks. His face got sort of crooked and he showed bad teeth.

"You're my mother," he said.

Shit. It's not like I'd been spending the last quarter century anticipating this Hallmark Moment.

I stood up and pointed into the house. "Want some espresso?"

MY CAT LOVES her babies; I once saw her attack a Doberman who got too close. The Doberman lost. But once the kittens hit puberty she won't have a thing to do with them, even chases them away. And she seems, in general, to be a better mom than my German shepherd, my quarter horse, my cow.

And then there's the birds. They'll die defending their nest—but if a baby falls out and lies there chirping, they just sit there and watch it die.

Motherhood. Donna Reed and Harriet Nelson and Jane Anderson tried to convince me it was the only reason I existed. Get born, grow up, get pregnant, have babies, raise them, have grandchildren, die. The last three thousand years of philosophy might have meant something to the lives of men, but my future was meant to be as uncomplicated as a brood mare's.

Maybe if everything had gone as planned I'd still be in Ohio, married, housewife, two sons in college, two daughters starting their own families. More likely I'd be divorced, trying to raise all those kids on minimum wage and minuscule child support, while my ex-husband the dentist drove his new wife around in a Lotus sport.

In fact, I bet Donna Reed's doctor divorced her for a trophy wife, and Harriet's raising grandchildren on her Social Security check, and Jane's in a nursing home that her kids never visit.

THE ROCK STAR sat at my kitchen table and briefly fooled with one of the dulcimers I build. He had musical talent—not that you could tell from his videos.

"You need something," I said.

"A guy can't wonder about his real mother?"

I shrugged. "You're twenty-five and look forty, you're covered with needle tracks and the kind of tattoos you have to be very drunk to hold still for . . . You don't strike me as the sentimental kind."

He grinned. "Right. You dropped me like a dog taking a dump and ran. My adoptive family raised me to be a little Republican 'til I was old enough to smoke and drink and screw around, and then they ditched me, too . . . I don't need anyone."

Like I said, a real Hallmark Moment.

"So what is it, bone marrow?"

"Close. How'd you like fifty grand?"

Well, hell. How'd I like to pay off the mortgage and the back debts? Selling homemade berry jam and dulcimers and playing flute in classy restaurants for tips isn't exactly financial security.

"What for?"

"Something you aren't using. Your eggs."

SOMETIMES—NOT OFTEN —I'd lie there in the night and wonder how my kid had turned out. I never regretted not raising him on my own. That wasn't one of the options you had in 1969.

Besides, I never liked kids. I hated baby-sitting, hated being at the kids' table at holiday dinners, didn't even think babies were cute. They were smelly and formless and boring. Until they got big enough to be smelly and unintelligible and demanding. Even now when some friend's two-year-old starts talking to me, I nod and fix a smile on my face and pray someone will rescue me.

Maybe if I'd met Mr. Right and lived a normal middle-class life I'd have eventually wanted to reproduce, and maybe I'd have wound up loving my kids the same way I get attached to stray cats. But I suspect I would have been a lousy mom, abusive or at best neglectful. Strung out on whatever prescription tranquilizer was *au courant*. Building job security for my kids' future psychotherapists.

When I wondered about my kid, I figured he'd have musical talent, like me, and like me at some point he might start thinking there was more to life than money and status and predictability.

Only when I discovered music in the Sixties it came with a philosophical background of love and peace. When Evan's time rolled around it was just sex 'n' drugs 'n' rock 'n' roll. Live fast, die young, leave a burned out body.

At twenty-five, when most kids from his background were finishing law or medical school, starting a career and a family, he'd somehow managed to get such bad alcoholic pancreatitis that now he was diabetic and dying. A real overachiever.

"I don't do well with insulin," he said. The groupies and the drugs tended to interfere with a regular diet and medication regimen. So it was in and out of hospitals with the various forms of diabetic coma.

"The docs say I have a year to live, maybe less. Maybe more if I clean up my act." He snorted derisively. *Yeah, like that could happen.*

I nodded, trying to look sympathetic. I've seen friends lose children; it seems like the worst thing that can happen. They never recover. Years later they're still haunted and bitter. It makes you wonder how people ever survived, back when half your kids routinely died.

Yet here my own son had just told me his death sentence, and it affected me no more than the news of the latest flood in Bangladesh: too bad, what's for dinner? He was a stranger to me.

"My only hope," he continued, "is a pancreas transplant."

"Well, go for it."

"It's not feasible," he said. "See, you have to at least pretend to clean up your act, something I'm no good at. Then you have to wait for someone right to die, and you take all these immunosuppressive drugs that make life unpleasant."

"Okay, so is this some find-yourself-before-you-die trip?"

He snorted again. "No way. I've got too much money to die.

I'm going for the best transplant—from my own body. From a clone."

He'd brought a video with his pet scientists giving the pitch. While I watched, he prowled around the house looking at pictures, noodling on my guitar, hassling the pets. I'd have been nervous if I'd had anything worth stealing.

I'd never thought about clones. I'd seen enough *Star Trek* to figure you just took any old cell from the human body—even hair or skin or blood, which it turns out don't even have enough DNA to work with—and grow one.

But it seems that only germ cells—eggs and sperm—have the appropriate DNA. Chromosomes are modified with methylation so the DNA of each cell line turns on in a specific way. That way liver cells can't grow into spleen cells, let alone become a baby.

To make matters more confused, even the chromosomes from egg or sperm alone aren't enough. There's something called genetic imprinting, meaning that you need both male and female contribution for the baby to turn out right. In illustration, the scientist went on and on about what happens when someone gets a wrong set of chromosome 14. If both come from Mom—it's called uniparental disomy, in the unlikely event anyone cares—the kid gets Prader Willi and he's retarded and fat. If both chromosomes come from Dad, then the kid has Angelman's syndrome, retarded and autistic.

The whole thing was incredibly complex, and since my tenth-grade bio was back in the dark ages I was lost.

I understood the bottom line, though. They needed *my* germ cell chromosomes to build a copy of Evan.

They'd give me a drug to make a bunch of eggs mature simultaneously, then harvest them laparascopically—Band-Aid surgery. Then they'd separate out the chromosomes they needed—the explanation for that was so technical I zoned out completely—and then add the dad's contribution, appropriate male chromosomes harvested from Evan.

"Whoa, more than oedipal," I remarked to the video.

They'd implant the fertilized egg in a host mother and let it grow. Just before six months they'd do a hysterectomy/abortion, dissect out the pancreas, and transplant the tiny islets of Langerhans into Evan, curing his diabetes. His own cells—a perfect match. He wouldn't need any immune suppressants.

"Two things," I told him after I'd stared at the blank TV awhile. "You can have the eggs. I'm not exactly using them. But I also want to be the host." I could use a hysterectomy. Menstruation has always struck me as a sexist God's punishment for lack of reproduction, and I was sick and tired of it. "Package deal, half a million bucks."

We haggled a couple hours, settled on a quarter million, and called the lawyers.

Two months later I was pregnant. *Déjà-vu.*

"I'M PREGNANT," said my friend Mary.

"You can't be!" We were whispering in the school rest room. She'd been puking, and I was supposed to be helping her get to the school nurse. "I mean, you can't get pregnant if you haven't . . ."

"I have."

"Wow." That stopped me. Back then, no one did.

"My folks'll kill me."

I didn't doubt it.

The father was one of the hippie poets in our class. He was terrified. Knocking someone up was grounds for reform school. For the girl it was a shotgun marriage, or an extended trip to some fictional relative out of state. In any event, you were grounded for the rest of your life.

Good girls didn't have sex. Everyone knew that. So if you did, and people found out, you were doomed. You'd never get a job or married. No decent person—including your own family—would ever talk to you again. You'd wind up a hooker in a seaport town and die of degradation or booze. No second chances. Absolute ruin.

The hippie poet got some money and found a guy who'd "take care of it." I borrowed the car, said we were going to the football game, and drove to the sleazy side of town. The father was too chicken to come along. He said he had to meditate.

Nowadays when you think of abortions, you think of a nice clean clinic with doctors, nurses, anesthesia, and assholes picketing outside. Back then abortions were in someone's kitchen, so dirty you would have refused to eat there let alone have surgery, and a guy with thick glasses and poor personal hygiene who claimed he knew how to do it. You didn't ask for credentials.

Mary got up on the table and spread her legs. She was crying.

"Shut up," he said offhandedly. "Hold her."

He had a metal speculum, not very shiny, and a few surgical tools that he wiped off with rubbing alcohol. Mary screamed.

"If you do that again, I'll stop."

She screamed again.

"Shut up, stupid bitch," he remarked. I was feeling pretty sick myself, and my hands hurt from where Mary was squeezing them. I gave her a rolled-up handkerchief to bite.

All in all, it wasn't much more sophisticated than a coat hanger. "You'll bleed for a few days," he said. "Tell anyone and I'll kill you."

"You have a lousy bedside manner," I told him as we left. That struck him as funny. I heard him laughing halfway down the stairs.

Mary bled all over the front seat. Try explaining that to your parents.

THE WORST BIT about being pregnant is the morning sickness. That sudden queasy feeling and, if you're lucky, a successful sprint for the toilet. Otherwise you just sit there and hate being alive and get sicker at the thought of food.

That was how I knew I was pregnant last time. I knew this time when I woke up puking.

I called the mad doctor in charge of the program. Frankie, I called him; he looked a little like a grown-up Frankie Avalon playing Dr. Frankenstein.

"I think I've got morning sickness."

"Great!"

"Easy for you to say."

"No, this means it took. You're pregnant."

"Look, just get me some phenergan or something."

"No, nothing that could cause birth defects."

"Who cares about that stuff? So it can screw up the heart or make the kid retarded—it's not like that matters. I want something for nausea!"

"No drugs. You're pregnant, remember?"

At that point I dropped the phone and ran for the sink. Frankie waited on the line, which ticked me off—it was long distance and I was paying.

I'D BEEN PLAYING guitar when Mary came over. I could play the folkie stuff, as long as none of it was antiwar, while my parents were home, but I had to save protest or hard-line rock for when they were out playing bridge.

"You don't look good."

"I'm sick," she moaned. She was hot to the touch, and she felt clammy and smelled bad.

"I'm still bleeding."

"He said you'd do that for a while."

"Yeah, but it's black and kind of stringy."

"Yuck . . . Maybe something's gone, you know, wrong. We could go to the hospital."

"No! They'd find out . . . I'll be okay. I just need to sleep, okay? Play some Dylan."

So I played "The Times They Are a Changing," which was our favorite because it stated the obvious, that our parents didn't know what we were up to, and "Subterranean Homesick Blues." She seemed to be asleep and then she had a seizure. I called the ambulance, but it was all over when they got there.

The cops grilled me, but I denied knowing anything. I got grounded for a month, anyway. I felt guilty, too. A couple years ago I told my doctor about it. "What if I'd made her go to the hospital, instead of waiting?"

"She'd have died anyway. Don't let it bother you."

Like you can let it not bother you, watching your best friend die on your bed from a botched abortion. Doctors are like that.

ROCK STAR CLONED! NATURAL MOTHER CARRIES TINY METAL MAN

The last people you'd expect to break a real story . . . I found out at the supermarket checkout stand, where I was loading up on

7-Up and soda crackers. It took reporters a while after that to locate me and expose my entire sleazy life story. No onus involved in getting pregnant when I was sixteen. No, now I was to be pilloried for not raising the kid. *Plus ça change, plus c'est le même chose.*

"How did it feel to give up your baby at birth?"

"I dunno, how did it feel to give up your journalistic integrity?"

A roadie had broke the story for ten grand. Evan's bikers broke him. Then Evan sent one of his toughs to keep reporters away from me. It was a real sweet gesture.

The biker's name was Tony. He was my age and on the wagon due to a mild case of cirrhosis and a moderate case of chronic bronchitis. Bikers have an early expiration date. Tony had a degree in philosophy from a Midwest aggie college, had learned to smoke and drink and shoot up in Nam, and had detoxed during his last stay in jail. His goal, he said, was to own a bar. Or a real old Harley.

He had a lot of interesting tattoos. We got friendly, and he showed them all to me.

I USED TO hang out at the record store and listen to all the new stuff as it came in. I loved the Doors, Hendrix, the psychedelics. There was this college guy working there that summer, and he liked the same groups I did.

One day I was in the booth listening to the new Cream when he told me he had a bootleg Dylan tape. Wow! It was illegal, but I could come over to his pad and listen . . .

This was still the Sixties. Girls didn't go to a guy's place to hear music. Guys then thought, you know, that if you came to their room it meant you were going to sleep with them.

They thought that if you said, yeah, you'd try some wine, you were going to sleep with them.

They thought if you said *No* it meant *Yes*, you were going to sleep with them.

They thought that it was no fun having sex with a virgin, it was a dirty job but someone had to do it. Sort of a civic duty.

So it was the worst afternoon of my life. And the guy came

out of it feeling like a boy scout who'd just helped an old lady across the street.

THE PROBLEM WITH beating up goons is it just makes them mad. So Evan's roadie called the reporters from the hospital and told them the whole story. I wasn't bearing Evan's clone because I was some California weirdo who never had the chance to raise her kid the first time. I was growing an organ donor.

Now it wasn't only reporters camping outside my place, scaring the livestock, running over my cat, annoying the hell out of the neighbors. It was right-to-life fanatics, too. They called me names you can't repeat in public even now. They threatened to kill me. Real life-affirming Christian types.

We hired rent-a-cops, changed my phone number, checked all mail for explosives. Tony and I alternated days of hiding in the house with days of sitting on the hood of my car and yelling back.

I was showing by then, wearing stretch pants and waddling when I went to feed the horse.

I'd bred her seven times. I was convinced she was smirking at me. Now I'd know what a pain motherhood was.

I DIDN'T TELL Mom and Dad about the rape. See, it didn't matter if you'd done it on purpose or not, ruin was ruin. I wasn't a virgin anymore, and that meant I was evil. A disgrace to the family. A whore.

Besides, I knew they'd take his side. I'd gone over to a guy's house to hear a bootleg Dylan tape. I'd asked for it!

I kept it secret because I didn't have a choice. When I'd gone without my period for two months and started puking every morning I knew I was doomed. I couldn't do what Mary'd done. I was too chicken. But it didn't matter, my parents would kill me anyway. And I deserved it.

FRANKIE CALLED ME. "We've got a little problem," he said. Namely his lab had been firebombed. It was almost funny. He was a fertility specialist. Other than his little deal with Evan, the vast majority of his work was devoted to helping people have babies. That 99 percent of his career goals coincided with theirs didn't stop the nuts from targeting him.

"And the hospital won't let me operate," he said.

"Find one that will." Evan had enough money, someone would give Frankie temporary privileges long enough for one lousy hysterectomy.

Then came the injunction.

I thought, you know, I'm an adult. I can do what I want with my body. No total stranger can go to court and sue for guardianship of a lump of tissue in my uterus.

Boy, was I naive.

Time was running out. It was five months. At six the annoying growth became a legal person, and I'd be stuck with him. *Shit*.

We had lawyers, they had lawyers. They dressed like yuppies and bragged like TV wrestlers before a match. That didn't give me much confidence.

I WAS SENT to visit "Aunt Martha in Missouri." I had no Aunt Martha in Missouri. What I had was a concentration camp where you did chores and got moral lectures from the nuns, with schoolwork in whatever spare time was left. By the time they were done with you, you had no doubt that you were a worthless piece of shit doomed to hell in this world and beyond. Unless you decided to become a nun yourself and atone by making other unlucky girls miserable.

Some people glow when they're pregnant. Some people say it's the best time of their life. I figure they must be insane. Even if you want the kid there's the nausea, the back pain, the forty extra pounds weighing you down. All leading up to the delightful experience of trying to shove an object the size of a watermelon through a hole the size of a needle.

I did it without anesthesia. Without the support of anyone who thought of me as anything more than a moral lesson.

On the upside, it's very easy to escape from a maternity hospital. No one expects it.

It's also easy to hitchhike to the Haight Ashbury, to change your name, to move into a commune and learn to make dulcimers and jam. It's easy to build a new life—until the old one finally catches up with you.

PREGNANCY SUCKED WHEN I was sixteen. The second time was worse. My back was already bad, my ankles swollen anyway; I didn't need the additional stress.

"If I don't get rid of this fetus next week, I'm going to be stuck with it," I said. We were all at my kitchen table, having a war conference.

"Don't worry, we'll take care of it," said the lawyer.

"So you've said. For three months. Why am I not reassured?"

"I need this damn clone," said Evan. "I'm dying, remember?"

"Worse comes to worst," said Tony, "we head to Mexico and get the surgery there."

"There's an injunction against me leaving the state."

"I've got a friend who smuggles dope, he'll fly us." Tony was very resourceful. "If we can't come back, hell, money goes further down there. I know some friends with a cantina in Baja." Practical too.

"I'm an officer of the court, don't say anything about breaking injunctions in front of me," said the lawyer. "I have a friend in San Diego who does a lot of work across the border, I could call him . . ."

"I need a drink," said Evan.

So we got in Tony's pickup truck and drove through the demonstrators to a crummy bar on the outskirts of town.

"I'm having a drink," I said.

"You're pregnant. You can't drink."

"Pregnant women have had a drink since the dawn of time and it hasn't hurt a damn thing. Gimme a bourbon."

For some reason this really ticked off Evan. "You bitch, did you drink when you were pregnant with me? Is that why I'm all screwed up?"

"Trust me, I would of if I could of."

"Oh yeah, you'd have liked it if I'd been retarded or had three arms or something."

"You can't hold your liquor," I said. "You never got that from me."

"What did I get from you?" Evan screamed. "A shitty life in the suburbs and a mom who never wanted me . . ."

"You can't speak to your mother like that," said Tony.

"I can say anything I want. I own you. Own you all!"

So Tony hit him over the head with a pool cue. And ran like hell. You shouldn't annoy a biker, even when he's sober.

THE ONLY TV shows the nuns let us watch were *The Flying Nun* and *Bewitched*. I still can't watch *Bewitched*. Think about it. The woman is a witch. When she gets married she's expected to give up her identity, her entire self, and just be a housewife. Whenever she does something bright, fixes things, she's betraying her husband. Go figure.

All I can do now is watch TV and hope the rent-a-cops keep the loonies out. Last week a drive-by maniac shot one of my dogs. Life-affirming, huh?

I got a postcard yesterday from Tony, somewhere down in Baja. Says he's drinking again, and woke up one day to find himself married and teaching philosophy to high school students. And I thought my life was hell.

I'm so damn pregnant I can barely move. I look like a balloon about to pop. Social Services tried to get me to go to Lamaze classes. I told them to get bent.

The baby will come. That's the thing about life, once that sperm hits that egg you've got no choice about it. You're going to take a risk and hurt like hell whatever way you go.

The lawyers are still fighting. Only now Evan's lawyers are squabbling with his adopted parents' lawyers over the estate. The baby could be born with a silver spoon up his nose. It seems that maybe the fetus is Evan's real heir—it's not only his illegitimate kid, but genetically it is him. This should break legal ground, they tell me. I could care less.

Some friends of mine, the ones who own the restaurant I play flute in, are desperate to have a kid. I don't know why, it's something genetic, I guess. But they like jam and dulcimers and stray dogs, so I've promised them the baby. If they get twenty million bucks with it, hey, good karma comes back to you.

I didn't want the kid twenty-five years ago, and I don't want him now. It's just that last time, society screwed me. This time, I did it to myself.

The Finger

RAY VUKCEVICH

*Ray Vukcevich lives in Eugene, Oregon, and recently sold his
first novel,* The Man of Maybe Half-a-Dozen Faces. *Reading through his many stories in our pages might lead one
to conclude that he views the world in an odd and rather
sardonic manner. So it is. Here he applies that worldview to
the men's movement and the results are . . . well, perhaps not
uplifting, but certainly upraised.*

BOBBY WANTED TO PRACTICE IT ON HIS MOTHER, BUT HE KNEW
her face would turn red, then purple, and he'd see all the veins
pulsing in her head. Smoke would pour from her ears and nose.
Her eyes would pinwheel, and sparks would fly. Her lips would
disappear in a tight mean line. She'd start vibrating and humming,
and the top of her head would blow off like the lid of a steam
kettle, and everything inside would run down her face, melting her
until there'd be nothing left but a puddle of Mom stuff. So Bobby
told her he was going out, instead.

He let the rusty spring on the screen door have its way as he
ran from the kitchen into the Arizona sunshine and summer bug
noise, and he was almost out of sight when he heard the satisfying
bang! that made all the peacocks scream.

Bobby lazed on down the street, Main Street, the only street,
a dirt road really, kicking rocks and looking for devils' horns.
Swarms of summertime flies buzzed around his head. He pulled at
his jeans and the shorts riding up in the crack of his butt. He kept
an eye out for whirlwinds to stand in as he practiced flipping birds,
the middle finger of his right hand snicking out like the blade of
a switchblade knife.

Do it once, then do it twice, then do it again. This was a necessary man-type skill his cousin fat Edward, who was thirteen and should know, had told him. Necessary for a gee man, Bobby thought (but never said) because that's what he was going to be—a gee man and maybe get himself a good golly molly. Twist and shout! Yes. He flipped off the sky.

And the sky said, "Hey!"

Bobby tipped his head back to see a man in a cage. The cage hung from a high branch of the biggest oak tree around. Jail tree. Everyone called the prisoner Robert; everyone knew he liked to drink whiskey and pinch the bottoms of bar girls. Bobby flipped him off.

Robert held the bars of the cage with both hands and glared down at Bobby. "Don't do that, Bobby B."

"That's not my name," Bobby said, and held up his fist and triggered his finger again. Just when his middle finger snapped into position, he jabbed at Robert with his whole hand—a nice bit of style, Bobby thought.

"I told you not to do that!" Robert yelled. He pumped his legs and the cage swung on its rope. Bobby showed him his bird again.

Robert had gotten the cage going around in a circle, and now he crashed it against the trunk of the oak tree. "You just wait till I get out of here!"

Bobby flipped him off again, and then as Robert slumped to the floor of the cage and broke into tears, Bobby ran off down Main Street.

What was it about this gesture, he wondered, that it could make a grown man cry? Such power and magic. It was like when he'd called his cousin Edward a cocksucker, a term he'd gotten from Edward in the first place. Edward had chased him around and around the barn yelling that he'd kill him if he ever got his hands around Bobby's pussy neck. Cats and chickens. It didn't make a lot of sense. There was something potent and dirty about sucking on roosters, but Bobby couldn't figure what it could be. Cock Robin. Or maybe something to do with devil worship; he'd heard they liked to kill things and drink blood, or maybe geeks, the way Edward said they liked to bite the heads off chickens and suck the eggs up through the bleeding top. But wouldn't that make it hensucking?

Bobby discovered a new refinement. As the middle finger of his right hand snicked out, he slapped the whole hand into his left palm, making a sharp smack that scared birds from the rooftops and set a snake to rattling right there in the middle of the road in front of him.

Coiled, pastel pink and blue and orange and green, the duckbill rattlesnake snarled, showing its daffy little needlesharp teeth. It swept its head left and right keeping its bright eyes on Bobby. The snake's dry rattle was so fast Bobby couldn't see the tail move. He stopped in his tracks and flipped off the snake.

The snake froze like it couldn't believe its eyes, then picked up its rattle twice as fast and hard as before. It hissed and spit at Bobby, who jumped to the side and jabbed his middle finger into the air, yelled "Yii!" then jumped again. The snake twisted around to follow Bobby, who kept moving and yelling and flipping it off. Just as Bobby thought he'd finally gotten the snake to knot itself, a car came barreling out of nowhere and honking its horn like crazy. Bobby jumped out of the way, and the car ran over the snake. Squashed it flat.

"No fair!" Bobby yelled, and when old Mr. Klein poked his head out of the side window to look back and shake his fist at Bobby, Bobby flipped a bird at him.

Mr. Klein braked hard, and the car skidded sideways and crashed into the Bait and Tackle Shop. Bobby hurried on down Main Street.

Mrs. Stokes stood hugging a brown paper bag on the steps of the Grocery Store. "Don't slouch so, Bobby," she said.

Bobby flipped her off.

Mrs. Stokes collapsed like she'd suddenly been unplugged.

Bobby jerked around like a gunfighter and flipped off the Dime Store, and the store exploded, spewing up electric trains and stuffed animals, comic books, and pieces of plastic airplane models.

Bobby flipped off the Bright White Church on the corner, and it jumped into the air then fell onto its side with a splintering crash and the sounds of breaking glass. Flipping fast and furious now, Bobby turned the Little Red Schoolhouse into a big pile of little red bricks.

Bobby flipped off the Court House, and smoke filled its windows. The mayor ran out screaming "Fire! Fire!"

Downtown was beginning to look war-torn, worse for wear, maybe tornado-struck.

"You're not being very nice, Bobby," said the West Witch, ugly as sin his father called her, where she sat on the boardwalk with her plastic bag of empty vegetable cans and bits of bright yarn and corked bottles of powders and potions. Bobby flipped her off.

The witch's eyes got big, then she grinned, and Bobby could see she had no teeth. "Maybe you just need something sweet to suck on. A sweet tooth. Or two." She wiggled her eyebrows up and down at him, and sweetness filled his mouth. Chocolate. He backed away, sucking at his teeth. His front teeth. His chocolate teeth, and they were getting smaller fast, dissolving.

The witch sat rocking and slapping her knees and laughing at him, and when he zapped her with the finger again, all he was able to do was knock off her ragged bonnet, and that just seemed to make her laugh harder.

Bobby swallowed the last of his chocolate and ran on down the street, tonguing the space where his top front teeth had been. He stopped in front of the still-standing Hardware Store where he knew there was a mirror in the window. He was so much older now, growing up before his very eyes. He watched in dismay as his new teeth came in. He was a chipmunk. How could he be a gee man if he looked like a big chipmunk? No, a beaver. Bobby the Beaver. There was something about beavers, too, something that put a sly smile on Edward's face. He'd never figure it out in time. You're always a day late and a dollar short, his father liked to say. Bobby flipped off the Hardware Store, reducing it to piles of lumber and nails, tools and electrical parts, pipes and toilet fixtures.

He let his shoulders slump, deliberate bad posture, and slouched on down the smoky street, getting bigger, stumbling into adolescence, feeling mean and shooting I-Meant-To-Do-That! glances around whenever he tripped over his own feet, kicking the town's rubble out of his way, taking time to flip off the county deputy and send his car tumbling with the tumbleweeds. Stinking black leather jacket and dirty jeans, torn basketball shoes, flattop, a cool fool, coming up on Molly, the East Witch, as beautiful as the other one was ugly, saying, hey baby. The once-over for this one in her tight purple skirt and lacy white deep-vee blouse, brown and white shoes and bobby sox. Once-over was not enough, so the twice-over. Her dog, a blond lab, sat by her side giving Bobby the eye, an Elvis sneer on its lips and a little rumbling growl coming from somewhere deep inside.

"Keep your eyes to yourself, Bobby B," Molly said.

So what could he do but flip her off?

She narrowed her eyes, said, "All right for you, Bobby. You asked for it." She raised an eyebrow.

What was it, he wondered, with these women and their eyebrows? Something pulled his eyes closed, and when he touched his face, he discovered that his eyelashes had grown long and heavy, so long, in fact, that they fell to his chest. He had to take a handful of eyelashes in each hand and pull them up and away from his eyes before he could see Molly standing there smirking with one hand on a cocked hip and a cigarette in the other. She blew a smoky kiss his way.

"I don't suppose you'd let me shine my gee man flashlight in your face?" Bobby asked.

"JC doesn't like that kind of talk, Bobby." She put her hand on the dog's head.

"You named your dog after Jesus Christ?"

"No. After Joseph Campbell."

Like that was his cue, the dog jumped up, circled around young Bobby B, and bit him in the seat of the pants.

Bobby dropped his eyelashes, but he could still see the sudden light. Teen epiphany. He was seized by a sudden need to rip off his clothes, run into the woods, and beat on a drum until his father came down out of the trees.

He turned and shouldered his way through the ragged refugees toward the end of Main Street and the wilderness beyond.

Just outside the remains of town, Edward jumped up from behind a big ocotillo and flipped Bobby off with both hands while doing a shimmy like he had a tail to wag. "Take that, beaver face!" he shouted.

"Same to you!" Bobby grinned and flipped Edward off so hard his cousin's ears were pinned back.

"All right!" Edward slugged Bobby in the shoulder, and the

two of them walked on, and as they walked, guys popped up from behind cacti to take potshots with that one-finger salute. Snick. Snick. Like a running gun battle, but Bobby and Edward were too fast, and the vanquished soon fell in behind them, and by the time the sun had set, a Society of Men had formed.

They built a fire. They killed and cooked some rabbits. The moon soon gave them the cold shoulder. Coyotes sang. Backslapping, spitting, and farting, the men squatted with their drums in a circle around Bobby, who would soon exclaim sweet gee manly poetry.

Lifeboat on a Burning Sea

BRUCE HOLLAND ROGERS

*Bruce Holland Rogers grew up in Colorado and recently
moved to Oregon after spending five years in Champaign,
Illinois. His short fiction has appeared in a variety of
magazines and anthologies, including* Century, Enchanted
Forests, The Fortune Teller, *and* Ellery Queen's
Mystery Magazine, *and he writes a regular column on the
writing life for* Speculations *magazine. This story—a
Nebula Award winner—takes us on an imaginative
trip into one of the eternal frontiers . . .*

DESERTERS.

When I can't see the next step, when I can't think clearly
about the hardware changes that TOS needs in order to become
the repository, the ark, the salvation of my soul, I think of deserters.

I think of men on the rail of a sinking tanker. For miles
around, there are no lights, only water black and icy. A lake of
flames surrounds the ship. Beyond the edge of the burning oil
slick, a man sits in the lifeboat looking at his comrades. The angle
of the deck grows steeper. The men at the rail are waving their
hands, but the one in the boat doesn't return. Instead, he puts his
back into rowing, rowing away. To the men who still wave, who
still hope, the flames seem to reach higher, but it's really the ship
coming down to meet the burning sea.

Or this:

The arctic explorer wakes from dreams of ice and wind to a

world of ice and wind. In the sleeping bag, his frostbite has thawed and it feels as though his hands and feet are on fire. It is almost more than he can endure, but he tells himself he's going to live. As long as his companion is fit enough to drive the sled, he's going to live. He hobbles from the tent, squints against the sunlight. When he finds the dogs and sled gone, he watches for a long time as the wind erases the tracks.

In these fantasies of mine, the dead bear witness.

From the bottom of the sea, dead sailors wave their arms.

Frozen into the ice, a leathery finger points, accuses.

THERE MUST HAVE been a time when I wasn't aware of the relentless tick of every heartbeat, but I don't remember it. My earliest memory is of lying awake in my bed, eyes open in the blackness, imagining what it was like to be dead.

I had asked my father. He was a practical man.

"It's like this," he said. He showed me a watch that had belonged to my grandfather, an antique watch that ran on a coiled spring instead of a battery. He wound it up. "Listen," he said.

Tick, tick, tick, I heard.

"Our hearts are like that," he said, handing me the watch. "At last, they stop. That's death."

"And *then* what?"

"Then, nothing," he told me. "Then we're dead. We just aren't anymore—no thought, no feeling. Gone. Nothing."

He let me carry the watch around for a day. The next morning, the spring had run down. I put the watch to my ear, and heard *absence*, heard *nothing*.

Even back then, lying awake in the dark with my thoughts of the void, I was planning my escape.

Tick, tick, tick, went my heart, counting down to zero.

I WASN'T ALONE. After my graduate work in neuronics, I found a university job and plenty of projects to work on, but research is a slow business.

Tick, tick, tick.

I was in a race, and by the time I was fifty-six, I knew I was falling behind. In fact, I felt lucky to have made it that far. We were living at the height of terrorist chic. The Agrarian Underground and Monetarists were in decline, but the generation of bombers that succeeded them was ten times as active, a hundred times as random in their selection of targets. Plastique, Flame, Implosion . . . They gave themselves rock-band names. And then there were the ordinary street criminals who would turn their splitter guns on you in the hope that your chip, once they dug it out of your skin, would show enough credit for a hit of whatever poison they craved.

Statistically, of course, it wasn't surprising that I was still alive. But whenever I tuned in to CNN Four, The Street Beat Source, the barrage of just recorded carnage made me wonder that *anyone* was still alive.

Fifty-six. That's when I heard from Bierley's people. And after I had met Bierley, after I had started to work with Richardson, I began to believe that I would hit my stride in time, that Death might not be quite the distance runner he'd always been cracked up to be.

I had known who Bierley was, of course. Money like his bought a high profile, if you wanted it. And I had heard of Richardson. He was hot stuff in analog information.

Bierley and Richardson were my best hope. Bierley and Richardson were magicians at what they did. And Bierley and Richardson—I knew it from the start—were unreliable.

Bierley, with his money and political charm, would stay with the project only until it bored him. And Richardson, he had his own agenda. Even when we were working well together, when we were making progress, Richardson never really *believed*.

In Richardson's office, he and I watched a playback of Bierley's press conference. It had been our press conference, too, but we hadn't answered many questions. Even Richardson understood the importance of leaving that to Bierley.

"A multicameral multiphasic analog information processor," Bierley said again on the screen, "but we prefer to call it TOS." He smiled warmly. "The Other Side."

From behind his desk, Richardson grumbled, "God. He makes what we've done sound like a séance."

"Come on," I said. "It's the whole point."

"Are you really so hot to live forever as a machine consciousness, if, fantasy of fantasies, it turns out to be possible?"

"Yes."

"Your problem," he said, pointing a finger, "is that you're too damned scared of death to be curious about it. That's not a very scientific attitude."

I almost told him he'd feel differently in another twenty years, but then I didn't. It might not be true. Since I had *always* seen death as the enemy, it was possible that someone like Richardson *never* would.

"Meanwhile," Richardson continued, "we've made a significant leap in machine intelligence. Isn't that worthy of attention in its own right without pretending that it's a step toward a synthesized afterlife?"

On the screen, Bierley was saying "Of all the frontiers humanity has challenged, death was the one we least expected to conquer."

"As if, Christ, as if we'd already *done* it!"

Bierley peered out from the screen. He had allowed only one video camera for the conference so that he'd know when he was looking his viewers in the eye. "Some of you watching now will never die. That's the promise of this research. Pioneers of the infinite! Who doesn't long to see the march of the generations? What will my grandchild's grandchildren be like? What lies ahead in one hundred years? A thousand? A million?" After a pause and another grandfatherly smile, a whisper. "Some will live to know."

Richardson blew a raspberry at the screen.

"All right," I admitted. "He oversells. But that's Bierley. Everything he says is for effect, and the effect is *funding!*"

On the screen, the silver-haired Bierley was rephrasing questions as only he could, turning the more aggressive queries in on themselves. Wasn't this a premature announcement *of a breakthrough bringing hope to millions?* Would Bierley himself turn a profit from this *conquest of humanity's oldest and cruelest foe?* Would he himself be among the first *to enter the possibly hazardous territory of eternity to make sure it was safe for others?*

Then he was introducing us, telling the reporters about my genius for hardware and Richardson's for analog information theory. We had sixty technicians and research assistants working with us, but Bierley made it sound like a two-man show. In some ways, it was. Neither of us could be replaced, not if you wanted the same synergy.

"Two great minds in a race for immortality," Bierley said, and then he gave them a version of what I'd told Bierley myself: Richardson was always two steps ahead of my designs, seeing applications that exceeded my intentions, making me run to keep up with him and propose new structures that would then propel him another two steps beyond me. I'd never worked with anyone who stimulated me in that way, who made me leap and stretch. It felt like flying.

What Bierley didn't say was that often we'd dash from thought to thought and finally look down to see empty air beneath us. Usually we discovered impracticalities in the wilder things we dreamed up together. Only rarely did we find ourselves standing breathless on solid ground, looking back at the flawless bridge we had just built. Of course, when that happened, it was magnificent.

It also frightened me. I worried that Richardson was indispensable, that after making those conceptual leaps with him, I could never go back to my solitary plodding or to working with minds less electric than his. *All* minds were less electric than his, at least when he was at his best. The only difficulty was keeping him from straying into the Big Questions.

The camera had pulled back, and Richardson and I both looked rumpled and plain next to Bierley's polish. On screen I stammered and adjusted my glasses as I answered a question.

Richardson was no longer watching the press conference video but had shifted his gaze to the flatscreen on his office wall. It showed a weather satellite image of the western hemisphere, time-lapsed so that the last 72 hours rolled by in three minutes. It was always running in Richardson's office, the only decoration there, unless you counted that little statue, the souvenir from India that he kept on his desk.

On the press conference tape, Richardson was answering a question. "We don't have any idea how we'd actually get a person's consciousness into the machine," he admitted. "We haven't even perfected the artificial mind that we've built. There's one significant glitch that keeps shutting us down for hours at a time."

At that point, Bierley's smile looked forced, but only for an instant.

"The best way to explain the problem," the recorded Richardson continued, "is to tell you that thoughts move through our hardware in patterns that are analogous to weather. Sometimes an information structure builds up like a tropical depression. If conditions are right, it becomes a hurricane. The processor continues to work, but at greatly reduced efficiency until the storm passes. So we're blacked-out sometimes. We can't talk to"—he paused, looking at Bierley, sort of wincing—"to TOS, until the hurricane has spent its energy."

"You don't like the name," I said in Richardson's office.

Richardson snorted. "The Other Side." He leaned back in his chair. "You're right about the money, though. He charms the bucks out of Congress, and that's not easy these days."

On the tape, I was telling the reporters about the warning lights I had rigged in the I/O room: they ran up a scale from Small Craft Advisory to Gale Warning to Hurricane, with the appropriate nautical flags painted onto the display. I had hoped for a bigger laugh than I got.

"Can we interview the computer?" a reporter asked.

I had started to say something about how the I/O wasn't up to that yet but that TOS itself was helping to design an appropriate interface to make itself as easy to talk to as any human being.

Bierley's image stepped forward in front of mine. "TOS is *not* a computer," he said. "Let's make this clear. TOS is an information structure for machine intelligence. TOS is interfaced with computers, can access and manipulate digital data, but this is an analog machine. Eventually, it will be a repository for human consciousness. If you want another name for it, you could call it a Mind Bank."

"No one gets it," Richardson said, "and this press conference isn't going to help." He looked at me. "You don't get it, do you, Maas?"

"I don't even know what you're talking about."

"Trying to synthesize self-awareness is an interesting project. And putting human consciousness into a box would be a neat trick, instructive. I mean, I'm all for trying even if we fail. I expect to fail. Even if we succeed, even if we find a *technical* answer, it begs the bigger question."

"Which is?"

"What does it *mean* to live? What does it *mean* to die? Until you get a satisfactory answer to that, then what's the point of trying to live forever?"

"The point is that I don't want to die." Then more quietly, I said, "Do you?"

Richardson didn't look at me. He picked up the Indian statue from his desk and leaned back in his chair to look at it. When he put it down again, he still hadn't answered.

The statue was a man dancing inside an arc of flames.

THE NEXT WEEK, Bierley deserted us.

"Brain aneurism in his sleep," one of the old man's attorneys told me via video link.

There had been no provision in Bierley's will to keep seed money coming. If he went first, we were on our own. The attorney zapped me a copy of the will so I could see for myself.

"Makes you think," the attorney said, "doesn't it?" He meant the sudden death. I thought about that, of course. As strong as ever, I could hear my pulse in my throat. *Tick, tick, tick.* But I was also thinking something else:

Bastard. *Deserter.*

He had left me to die.

WEEKS LATER IN the I/O room, I said to Richardson, "We're in trouble."

He and a technician had been fiddling with TOS's voice, and he said, "TOS, what do you think of that?"

"I don't know what to think of it," said the machine voice. The tone was as meaningfully modulated as any human voice, but there was still something artificial about the sound—too artificial, still, for press exposure. "I don't know enough of what Dr. Maas means by 'trouble.' I'm unsure of just how inclusive 'we' is intended to be."

"My bet," Richardson said, "is that he's going to say our project has funding shortfalls up the yaya."

"Yaya?" said TOS.

"Wazoo," Richardson said.

"Oh." A pause. "I understand."

Richardson grinned at me. "English as she is spoke."

I waved off his joke. "There's talk of cutting our funding in Congress. I've been calling the reps that were in Bierley's pocket, but I can't talk to these people. Not like he could. And I sure as hell can't start a grass-roots ground swell."

"How about that lobbyist we hired?"

"She's great at phoning, full of enthusiasm, to tell me how bad things are. She says she's doing her best." I dropped into a chair. "Damn Bierley for dying." And for taking us with him, I thought. Didn't those bastards in Washington understand what the stakes were here? This wasn't basic science that you could throw away when budgets were tight. This was life and death!

Tick, tick, tick.

My life. *My* death!

Richardson said, "How desperate are we?"

"Plenty."

"Good." Richardson smiled. "I have a desperation play."

WE PLAYED IT close to the edge. Our funding was cut in a House vote, saved by the Senate, and lost again in conference committee. Two weeks later, we also lost an accountant who said he wouldn't go to jail for us, but by then we had figured out that the best way to float digital requisition forms and kite electronic funds transfers was with TOS. We couldn't stay ahead of the numbers forever, but TOS, with near-human guile and digital speed, bought us an extra week or two while the team from Hollywood installed the new imaging hardware.

The technicians and research assistants kept TOS busy with new data to absorb, to *think about*, and I worked to add "rooms" to the multicameral memory, trying to give TOS the ability to suppress the information hurricanes that still shut us down at unpredictable intervals. The first rooms had each been devoted to a specific function—sensory processing, pattern recognition, mem-

ory sorting—but these new ones were basically just memory mod-
ules. Meanwhile, Richardson paraded people who had known
Bierley through the I/O room for interviews with TOS.

The day of the press conference, I deflected half a dozen calls
from the Government Accounting Office. Even as the first reporters were filing into our press room, I kept expecting some suits
and crewcuts to barge in, flash badges, and say, "FBI."

I also worried about hurricanes, but TOS's storm warning
lights stayed off all morning, and the only surprise of the press
conference was the one Richardson and I had planned. While
stragglers were still filing into the room—security-screening and
bomb-sniffing that many people took some time—the video behind the podium flicked on.

"BIERLEY, REGRETTABLY, *is dead*," said Bierley's image. He was re-
sponding to the first question after his prepared statement.
"There's no bringing him back, and I regret that." Warm smile.

The press corps laughed uncertainly.

"But you're his memories?" asked a reporter.

"Not in the sense that you mean it," Bierley said. "Nobody
dumped Bierley's mind into a machine. We can't do that." Dra-
matic pause. "Yet." Smile. "What I am is a personality construct
of *other* people's memories. Over one hundred of Bierley's closest
associates were interviewed by TOS. Their impressions of Bierley,
specific examples of things he had said and done, along with digital
recordings of the man in action, were processed to create me. I
may not be Jackson Bierley as he saw himself, but I'm Jackson
Bierley as he was seen by others."

Bierley chose another reporter by name.

The reporter looked around herself, then at the screen. "Can
you see me?" she said. "Can you see this room?"

"There's a micro camera," said the image, "top and center of
this display panel. Really, though"—he flashed the grandfatherly
Bierley smile—"that's a wasted question. You must have had a
harder one in mind."

"Just this," she said. "Are you self-aware?"

"I certainly seem to be, don't I?" said the image. "There's
liable to be some debate about that. I'm no expert, so I'll leave the

final answer up to Doctors Maas and Richardson. But my opinion is that, no, I am not self-aware."

A ripple of laughter from the reporters who appreciated paradox.

"How do we know," said a man who hadn't laughed, "that this isn't some kind of fake?"

"How do you know I'm not *some incredibly talented actor who's wearing undetectable makeup and who studied Jackson Bierley's every move for years in order to be this convincing?*" Undetectably, unless you were looking for it, Bierley's pupils dilated a bit, and the effect was to broadcast warmth and openness. We had seen the real Bierley do that in recorded addresses. "I guess you have to make up your own mind."

Then he blinked. He smiled. Jackson Bierley didn't intend to make a fool of anyone, not even a rude reporter.

"What does Bierley's family think of all this?" asked someone else.

"You could ask them. I can tell you that they cooperated— they were among those interviewed by TOS. They have me back to an extent. I'll be here to meet those great-great grandchildren I so longed to greet one day. Unfortunately . . ." And suddenly he looked sad. "Unfortunately, those kids will know Bierley, but Bierley won't know them. Only much more research can hold out the promise that one day, a construct like me really will be self-aware, will remember, will *be* the man or woman whose life he or she extends into eternity."

He didn't mention the licensing fee his family was charging us for the exclusive use of his image, any more than Bierley himself would have mentioned it.

"Are the Bierleys funding this project?"

"I know a billion sounds like a lot of money, but when it's divided up among as many heirs as I have . . ." He paused, letting the laughter die. "No. They are not. This project is more expensive than you can imagine. In the long run, it's going to take moon-shot money to get eternity up and running."

"And where's that money going to come from, now that your federal funds have been cut off?"

"Well, I can't really say much about that. But I'll tell you that it will be much easier for me to learn Japanese or Malay as a construct than it would have been for the real Jackson Bierley." He smiled, but there was a brief tremor to the smile, and it didn't take a genius to see that Jackson Bierley, personality construct or not, was one American who didn't want to hand yet another technological advantage across the Pacific.

"In these times, it's understandable that the American taxpayer wants his money spent on hiring police," Bierley went on. "Why think about eternal life when you're worried about getting home from work alive? It's too bad that *both* can't be a priority. Of course, with the appropriate hardware attached, a machine like TOS could be one hell of a security system—a very smart guard who never sleeps." As if a TOS system could one day be in everyone's home.

Richardson and I stepped to the podium then, and for once I was happy to have no public speaking skills. The Bierley construct jumped in with damage control whenever I was about to say something I shouldn't. He made jokes when Richardson dryly admitted that, in all honesty, the construct was closer to a collaborative oil painting than it was to the real Jackson Bierley. Of the three of us up on the platform, the one who seemed warmest, funniest, most human, was the one inside the video screen.

After the conference, we got calls from the Secretary of Commerce, the Speaker of the House, and both the Majority and Minority Leaders in the Senate. Even though they were falling all over themselves to offer support for funding, Richardson and I knew we could still screw it up, so we mostly listened in while the Bierley construct handled the calls.

It was Richardson who had pulled our fat out of the fire, but even I was caught up in the illusion. I felt grateful to *Bierley*.

ONCE WE'D RESTORED our funding, I expected things to return to normal. I thought Richardson would be eager to get back to work, but he wouldn't schedule meetings with me. Day after day, he hid out in his office to tie up what he said were "loose ends."

I tried to be patient, but finally I'd had enough.

"It's time you talked to me," I said as I jerked open his office door. I stormed up to his desk. "You've been stalling for two weeks. This project is supposed to be a collaboration!"

Without looking up from his phone screen, he said, "Come in," which was supposed to be funny.

"Richardson," I told him, not caring who he might be talking to, "you were brilliant. You pulled off a coup. Great! Now let's get back to work. I can sit in my office and dream up augmentations for TOS all day, but it doesn't mean squat if I'm not getting your feedback."

"Have a seat."

"I'd prefer to stand, damn it. We're funded. We're ready to go. Let's get something done!"

He looked up at last and said, "I'm not a careerist, Maas. I'm not motivated by impressing anyone."

"And I am?" I sat down, tried to catch his eye. "I want to get to work for my own reasons, all right? The Bierley construct is incredible. Now what can we do next?"

"What indeed?"

"Yes," said the voice of Jackson Bierley. "I'm going to be a pretty hard trick to top, especially once you've got me in 3-D." The phone screen was at an acute angle and hard for me to see, but now I noticed the silver hair.

"Is that it?" I said. "You spend your day on the phone, chatting with the construct?"

Richardson said, "Bye, Jackson," and disconnected. "The construct is interesting. This is a useful tool we've invented."

"It is," I agreed. "It's something we can build on."

"It's something lots of people can build on." He folded the phone screen down. "A week ago I got a call from a Hollywood agent. He wanted to talk to me about some ideas. Constructs for dead singers—they could not only do new recordings, but grant interviews. Dead actor constructs. TOS-generated films scripted by dead writers and directed by Hitchcock or Huston or Spielberg or any other dead director you'd care to name. TOS is getting so good at imaging, you'd never need to build a set or hire a vid crew."

"Is *that* what you've spent all this time on?"

"Of course not. It's a good idea from the agent's perspective— as he sees it, he'd represent all of the virtual talent and practically own Hollywood. But it sounds to me like a waste of resources."

"Good."

"I'm just pointing out that everybody who hears about what TOS can do will see it in terms of meeting his or her own needs. The agent sees dead stars. You see a stepping-stone to immortality. I see a tool for making my own inquiries."

"What inquiries?"

"We've had that discussion." He pointed at his wall. "They've always had a better handle on it than we have."

I looked where he was pointing but just saw the usual time-lapse satellite image of weather systems crossing the globe. Then I realized that something was different. The display wasn't of the western hemisphere but of the eastern.

Richardson picked up the statue on his desk. "Shiva," he said. "This arc of flames that surrounds him is life and death. Flames for life. Spaces between the flames for death. The one and the zero. Reincarnation."

For once it was my turn to be the skeptic. "You find that consoling? An afterlife that can't be verified? It's superstition, Richardson."

"It's religion," he said, "and I don't have any more faith than you do that I'll be reborn after I die. Maybe I don't *dis*believe it as much as you do. Since it can't be falsified, it's not subject to any scientific test. But as a metaphor, I find it fascinating."

"What are you talking about?"

"Maas, what if you really *knew* death? What if you and death were intimate?"

"I still don't follow you."

"You're so interested in synthetic consciousness. What about synthesized death? If you knew more about death, Maas, would you still have this unreasoning fear of it?"

I snapped, "What do you mean, 'unreasoning'?"

"Forget it. I guess it's not your cup of tea. Why don't you think about this instead: Could a TOS construct replace you?"

"Replace me?"

"The way we replaced Bierley. The Bierley construct works for us every bit as well as the original did. So what about you? If I built a Maas construct, could it work on augmenting TOS as well as you do? It could sound like you, it could interact with other people convincingly, but could it think like you, design like you?"

"I don't know," I said. "I doubt it. A construct mimics social impressions. The pattern of thought that produces the behavior in the construct isn't sequenced quite like the thought in our heads. But you know that. Hell, what are you asking me for? You're the information expert."

"Well, if the behavior is the same, if the behavior is the production of good ideas, then maybe all we'd have to do is teach the machine to go through the motions that produce that behavior. We'd get the construct to act out whatever it is that you do when you're producing a good idea. Maybe it would kick out quality results as a sort of by-product."

I chewed my lip. "I don't think so."

"Works with Bierley."

"That's social skills. Not the same."

"You doubt the machine intelligence is sufficiently sophisticated, right?" Richardson said. "You're investing all this hope in TOS as a repository of consciousness, but you're not sure that we can even *begin* to synthesize creative thinking.

"Bierley makes for some interesting speculation," he went on. "Don't you think so? The original is dead. Jackson Bierley, in that sense, is complete. What we're left with is our memories of him. That's what we keep revising. And isn't that always true?

"My father died fifteen years ago," he said, "and I still feel as though my relationship with him changes from year to year. A life is like a novel that burns as you read it. You read the last page, and it's complete. You think about it, then, reflect on the parts that puzzle you. You feel some loss because there aren't any pages left to turn. You can remember only so many of the pages. That's what the construct is good for—remembering pages."

He smiled. "And here's the metaphysics: while you're trying to remember the book that's gone, maybe the author is writing a new one."

He put the statue of Shiva down on his desk. "Give me some more time, Maas. I'm not sitting on my hands, I promise you that. I'm working on my perspective."

"Your perspective."

"That's what I said."

I exhaled sharply. "I've been thinking about your suggestion that we tie building security into TOS. I could do that. And I guess I could work on getting rid of the hurricanes once and for all. But that's not just a hardware problem."

"All right. I'll give you an hour a day on that. Okay?"

I didn't tell him what I really thought. If I thoroughly pissed him off, who knew how long it would take for us to get back to our real work? I said, "Get your perspective straight in a week."

IN A WEEK, he was gone.

One of the research assistants, somewhat timidly, brought me the news. She had been watching CNN Four and saw a bombing story across town, and she was certain that she had seen Philip Richardson among the dead.

She followed me into my office, where I switched on the TV. CNN Four recycles its splatter stories every twenty minutes, so we didn't have long to wait.

The bomb had gone off in a subway station. Did Richardson ride the subway? I realized I didn't know where the man lived or how he got back and forth from work.

The station would have channeled the energy up through its blast vents—everything in the city was designed or redesigned these days with bombs in mind. But that saved structures, not people. Images of the station platform showed a tangle of twisted bodies. The color, as in all bomb-blast scenes, seemed wrong; the concussion turns the victims' skin slightly blue.

The camera panned across arms and legs, the faces turned toward the camera and away.

"Three terrorist groups, Under Deconstruction, Aftershock, and The Last Wave, have all claimed responsibility for the bombing," said the news reader.

There, at the end of the pan, was Philip Richardson, discolored like the rest. At the end of the story, I ran back the television's memory cache and replayed the images. I froze the one that showed Richardson.

"Get out," I told the research assistant. "Please."

I called the police.

"Are you family?" asked the desk sergeant when I told her

what I wanted. "We can't make a verification like that until the next of kin have been notified."

"His goddam face was just on the goddam TV!"

"Rules are rules," she said. "Hang on." Her gaze shifted from the phone to another monitor as she keyed in the query. "No problem, anyway. This is cleared to go out. And, yeah, sorry. The list of fatalities includes your friend."

I broke the connection.

"He was no friend of mine."

Deserter.

AT FIRST I dismissed the thought of making a Richardson personality construct. It wasn't the personality I needed but the mind. Substance, not surface.

But how different were they, really?

Maybe, Richardson had said, *all we'd have to do is teach the machine to go through the motions. Maybe it would kick out results as a by-product.*

I went to the I/O room where the hologram generator—Richardson's idea—had been installed. I called up Bierley.

"Hello, Maas," he said.

"Hi, Jackson."

"First names?" Bierley arched an eyebrow. "That's a first for you." Except for distortion flecks that were like a fine dust floating around him, Bierley was convincingly present.

"Well," I said, "let's be pals."

His laugh was ironic and embracing at the same time. "All right," he said. "Let's."

"Jackson, what's the product of 52,689 and 31,476?"

"My net worth?"

"No. Don't kid. What's the product?"

"What were those numbers again?"

"You're shading me, Jackson. You can't have forgotten."

About then, the Small Craft Advisory light came on, but I ignored it. Chaotic disturbances hardly ever built to hurricane force anymore. Sure enough, the light went out soon after it had come on.

"What's this about?" Bierley asked me.

"Did you calculate the product on the way to deciding how you'd respond to the question? Or did you jump straight to an analysis of what Bierley would say?"

"*I* did neither," Bierley said. Which was true. There wasn't an "I" there, except as a grammatical convention. "Don't confuse me with your machine, Dr. Maas. You're the scientist. You know what I'm talking about." He brushed the lapel on his jacket. "I'm an elegant illusion."

"Would you give me some investment advice, Jackson?"

The hologram smiled. "My forte was always building companies," he said, "not trading stocks. Best advice that I could give you about stocks is some I got at my daddy's knee. He said you don't go marrying some gal just because another fool loves her."

I smiled, and then I wondered if Bierley's father had actually said that. If it sounded good, that's what would matter to the construct. But that's just what would have mattered to the real Bierley, too.

That is, what had mattered to the real Bierley and what mattered now to the construct was that the story have its effect. He had made me smile, made me think that Bierley the billionaire was just a regular guy.

What if a Richardson construct could work the same way? The effect that Richardson had produced, the one I wanted to duplicate, was an effect on me. I wanted to stretch my thinking. What if that depended more on the emotional state he generated in me than on his actual ideas?

No, I thought. That was ridiculous.

WHAT DECIDED ME was the phone call.

"Are you Maas?" the woman said. Her hair was long and black, but disarrayed. Her eyes were red-rimmed. On her face was the blankness that comes after too many days of anger or grief or worry, when the muscles can't hold the form of feeling any longer, but the feeling persists. "I'm Phillips," I thought she said. That is, I thought she was saying her name was Phillips. But she was only pausing to search for the next word.

"I'm Philip's . . . widow," she said.

I hadn't known Richardson was married. I wasn't the only one he had deserted.

"Yes," I said, and then again, more gently: "Yes, Mrs. Richardson. I'm Dr. Maas." An infant wailed in the background, and Mrs. Richardson seemed not to have noticed. "I'm Elliot Maas."

"Do you know where he is?" she asked.

Was she really asking what I thought she was? I opened, then closed my mouth. What would I tell her? *He's dead, Mrs. Richardson. Death is not a location. Where is he? He isn't anywhere. Mrs. Richardson, he is not. Mrs. Richardson, your husband doesn't exist. Where he used to be, there is nothing. Mrs. Richardson . . .*

"I'm sorry," she said. "I'm not being very clear." She put her hand to her forehead and closed her eyes. "The ashes, Dr. Maas. Have the ashes been delivered to you?"

I stared stupidly at the screen.

"The coroner's office says they had the ashes delivered to me, but they didn't. I thought perhaps they had made a mistake and sent them to Philip's work address." She opened her eyes. "Did the coroner's office make a delivery?" In the background, the infant cried more lustily.

"I don't know," I said. "I could check, I suppose."

"They used to . . ." Her mouth trembled, and she pursed her lips. Her eyes glistened. "They used to let you make your own arrangements," she said. "But they don't do that anymore because there are so many bombs and so many . . . I never saw him. I never got to say good-bye and now they can't even find his ashes."

"I'll make inquiries."

"His mother's been here, trying to help out, but she . . ." Richardson's wife blinked, as if waking. "Oh, God. The baby. I'm so sorry."

The phone went black, then the screen showed the Ameritech logo and the dial tone began to drone.

I made sure that the ashes hadn't been delivered to us, and I called the coroner's office where they swore that the ashes had been processed and delivered to Richardson's home address days earlier. They had a computer record of it.

When I called Mrs. Richardson back, it was the other Mrs. Richardson—his mother—who answered. She looked worn out, too. One more person that Richardson had abandoned.

But she would manage to get by in whatever way she had managed before. I was the one he had hurt the most. I was the one with the most to lose.

When Richardson's wife came to the phone, I told her that I'd struck out with the coroner. "But I think there is a way that I can help you," I said. I even admitted that it might be of some use to me, as well.

WHO KNOWS WHETHER the construct brought Sharon Richardson any consolation? She came by from time to time as the construct evolved, and she usually brought the baby. That actually caused a problem the first time she did it—I had cleared her through the building's recognition system, but TOS didn't want to let Richardson's infant daughter, a stranger, inside without my authorization. The door refused to open. TOS-mediated security still needed some tinkering.

In the I/O room, Sharon Richardson told the construct, "We miss you."

"He loved you," the construct told her.

"We miss you," she said again.

"I'm not really him."

"I know."

"What do you want me to say?"

"I don't know. There's something that never got said, but I don't know what it is."

"Everything passes away. Nothing lasts," the construct said. "That's the thing he carried with him every moment. Nothing lasts, and that's the thing we have to hold on to. That's the thing we have to understand, that we're as transitory as thoughts. Butterflies or thoughts. When we really understand that, then we're beautiful."

Defeatist, I thought. *Deserter*.

"That's not it," she said. "I heard him say that. More than once."

"What do you want me to say?" the construct repeated.

She looked at me, self-conscious, then turned away.

"He was selfish," she said to the floor. "I want to hear him . . . I want you to say you're sorry."

The construct sighed. "Do you think he died on purpose?"

"Did he?" she said. "I *loved* him!"

"Nothing lasts."

"Say it!"

The image of Philip Richardson closed his eyes, hung his head, and said, "Death comes. Sooner or later, it comes."

Sharon Richardson didn't leave looking any more prepared for life without Philip than she had looked when she first called me, looking for his ashes.

I wasn't any more satisfied than she was. That the construct wasn't finished yet was the one thing that gave me hope. But not much.

Using the Bierley construct as the interviewer, TOS had talked to Sharon, to Richardson's mother, his brother, and his two sisters. The interviews took place in the I/O room where the hologram made Bierley more convincingly warm, caring, and real. He extracted insights, anecdotes, and honest appraisals from every technician who had worked with Richardson on TOS. I flew in Richardson's grad school peers and colleagues from his stints at MIT and Stanford. They all talked to Bierley, and Bierley interviewed me, too. I was as exhaustive and as honest as I could be in conveying my impressions of Richardson. Everything about him mattered—even whatever had irritated me. It was all part of the pattern that made him Philip Richardson. After the interviews, I'd stay in the I/O room talking to the construct as it developed. That made for late nights.

Irritatingly, TOS started to suffer again from hurricanes. Those chaos storms in the information flow started to shut down the Richardson construct around one in the morning, regularly.

"It's like you're too much contradiction for TOS to handle," I told the construct late one night. "A scientist and a mystic."

"No mystic," Richardson said. "I'm more scientist than you are, Maas. You're in a contest with the universe. You want to *beat* it. If someone gave you the fountain of youth, guaranteed to keep you alive forever with the proviso that you'd never understand how it worked, you'd jump at the chance. Science is a means to you. You want results. You're a mere technologist."

"I have a focus. You could never keep yourself on track."

"You have an obsession," the construct countered. "You're

right that I can never resist the temptation of the more interesting questions. But that's what matters to me. What does all of this—" He swept his hand wide to encompass the universe with his gesture, and his hand came to rest on his own chest. "What does it all mean? That's my question, Maas. I never stop asking it."

"You sound like him. Sometimes I forget what you are."

"I'm a dead loss, that's what I am," the construct said with a smile. "I probably argue as well as Richardson, but when it comes to conceptualizing, I'm just TOS. Not that the machine is chopped liver, but you haven't resurrected Philip Richardson."

The Small Craft Advisory light had been on for an hour, but now the next light in the sequence came on. Gale Warning.

"We'd better talk fast," said Richardson. "I don't have much time." He smiled again. "Memento mori."

I said nothing but stared at him. The hologram generator had been improved a bit recently, and for minutes at a time, I could detect no flaw in his appearance. The eye was so easy to fool.

This was the fifth night in a row with a hurricane. They always came after midnight. *Tick, tick, tick.* Like clockwork.

But TOS hurricanes were a function of chaos. Why would they suddenly behave so predictably?

And then I thought again, *The eye is so easy to fool.*

The ashes never *had* turned up.

"Son of a bitch!" I said aloud.

That's when the hurricane light came on and the hologram of Philip Richardson winked out.

I SAT THINKING for five minutes in the quiet building, the building that was down to just two overnight guards—a skeleton crew— since TOS oversaw security and controlled all the locks inside and out. A big, silent building. For five minutes, I considered what I needed to do. Then I went to the part of the building that housed the TOS memory.

The multicameral design of TOS made it relatively easy to isolate various functions from one another. I could pull all the sensory "rooms" off-line and make changes in them, and the rest of TOS wouldn't know what I was doing. It would be like slicing the corpus callosum in the human brain—the left hemisphere wouldn't know what the right was doing, wouldn't know that things were being monkeyed with in the other hemisphere. But TOS was self-programming, so I needed instructions from the left hemisphere to reprogram the right. Getting the job done without tripping whatever safeguards Richardson had programmed in meant pulling out one room at a time, giving it a function, downloading the result of the function as a digital record, then emptying the room of any traces of what it had just done before I connected it back to the whole. One room at a time, I captured the instructions that would let me generate false data for the sensory rooms.

The process would have taken thirty seconds if I could have just told TOS what I wanted to do, but it wouldn't have worked that way. Doing it the slow way took an hour.

I went back to the I/O room and said, "I'm going home." TOS started to process the words, and the phrase tugged at the tripwires I had just programmed.

To the rest of TOS, the sensory rooms sent sounds and images of my walking out of the room, closing the door, walking down the corridor, down the stairs, out of the building, and across the parking lot. TOS saw me get into my car and drive away.

And TOS didn't just see this. It heard, felt, and smelled it, too.

Meanwhile, the sensory rooms suppressed the data that was coming from the I/O room, data that said I was still there, at the back of the room, hiding behind file cabinets with the lights out. Otherwise, everything ran as it normally would.

The eye was easy to fool. Yes, and so was the ear. So was the motion detector. So was the air sampler.

HE CAME IN at about four o'clock. The hall lights at his back showed that he was dressed in something baggy. He said, "Lights," and the lights came on in the room. It was a sweat suit. A gray one. He said, "The one and the zero," his code, I suppose, for "System Restore," and the Hurricane, Gale Warning, and Small Craft Advisory lights clicked off in quick succession.

He called up the construct and said to it, in a flat voice, "Hello, Richardson."

And the construct answered, mimicking the tone, "Hello,

Richardson." The construct shook his head. "You sound hollow." Then he smiled. "Death warmed over, eh?"

The man in the sweat suit sat down with his back to me and watched the construct without answering.

"So tell me what it's like," said the construct. "You give *me* some information for a change."

"It's more real than you could believe. He's more dead than you can imagine."

"Of course." Big smile. "I'm a construct. I only *seem* to imagine."

"Richardson is more dead than even Richardson could have imagined."

"Wasn't that the point of this exercise?"

The man in the sweat suit didn't answer.

"I don't understand why you're not excited. This is a breakthrough!"

"I suppose it is." He took a deep breath and let it out. "Give me Bierley."

"Cheer up," the construct said. "It's the great adventure. You'll make the journey with your memory intact."

"Shut your trap and give me Bierley."

The Richardson construct hesitated a moment longer. Then, without transition, it was Bierley in the hologram.

"Hi," Bierley said.

"Hi, Jackson."

"You don't look so good."

"So I've been told."

"Want to start with easy questions?" asked Bierley. "His favorite color, that sort of thing?"

"I'm through with the construct. It doesn't interest me anymore." He stood up. "I just came by to tell you that it's time for me to move on."

"That's enough," I said.

He jumped at the sound of my voice, but he didn't turn around.

"Richardson," I told him, "you are a son of a bitch."

"Richardson's dead."

"So you've told me," said Bierley.

"I was talking to Maas," he said, his voice still flat.

"Maas went home over an hour ago," said the construct.

"Turn the construct off," I told him. "I built a sensory barricade. TOS doesn't know I'm in the building, and won't know it until I leave this room."

"Clever."

"What is?" said Bierley.

I said, "No more clever than splicing yourself into the image bank at CNN Four. No more clever than hacking your way into records at the coroner's office and police department."

"TOS did most of the work."

"Most of what work?" said the construct.

"Turn it off," I said again.

"Bierley," he said, "give me Richardson again."

The hologram flipped immediately to the other man's image. "You want Richardson? There he is. That's the closest anyone can get. Not the real thing, of course, but more Richardson than I am." But then he did shut the construct down. Again he said, "Richardson is dead."

"You used me. You planted the idea. You knew I'd build the construct."

"I'm not him. I'm the space in between. I'm the void." He edged toward the door as I stepped closer to him, close enough to see his profile. He still didn't turn to face me.

"I want to kick your living, breathing ass," I said. "We've lost a lot of time on this."

I nodded at the empty space above the hologram projector. I said, "So you've met him. You've had a chance to see yourself as others saw you. Was it worth it?"

He said nothing at first. "The curious thing," he said at last, "was that the construct wasn't surprised to meet me."

"Nothing much fazes you, Richardson. Why should your construct be any different?"

"I don't think that's it," he said. "I think it was something others knew about Richardson, that he would do anything to know . . ."

"What do you do during the day? Do you watch the building?"

He was silent.

"Have you seen your wife come here? Doesn't look good, does

she? She paid a price for your little experiment, wouldn't you say? Have you been keeping up?"

"Every day," he said, "I'm aware of the zero where Richardson used to be. Every day, I'm face to face with his absence."

I clenched my fists. "Do you have any idea what it's been like for me to think that you were gone?"

"I know she . . ." For a moment, he was at a loss. "He loved her very much."

"What about me? I can't bring TOS to its potential on my own. You left me without hope!"

"Richardson did that," he said. And again, flatly: "Richardson is dead."

"Why did you have to do it like this? We could have made you a construct! Do you think you need to be dead for people to say what they really think of you?" I pounded my fist on the hologram console. "Damn it, I'd have done whatever you wanted me to. Whatever it takes, whatever you need. But it didn't have to be like this!"

"Richardson wanted to bring you along," he said. He took another sideways step toward the door. "He thought it would help you if you had a closer look at what you were afraid of."

I sat down. I tried to take the anger out of my voice. "Whatever you need," I said, "however strange, you just ask for it from now on. Understand? After we get this straightened out, assuming I can keep you out of prison, you tell me about how you want to use TOS, and we'll do that. Just so you give some attention to the things that *I* am interested in."

"I don't think you understand. You can't bring him back from the dead. The construct was for the bardo."

"The what?"

"The in-between time. Before its next life, the soul looks back, understands. Looks back, but there's no *going* back. There's only the next life, and forgetfulness."

He turned his face to me. His expression was blank, so blank that in truth he didn't look like himself.

"I'm the soul who doesn't forget. I'll have a new life, the life of a man who *understands* death. I have died. I am dead. And I will live again." He looked at his hands. "What a thing to long for."

He was right. I hadn't understood. I had thought this whole

thing was like the story of the man who stages his own funeral so he can hear what the mourners will have to say about him. But there was more to it than that.

I said, "You're not going anywhere."

He stepped closer to the door. "I'll have another life."

"Got TOS to make an electronic funds transfer, did you? You're a rich man?"

"It's not like that. I'm going naked. I'm taking nothing along."

"I see. Taking no baggage but your worthless skin and your newfound wisdom."

"Memory."

"How about your wife, then? Did you and TOS arrange some little windfall for her?"

"Richardson's wife!" he shouted. "I'm not him! Richardson is dead!"

He ran then. I followed him out of the I/O room, but I didn't bother to run.

As soon as I was out in the hallway, TOS did what I knew it would do. I had just materialized out of thin air, and TOS could only conclude, recognizing me or not, that some sort of security breach had taken place.

All over the building, doors locked. The alarm rang at the security guards' desks. Through the glass wall along the corridor, I could see one of the guards in the other wing looking up at the lights on our floor.

Richardson tried the stairwell door. It wouldn't budge.

"Richardson," I said gently as I approached. "Philip."

He ran down the side corridor but was blocked by a fire door.

"It's over," I said when I had turned the corner. "Let it be over."

He whirled to face me. "I won't bring him back!" he said. "Forever is *your* obsession, not mine!" Then, pleading: "I *can't* bring him back! It can't be done!"

"Surely," I said, "you've seen whatever you needed to see. Surely you have come to understand whatever it is that you needed to understand."

"I won't help you!"

I grabbed the front of his sweat shirt. "When they arrest you, Philip, when the truth comes out . . ."

He masked his face with shaking hands and slumped against the fire door.

"When the truth comes out, I can help you or I can hurt you, Richardson."

"Dead," he said through his hands. "He's dead."

"You can get your life back. It's going to be a bit smashed up. It's going to take some piecing back together. But you can have it back."

He pressed his hands hard against his face.

BIERLEY SAVED HIS ass.

The construct was making calls to our politicos before the police had taken Richardson from the building, and before sunrise, there were thirty spin doctors in different parts of the country finding ways to put what Richardson had done in the best possible light.

The press verdict, basically, was genius stretched to the limit. He'd pushed himself too hard doing work vital to national interests. The courts ordered rest, lots of psychological evaluations, and release under his own recognizance. Eventually, he received a suspended sentence for data fraud.

And Sharon Richardson took him back. I wouldn't have, if he'd been replaceable. It was hard to imagine an infidelity worse than his. I had to welcome him back. But she chose to.

DESERTERS. When the work is hard, I think of deserters. And the work is often hard. We've been at it again for months now, but Richardson and I don't throw off sparks the way we once did. We talk about technical problems with TOS, and we bounce ideas off each other, but something's gone.

No more conceptual leaps. No more flying from breakthrough to breakthrough.

I think of men on the rail of a sinking tanker. I think of the arctic explorer stranded on the ice.

I think of deserters. What are they afraid of?

Maybe they are afraid of the wrong thing.

The dead bear witness.

From the bottom of the sea, dead sailors wave their arms.

It's not that Richardson has gone dull. If anything, his mind has more edge than before. But we'll be arguing some point of memory structures and I'll happen to catch his eye and see . . .

There's someone else looking back.

"Philip Richardson," he likes to remind me, "is dead."

I'd be a damned fool to believe him.

There are a lot of damned fools in the world.

I still hear the *tick*, *tick*, *tick* of my heart, the one, one, one that counts down to zero. I still believe that there's a chance, just a chance, that I can find a door into eternity. When Richardson and I were at our best, there were days when I thought I had glimpsed that door.

But I don't work with the same focus I once did. Whatever I'm doing, there's something that flutters at the edge of my consciousness.

When, at quiet moments, I hear the blood rush in my ears, when I feel my heart thumping in my chest, it's not just the numbers counting down that I think of. It's also the numbers already counted. Bierley, gone. Richardson . . . different.

I am fifty-nine years old.

What if I succeed? What if I reside in TOS, eternal, separate, watching the living die and die and die?

Often I think of the man in the lifeboat. He has rowed himself to safety, beyond the burning oil, beyond the fire's reach. Through the smoke and flames, he can see the others waving to him, holding out their arms. Do they think he'd row back across the fire in a wooden boat?

Crowded at the rail, the sailors wave and sink. Each drowns alone, but they sink together.

There's no comfort in a common grave, I tell myself.

But on days when I can't think clearly, I sit and look at my hands, the hands of a man who is rowing himself to safety, and I know that the sea around him is wide. And black. And cold. And empty.

Gone

JOHN CROWLEY

*John Crowley is one of the most significant fantasists at work
today. His novels* Engine Summer *and* Little, Big *have had
a tremendous impact on the fantasy genre, and his new novel,*
Dæmonomania *(being the third book in the sequence begun
in* Ægypt *and continued in* Love & Sleep*) is very eagerly
awaited. His short SF and fantasy stories, which appear all
too infrequently, have been collected in* Novelty *and in*
Antiquities. *"Gone" is an alien invasion story that
approaches the human condition from an unusual angle.*

ELMERS AGAIN. YOU WAITED IN A SORT OF EXASPERATED
amusement for yours, thinking that if you had been missed last
time yours would likely be among the households selected this
time, though how that process of selection went on no one knew,
you only knew that a new capsule had been detected entering the
atmosphere (caught by one of the thousand spy satellites and
listening-and-peering devices that had been trained on the big
Mother Ship in orbit around the moon for the past year) and
though the capsule had apparently burned up in the atmosphere,
that's just what had happened the time before, and then elmers
everywhere. You could hope that you'd be skipped or passed over
—there were people who had been skipped last time when all
around them neighbors and friends had been visited or afflicted,
and who would appear now and then and be interviewed on the
news, though having nothing, after all, to say, it was the rest of us
who had the stories—but in any case you started looking out the
windows, down the drive, listening for the doorbell to ring in the
middle of the day.

Pat Poynton didn't need to look out the window of the kid's bedroom where she was changing the beds, the only window from which the front door could be seen, when her doorbell rang in the middle of the day. She could almost hear, subliminally, every second doorbell on Ponader Drive, every second doorbell in South Bend go off just at that moment. She thought: Here's mine.

They had come to be called elmers (or Elmers) all over this country, at least, after David Brinkley had told a story on a talk show about how when they built the great World's Fair in New York in 1939, it was thought that people out in the country, people in places like Dubuque and Rapid City and South Bend, wouldn't think of making a trip East and paying five dollars to see all the wonders, that maybe the great show wasn't for the likes of them; and so the fair's promoters hired a bunch of people, ordinary-looking men with ordinary clothes wearing ordinary glasses and bow ties, to fan out to places like Vincennes and Austin and Brattleboro and just talk it up. Pretend to be ordinary folks who had been to the fair, and hadn't been high-hatted, no sirree, had a wonderful time, the wife too, and b'gosh had Seen the Future and could tell you the sight was worth the five dollars they were asking, which wasn't so much since it included tickets to all the shows and lunch. And all these men, whatever their real names were, were all called Elmer by the promoters who sent them out.

Pat wondered what would happen if she just didn't open the door. Would it eventually go away? It surely wouldn't push its way in, mild and blobby as it was (from the upstairs window she could see that it was the same as the last ones), and that made her wonder how after all they had all got inside—as far as she knew there weren't many who had failed to get at least a hearing. Some chemical hypnotic maybe that they projected, calming fear. What Pat felt standing at the top of the stair and listening to the doorbell pressed again (timidly, she thought, tentatively, hopefully) was amused exasperation, just like everyone else's: a sort of oh-Christ-no with a burble of wonderment just below it, and even expectation: for who wouldn't be at least intrigued by the prospect of his, or her, own lawn-mower, snow-shoveler, hewer of wood and drawer of water, for as long as it lasted?

"Mow your lawn?" it said when Pat opened the door. "Take out trash? Mrs. Poynton?"

Now actually in its presence, looking at it through the screen door, Pat felt most strongly a new part of the elmer feeling: a giddy revulsion she had not expected. It was so not human. It seemed to have been constructed to resemble a human being by other sorts of beings who were not human and did not understand very well what would count as human with other humans. When it spoke its mouth moved *(mouth-hole must move when speech is produced)* but the sound seemed to come from somewhere else, or from nowhere.

"Wash your dishes? Mrs. Poynton?"

"No," she said, as citizens had been instructed to say. "Please go away. Thank you very much."

Of course the elmer didn't go away, only stood bobbing slightly on the doorstep like a foolish child whose White Rose salve or Girl Scout cookies haven't been bought.

"Thank you very much," it said, in tones like her own. "Chop wood? Draw water?"

"Well gee," Pat said, and, helplessly, smiled.

What everyone knew, besides the right response to give to the elmer, which everyone gave and almost no one was able to stick to, was that these weren't the creatures or beings from the Mother Ship itself up above (so big you could see it, pinhead sized, crossing the face of the affronted moon) but some kind of creation of theirs, sent down in advance. An artifact, the official word was; some sort of protein, it was guessed; some sort of chemical process at the heart of it or head of it, maybe a DNA-based computer or something equally outlandish, but no one knew because of the way the first wave of them, flawed maybe, fell apart so quickly, sinking and melting like the snowmen they sort of resembled after a week or two of mowing lawns and washing dishes and pestering people with their Good Will Ticket, shriveling into a sort of dry flocked matter and then into nearly nothing at all, like cotton candy in the mouth.

"Good Will Ticket?" said the elmer at Pat Poynton's door, holding out to her a tablet of something not paper, on which was written or printed or anyway somehow indited a little message. Pat didn't read it, didn't need to, you had the message memorized by the time you opened your door to a second-wave elmer like Pat's. Sometimes lying in bed in the morning in the bad hour before the kids had to be got up for school Pat would repeat like a prayer the little message that everybody in the world it seemed was going to be presented with sooner or later:

Good Will
You Mark Below
All All Right With Love Afterwards
Why Not Say Yes
☐ Yes

And no box for No, which meant—if it was a sort of vote, and experts and officials (though how such a thing could have been determined Pat didn't know) were guessing that's what it was, a vote to allow or to accept the arrival or descent of the Mother Ship and its unimaginable occupants or passengers—that you could only refuse to take it from the elmer: shaking your head firmly and saying No clearly but politely, because even *taking* a Good Will Ticket might be the equivalent of a Yes, and though what it would be a Yes *to* exactly no one knew, there was at least a groundswell of opinion in the think tanks that it meant acceding to or at least not resisting World Domination.

You weren't, however, supposed to shoot your elmer. In places like Idaho and Siberia that's what they were doing, you heard, though a bullet or two didn't seem to make any difference to them, they went on pierced with holes like characters in the Dick Tracy comics of long ago, smiling shyly in at your windows, Rake your leaves? Yardwork? Pat Poynton was sure that Lloyd would not hesitate to shoot, would be pretty glad that at last something living or at least moving and a certified threat to freedom had at last got before him to be aimed at. In the hall-table drawer Pat still had Lloyd's 9mm Glock pistol, he had let her know he wanted to come get it but he wasn't getting back into this house, she'd use it on him herself if he got close enough.

Not really, no, she wouldn't. And yet.

"Wash windows?" the elmer now said.

"Windows," Pat said, feeling a little of the foolish self-consciousness people feel who are inveigled by comedians or MCs into having conversations with puppets; wary in the same way too, the joke very likely being on her. "You do windows?"

It only bobbed before her like a big water toy.

"Okay," she said, and her heart filled. "Okay, come on in."

Amazing how graceful it really was; it seemed to navigate through the house and the furniture as though it were negatively charged to them, the way it drew close to the stove or the refrigerator and then was repelled gently away, avoiding collision. It seemed to be able to compact or compress itself, too, make itself smaller in small spaces, grow again to full size in larger spaces.

Pat sat down on the couch in the family room and watched. It just wasn't possible to do anything else but watch. Watch it take the handle of a bucket; watch it open the tops of bottles of cleansers and seem to inhale their odors to identify them; take up the squeegee and cloth she found for it. The world, the universe, Pat thought (it was the thought almost everyone thought who was just then taking a slow seat on his or her davenport in his or her family room or in his or her vegetable garden or junkyard or wherever and watching a second-wave elmer get its bearings and get down to work): how big the world, the universe is, how strange; how lucky I am to have learned it, to be here now seeing this.

So the world's work, its odd jobs anyway, were getting done as the humans who usually did them sat and watched, all sharing the same feelings of gratitude and glee, and not only because of the chores being done: it was that wonder, that awe, a universal neap tide of common feeling such as had never been experienced before, not by this species, not anyway since the days on the old old veldt when every member of it could share the same joke, the same dawn, the same amazement. Pat Poynton, watching hers, didn't hear the beebeep of the school-bus horn.

Most days she started watching the wall clock and her wristwatch alternately a good half hour before the bus's horn could be expected to be heard, like an anxious sleeper who continually awakes to check his alarm clock to see how close it has come to going off. Her arrangement with the driver was that he wouldn't let her kids off before tooting. He promised. She hadn't explained why.

But today the sounding of the horn had sunk away deeply into her back brain, maybe three minutes gone, when Pat at last reheard it or remembered having heard and not noticed it. She leapt to her feet, an awful certainty seizing her; she was out the door as fast as her heartbeat accelerated, and was coming down the front steps just in time to see down at the end of the block the kids disappearing into and slamming the door of Lloyd's classic Camaro (whose macho rumble Pat now realized she had also been hearing for some minutes). The cherry-red muscle car, Lloyd's other and more beloved wife, blew exhaust from double pipes that stirred the gutter's leaves, and leapt forward as though kicked.

She shrieked and spun around, seeking help; there was no one in the street. Two steps at a time, maddened and still crying out, she went up the steps and into the house, tore at the pretty little Hitchcock phone table, the phone spilling in parts, the table's legs leaving the floor, its jaw dropping and the Glock 9mm nearly falling out: Pat caught it and was out the door with it and down the street calling out her ex-husband's full name, coupled with imprecations and obscenities her neighbors had never heard her utter before, but the Camaro was of course out of hearing and sight by then.

Gone. Gone gone gone. The world darkened and the sidewalk tilted up toward her as though to smack her face. She was on her knees, not knowing how she had got to them, also not knowing whether she would faint or vomit.

She did neither, and after a time got to her feet. How had this gun, heavy as a hammer, got in her hand? She went back in the house and restored it to the raped little table, and bent to put the phone, which was whimpering urgently, back together.

She couldn't call the police; he'd said—in the low soft voice he used when he wanted to sound implacable and dangerous and just barely controlled, eyes rifling threat at her—that if she got the police involved in his family he'd kill all of them. She didn't entirely believe it, didn't entirely believe anything he said, but he had said it. She didn't believe the whole Christian survivalist thing he was supposedly into, though he would not probably take them to a cabin in the mountains to live off elk as he had threatened or promised, would probably get no farther than his mother's house with them.

Please Lord let it be so.

The elmer hovered grinning in her peripheral vision like an accidental guest in a crisis as she banged from room to room, getting her coat on and taking it off again, sitting to sob at the kitchen table, searching yelling for the cordless phone, where the hell had it been put this time. She called her mother, and wept. Then, heart thudding hard, she called his. One thing you didn't know about elmers (Pat thought this while she waited for her mother-in-law's long cheery phone-machine message to get over) was whether they were like cleaning ladies and handymen, and you were obliged not to show your feelings around them; or whether you were allowed to let go, as with a pet. Abstract question, since she had already.

The machine beeped and began recording her silence. She punched the phone off without speaking.

TOWARD EVENING SHE got the car out at last and drove across town to Mishiwaka. Her mother-in-law's house was unlit, and there was no car in the garage. She watched a long time, till it was near dark, and came back. There ought to have been elmers everywhere, mowing lawns, taptapping with hammers, pulling wagonloads of kids. She saw none.

Her own was where she had left it. The windows gleamed as though coated with silver film.

"What?" she asked it. "You want something to do?" The elmer bounced a little in readiness and put out its chest—so, Pat thought, to speak—and went on smiling. "Bring back my kids," she said. "Go find them and bring them back."

It seemed to hesitate, bobbing between setting off on the job it had been given and turning back to refuse or maybe to await further explanation; it showed Pat its three-fingered cartoon hands, fat and formless. You knew, about elmers, that they would not take vengeance for you, or right wrongs. People had asked, of course they had. People wanted angels, avenging angels; believed they deserved them. Pat, too: she knew now that she wanted hers, wanted it right now.

She stared it down for a time, resentful; then she said forget it, sorry, just a joke, sort of; there's nothing really to do, just forget it, nothing more to do. She went past it, stepping first to one side as it did too and then to the other side; when she got by she went into the bathroom and turned on the water in the sink full force, and after a moment did finally throw up, a wrenching heave that produced nothing but pale sputum.

Toward midnight she took a couple of pills and turned on the TV.

What she saw immediately was two spread-eagled skydivers circling each other in the middle of the air, their orange suits rippling sharply in the wind of their descent. They drifted closer together, put gloved hands on each other's shoulders. Earth lay far below them, like a map. The announcer said it wasn't known just what happened, or what grievances they had, and at that moment one clouted the other in the face. Then he was grabbed by the other. Then the first grabbed the second. Then they flipped over in the air, each with an arm around the other's neck in love or rage, their other arms arm-wrestling in the air, or dancing, each keeping the other from releasing his chute. The announcer said thousands on the ground watched in horror, and indeed now Pat heard them, an awful moan or shriek from a thousand people, a noise that sounded just like awed satisfaction, as the two skydivers—locked, the announcer said, in deadly combat—shot toward the ground. The helicopter camera lost them and the ground camera picked them up, like one being, four legs thrashing; it followed them almost to the ground, when people rose up suddenly before the lens and cut off the view: but the crowd screamed, and someone right next to the camera said *What the hell.*

Pat Poynton had already seen these moments, seen them a couple of times. They had broken into the soaps with them. She pressed the remote. Demonic black men wearing outsize clothing and black glasses threatened her, moving to a driving beat and stabbing their forefingers at her. She pressed again. Police on a city street, her own city she learned, drew a blanket over someone shot. The dark stain on the littered street. Pat thought of Lloyd. She thought she glimpsed an elmer on an errand far off down the street, bobbing around a corner.

Press again.

That soothing channel where Pat often watched press conferences or speeches, awaking sometimes from half sleep to find the meeting over or a new one begun, the important people having left or not yet arrived, the backs of milling reporters and government people who talked together in low voices. Just now a senator with white hair and a face of exquisite sadness was speaking on the Senate floor. "I apologize to the gentleman," he said. "I wish to withdraw the word *snotty*. I should not have said it. What I meant by that word was: arrogant, unfeeling, self-regarding; supercilious; meanly relishing the discomfiture of your opponents and those hurt by your success. But I should not have said *snotty*. I withdraw *snotty*."

She pressed again, and the two skydivers again fell toward earth.

What's wrong with us? Pat Poynton thought.

She stood, black instrument in her hand, a wave of nausea seizing her again. What's wrong with us? She felt as though she were drowning in a tide of cold mud, unstoppable; she wanted not to be here any longer, here amid this. She knew she did not, hadn't ever, truly belonged here at all. Her being here was some kind of dreadful sickening mistake.

"Good Will Ticket?"

She turned to face the great thing, gray now in the TV's light. It held out the little plate or tablet to her. All all right with love afterwards. There was no reason at all in the world not to.

"All right," she said. "All right."

It brought the ticket closer, held it up. It seemed to be not something it carried but a part of its flesh. She pressed her thumb against the square beside the YES. The little tablet yielded slightly to her pressure, like one of those nifty buttons on new appliances that feel, themselves, like flesh to press. Her vote registered, maybe.

The elmer didn't alter, or express satisfaction or gratitude, or express anything except the meaningless delight it had been expressing, if that's the word, from the start. Pat sat again on the couch and turned off the television. She pulled the afghan (his mother had made it) from the back of the couch and wrapped herself in it. She felt the calm euphoria of having done something irrevocable, though what exactly she had done she didn't know. She slept there awhile, the pills having grown importunate in her bloodstream at last; lay in the constant streetlight that tiger-striped the room, watched over by the unstilled elmer till gray dawn broke.

IN HER CHOICE, in the suddenness of it, what could almost be described as the insouciance of it if it had not been experienced as so urgent, Pat Poynton was not unique or even unusual; world-wide, polls showed, voting was running high against life on Earth as we know it and in favor of whatever it was that your YES was said to, about which opinions differed. The alecks of TV smart and otherwise detailed the rising numbers, and an agreement seemed to have been reached among them all, an agreement shared in by government officials and the writers of newspaper editorials, to describe this craven unwillingness to resist as a sign of decay, social sickness, repellently nonhuman behavior: the newspeople reported the trend toward mute surrender and knuckling under with the same faces they used for the relaying of stories about women who drowned their children or men who shot their wives to please their lovers, or of snipers in faraway places who brought down old women out gathering firewood: and yet what was actually funny to see (funny to Pat and those like her who had already felt the motion of the soul, the bone-weariness, too, that made the choice so obvious) was that in their smooth tanned faces was another look never before seen there, seen before only on the faces of the rest of us, in our own faces: a look for which Pat Poynton anyway had no name but knew very well, a kind of stricken longing: like, she thought, the bewildered look you see in kids' faces when they come to you for help.

It was true that a certain disruption of the world's work was becoming evident, a noticeable trend toward giving up, leaving the wheel, dropping the ball. People spent less time getting to the job, more time looking upward. But just as many now felt themselves more able to buckle down, by that principle according to which you get to work and clean your house before the cleaning lady comes. The elmers had been sent, surely, to demonstrate that peace and cooperation were better than fighting and selfishness and letting the chores pile up for others to do.

For soon they were gone again. Pat Poynton's began to grow a little listless almost as soon as she had signed or marked or accepted her Good Will Ticket, and by evening next day, though it had by then completed a list of jobs Pat had long since compiled but in her heart had never believed she would get around to, it had slowed distinctly. It went on smiling and nodding, like an old person in the grip of dementia, even as it began dropping tools and bumping into walls, and finally Pat, unwilling to witness its dissolution and not believing she was obliged to, explained (in the somewhat overdistinct way we speak to not real bright teenage baby-sitters or newly hired help who have just arrived from elsewhere and don't speak good English) that she had to go out and pick up a few things and would be back soon; and then she drove aimlessly out of town and up toward Michigan for a couple of hours.

Found herself standing at length on the dunes overlooking the lake, the dunes where she and Lloyd had first. He not the only one, though, only the last of a series that seemed for a moment both long and sad. Chumps. Herself, too, fooled bad, not once or twice, either.

Far off, where the shore of the silver water curved, she could see a band of dark firs, the northern mountains rising. Where he had gone or threatened to go. Lloyd had been part of a successful class-action suit against the company where he'd worked and where everybody had come down with Sick Building Syndrome, Lloyd being pissed off enough (though not ever really deeply affected as far as Pat could ever tell) to hold out with a rump group for a higher settlement, which they got, too, that was what got him the classic Camaro and the twenty acres of high woods. And lots of time to think.

Bring them back, you bastard, she thought; at the same time thinking that it was her, that she should not have done what she did, or should have done what she did not do; that she loved her kids too much, or not enough.

They would bring her kids back; she had become very sure of that, fighting down every rational impulse to question it. She had voted for an inconceivable future, but she had voted for it for only one reason: it would contain—had to contain—everything she had lost. Everything she wanted. That's what the elmers stood for.

She came back at nightfall and found the weird deflated spill of it strung out through the hallway and (why?) halfway down the stairs to the rec room, like the aftermath of a foam fire-extinguisher accident, smelling (Pat thought, others described it differently) like buttered toast; and she called the 800 number we all had memorized.

And then nothing. There were no more of them. If you had been missed you now waited in vain for the experience that had happened to nearly everyone else, uncertain why you had been excluded but able to claim that you, at least, would not have succumbed to their blandishments; and soon after it became apparent that there would be no more, no matter how well they would be received, because the Mother Ship or whatever exactly it was that was surely their origin also went away: not *away* in any trackable or pursuable direction, just away, becoming less distinct on the various tracking and spying devices, producing less data, fibrillating, becoming see-through finally and then unable to be seen. Gone. Gone gone gone.

And what then had we all acceded to, what had we betrayed ourselves and our leadership for, abandoning all our daily allegiances and our commitments so carelessly? Around the world we were asking questions like that, the kind that result in those forlorn religions of the abandoned and forgotten, the religions of those who have been expecting big divine things any moment and then find out they are going to get nothing but a long, maybe a more than lifelong, wait and a blank sky overhead. If their goal had been to make us just dissatisfied, restless, unable to do anything at all but wait to see what would now become of us, then perhaps they had succeeded; but Pat Poynton was certain they had made a promise and would keep it: the universe was not so strange, so unlikely, that such a visitation could occur and come to nothing. Like many others she lay awake looking up into the night sky (so to speak, up into the ceiling of her bedroom in her house on Ponader Drive, above or beyond which the night sky lay) and said over to herself the little text she had assented or agreed to: *Good will. You sign below. All all right with love afterwards. Why not say yes?*

At length she got up and belted her robe around her; she went down the stairs (the house so quiet, it had been quiet with the kids and Lloyd asleep in their beds when she had used to get up at five and make instant coffee and wash and dress to get to work but this was quieter) and put her parka on over her robe; she went out barefoot into the backyard.

Not night any longer but a clear October dawn, so clear the sky looked faintly green, and the air perfectly still: the leaves falling nonetheless around her, letting go one by one, two by two, after hanging on till now.

God, how beautiful, more beautiful somehow than it had been

before she decided she didn't belong here; maybe she had been too busy trying to belong here to notice.

All all right with love afterwards. When though did afterwards start? When?

There came to her as she stood there a strange noise, far off and high up, a noise that she thought sounded like the barking of some dog pack, or maybe the crying of children let out from school, except that it wasn't either of those things; for a moment she let herself believe (this was the kind of mood a lot of people were understandably in) that this was it, the inrush or onrush of whatever it was that had been promised. Then out of the north a sort of smudge or spreading dark ripple came over the sky, and Pat saw that overhead a big flock of geese was passing, and the cries were theirs, though seeming too loud and coming from somewhere else or from everywhere.

Going south. A great ragged V spread out over half the sky.

"Long way," she said aloud, envying them their flight, their escape; and thinking then, No, they were not escaping, not from Earth, they were of Earth, born and raised, would die here, were just doing their duty, calling out maybe to keep their spirits up. Of Earth as she was.

She got it then, as they passed overhead, a gift somehow of their passage, though how she could never trace afterwards, only that whenever she thought of it she would think also of those geese, those cries, of encouragement or joy or whatever they were. She got it: in pressing her Good Will Ticket (she could see it in her mind, in the poor dead elmer's hand) she had not acceded or given in to something, not capitulated or surrendered, none of us had though we thought so and even hoped so: no she had made a promise.

"Well, yes," she said, a sort of plain light going on in her back brain, in many another, too, just then in many places, so many that it might have looked—to someone or something able to perceive it, someone looking down on us and our Earth from far above and yet able to perceive each of us one by one—like lights coming on across a darkened land, or like the bright pinpricks that mark the growing numbers of Our Outlets on a TV map, but that were actually our brains, Getting It one by one, brightening momentarily, as the edge of dawn swept westward.

They had not made a promise, she had: good will. She had said yes. And if she kept that promise it would all be all right, with love, afterwards: as right as it could be.

"Yes," she said again, and she raised her eyes to the sky, so vacant, more vacant now than before. Not a betrayal but a promise; not a letting go but a taking hold. Good only for as long as we, all alone here, kept it. All all right with love afterwards.

Why had they come, why had they gone to such effort, to tell us that, when we knew it all along? Who cared that much, to come to tell us? Would they come back, ever, to see how we'd done?

She went back inside, the dew icy on her feet. For a long time she stood in the kitchen (the door unshut behind her) and then went to the phone.

He answered on the second ring. He said hello. All the unshed tears of the last weeks, of her whole life probably, rose up in one awful bolus in her throat; she wouldn't weep though, no not yet.

"Lloyd," she said. "Lloyd, listen. We have to talk."

First Tuesday

ROBERT REED

Robert Reed published his first novel, The Leeshore, *in 1987 and since then he has published seven more novels, including* Black Milk, Beyond the Veil of Stars, *and* Beneath the Gated Sky. *In addition to writing all those novels, he has been extremely prolific at shorter lengths—in most years of the past decade, Gardner Dozois has remarked on the difficulty of choosing only one or two of Bob's stories for his annual* Year's Best SF *collection from the many worthy stories published in that particular year. Dozois certainly got our sympathies when we were making the selections for this anthology, but ultimately "First Tuesday" won out because of its uncommon approach to American politics; whereas most political SF has a prescriptive quality to it, this story is more interested in examining the effects of politics (and technology) on ordinary citizens.*

AFTER A LOT OF PESTERING, MOM TOLD STEFAN, "FINE, YOU CAN pick the view." Only it wasn't an easy job, and Stefan enjoyed it even more than he'd hoped. Standing on the foam-rock patio, he spoke to the house computer, asking for the Grand Canyon, then Hawaii's coast, then Denali. He saw each from many vantage points, never satisfied and never sure why not. Then he tried Mount Rushmore, which was better. Except Yancy saw the six stone heads, and he stuck his head out long enough to say "Change it. Now." No debate; no place for compromise. Stefan settled on the Grand Canyon, on a popular view from the North Rim, telling himself that it was lovely and appropriate, and he hoped their guest would approve, and how soon would he be here? In another couple seconds, Stefan realized. *Jesus, now!*

A figure appeared on the little lawn. He was tall, wearing a fancy suit, that famous face smiling straight at Stefan. And the boy jumped into the house, shouting with glee:

"The President's here!"

His stepfather muttered something.

Mom whined, "Oh, but I'm not ready."

Stefan was ready. He ran across the patio, leaping where it ended. His habit was to roll down the worn grassy slope. But he was wearing good clothes, and this evening was full of civic responsibilities. Landing with both feet solidly under him, he tried very hard to look like the most perfect citizen possible.

The President appeared solid. Not real, but nearly so.

The face was a mixture of Latin and African genes. The dreadlocks were long enough to kiss his broad shoulders. Halfway through his second term, President Perez was the only president that Stefan could remember, and even though this was just a projection, an interactive holo generated by machines . . . it was still an honor to have him here, and Stefan felt special, and for more reasons than he could count, he was nervous. In good ways, and in bad ways too.

"Hello?" chirped the eleven-year-old boy. "Mr. President?"

The projection hadn't moved. The house computer was wrestling with its instructions, fashioning a personality within its finite capacity. There was a sound, a sudden "Sssss" generated by speakers hidden in the squidskin fence and sky. The projection opened its mouth; a friendly, reedy voice managed, "Ssssstefan." Then the President moved, offering both hands while saying "Hello, young man. I'm so very glad to meet you."

Of course he knew Stefan's name. The personality could read the boy's public files. Yet the simple trick impressed him, and in response he shouted, "I'm glad to meet you, Mr. President."

The brown hands had no substance, yet they couldn't have acted more real. Gripping Stefan's pale little hand, they matched every motion, the warmth carried by the bright eyes and his words. "This is an historic moment, Stefan. But then you already know that, I'm sure."

The first nationwide press conference, yes. Democracy and science joined in a perfect marriage. President Perez was invited here for a symbolic dinner, and he was everywhere else at the same time. It was a wondrous evening . . . magical!

"A lovely yard," said the President. The eyes were blind, but the personality had access to the security cameras, building appropriate images as the face moved. With a faraway gaze, he announced, "I do like your choice of view."

"Thank you, Mr. President."

"Very nice indeed!"

Holo projectors and squidskin fabrics created the illusion of blue skies and rugged geology. Although nothing was quite as bright as it would appear in the real outdoors, of course. And the squidskin rocks and the occasional bird had a vagueness, a dreamy imprecision, that was the mark of a less-than-good system. Sometimes, like now, the antinoise generators failed to hide unwanted sounds. Somewhere beyond the President, neighbors were applauding, and cheering, making it seem as if ghosts inhabited the ghostly canyon.

President Perez seemed oblivious to the imperfections. Gesturing at their garden, he said, "Oh, I see you're doing your part. How close are you to self-sufficiency?"

Not close at all, really.

"Beautiful eggplants," said the guest, not waiting for a response. "And a fish pond too!"

Without fish. A problem with the filter, but the boy said nothing, hoping nothing would be noticed.

The President was turning in a circle, hunting for something else to compliment. For some reason, the house wasn't wearing its usual coat of projected paints and architectural flourishes. Their guest was too complicated, no doubt. Too many calculations, plus the computer had to show the Grand Canyon . . . and the real house lay exposed in all its drabness. Glass foams and cardboard looked gray and simple, and insubstantial, three walls inside the yard and the fourth wall pointed toward the outdoors, the brown stains on the sky showing where rainwater had damaged the squidskin.

To break the silence, Stefan blurted out a question. "Mr. President, where do you stand on the economy?"

That's how reporters asked questions.

But the great man didn't respond in the expected way. His smile changed, remaining a smile but encompassing some new, subtly different flavor of light. "I'll stand on the economy's head," he replied. "With my feet apart, ready for anything."

Was that a genuine answer?

Stefan wasn't sure.

Then the President knelt, putting his head below the boy's, saying with a happy, self-assured voice "Thank you for the question. And remember, what happens tonight goes both ways. You can learn what I'm thinking, and in a different way I'll learn what's on your mind."

Stefan nodded, well aware of the principles.

"When I wake," said the handsome brown face, "I'll read that this many people asked about the economy, and how they asked it, and what they think we should be doing. All that in an abbreviated form, of course. A person in my position needs a lot of abbreviations, I'm afraid."

"Yes, sir." Stefan waited for a moment, then blurted, "I think you're doing a good job with the economy, sir. I really do."

"Well," said the guest, "I'm very, very glad to hear it. I am."

AT THAT MOMENT, the genuine President Perez was inside a government hospital, in a fetal position, suspended within a gelatin bath. Masses of bright new optical cable were attached to his brain and fingers, mouth and anus, linking him directly with the Net. Everything that he knew and believed was being blended with his physical self, all elements reduced to a series of numbers, then enlarged into a nationwide presence. Every household with an adequate projection system and memory was being visited, as were public buildings and parks, stadiums and VA facilities. If it was a success, press conferences would become a monthly event. Political opponents were upset, complaining that this was like one enormous commercial for Perez; but this was the President's last term, and it was an experiment, and even Stefan understood that these tricks were becoming cheaper and more widespread every day.

In the future, perhaps by the next election, each political party would be able to send its candidates to the voters' homes.

What could be more fair? thought the boy.

Stefan's stepfather had just stepped from the drab house, carrying a plate full of raw pink burgers.

In an instant, the air seemed close and thick.

"Mr. Thatcher," said the projection, "thank you for inviting me. I hope you're having a pleasant evening!"

"Hey, I hope you like meat," Yancy called out. "In this family, we're carnivores!"

Stefan felt a sudden and precise terror.

But the President didn't hesitate, gesturing at the buffalo-augmented soy patties. Saying "I hope you saved one for me."

"Sure, Mr. President. Sure."

For as long as Stefan could remember, his stepfather had never missed a chance to say something ugly about President Perez. But Mom had made him promise to be on his best behavior. Not once, but on several occasions. "I don't want to be embarrassed," she had told him, using the same tone she'd use when trying to make Stefan behave. "I want him to enjoy himself, at least this once. Will you please just help me?"

Yancy Thatcher was even paler than his stepson. Blond hair worn in a short, manly ponytail; a round face wearing a perpetually sour expression. He wasn't large, but he acted large. He spoke with a deep, booming voice, and he carried himself as if endowed with a dangerous strength. Like now. Coming down the slope, he was walking straight toward their guest. The President was offering both hands, in his trademark fashion. But no hand was offered to him, and the projection retreated, saying "Excuse me," while deftly stepping out of the way.

"You're excused," Yancy replied, laughing in a low, unamused fashion. Never breaking stride.

Mom wasn't watching; that's why he was acting this way.

Things worsened when Yancy looked over his shoulder, announcing, "I didn't want you coming tonight, frankly. But the kid's supposed to do an assignment for school, and besides, I figured this was my chance to show you my mind. If you know what I mean . . ."

President Perez nodded, dreadlocks bouncing. "Feedback is the idea. As I was just telling Stefan—"

"I'm an old-fashioned white man, Mr. President."

The boy looked at the drab house, willing Mom to appear.

But she didn't, and Yancy flung open the grill and let the biogas run too long before he made a spark, a soft blue explosion causing Stefan to back away. Nobody spoke. Every eye, seeing or blind, watched the patties hit the warming rack, sizzling quietly but with anger, Yancy mashing them flat with the grimy spatula that he'd gotten for Christmas last year.

Then the President spoke, ignoring that last comment.

"It's a shame this technology won't let me help you," he declared with a ring of honesty.

Yancy grimaced.

The patties grew louder, the flames turning yellow.

Obstinately ignoring the tensions, the President looked at his own hands. "A poverty of physicality," he declared, laughing to himself.

That was it. Something snapped, and Yancy barked, "Know what I like, Mr. President? About tonight, I mean."

"What do you like?"

"Thinking that the real you is buried in goo, a big fat glass rope stuck up your ass."

Stefan prayed for a systems failure, or, better, a war. Anything that would stop events here. His fear of fears was that the President would awaken to learn that Yancy Thatcher of Fort Wayne, Indiana, had insulted him. Because the boy couldn't imagine anyone else in the country having the stupid courage to say such an awful thing.

Yet their guest wasn't visibly angry. He actually laughed, quietly and calmly. And all he said was, "Thank you for your honesty, sir."

Yancy flipped burgers, then looked at Stefan. "Tell your mom it'll be a few minutes. And take *him* with you."

It was such a strange, wondrous moment.

The boy looked at his President, at his smile, hearing the conjured voice saying, "Yes. That's a fine idea." Built of light and thought, he seemed invulnerable to every slight, every unkind word.

Stefan had never envied anyone so much in his life.

.   .   .

MOM WAS A BLIZZARD of activity, hands blurring as they tried to assemble a fancy salad from ingredients grown in the garden, then cleaned and cut into delicate, artful shapes. She loved salads, planning each with an artist's sensibilities, which to Mom meant that she could never predict preparation times, always something to be done too fast at the end. When she saw Stefan inside, she whined, "I'm still not ready." When she saw President Perez fluttering for that instant when he passed from the outside to the kitchen projectors, she gave a little squeal and threw spinach in every direction. Then she spoke, not leaving enough time to think of proper words. "You've lost weight," she blurted. "Since the election, haven't you?"

Embarrassed again, Stefan said, "The President of the United States," with a stern voice. In warning. Didn't Mom remember how to address him?

But the President seemed amused, if anything. "I've lost a couple of kilos, yes. Job pressures. And the First Lady's antiequatorial campaign, too."

The joke puzzled Stefan until he stopped thinking about it.

"A drink, Mr. President? I'm having a drop for myself."

"Wine, please. If that's not too much trouble."

Both adults giggled. Touching a control, Mom ordered an elegant glass to appear on the countertop, already filled with sparkling white wine, and their guest went through the motions of sipping it, his personality given every flavor along with an ethanol kick. "Lovely," he declared. "Thanks."

"And how is the First Lady?"

It was a trivial question; Stefan was within his rights to groan.

Mom glared at him, in warning. "Go find Candace, why don't you?" Then she turned back to their guest, again inquiring about his dear wife.

"Quite well, thank you. But tired of Washington."

Mom's drink was large and colorful, projected swirls of red and green never mixing together. "I wish she could have come. I *adore* her. And oh, I love what she's done with your house."

The President glanced at his surroundings. "And I'm sure she'd approve of your tastes, Mrs. Thatcher."

"Helen."

"Helen, then."

The kitchen walls and ceiling were covered with an indoor squidskin, and they built the illusion of a tall room . . . except that voices and any sharp sound echoed off the genuine ceiling, flat and close, unadorned by the arching oak beams that only appeared to be high overhead.

Mom absorbed the compliment and the sound of her own name, then noticed Stefan still standing nearby. "Where's Candace? Will you *please* go find your sister, darling?"

Candace's room was in the basement. It seemed like a long run to a boy who would rather be elsewhere, and worse, her door was locked. Stefan shook the knob, feeling the throb of music that seeped past the noise barriers. "He's here! Come on!" Kicking the door down low, he managed to punch a new hole that joined half a dozen earlier kickholes. "Aren't you coming up to meet him?"

"Open," his sister shouted.

The knob turned itself. Candace was standing before a mirrored portion of squidskin, examining her reflection. Every other surface showed a fantastic woodland, lush red trees interspersed with a thousand Candaces who danced with unicorns, played saxophones, and rode bareback on leaping black tigers. The images were designed to jar nerves and exhaust eyes. But what Stefan noticed was the way his sister was dressed, her outfit too small and tight, her boobs twice their normal size. She was ready for a date, and he warned her, "They won't let you go. It's only Tuesday."

Candace gave her little brother a cutting worldly look. "Go lose yourself."

Stefan began to retreat, gladly.

"Wait. What do you think of these shoes?"

"They're fine."

She kicked them off, without a word, then opened the door behind the mirror, mining her closet for a better pair.

Stefan shot upstairs.

Their honored guest and Mom remained in the kitchen. She was freshening her drink, and talking.

"I mean I really don't *care*," she told him. "I *know* I deserve the promotion, that's what matters." She gave her son a quick, troubled glance. "But Yankee says I should quit if they don't give it to me—"

"Yankee?"

"Yancy, I mean. I'm sorry, it's my husband's nickname."

The President was sitting on a projected stool, watching Mom sip her swirling drink once, then again.

"What do you think I should do? Quit, or stay."

"Wait and see," was the President's advice. "Perhaps you'll get what you deserve."

Mom offered a thin, dissatisfied smile.

Stefan thought of his comppad and his list of important questions. Where was it? He wheeled around and ran to his room, finding the pad on his unmade bed, its patient voice repeating the same math problem over and over again. Changing functions, he returned to the kitchen. There'd been enough noise about decorating and Mom's job, he felt. "Mr. President? Are we doing enough about the space program?"

"Never," was the reply. "I wish we could do more."

Was the comppad recording? Stefan fiddled with the controls, feeling a sudden dull worry.

"In my tenure," the voice continued, "I've been able to double our Martian budget. Spaceborn industries have increased twelve percent. We're building two new observatories on the moon. And we just found life on Triton—"

"Titan," the boy corrected, by reflex.

"Don't talk to him that way!" Mom glowered, thoroughly outraged.

"Oh, but the fellow's right, Helen. I misspoke."

The amiable laugh washed over Stefan, leaving him warm and confident. This wasn't just an assignment for school, it was a mission, and he quickly scrolled to the next question. "What about the oceans, Mr. President?"

A momentary pause, then their guest asked, "What do you mean?"

Stefan wasn't sure.

"There are many issues," said the President. "Mineral rights. Power production. Fishing and farming. And the floating cities—"

"The cities."

"Fine. What do you think, Stefan? Do they belong to us, or are they free political entities?"

Stefan wasn't sure. He glanced at his pad, thinking of the islands, manmade and covered with trim, modern communities. They grew their own food in the ocean, moved where they wanted, and seemed like wonderful places to live. "They should be free."

"Why?"

Who was interviewing whom?

The President seemed to enjoy this reversal in roles. "If taxes pay for their construction—your tax money, and mine—then by what right can they leave the United States?" A pleasant little laugh, then he added, "Imagine if the First Lady and I tried to claim the White House as an independent nation. Would that be right?"

Stefan was at a loss for words.

Then Mom sat up straight, giving a sudden low moan.

Yancy was coming across the patio. Stefan saw him, and an instant later, Mom jumped to her feet, telling her son and guest, "No more politics. It's dinnertime."

Yancy entered the kitchen, approaching the projection from behind.

The President couldn't react in time. Flesh-and-bone merged with him; a distorted brown face lay over Yancy's face, which was funny.

"Why are you laughing?" snapped Yancy.

"No reason," the boy lied.

His stepfather's temper was close to the surface now. He dropped the plate of cooked burgers on the countertop, took an enormous breath, then said, "Show your guest to the dining room. Now."

Taking his comppad, Stefan obeyed.

The President flickered twice, changing projectors. His voice flickered, too, telling the boy the story of some unnamed Senator who threw a tantrum whenever rational discourse failed him. "Which is to say," he added, "I have quite a lot of practice dealing with difficult souls." And with that he gave a little wink and grin, trying to bolster the boy's ragged mood.

Stefan barely heard him; he was thinking of floating cities.

It occurred to him that he'd answered, "Yes, they should be free," for no other reason than that was his stepfather's opinion, voiced many times. The cities were uncrowded. Some allowed only the best kinds of people. And Stefan had spoken without thinking,

Yancy's ideas worming their way inside him. Embarrassed and
confused, he wondered what he believed that was really his own.
And did it ever truly matter?

Even if Stefan could think what he wanted, how important
could his opinions ever be?

The table was set for five, one place setting built from light.
The President took his seat, and Stefan was across from him,
scrolling through the comppad in search of new questions. Most
of these came from his social studies teacher—a small, handsome
Nigerian woman who didn't know Yancy. *Why do we keep our open
border policy?* He didn't dare ask it. Instead he coughed, then inquired, "How are your cats, Mr. President?"

Both of them seemed happy with the new topic. "Fine, thank
you." Another wink and grin. "The jaguars are fat, and the cheetah
is going to have triplets."

Miniature breeds. Declawed and conditioned to be pets.

They spoke for a couple minutes about preserving rare species,
Stefan mentioning his hope to someday work in that field. Then
Mom burst into the room with her completed salad, and Yancy
followed with some bean concoction, making a second trip for the
burgers. Somewhere en route he shouted, "Candace!" and she appeared an instant later, making her entrance with a giggle and a
bounce.

If anything her boobs were even bigger. And the room's holo
projectors changed her skin, making it coffee-colored.

Mom saw the clothes and her color, then gave a shocked little
groan. But she didn't dare say anything with the President here.
Yancy entered the little room, paused and grimaced . . . then almost smiled, glancing at their guest with the oddest expression.

Why wasn't he saying anything?

The President glanced at Candace, for half a second. Then he
looked straight ahead, eyes locked on Stefan. Big, worried eyes.
And his projection feigned a slow sigh.

With her brown boobs spilling out, Candace sat beside President Perez.

Mom glared at her, then at Yancy. But Yancy just shook his
head, as if warning her to say nothing.

Seven burgers were on the plate. The real ones were juicy; the one built from light resembled a hard lump of charcoal.

Stefan realized that he was growing accustomed to being ashamed.

Candace took nothing but a small helping of salad, giggling and looking at their guest with the same goofy flirtatious face that she used on her infinite boyfriends. "Hey, are you having a good time?"

"Mr. President," Stefan added.

His sister glared at him, snapping, "I know *that*."

"I'm having a fine time." The apparition never quite looked at her, using his spoon to build a mound of phantom beans on the phantom plate. "You have a lovely home."

Mom said, "Thank you."

Candace giggled, like an idiot.

But she wasn't stupid, her brother wanted to say. To shout.

Yancy was preparing two burgers, slipping them into their pouches of bread and adding pickles, mustard, and sugar corn. Then after a first oversized bite, he grinned, telling the house computer to give them scenery. "Mount Rushmore," he demanded. "The original."

Squidskin re-created the four-headed landmark. President Barker and Yarbarro were notably absent.

The current President was staring at his plate. For the first time, he acted remote. Detached. A bite of his charred burger revealed its raw red interior, blood flowing as if from an open wound. After a long pause, he looked at Stefan again and with a certain hopefulness asked, "What's your next question, please?"

Candace squealed, "Let me ask it!"

She shot to her feet, reaching over the table, her boobs fighting for the privilege of bursting out of her shirt. Before Stefan could react, she'd stolen his comppad, reading the first question aloud.

"Why do we keep our open border policy?"

The pause was enormous, silence coming from every direction at once. Mom stared at Yancy, pleading with her eyes. Everyone else studied the President, wondering how he would respond. Except he didn't. It was Yancy who spoke first, in a voice almost mild. Almost.

"I don't think it matters," he replied. "I think if we want to do some good, we've got to turn the flow back the other direction. If you know what I mean."

"I think we do," said President Perez.

"Fifty years of inviting strangers into our house. Fifty idiotic years of making room, making jobs, making allowances . . . and always making due with less and less. That's what the great Barker gave us. Her and her damned open border bullshit!"

Stefan felt sick. Chilled.

Mom began, "Now, Yancy—"

"My grandfather owned an acreage, Mr. President. He ate meat three times a day, lived in a big house, and worked hard until he was told to go half time, some know-nothing refugee given the other half of his job, and his paycheck!"

"Employment readjustments." Their guest nodded, shrugged. "That's a euphemism, I know. There were problems. Injustices. But think of the times, Mr. Thatcher. Our government was under enormous pressures, yet, we managed to carry things off—"

"Some know-nothing refugee!" Yancy repeated, his face red as uncooked meat. "And your party took his home, his land, needing the room for a stack of apartment buildings."

Stefan tried not to listen. He was building a careful daydream where he had a different family, and he was sitting with the President, everyone working to make his visit productive, and fun.

Yancy pointed at the old Rushmore. "A great nation built it—"

"An individual built it," the President interrupted. "Then his grateful nation embraced it."

"A free nation!"

"And underpopulated, speaking relatively."

Pursing his heavy pink lips, Yancy declared, "We should have let you people starve. That's what I think." He took a huge breath, held it, then added, "You weren't our responsibility, and we should have shut our borders. Nothing in. Not you. Not a rat. Not so much as a goddamn fly . . . that's my opinion!"

President Perez stared at his own clean plate. Eyes narrowed. The contemplative face showed a tiny grin, then he looked up at Yancy, eyes carved from cold black stone.

With a razored voice, he said, "First of all, sir, I'm a third-generation U.S. citizen. And second of all, I believe that you're an extraordinarily frightened man." A pause, a quiet sigh. "To speak that way, your entire life must be torn with uncertainty. And probably some deep, deep sense of failure, I would guess."

Stefan sat motionless, in shock.

"As for your opinions on national policy, Mr. Thatcher . . . well, let me just say this. These are the reasons why I believe you're full of shit."

THE REBUKE WAS steady, determined, and very nearly irresistible.

President Perez spoke calmly about war and famine, a desperate United Nations, and the obligations of wealthy people. He named treaties, reciting key passages word for word. Then he attacked the very idea of closing the borders, listing the physical difficulties and the economic costs. "Of course it might have worked. We could have survived. An enclave of privilege and waste, and eventually there would have been plagues and a lot of quiet hunger on the outside. We'd be left with our big strong fences, and beyond them . . . a dead world, spent and useless to us, and to the dead." A brief pause, then he spoke with a delicate sorrowful voice, asking "Are you really the kind of man who could live lightly with himself, knowing that billions perished . . . in part because you deserved a larger dining room?"

Yancy had never looked so tired. Of those at the table, he seemed to be the one composed of light and illusion.

The President smiled at everyone, then focused on Stefan. "Let's move on, I think. What's your next question?"

The boy tried to read his comppad, but his brain wouldn't work.

"Perhaps you can ask me 'What do you think about this hallmark evening?' "

"What do you think?" Stefan muttered.

"It should revolutionize our government, which isn't any surprise. Our government was born from a string of revolutions." He waited for the boy's eyes, then continued. "I love this nation. If you want me angry, say otherwise. But the truth is that we are diverse and too often divided. My hope is that tonight's revolution

will strengthen us. Judging by these events, I'd guess that it will
make us at least more honest."

Yancy gave a low sound. Not an angry sound, not anything.

"Perhaps I should leave." The President rose to his feet. "I
know we've got another half hour scheduled—"

"No, please stay!" Mom blurted.

"Don't go," begged Candace, reaching for his dreadlocks.

Mom turned on her. At last. "Young lady, I want you out of
those clothes—!"

"Why?"

"—and drain those breasts. You're not fooling anyone here!"

Candace did her ritual pout, complete with the mournful
groan and the teary run to the basement.

Mom apologized to their guest, more than once. Then she
told Yancy, "You can help Stefan clear the table, please. *I* will show
our President the rest of *my* house."

Stefan worked fast. Scraps went into the recyke system; dishes
were loaded in the sonic washer. Through the kitchen window, he
saw the Grand Canyon passing into night, its blurry, imperfect
edges more appropriate in the ruddy half-light. And it occurred to
him that he was happy with this view, even if it wasn't real. Happier than he'd feel on any ordinary plot of real ground, surely.

His stepfather did no work. He just stood in the middle of the
room, his face impossible to read.

Stefan left him to set the controls. Mom and the President
were in the front room, looking outside. Or at least their eyes were
pointed at the lone window. With a soft, vaguely conspiring tone,
the President said, "It's not my place to give advice. Friends can.
Counselors and ministers should. But not someone like me, I'm
sorry."

"I know," his mother whispered. "It's just ... I don't
know ... I just wish he would do something awful. To me, of
course. Just to make the choice simple."

What choice? And who was she talking about?

"But really, he only sounds heartless." She tried to touch their
guest, then thought better of it. "In five years, Yankee hasn't lifted
his hand once in anger. Not to the kids, or me. And you're right,
I think. About him being scared, I mean ..."

Stefan listened to every word.

"When you come next month," Mom inquired, "will you remember what's happened here?"

President Perez shook his head. His face was in profile, like on a coin. "No, I won't. Your computer has to erase my personality, by law. And you really don't have room enough to hold me. Sorry."

"I guess not," Mom allowed.

They looked outside, watching an air taxi riding its cable past the window. The building across the street mirrored theirs, houses stacked on houses, each one small and efficient, and lightweight, each house possessing its own yard and the same solitary window facing the maelstrom that was a city of barely five million.

Several Presidents were visible.

They waved at each other, laughing with a gentle, comfortable humor.

Then their President turned, spotting the boy at the other end of the little room, and when he smiled at Stefan with all of his original charm and warmth, nothing else seeming to matter.

Mom turned and shouted, "Are you spying on us?"

"I wasn't," he lied. "No, ma'am."

The President said, "I think he just came looking for us." Then he added, "Dessert. I feel like a little dessert, if I might be so bold."

Mom wasn't sure what to say, if anything.

"Perhaps something that looks delicious, please. In the kitchen. I very much liked your kitchen."

THEY GATHERED AGAIN, a truce called.

Candace was dressed as if ready for school, looking younger and flatter, and embarrassed. Yancy had reacquired a portion of his old certainty, but not enough to offer any opinions. Mom seemed wary, particularly of Stefan. What had he heard while eavesdropping? Then the President asked for more questions, looking straight at Yancy, nothing angry or malicious in his dark face.

Crossing his arms, Yancy said nothing.

But Stefan thought of a question. "What about the future?"

It wasn't from his comppad's list; it was an inspiration. "Mr. President? How will the world change?"

"Ah! You want a prediction!"

Stefan made sure that the comppad was recording.

President Perez took a playful stab at the layered sundae, then spoke casually, with an easy authority.

"What I'm going to tell you is a secret," he said. "But not a big one, as secrets go."

Everyone was listening. Even Yancy leaned closer.

"Since the century began, every President has had an advisory council, a team of gifted thinkers. They know the sciences. They see trends. They're experts in new technologies, history, and human nature. We pay them substantial fees to build intelligent, coherent visions of tomorrow. And do you know what? In eighty years, without exception, none of their futures has come true." He shook his head, laughing quietly. "Predicted inventions usually appear, but never on schedule. And the more important changes come without warning, ruining every one of their assessments." A pause, then he added, "My presence here, for instance. Not one expert predicted today. I know because I checked the records myself. No one ever thought that a President could sit in half a billion kitchens at once, eating luscious desserts that will never put a gram on his waist."

Yancy growled, asking "Then why do you pay the bastards?"

"Habit?" The President shrugged his shoulders. "Or maybe because nothing they predict comes true, and I find that instructive. All these possible futures, and I don't need to worry about any of them."

A long, puzzled silence.

"Anyway," said the President, "my point is this: Now that we've got this technology, every prediction seems to include it. In fact, my experts are claiming that in fifty years, give or take, all of us will spend our days floating in warm goo, wired into the swollen Net. Minimal food. No need for houses or transportation. Maximum efficiency for a world suddenly much less crowded." He gazed at Stefan, asking "Now does that sound like an appealing future?"

The boy shook his head. "No, sir."

"It sounds *awful*," Mom barked.

Candace said, "Ugh."

Then Yancy said, "It'll never happen. No."

"Exactly," said their guest. "It's almost guaranteed not to come true, if the pattern holds." He took a last little bite of his sundae, then rose. "You asked for a prediction, son. Well, here it is. Your life will be an unending surprise. If you're lucky, the surprises will be sweet and come daily, and that's the best any of us can hope for. I think."

The silence was relaxed. Contemplative.

Then the President gestured at the projected clock high above their stove. "Time to leave, I'm afraid. Walk me out?"

He was speaking to Stefan.

Hopping off his stool, the boy hugged himself and nodded. "Sure, Mr. President. Sure."

THE GRAND CANYON was dark, the desert sky clear and dry. But the genuine air was humid, more like Indiana than Arizona. There were always little clues to tell you where you were. Stefan knew that even the best systems fell short of being *real*.

In a low, hopeful voice, he said, "You'll come back in a month. Won't you, sir?"

"Undoubtedly." Another smile. "And thank you very much. You were a wonderful host."

What else? "I hope you had a good time, sir."

A pause, then he said, "It was perfect. Perfect."

Stefan nodded, trying to match that smile.

Then the image gave a faint "Good-bye" and vanished. He suddenly just wasn't there.

Stefan stared at the horizon for a long moment, then turned and saw that the house was whole again. Their computer had enough power to add color and all the fancy touches. Under the desert sky, it looked tall and noble, and he could see the people sitting inside, talking now. Just talking. Nobody too angry or too sad, or anything. And it occurred to Stefan, as he walked up toward them, that people were just like the house, small inside all their clothes and words and big thoughts.

People were never what they appeared to be, and it had always been that way. And always would be.

The Fool, the Stick, and the Princess

RACHEL POLLACK

Rachel Pollack's first novel, Golden Vanity, *appeared in 1980, but it wasn't until her fantasy novel* Unquenchable Fire *came out in 1988 that her impact on the field was felt strongly. Since then she has published two more novels,* Temporary Agency *and the World Fantasy Award–winning* Godmother Night, *along with a collection of short fiction entitled* Burning Sky, *and she is widely regarded as one of the most distinctive fantasists writing today. She is also a noted expert on the Tarot and has written for such comic books as* Doom Patrol *and* Tomahawk. *The following fairy tale shows her mastery of blending the mythic and the mundane.*

THERE WERE ONCE THREE BROTHERS WHO LIVED IN A POOR COUNTRY far away. The two older brothers were very clever and everyone said they would do well in the world, even in a land with so few opportunities. But the youngest was nothing but a fool. He had never learned to read, and even the simplest tasks eluded him. Told to fetch wood, he would set out determined to get it right, but before he got to the back of the house and the woodpile he might see a rabbit and try to imitate its hop until he fell over laughing, the woodpile long forgotten. Or worse, he might see a rainbow and fling the wood in the air as he lifted his arms in happiness. The Fool, as everyone called him, simply loved rainbows. Whenever he saw one he would throw his arms high above his head, no matter what else was happening. People would shake their heads and worry what would become of him.

As time went on, the family became poorer and poorer, despite all the efforts of the mother and father and the elder brothers. Finally, the oldest brother announced that there were just no opportunities for an ambitious young man in a country where people told legendary stories about eating more than one meal a day. He must leave home and seek his fortune. He kissed his parents, told his second brother to take care of the Fool, and set out on a sunny morning across the cracked clay of their poor farm.

He had gone no more than a day's journey when he spotted something along the side of the road, half hidden under a burned-out bush. At first glance it looked like a plain stick, about waist high, but the sharp-eyed brother noticed a glow of light all around it. "A magic staff!" he cried excitedly, and seized it. Power surged through him and he shook the stick at the sky. "Now nothing can stop me!" he cried. "I will make my fortune and return home to rescue my family."

Just as he was striding off, he heard a terrible roar. He turned and saw an ogre about to rush at him. The ogre stood ten feet tall, with shoulders like rocks, and thick scales for skin, and teeth like sharpened iron stakes. Though he shook with fear, the eldest brother told himself he had no reason to worry. He pointed the magic stick at the ogre and shouted, "Stop this monster from devouring me!" A blast of light streaked from the stick—but instead of striking the ogre, it ran all through the eldest brother. In an instant his entire body had turned to stone. Furious, the hungry ogre lumbered away.

A year went by. When Spring came once more, the second brother looked one day at the scraps of bread on the table and shook his head. "It's no use," he told his parents. "Something terrible must have happened to my brother or he would have returned by now. We have become more wretched than ever. I must go seek my fortune." His parents begged him not to go. If he didn't come back, they said, and they died, who would take care of the Fool? But he only kissed them and shook his head sadly at his younger brother. Then he left.

Three days from home he came upon his petrified brother. The magic stick still lay at his stone feet. "Oh, my poor poor brother," he cried. "He must have found this magic stick and tried to use it and it turned against him." He picked up the stick. The power in it made him tremble all over. "Well," he said. "Luckily I am much cleverer than my brother. Besides, he always wanted glory. I just want to feed my family. As long as I don't make any mistakes I can use this stick to make my fortune."

He had gone no more than a day's journey when he heard a roar. An ogre was rushing at him. Its mouth drooled with thick black slime. The brother raised his stick. He could see fire run along its length in its eagerness to unleash itself. "Prevent this creature from devouring me!" he ordered the stick. Just as the ogre reached him he turned all to stone.

Another year passed. One day the Fool said, "Didn't my brothers leave some time ago? I remember something about that." His parents nodded. "They haven't come back, have they?" His parents shook their heads. "Oh," said the Fool, "I guess that means I'll have to go seek my fortune."

"No!" his parents cried. They knew he could hardly find his way out the door. But nothing they said could dissuade him. Maybe he'd forget. They tried to distract him, with stories, and games, and a bunch of flowers that his mother begged from a neighbor who had managed to grow a small garden. The next morning, however, the Fool tied a change of clothes in a large cloth and set out.

No sooner had he left the house than he saw a rainbow. "Oh, look!" he cried, and raised his arms, flinging his bundle away from him. His poor father had to run after it or the Fool would have forgotten it entirely. As the Fool wandered up the road, his parents held each other and wept loudly.

The Fool had traveled several days, with detours to follow various small animals, when he came upon his petrified eldest brother. "How wonderful," he said. "Here we all thought something terrible must have happened, but instead someone's made a statue of him. He must be famous. How nice. He always wanted to be famous."

Several more days later, he discovered his second brother. "Now our family has really done well," he said. "Statues of both my brothers. Won't my parents be happy. Maybe someone will make a statue of me someday." As soon as he said it, the idea struck him as so ludicrous he bent over laughing. With his face close to the ground like that, he discovered the stick at his brother's feet.

"Oh, look," he said. "Just what I need to carry my bundle." He tied his cloth to the end of the stick and lifted it to his shoulder. A tickle ran all through his body. "What a nice breeze," he said to himself.

That night he used his stick to dig up some roots for his dinner. To his surprise they tasted like a marvelous feast, with flavors from roast quail to wild strawberries crème de menthe. "What amazing roots," he thought. "I'll have to tell my brothers about this." With the stick he drew an outline of a bed on the dirt. When he lay down on it he found it as soft as baby goose feathers. He smiled and fell asleep.

He had hardly set out the next morning when the ground shook with a great roar. "Thunder," he said to himself. "I hope the rain falls on something else and not me." Behind him, a sudden burst of rain like knives fell on the ogre who had just opened his mouth wide to bite off the Fool's head. As the rain hit him the ogre screamed, for ogres cannot stand water. He thrashed about but it was no use. The scales cracked, the skin underneath sizzled and burned. Finally the creature fell down dead.

"I wonder what all that noise was," the Fool said. He walked away without turning around.

For several weeks he wandered. Each day his stick dug up banquets in the form of roots, and every night he slept peacefully in his outline of a bed, untouched by animals or storms or even damp.

One day he came to a river. Beyond it he could see houses and fields, even a city, and somewhere near the city what looked like a tower of light. He wondered how he could get across. It was too far to swim and he could not see a bridge. "If only I was clever like my brothers and not such a fool," he thought, "I would know what to do." In a rare burst of annoyance he struck his stick against a tree. "I wish I had a boat!" he said. He heard a crackle, and when he turned around the tree had gone and in its place lay a fine rowboat. "How nice," the Fool said, as he got in and began rowing. "Someone just left this for strangers. What a generous land. Maybe here I can find my fortune."

When he reached the other side he found signs posted up and down the riverbank. Since he could not read he paid them no attention, and began walking toward the tower of light, which shimmered and flickered in the bright sun. In fact, the signs were all about the tower.

The king and queen of this land had a daughter who was so beautiful that princes from lands as exotic as Cathay, Persia, and England all sent delegations asking for her hand in marriage. Some even came in person and bowed down with great flourishes (and expensive presents) to press their case. Her parents considered the princess a gift from heaven itself, for they could pick a husband who would bring even more wealth and power to their kingdom. Empire, they told each other. Through their daughter's marriage they would change from mere king and queen to emperor and empress.

Unfortunately, when they had calculated the best possible match for the princess, they discovered that the gods had played an awful trick on them. Their daughter refused to marry! At first, they thought they might have gone a little too far in their choice. The prospective husband was not exactly young, and the warts on his bent nose and saggy chin ruled out any suggestion of handsome. So they found a prince whose good looks caused young women to faint any time he walked down an open street (newspaper editorials suggested he wear a veil, or simply stay home, but the prince only laughed). Again the princess refused.

"What do you want?" her parents shouted at her. "Just tell us."

"I want to study," she said.

They stared at her. Study? They knew she spent a great deal of time with her books, rather odd books, in fact, but study? They'd always assumed she'd read all those books because she was bored and waiting to get married. Study rather than a husband?

They arranged one match after another. The princess refused to see them. Now they became truly angry. They told her they would choose a husband for her and she would marry the man, even if the palace slaves had to drag her from her precious library.

For the first time the princess became frightened. Until now she'd thwarted them by her will and by the good sense of prospective husbands who knew how miserable an unwilling wife could make them. But suppose her parents chose some brute who would relish forcing his wife to obey him? Suppose he took away her books?

Usually the princess did not study anything very practical. She preferred instead to ponder the mysteries of creation and the secret discoveries of ancient philosophers. Nevertheless, some of her books did contain a few magic formulas, if only to show the writer's disdain for such ordinary concerns. For days she searched through her books (she'd never gotten around to putting them in any order) until at last she came upon something truly useful.

While the palace slept the princess secretly borrowed a wheelbarrow from the gardener and carted all her books out to an open field. Standing in the middle of them, she cast a spell. A glass tower rose up beneath her, so steep and smooth that no one could possibly climb it. On top of it sat the delighted princess and all her books. Safe! She clapped her hands in joy. A moment later, she had opened one of her favorite works, a treatise on creation told from the viewpoint of trees instead of people.

Several hours later a noise disturbed her. She peered down the edge of the tower to see her parents there, waving their arms and stamping their feet. They screamed, they cursed, they threatened to tear down the glass mountain chip by chip. She paid no attention. Finally her mother pointed out that she had taken no food with her. If she didn't come down and obey them she would starve.

Not so, the princess knew. As part of her years of study, she had learned the language of the birds. In a pure voice she sang out to them, and they brought her whatever she needed. When her parents heard her song and saw the birds deliver her fruits and fish eggs and delicacies stolen from wealthy tables, they finally knew she had beaten them.

Still they would not give up entirely. They sent out messages to all the princes and kings they could reach that whoever could climb the glass tower and bring down the princess could marry her on the spot. They even put up signs all about the land to announce this challenge. Secretly they hoped some lout would be the one to get her. It would serve her right, they told themselves.

The Fool knew none of this, for signs meant nothing to him. Music, however— Just as the Fool started toward the glass tower the princess began her song. The Fool stopped and closed his eyes. Tears spilled out from beneath the lids to slide down into his wide smile. Never, never, had he heard such a wondrous sound. When it ended, and he opened his eyes, he saw birds of all colors and sizes, condors, parrots, hummingbirds, all of them in a great swirl around the top of the tower. Quickly he walked toward the light and the birds.

As he approached it he saw men, more and more of them as he got closer, most of them injured in some way, and all of them miserable. They hobbled about on crutches, they held bandaged heads in their hands, a few lay on the ground in the middle of broken contraptions. One man had strapped giant wood and cloth wings to his back, then jumped off a tree, hoping to flap his way up the tower. He'd only fallen on his head. Another had made shoes with wire springs so that he might bounce high enough to reach the princess. He'd only crashed into the side of the glass.

The Fool looked around at all these sad figures. "What happened to all of you?" he asked.

One of the men stopped groaning long enough to look up at the Fool's cheerful face. "What are you?" he said, "Some kind of fool?"

The Fool nodded happily. "That's right," he said. He thought he might have found a friend but the man only groaned more loudly and turned away.

"Well," the Fool said to himself, "if I want to climb to the top I better get started." He set the stick down on the base of the tower in order to brace himself. A step formed in the glass. He placed the stick a little ways up and then another step formed. "This is easy," he said. "I don't know why all those men made such a fuss. I'm just a Fool, but even I can find my way up a bunch of steps."

When he reached the top the princess stood there. She was furious! She pulled at her hair, she twisted her face in anger, she hopped up and down. Even so, the Fool thought her the most wonderful being he had ever seen.

"What are you doing here?" she shouted. "Why can't anyone ever leave me alone? How did you get up the tower?"

Her fury so startled the Fool he could hardly speak. "I . . . I just climbed up the steps. It wasn't very hard. Really it wasn't."

Now the princess stared at the glass steps. Then she looked at the Fool, and then at his stick, which shone with a soft pink glow. She nodded to herself. Again she looked at the Fool.

She could see a light in him purer than the magic of his stick.

Still she refused to let go of her anger. "So," she said. "Now you expect me to marry you?"

"Marry you?" the Fool said. "*Marry* you? I could never think to marry someone as wise and wonderful as you. I'm just a Fool. I only came here because of the singing. I just wanted to hear you sing with the birds." He began to cry.

The princess felt her heart dissolve and flow out of her body. No, she told herself, she would not allow any tricks. "Right," she said sarcastically. "And I suppose you didn't see all the signs my father has planted everywhere."

The Fool said "I saw them, but I don't know what they said. I can't read."

The princess's mouth fell open. She stared and stared at him. How sweet he looked, how kind, how honest. "Will you marry me?" she blurted.

"What?" the Fool said. He looked around at the piles and piles of books, some as high as a house, some arranged like a table or a bed. "Marry you? I . . . How could I marry you? I just told you, I can't read."

"That's so wonderful," the princess cried. "I read more than enough for any two people. We will be perfect together." She began to sing the song a partridge hen sings when she has found the perfect mate. The Fool closed his eyes and became so swept up in joy he would have fallen right off the tower if the princess had not held on tightly to him. She stopped singing finally and kissed him. "We will be so happy," she said.

"Oh yes," he told her. "Yes!"

Before they went down from the tower, the princess looked at her beloved Fool and his ragged clothes. "Hmm," she said: To her he was perfect in every way, but she knew what her father would think of such a husband, and even though the king had said he would marry her to whoever climbed the tower, she feared he would try to stop them. "Do you have any other clothes?" she asked him.

He looked at the bundle on the end of the stick. "Well," he said. "I did bring an extra shirt and trousers, just in case I had to give these to somebody who needed them more than me. But I'm afraid my other clothes have just as many holes as the ones I am

wearing." He reached down and untied the bundle for the first
time since he'd placed it on his stick. Then he gasped in surprise.
His ragged clothes had vanished and in their place lay the softest
and most elegant tunic and leggings anyone had ever seen, softer
than silk, stronger than wool, with a river of colors woven into the
fabric. The Fool scratched his head. "Now where did this come
from?" he said.

Once the Fool had dressed, the princess called the larger birds,
the condors and rocs and vultures, and asked them if they would
carry her books down to the ground. Then she took her sweet
Fool's hand and together they walked down the steps of the tower.

The king and queen were delighted to see their daughter married at last, and to such a fine prince—or so they thought, for
when they asked him his kingdom he just waved his stick and said,
"Oh, over there," and each of them saw a vision of fields of dia-
monds growing like berries and castles as large as mountains. They
offered to have the Fool and their daughter live with them, but
their new son-in-law said, "No, thank you. I promised my mother
and father I'd come right home as soon as I made my fortune."
He wondered why the king and queen laughed, but he thought it
rude to ask too many questions (he so rarely understood the things
other people said anyway), so he said nothing. They set out with
seven horses, one for the Fool, one for the princess, one for the
treasures the king and queen were sending to the Fool's parents,
and four for the princess's books.

Just as they approached the river, the ground shook and they
heard a roar like the earth itself breaking in two. The princess
turned around and saw a whole army of ogres racing toward them!
Word had gotten to the creatures of their brother's destruction
and now they wanted revenge. *They'll tear us to shreds*, the princess
thought. *We have to do something*. But what could they do? There
stood the river, too wide for them to swim across, and besides,
what would happen to her books in the water? She looked up at
the sky but there were no birds near enough to come to their
rescue. Knowing that the ogres would reach them in just a few
minutes, she began frantically to search through her books for the
ones on magic. If only, she thought, as she raced from horse to
horse, she had paid more attention to practical issues.

The Fool meanwhile paid no attention at all to any of these

events. He did hear the noise and felt the ground shake but thought it might be a herd of animals running back and forth to enjoy the day. And he did wonder why his bride kept dashing from one horse to another, but trusted her totally, for after all, she was so much wiser than he. He might have wondered how they would cross the river, for someone had taken away the rowboat, except that right then, on the other side of the river, he saw his favorite sight in all the world (after his wife, of course). A rainbow!

The Fool did what he always did when he saw a rainbow, he raised his arms above his head to greet it. This time, however, he held the stick in his hand. The moment he lifted his arms, the entire river separated before him. The water rose up on either side, huge walls of water high enough to block the sky. You see, the Fool's stick was a very *old* magic stick, and it knew some very special tricks.

"Hurry," the princess urged as she spurred her horse, and the pack horses, across the passageway between the walls of water. The Fool laughed, thinking his wife wanted to exercise the horses, and so he galloped alongside her.

The princess looked over her shoulder. There came the ogres, filling the path, coming closer and closer. By the time she and the Fool and their horses reached the other side the entire army of ogres raced between the watery walls. *What can we do?* she thought. *They'll swallow us.*

The Fool glanced back, curious to see what his wife was looking at with such distress. All he could make out was a cloud of dust. "Now that's not right," he said to himself. "People depend on this river. What will happen if the water just stays piled up like that? I sure wish the river would come back down again." The moment he said it, the walls of water crashed down in a furious whirl of waves. The entire army of ogres washed away and was never heard from again.

Now they set out happily for home. Anytime the Fool got lost (at least four or five times a day) the princess called a hawk or a raven to look ahead and return them to the path. They were two days from home when they came upon the Fool's second brother, still fixed in stone in the act of trying to cast a spell. "Look," the Fool said to his wife. "Not everyone in my family is a fool. My second brother has become so famous someone has made a statue of him." With his stick he tapped twice on the shoulder.

Instantly his brother came to life, falling to the ground where he looked up confused. "What. . . ." he said. "Where am I?"

"Brother!" cried the Fool, and gave him a big hug. "What a nice surprise. Look, this is my wife, she's a princess, imagine that. Your foolish brother married to a genuine princess. And look, here's our treasure, a whole lot of it, or so my wife tells me, and here are all her books." He helped his confused brother onto his own horse and walked alongside, caught up in a happy chatter. Just as the path turned around the side of a hill, the Fool glanced back. To himself he said, "I wonder what happened to that statue?"

A day later they came to the first brother. Once again the Fool tapped the shoulder with the stick, and once again his brother came to life. Now they all traveled together, and when the Fool's parents saw them they wept with joy. With one of the jewels from the treasure chest they bought food and laid out a feast. Just as they all sat down to eat, the oldest brother suddenly remembered what had started them all on their adventures. "The staff," he said, "what happened to the magic staff?"

"Do you mean my walking stick?" the Fool said. "When we came close to home I realized I didn't need it anymore, so I threw it away."

"You threw it away?" both brothers repeated. "Where?"

The Fool shrugged. He saw his wife look at him with laughter and love and smiled back at her. "I don't remember," he said. "I just tossed it in some bushes."

And there it remains to this very day.

A Birthday

ESTHER M. FRIESNER

*Known best for her funny fantasy stories and novels, Esther
Friesner also writes horror and science fiction frequently.
"A Birthday" is a bit of both, and the chilling results earned
her a Nebula Award.*

I WAKE UP KNOWING THAT THIS IS A SPECIAL DAY. TODAY IS
Tessa's birthday. She will be six. That means she will start school
and I won't see her during the day at all.

My friends will have a party for Tessa and for me. The invitation sits on my bedside table, propped up against the telephone
so I can't possibly forget it. I wish I could. There are pink pandas
tumbling around the borders of the card and inside my friend
Paula has written in the details of time and place in her beautiful
handwriting. I get up, get dressed, get ready for the day ahead.
Before I leave the apartment I make sure that I haven't locked
Squeaker in the closet again. Squeaker is my cat. You'd think it
would be hard for a cat to hide in a studio apartment, but Squeaker
manages. Tessa loves cats and pandas, just like me. She told me
so.

I am almost out the door when I remember the invitation.
Tessa hasn't seen it yet. Today will be my last chance to show it
to her. I keep forgetting to take it with me, not because I want to
deprive my daughter of anything but because of what this birthday
means to us both. I don't like to think about it. I tuck the invitation
into my purse and go to work.

I arrive a little before nine. Mom always said I never plan
ahead, but I do now. There are flowers on my desk at work, six

pink fairy roses in a cut-glass bud vase with a spill of shiny white ribbon tied around its neck. There is a freedom card propped open on the keyboard in front of my terminal, signed by most of the women in the office. I hang up my jacket and check my IN box for work, but there is nothing there, no excuse to turn on my terminal. Still, a good worker finds work to do even when there's none, and I do so want to touch the keys.

I sit down and reach for a sampler sheet to rub over my thumb and slip into the terminal. Damn, the pad's empty! I know I had some left yesterday; what happened? I can't turn on my terminal without giving it a sample of my cell-scrapings so the system knows it's me. Who's been getting at my things? I'll kill her!

No. I mustn't lose my temper like this. I have to set a good example for my girl. It's important for a woman to make peace, to compromise. No one wins a war. Maybe whoever took the last of my sampler sheets needed it more than I do. Maybe she had to stay late, work overtime, and everyone else locked their pads away in their desks so she had to help herself to mine.

"Good morning, Linda." It's my boss, Mr. Beeton. His melon face is shiny with a smile. "I see you've found my little surprise."

"Sir?" I say.

"Now, now, I know what day this is just as well as you do. Do you think the ladies are the only ones who want to wish you the best for the future? Just because there's a door on my office, it doesn't mean I'm sealed inside, ignorant of my girls' lives." He pats me on the back and says, "I'm giving you the day off, with pay. Have fun." And then he is gone, a walrus in a blue-gray suit waddling up the aisle between the rows of terminals.

I don't want to have the day off. What will I do?

Where will I go? The party isn't until six o'clock tonight. There is so much I need to say to her before then. I suppose I could go to the bank, but that's only ten seconds' worth of time. It's nowhere near enough. Here at work I could keep finding excuses to—

Mr. Beeton is at the end of the aisle, staring at me. He must be wondering why I'm still sitting here, staring at a blank screen. I'd better go. I put on my jacket and walk away from my terminal. It will still be here tomorrow. So will part of me.

I hear the murmurs as I walk to the door. The women are

smiling at me as I pass, sad smiles, encouraging smiles, smiles coupled with the fleeting touch of a hand on mine. "I'm so happy for you," they say. "You're so strong."

"I've been praying for you."

"Have a good time."

"Have a good life."

"See you tomorrow."

But what will they see? I think about how many sick days I have left. Not enough. I will have to come back tomorrow, and I will have to work as if everything were still the same.

As I walk down the hall to the elevator I have to pass the Ladies' Room. I hear harsh sounds, tearing sounds.

Someone is in there, crying. I don't have to work today; I can take the time to go in and see who it is, what's wrong. Maybe I can help. Maybe this will kill some time.

The crying is coming from one of the stalls. "Who's there?" I call. The crying stops. There is silence, broken only by the drip of water from a faucet and a shallow, sudden intake of breath from the stall.

"What's wrong?" I ask. "Please, I can help you."

"Linda?" The voice is too fragile, too quavery for me to identify. "Is that you? I thought Beeton gave you the day off."

"He did," I tell whoever it is in there. "I was just on my way out."

"Go ahead, then." Now the voice is a little stronger, a little surer when giving a direct command. "Have fun." Another shudder of breath frays the edges of her words.

I think I know who it is in there now. Anyway, it's worth a guess. "Ms. Thayer?" What is she doing in here? The executives have their own bathrooms.

A latch flicks; the stall door swings open. Ms. Thayer is what I dreamed I'd be someday, back when I was a business major freshman in college: a manager never destined to waste her life in the middle reaches of the company hierarchy, a comer and a climber with diamond-hard drive fit to cut through any glass ceiling her superiors are fool enough to place in her way. Sleekly groomed, tall and graceful in a tailored suit whose modest style still manages to let the world know it cost more than my monthly take-home pay, Ms. Thayer is a paragon. Every plane of expensive fabric lies

just so along a body trimmed and toned and tanned to perfection.
Only the front of her slim blue skirt seems to have rucked itself a
little out of line. It bulges just a bit, as if—as if—

Oh.

"Would you like me to come with you?" I ask her. I don't
need to hear confessions. "If it's today, I mean." If I'm wrong,
she'll let me know.

She nods her head. Her nose is red and there is a little trace
of slime on her upper lip. Her cheeks are streaked with red, her
eyes squinched half shut to hold back more tears. "I called," she
tells me. "I have a four o'clock appointment. Upstairs, they think
I'm going to the dentist."

"I'll meet you in the lobby, then, at three-thirty," I promise.
And I add, because I know this is what she needs to hear more
than anything. "It's not so bad." She squeezes my hand and flees
back into the shelter of the stall. I hear the tears again, but they
are softer this time. She is no longer so afraid.

I could take her sorrow from her as I took her fear by telling
her there are ways to make what lies ahead a blessing, but I won't
do that. She'd never believe me, anyhow. I know I would never
have believed anyone when it was me. Besides, I was in college. I
knew it all, better than anyone who'd been there, and the evening
news was full of stories to back up my conviction that I'd chosen
purgatory over hell. You're supposed to be able to survive purgatory.

I should have known better. Surviving isn't living, it's only
breath that doesn't shudder to a stop, a heart that keeps lurching
through beat after beat after beat long after it's lost all reason to
keep on beating. I was wrong. But I was in college, Mom and Dad
had given up so much to provide the difference between my mea-
ger scholarship and the actual cost of tuition, books, room and
board. They said, "Make us proud."

When I dropped out in junior year and got this job as a secretary, they never said a word.

I think I need a cup of coffee. I know I need a place to sit and
think about what I'll do to fill the hours between now and three-
thirty, three-thirty and six. There's a nice little coffee shop a block
from the office, so I go there and take a booth. The morning rush
is over; no one minds.

The waitress knows me. Her name is Caroline. She is twenty-six, just two years older than me. Usually I come here for lunch at the counter, when there's lots of customers, but we still find time to talk. She knows me and I know her. Her pink uniform balloons over a belly that holds her sixth baby. She admires me for the way I can tease her about it. "Isn't that kid here *yet*?" I ask.

"Probably a boy," she answers. "Men are never on time." We both laugh.

"So how far along are you?"

"Almost there. You don't wanna know how close."

"No kidding? So why are you still . . ."

"Here? Working?" She laughs. "Like I've got a choice!" She takes my order and brings me my food. I eat scrambled eggs and bacon and toast soaked with butter. I drink three cups of coffee, black. I don't want to live forever. I leave Caroline a big tip because it's no joke having five—six kids to raise at today's prices, and a husband who doesn't earn much more than minimum wage.

I get a good idea while I am smearing strawberry jam over my last piece of toast: The Woman's Center. I do weekend volunteer work there, but there's no reason I can't go over today and see if they can use me. I'm free.

I try to hail a cab but all of them are taken, mostly by businessmen. Once I see an empty one sail past, but he keeps on going when I wave. Maybe he is nearsighted and can't see me through the driver's bulletproof bubble. Maybe he is out of sampler sheets for his automatic fare-scan and is hurrying to pick up some more. Maybe he just assumes that because I am a woman of a certain age I really don't want to ride in a cab at all.

I walk a block west and take the bus. Busses don't need fare-scan terminals because it always costs the same for every ride and you don't need to key in the tip. Tokens are enough. I ride downtown across the aisle from a woman with two small children, a boy and a girl. The boy is only two or three years old and sits in his mother's lap, making *rrrum-rrrum* noises with his toy truck. The little girl looks about four and regards her brother scornfully. She sits in her own seat with her hands folded in the lap of her peach-colored spring coat. She wants the world to know that she is all grown up and impatient to leave baby things behind. I wonder if she'll like kindergarten as much as Tessa did? She didn't cry at all when it was time to go, even though it meant I couldn't see her in the mornings.

Things are pretty quiet at the Woman's Center. After all, it is a weekday, a workday. You have to work if you want to live. But Oralee is there. Oralee is always there, tall and black and ugly as a dog's dinner, the way my mom would say. She is the Center manager. It doesn't pay much, but it's what she wants to do. She is seated at her desk—an old wooden relic from some long-gone public school—and when she sees me she is surprised.

Then she remembers.

"Linda, happy freedom!" She rises from her chair and rushes across the room to embrace me. Her skin is very soft and smells like lilacs. I don't know what to do or say. Oralee lives with her lover Corinne, so I don't feel right about hugging her back, no matter how much I like her or how grateful I am for all she's done for me over the years. It would be easier if she hadn't told me the truth about herself. A lesbian is a lesbian. I have no trouble hugging Corinne, but what Oralee is scares me. She clings to Corinne not because she loves her, but because it's safe, because she'll never have to risk anything that way, because her body craves touching. Oralee is always telling us we have to be brave, but she is a coward, pretending she's something she's not, out of fear. I can understand, but I can't like her for it.

Oralee leads me back to her desk and motions for me to sit down. She leans forward, her elbows on the blotter, a pen twiddling through her fingers. "So, to what do we owe the honor?" she asks, a grin cutting through the scars that make her face look like a topographical map with mountains pinched up and valleys gouged in. Today she wears the blue glass eye that doesn't match her working brown one and that startles people who don't know her.

"My boss gave me the day off," I tell her. "With pay."

"Well, of course he did. Soul-salving bastard."

"I have to be somewhere at three-thirty, but I thought that until then you might have something for me to do here."

Oralee pushes her chair a little away from her desk. The casters squeak and the linoleum floor complains. She runs her fingers over her shaven skull in thought. "Well, Joan and Cruz are already handling all the paperwork. . . . Our big fund-raising drive's not on until next week, no need for follow-up phone calls, the envelopes are all stuffed and in the mail . . ."

My heart sinks as she runs down a list of things that don't want doing. I try not to think about the empty hours I'll have to face if Oralee can't use me. To distract myself while I await her verdict, I look at all the things cluttering up her desktop. There is an old soup can covered with yellow-flowered shelving paper, full of paper clips, and another one full of pens and pencils. Three clay figurines of the Goddess lie like sunbathers with pendulous breasts and swollen bellies offered up to the shameless sky. Oralee made the biggest one herself, in a ceramics class. She uses Her for a paperweight. Oralee says she is a firm believer in making do with what you've got. Mr. Beeton would laugh out loud if he could see the antiquated terminal she uses. All you need to access it is a password that you type in on the keys so just anyone can get into your files if they discover what it is. At least this way the Woman's Center saves money on sampler pads, even if that's not the real reason.

The photo on the desk is framed with silver, real silver. Oralee has to polish it constantly to keep the tarnish at bay. The young black woman in the picture is smiling, her eyes both her own, her face smooth and silky-looking as the inner skin of a shell, her hair a soft, dark cloud that enhances her smile more beautifully than any silver frame.

At the bottom of the frame, under the glass with the photograph, there is a newspaper clipping. It's just the headline and it's not very big. The event it notes was nothing extraordinary enough to merit more prominent placement on the page: ABORTION CLINIC BOMBED. TWO DEAD, THREE INJURED. The clipping came from a special paper, more like a newsletter for the kind of people who would read TWO DEAD, THREE INJURED and smile. Oralee tells us that most of the papers weren't like that; they used to call them birth control clinics or family planning clinics or even just women's clinics. As if we're none of us old enough to remember when it changed! She talks about those days—the times when the bombings were stepped up and the assaults on women trying to reach the clinics got ugly and the doctors and sometimes their families were being threatened, being killed—as if they'd lasted as long as the Dark Ages instead of just four years. Thank goodness everything's settled down. We're civilized people, after all. We can compromise.

"I know!" Oralee snaps her fingers, making me look up. "You can be a runner. That is—" She hesitates.

"Yes, I can do that," I tell her.

"Are you sure?"

"Just give me what I need and tell me where I have to go. It's all right, really. I need to go to the bank myself anyway."

"Are you *sure?*" she asks again. Why does she doubt me? Do I look so fragile? No. I take good care of my body, wash my hair every day, even put on a little lipstick sometimes. It's not like before, that hard time when I first came to the city, when I was such a fool. I almost lost my job, then, because I was letting myself go so badly. I know better, now. It's my duty to set a good example. Children past a certain age start to notice things like how Mommy looks and how Mommy acts. I've read all the books. You get the child you deserve.

Oralee goes into the back room where they keep the refrigerator. She comes back with a compartmentalized cold pack the size of a clutch purse, a factory-fresh sampler pad, and a slip of paper. "You can put this in your pocketbook if you want," she tells me, giving me the cold pack. "Make sure you only keep it open long enough to take out or put in one sample at a time. And for the love of God, don't mix up the samples!"

I smile at how vehement she sounds. "I've done this before, Oralee," I remind her.

"Sure you have; sorry. Here are the names and addresses. Bus tokens are in the clay pot on the table by the front door. You don't have to bring back the pack when you're done; just drop it off next time you're here." She cocks her head. "If you *are* coming back?"

"Of course I am," I say, surprised that she'd think I wouldn't.

"Oh," she says. "Because I thought—you know—after today's over—Well, whatever. Good luck."

There are five names on the list, most of them in the neighborhood close to the Woman's Center, only one of them farther uptown. It's a glorious spring day. Soon it will be Easter. The holiday came late this year, almost the end of April. I think April is a pretty name to give a girl—April, full of hope and promise, full of beauty. Maybe I should have named my daughter April. I laugh away the thought. What's done is done, too late now to change Tessa's name. Too late.

When I get to the first place I'm surprised by how old the woman is who answers the door. I introduce myself and say that the Woman's Center sent me. I show her the cold pack and the sampler pad, telling her what I'll do for her at the bank. She has black hair that is so shot through with silver threads it looks gray, and her fingers are stained with tobacco. She stands in the doorway, stony-eyed, barring me from the dark apartment beyond, making me stand in the hall while I run through my entire explanation.

After I have finished and I'm standing there, holding out one sampler sheet, she speaks: "I'm not Vicky," she says. "I'm her mother. God will judge you people. You go to hell." And she slams the door in my face.

I feel like a fool, but by the time I reach the next address on the list the feeling has faded. It's better here. The woman's name is Maris and she lives alone. She urges me to come in, to have a cup of tea, some cookies, anything I'd like. Her apartment is small but tasteful, a lot of wicker, a lot of sunlight. "God bless you," she says. "I was just about at my wits' end. I thought if I had to go through that one more time I'd go crazy. It's supposed to get easier with time, but it just gets harder. I've got three more years to go before I'm free. Never again, believe me; never again."

She rubs the sampler sheet over her thumb and watches like a hawk as I fumble it into its thin plastic envelope. The envelope goes into the cold pack and the cold pack goes back into my purse. "Are you sure you remember my password?" she asks as she sees me to the door.

"Yes, but please change it after today," I tell her.

The third and fourth women are not as hospitable as Maris, but there is no one there to tell me to go to hell. One of them is an artist, the other lost her job, and Maris, I recall, told me she'd taken a sick day off from work just on the off chance the Woman's Center could find a runner to come help her. It feels very strange to me, sitting in rooms freckled with spring sunshine, to be talking with strange women when I would normally be at work. In the course of these three visitations I drink three cups of tea and also share a little gin with the woman who has lost her job. My head spins with passwords and special instructions, my hands clasp a pile of three plain brown self-addressed stamped envelopes by the time I teeter out the door in search of my final contact.

I take the bus uptown. Out the window I see new leaves unfurl in blurs of green made more heartstoppingly tender by the gin. It was a mistake to drink, but if I looked into the glass I didn't have to look into the woman's eyes. I decide to get off the bus a few blocks away from my stop. A walk will clear my head.

The blue and red and white lights flash, dazzling me. Two police cars and a crowd have gathered outside a restaurant that's trying to be a Paris sidewalk café. A man is clinging to the curlicued iron fence around one of the trees in front of the place, his face a paler green than the leaves above his head. I smell vomit, sour and pungent. I watch where I step as I try to make my way through the crowd.

One of the policemen is holding a shopping bag and trying to make the crowd back away. The bottom of the shopping bag looks wet. Another one is telling the people over and over that there is nothing here for them to see, but they know better.

A third stands with pad in hand, interviewing a waiter. The waiter looks young and frightened. He keeps saying "I didn't know, I had no idea, she came in and ordered a Caesar salad and a cup of tea, then she paid the bill and started to go. I didn't even notice she'd left that bag under the table until that man grabbed it and started to run after her." He points to the man embracing the iron girdle of the tree. "I didn't know a thing."

The girl is in the fourth policeman's custody. I think she must be sixteen, although she could be older and small for her age. Her face is flat, vacant. What does she see? The policeman helps her into the back of his squad car and slams the door. "Said she couldn't face it, going to a clinic, having it recorded like a decent woman. Bitch," I hear him mutter. "Murderer."

As I walk past, quickening my step as much as I can without beginning to run, I hear the waiter's fluting voice say, "I don't think it was dead when she got here."

A man answers the door when I ring the bell at my last stop. "Frances Hughes?" I ask nervously. Has a prankster called the Woman's Center, giving a man's name that sounds like a woman's?

Oralee says it's happened before. Sometimes a prank call only leads to a wild goose chase, but sometimes when the runner arrives they're waiting for her. Trudy had her wrist broken and they destroyed all the samples she'd collected so far. It was just like those stories about Japanese soldiers lost for years on small islands in the Pacific, still fighting a war that was over decades ago.

The man smiles at me. "No, I'm her husband," he says. "Won't you come in?"

Frances Hughes is waiting for me in the living room. She is one of those women whose face reflects years of breeding and who looks as if she were born to preside over a fine china tea service on a silver tray. If I drink one more cup of tea I think I'll die, but I accept the cup she passes to me because she needs to do this.

"We can't thank you enough," her husband says as he sits down in the Queen Anne armchair across from mine. Frances sits on the sofa, secure behind a castle wall of cups and saucers, sliced lemons and sugar cubes and lacy silver tongs. "I wanted to do it, but Frances insisted we call you."

"You know you couldn't do it, George," says Frances. "Remember how hard it was for you in the clinic, and after?"

"I *could* do it," he insists stubbornly.

"But you don't have to," she tells him softly. "Spare yourself, for me." She reaches over to stroke his hand. There is an old love between them and I feel it flow in waves of strength from her to him.

I leave their building still carrying just three brown envelopes. They don't want me to mail them any cash, like the others; they only want me to close Frances's personal account and transfer the funds into George's.

I also have a check in my wallet from Mr. George Hughes made out to the Woman's Center. He gave it to me when I was leaving the apartment, while I set my purse aside on a miniature bookcase and rebuttoned my jacket. He said, "We were very wrong." I didn't know what he meant. Then, just as I was picking up my purse, my eye lit on the title of one of the volumes in that bookcase.

"No Remorse?"

It is the book that changed things for good, for ill. You can still find it for sale all over. My aunt Lucille gave a copy to my mother. My mother has not spoken to her since. They study it in schools with the same awe they give to *Uncle Tom's Cabin* and *Mein Kampf.* Some say, "It stopped the attacks, the bombings, it saved lives." Others say, "It didn't stop the deaths. So what if they're forced to suffer? It still sanctioned murder." Some reply, "It threw those damned extremists a sop, it truly freed women." And others yet say, "It sold out our true freedom for a false peace, it made us terror's slaves." I say nothing about it at all. All I know is what it did to me.

I looked at Frances's husband and I wanted to believe that the book had come there by accident, left behind by a caller who was now no longer welcome under that roof. But when he looked away from me and his face turned red, I knew the truth. I took the check. "You go to hell," I told him, the same way Vicky's mother said it to me.

I will not use Frances Hughes's password and sample to steal. I could, but I won't. I will not betray as I hope not to be betrayed. But George Hughes doesn't know that. Let him call ahead to his bank, change the password. Let him be the one to come down and face the truth of what he's helped to bring about, this dear-won, bloodyminded peace. Let him twist in the wind.

There is almost no line worth mentioning at the bank. It is a small branch office with only one live employee to handle all transactions past a certain level of complexity. All others can be taken care of through the ATMs. There is only one ATM here. As I said, this is a small branch.

I prefer small banks. Larger ones sometimes have live employees on duty whose only job is to make sure that no one uses the ATMs to perform transactions for a third party. That would be cheating.

I stand behind a man who stands behind a woman. She looks as if she is at least fifty years old, but when it is her turn she does not take one of the sampler sheets from the dispenser. Instead she opens her purse and takes out a cold pack like mine, a little smaller. Her hands are shaking as she extracts the sheet, inserts it, and types in the password.

The child is no more than nine months old. It can coo and gurgle. It can paw at the screen with its plump, brown hands. "Hi, sugar," the woman says, her voice trembling. "It's Nana, darlin', hi. It's your nana. Your mama couldn't come here today; she sick. She'll come see you soon, I promise. I love you, baby. I love—"

The screen is dark. A line of shining letters politely requests that the woman go on with her transaction. She stares at the screen, tight-lipped, and goes on. Bills drop one after another into the tray. She scoops them out without even bothering to look down, crams them into her purse, and walks out, seeing nothing but the door.

The man ahead of me dashes a sampler sheet over his thumb, inserts it, and does his business. He looks young, in his twenties. He is handsome. The girls must have a hard time resisting him, especially if he knows how to turn on the charm. He may have the ability to make them think he is falling in love with them, the passion of novels, spontaneous, intense, rapture by accident.

Accidents happen. Accidents can change your life, but only if you let them. While he is waiting for the ATM to process his transaction, he turns his head so that I can see his profile. He looks like a comic book hero, steadfast and noble, loyal and true. If there was an accident, he would accompany her to the clinic. He would hold her hand and stay with her for as long as the doctors allowed. And then it would all be over for him and he could go home, go about his business. No one would insist on making sure he stayed sorry for what was done.

There is no picture on the screen for him.

I am next. I do the other transactions first. Maris has a little three-year-old boy, like the one I saw on the bus. He can talk quite well for his age. He holds up a blue teddy bear to the screen. "T'ank you, Mommy," he says. "I name him Tadda-boy. Give Mommy a big kiss, Tadda-boy." He presses the bear's snout to the glass.

The artist's little girl is still only a few months old. This is easy. I never had any trouble when Tessa was this young. I could pretend I was watching a commercial for disposable diapers on the TV. It got harder after Tessa learned to do things, to roll over, to push herself onto hands and knees, to toddle, to talk . . .

The woman who lost her job has a one-year-old with no hair and the bright, round eyes of the blue teddy bear. I can't tell whether this is a boy or a girl, but I know he or she will be blond. Tessa is blond. She looked like a fuzzy-headed little duckling until she was almost two.

I see why Frances Hughes did not let George handle this. The child lies on its back, staring straight up with dull eyes. It must be more than a year old, judging from its size, but it makes no attempt to move, not even to turn its head. I feel sorry for Frances. Then I remember the book in their house and for a moment I am tempted to believe that there is a just God.

Of course I know better.

It's my turn. I glance over my shoulder. A line has formed behind me. Four people are waiting. They look impatient. One of them is a woman in her sixties. She looks angry. I guess they have been standing in line long enough to notice that I am not just doing business for myself.

I leave the ATM and walk to the back of the line. As I pass the others I murmur how sorry I am for making them wait, how there was no one waiting behind me when I began my transactions. The three people who were merely impatient now smile at me. The woman in her sixties is at the end of the line. She waits until I have taken my place behind her, then she turns around and spits in my face.

"Slut!" she shouts. "Murdering bitch! You and all the rest like you, baby killers, damned whores, can't even face up to your sins! Get the hell out—"

"I'm sorry, ma'am, but I'm going to have to ask you to leave." The bank's sole live employee is standing between us. He is a big man, a tall man. I have yet to see one of these small branches where the only live worker is not built like a bodyguard. That is part of the job, too.

"You should toss her out, not me!" the woman snaps. She lunges for me, swatting at me with her purse. I take a step backward, holding the envelopes tight to my chest. I am afraid to drop them. She might get her hands on one and tear it up.

The man restrains her. "Ma'am, I don't want to have to call the police."

This works. She settles down. Bristling, she stalks out of the bank, cursing me loudly. The man looks at me but does not smile.

"In the future, please limit yourself to personal transactions," he says.

"Thank you," I say, dabbing the woman's spittle from my cheek with a tissue.

It is my turn again. I want to kiss the sampler sheet before I run it across my thumb, but I know that if I do that, I will not be able to access my account. I wonder how long we will have together? Sometimes it is ten seconds, sometimes fifteen. Maybe they will give us twenty because it's Tessa's birthday. I take a deep breath and insert the sampler sheet, then enter my password.

There she is! Oh my God, there she is, my baby, my daughter, my beautiful little girl! She is smiling, twirling to show off her lovely pink party dress with all the crisp ruffles. Her long blond hair floats over her shoulders like a cloud. "Hi, Mama!" she chirps.

"Hi, baby." My hand reaches out to caress her cheek. I have to hold it back. Touching the screen is not allowed. It cuts off the allotted seconds entirely, or cuts them short, or extends them for an unpredictable amount of time. Few risk the gamble. I can't; not today.

I take out the invitation and hold it up so that Tessa can see it. "Look, honey," I say. "Pandas!"

"I'm going to school tomorrow," Tessa tells me. "I'm a big girl now. I'm almost all grown up."

"Baby . . ." My eyes are blinking so fast, so fast! Tessa becomes a sweet pink and gold blur. "Baby, I love you so much. I'm sorry, I'm so sorry for what I did, but I was so young, I couldn't— Oh, my baby!"

And I *will* touch her, I *will!* It's all lies they tell us anyway, about how touching the screen will affect how long we may see our children, about how now we are safe to choose, about how our compromise was enough to stop the clinic bombings and the assassinations of doctors and the fear. I don't believe them! I will hold my child!

Glass, smooth and dark.

"I'm sorry, ma'am, but I'm going to have to ask you to leave."

I go with my own business left undone. The man takes a spray bottle of glass cleaner and a cloth from his desk and wipes away the prints of my hands, the image of my lips.

There is another small bank that I like on the east side. I think I'll go there. I start to walk. It's getting late. Paula must be making all kinds of last-minute phone calls, settling the details of my party. They call it freedom. I call it nothing.

At first I hated her, you know. I hated my own child. She was there, always there, on every CRT device I chose to use in college, in public, at home. After the procedure, the college clinic forwarded the developmental information that the central programming unit needed to establish her birth date. The tissue was sent along, too, so that they could project a genetically accurate image of my child. She wasn't there until her birth date, but then . . . !

Then there was no escaping her. Not if I wanted to use a computer, or an ATM, or even turn on any but the most antiquated model of a television set. I hated her. I hated her the way some hate the children of rape who also live behind the glass, after. But they exult in what they've done, how they've had the last laugh, how they've cheated their assailants of the final insult. I have seen them in the banks, at the ATMs, even at work, once. *Who's got the power now?* they shout at the children, and they laugh until they cry. Sometimes they only cry.

I fled her. I ran away—away from college, away from home, away from so much that had been my life before. Away from Tessa. A mandatory sentence of six years of persecution for one mistake, one accident, seemed like an eternity. She was almost the end of my future and my sanity.

And then, one day, it changed. One day I looked at her and she wasn't a punishment; she was my little girl, my Tessa with her long, silky blond curls and her shining blue eyes and her downy cheeks that must smell like roses, like apples. One day I was tired of hating, tired of running. One day I looked at her and I felt love.

Now they're taking my baby away.

No.

I find a phone booth. "Hello, Ms. Thayer? I'm sorry, something's come up. I can't go with you to the clinic today . . . Yes, this is Linda . . . No, really, you'll be all right. No one will bother you; it's against the law. And after, you'll handle it just fine . . . Sure, you will. I did."

"Hello, Mr. Beeton? This is Linda. I don't think I'll be in

tomorrow . . . Yes, I know you can't give me two days off with pay. That's all right."

"Hello, Paula? Linda. Listen, there's a spare key with my neighbor, Mrs. Giancarlo. Feed Squeaker . . . No, just do it, I can't talk now. And for God's sake, don't let him hide in the closet. I have to go. Good-bye."

I am walking east. I realize that I am still holding the envelopes full of all the money the women need. Singly they are small sums, but put them all together . . . I could buy a lot of pretty things for Tessa with so much money. I could afford to keep her, if I were rich as Frances Hughes.

There are no mail boxes near the river. I'm letting them all down, all of them except for Frances Hughes and her husband. I'm sorry. Maybe I should call Oralee? No. She's a coward. I despise her. If I turn back to find a mail box, I might turn back forever. Then I'll be a coward, too. It's Tessa who's been so brave, so loving, so alone for so long, and still she smiles for me. Tessa is the only one that matters.

I lean against the railing and see another shore. Gulls keen and dip their wings above the river. Starveling trees claw the sky. The envelopes flutter from my hands, kissing the water. No one is near. I take off my shoes to help me step over the railing. The concrete is cold through my stockings.

There she is. I see her as I have always seen her, smiling up at me through the sleek, shining surface that keeps us apart. She is giggling as she reaches out for the envelopes. Oh, greedy little girl! You can't spend all that. Now that you're six, maybe Mama will give you an allowance, just like the big girls. After all, you're going to school tomorrow. But first, let Mama give you a kiss.

We fly into each other's arms. Oh, Tessa, your lips are so cool! Your laughter rushes against my ears. I breathe in, and you fill my heart.

Happy birthday, my darling.

Sensible City

HARLAN ELLISON

*Harlan Ellison is many things—award-winning screenwriter,
critic, spoken word performer, anthologist, our longtime film
editor, and one of the most acclaimed short story writers in
the history of the SF field. One thing he is not, however, is
"a cruise kind of guy," so when he found himself on board a
cruise ship with his wife, Susan, he took to his stateroom and
gifted us with this sharp tale.*

DURING THE THIRD WEEK OF THE TRIAL, SWORN UNDER OATH,
one of the Internal Affairs guys the DA's office had planted un-
dercover in Gropp's facility attempted to describe how terrifying
Gropp's smile was. The IA guy stammered some; and there seemed
to be a singular absence of color in his face; but he tried valiantly,
not being a poet or one given to colorful speech. And after some
prodding by the Prosecutor, he said:

"You ever, y'know, when you brush your teeth . . . how when
you're done, and you've spit out the toothpaste and the water, and
you pull back your lips to look at your teeth, to see if they're
whiter, and like that . . . you know how you tighten up your jaws
real good, and make that kind of death-grin smile that pulls your
lips back, with your teeth lined up clenched in the front of your
mouth . . . you know what I mean . . . well . . ."

Sequestered that night in a downtown hotel, each of the twelve
jurors stared into a medicine cabinet mirror and skinned back a
pair of lips, and tightened neck muscles till the cords stood out,
and clenched teeth, and stared at a face grotesquely contorted.
Twelve men and women then superimposed over the mirror reflection the face of the Defendant they'd been staring at for three

weeks and approximated the smile they had *not* seen on Gropp's face all that time.

And in that moment of phantom face over reflection face, Gropp was convicted.

Police Lieutenant W. R. Gropp. Rhymed with *crop*. The meatman who ruled a civic smudge called the Internment Facility when it was listed on the City Council's budget every year. Internment Facility: dripping wet, cold iron, urine smell mixed with sour liquor sweated through dirty skin, men and women crying in the night. A stockade, a prison camp, stalag, ghetto, torture chamber, charnel house, abattoir, duchy, fiefdom, Army co-op mess hall ruled by a neckless thug.

The last of the thirty-seven inmate alumni who had been supoenaed to testify recollected, "Gropp's favorite thing was to take some fool outta his cell, get him nekkid to the skin, then do this *rolling* thing t'him."

When pressed, the former tenant of Gropp's hostelry—not a felon, merely a steamfitter who had had a bit too much to drink and picked up for himself a ten-day Internment Facility residency for D&D—explained that this "rolling thing" entailed "Gropp wrappin' his big, hairy sausage arm aroun' the guy's neck, see, and then he'd *roll him* across the bars, real hard and fast. Bangin' the guy's head like a roulette ball around the wheel. Clank clank, like that. Usual, it'd knock the guy flat out cold, his head clankin' across the bars and spaces between, wham wham wham like that. See his eyes go up outta sight, all white; but Gropp, he'd hang on with that sausage aroun' the guy's neck, whammin' and bangin' him and takin' some goddam kinda pleasure mentionin' how much bigger this criminal bastard was than *he* was. Yeah, fer sure. That was Gropp's fav'rite part, that he always pulled out some poor nekkid sonofabitch was twice his size.

"That's how four of these guys he's accused of doin', that's how they croaked. With Gropp's sausage 'round the neck. I kept my mouth shut; I'm lucky to get outta there in one piece."

Frightening testimony, last of thirty-seven. But as superfluous as feathers on an eggplant. From the moment of superimposition of phantom face over reflection face, Police Lieutenant W. R. Gropp was on greased rails to spend his declining years for Brutality While Under Color of Service—a *serious* offense—in a maxi-

galleria stuffed chockablock with felons whose spiritual brethren
he had maimed, crushed, debased, blinded, butchered, and killed.

Similarly destined was Gropp's gigantic Magog, Deputy Sergeant Michael "Mickey" Rizzo, all three hundred and forty pounds
of him; brainless malevolence stacked six feet four inches high in
his steel-toed, highly polished service boots. Mickey had only been
indicted on seventy counts, as opposed to Gropp's eighty-four
ironclad atrocities. But if he managed to avoid Sentence of Lethal
Injection for having crushed men's heads underfoot, he would certainly go to the maxi-galleria mall of felonious behavior for the
rest of his simian life.

Mickey had, after all, pulled a guy up against the inside of the
bars and kept bouncing him till he ripped the left arm loose from
its socket, ripped it off, and later dropped it on the mess hall steam
table just before dinner assembly.

Squat, bullet-headed troll, Lieutenant W. R. Gropp, and the
mindless killing machine, Mickey Rizzo. On greased rails.

So they jumped bail together, during the second hour of jury
deliberation.

Why wait? Gropp could see which way it was going, even
counting on Blue Loyalty. The city was putting the abyss between
the Dept., and him and Mickey. So, why wait? Gropp was a sensible guy, very pragmatic, no bullshit. So they jumped bail together, having made arrangements weeks before, as any sensible
felon keen to flee would have done.

Gropp knew a chop shop that owed him a favor. There was a
throaty and hemi-speedy, immaculately registered, four-year-old
Firebird just sitting in a bay on the fifth floor of a seemingly abandoned garment factory, two blocks from the courthouse.

And just to lock the barn door after the horse, or in this case
the Pontiac, had been stolen, Gropp had Mickey toss the chop
shop guy down the elevator shaft of the factory. It was the sensible
thing to do. After all, the guy's neck *was* broken.

By the time the jury came in, later that night, Lieut. W. R.
Gropp was out of the state and somewhere near Boise. Two days
later, having taken circuitous routes, the Firebird was on the other
side of both the Snake River and the Rockies, between Rock
Springs and Laramie. Three days after that, having driven in large

circles, having laid over in Cheyenne for dinner and a movie, Gropp and Mickey were in Nebraska.

Wheat ran to the sun, blue storms bellowed up from horizons, and heat trembled on the edge of each leaf. Crows stirred inside fields, lifted above shattered surfaces of grain and flapped into sky. That's what it looked like: the words came from a poem.

They were smack in the middle of the Plains state, above Grand Island, below Norfolk, somewhere out in the middle of nowhere, just tooling along, leaving no trail, deciding to go that way to Canada, or the other way to Mexico. Gropp had heard there were business opportunities in Mazatlán.

It was a week after the jury had been denied the pleasure of seeing Gropp's face as they said, "Stick the needle in the brutal sonofabitch. Fill the barrel with a very good brand of weed-killer, stick the needle in the brutal sonofabitch's chest, and slam home the plunger. Guilty, your honor, guilty on charges one through eighty-four. Give 'im the weed-killer and let's watch the fat scumbag do his dance!" A week of swift and leisurely driving here and there, doubling back and skimming along easily.

And somehow, earlier this evening, Mickey had missed a turn-off, and now they were on a stretch of superhighway that didn't seem to have any important exits. There were little towns now and then, the lights twinkling off in the mid-distance, but if they were within miles of a major metropolis, the map didn't give them clues as to where they might be.

"You took a wrong turn."

"Yeah, huh?"

"Yeah, *exactly* huh. Keep your eyes on the road."

"I'm sorry, Looten'nt."

"No. Not Lieutenant. I told you."

"Oh, yeah, right. Sorry, Mr. Gropp."

"Not Gropp. Jensen. Mister *Jensen*. You're *also* Jensen; my kid brother. Your name is Daniel."

"I got it, I remember: Harold and Daniel Jensen is us. You know what I'd like?"

"No, what would you like?"

"A box'a Grape-Nuts. I could have 'em here in the car, and when I got a mite peckish I could just dip my hand in an' have a mouthful. I'd like that."

"Keep your eyes on the road."

"So whaddya think?"

"About what?"

"About maybe I swing off next time and we go into one'a these little towns and maybe a 7-Eleven'll be open, and I can get a box'a Grape-Nuts? We'll need some gas after a while, too. See the little arrow there?"

"I see it. We've still got half a tank. Keep driving."

Mickey pouted. Gropp paid no attention. There were draw-backs to forced traveling companionship. But there were many culs-de-sac and landfills between this stretch of dark turnpike and New Brunswick, Canada, or Mazatlán, state of Sinaloa.

"What is this, the southwest?" Gropp asked, looking out the side window into utter darkness. "The Midwest? What?"

Mickey looked around, too. "I dunno. Pretty out here, though. Real quiet and pretty."

"It's pitch dark."

"Yeah, huh?"

"Just drive, for godsake. Pretty. Jeezus!"

They rode in silence for another twenty-seven miles, then Mickey said, "I gotta go take a piss."

Gropp exhaled mightily. Where were the culs-de-sac, where were the landfills? "Okay. Next town of any size, we can take the exit and see if there's decent accommodations. You can get a box of Grape-Nuts and use the toilet; I can have a cup of coffee and study the map in better light. Does that sound like a good idea, to you . . . Daniel?"

"Yes, Harold. See, I remembered!"

"The world is a fine place."

They drove for another sixteen miles and came nowhere in sight of a thruway exit sign. But the green glow had begun to creep up from the horizon.

"What the hell is that?" Gropp asked, running down his power window. "Is that some kind of a forest fire, or something? What's that look like to you?"

"Like green in the sky."

"Have you ever thought how lucky you are that your mother abandoned you, Mickey?" Gropp said wearily. "Because if she hadn't, and if they hadn't brought you to the county jail for temporary housing till they could put you in a foster home, and I hadn't taken an interest in you, and hadn't arranged for you to live with the Rizzos, and hadn't let you work around the lockup, and hadn't made you my deputy, do you have any idea where you'd be today?" He paused for a moment, waiting for an answer, realized the entire thing was rhetorical—not to mention pointless—and said, "Yes, it's green in the sky, pal, but it's also something odd. Have you ever seen 'green in the sky' before? Anywhere? Any time?"

"No, I guess I haven't." Gropp sighed, and closed his eyes.

They drove in silence another nineteen miles, and the green miasma in the air had enveloped them. It hung above and around them like sea fog, chill and with tiny droplets of moisture that Mickey fanned away with the windshield wipers. It made the landscape on either side of the superhighway faintly visible, cutting the impenetrable darkness, but it also induced a wavering, ghostly quality to the terrain.

Gropp turned on the map light in the dome of the Firebird, and studied the map of Nebraska. He murmured, "I haven't got a rat's-fang of any idea where the hell we *are*! There isn't even a freeway like this indicated here. You took some helluva wrong turn 'way back there, pal!" Dome light out.

"I'm sorry, Loo-Harold . . ."

A large reflective advisement marker, green and white, came up on their right. It said: **FOOD   GAS   LODGING   10 MILES.**

The next sign said: **EXIT   7 MILES.**

The next sign said: **OBEDIENCE   3 MILES.**

Gropp turned the map light on again. He studied the venue. "Obedience? What the hell kind of 'obedience'? There's nothing like that *anywhere*. What is this, an old map? Where did you get this map?"

"Gas station."

"Where?"

"I dunno. Back a long ways. That place we stopped with the root beer stand next to it."

Gropp shook his head, bit his lip, murmured nothing in particular. "Obedience," he said. "Yeah, huh?"

They began to see the town off to their right before they hit the exit turnoff. Gropp swallowed hard and made a sound that caused Mickey to look over at him. Gropp's eyes were large, and Mickey could see the whites.

"What'sa matter, Loo . . . Harold?"

"You see that town out there?" His voice was trembling.

Mickey looked to his right. Yeah, he saw it. Horrible.

Many years ago, when Gropp was briefly a college student, he had taken a warm-body course in Art Appreciation. One oh one, it was; something basic and easy to ace, a snap, all you had to do was show up. Everything you wanted to know about Art from aboriginal cave drawings to Diego Rivera. One of the paintings that had been flashed on the big screen for the class, a sleepy 8:00 A.M. class, had been *The Nymph Echo* by Max Ernst. A green and smoldering painting of an ancient ruin overgrown with writhing plants that seemed to have eyes and purpose and a malevolently jolly life of their own, as they swarmed and slithered and overran the stone vaults and altars of the twisted, disturbingly resonant sepulcher. Like a sebaceous cyst, something corrupt lay beneath the emerald fronds and hungry black soil.

Mickey looked to his right at the town. Yeah, he saw it. Horrible.

"Keep driving!" Gropp yelled as his partner-in-flight started to slow for the exit ramp.

Mickey heard, but his reflexes were slow. They continued to drift to the right, toward the rising egress lane. Gropp reached across and jerked the wheel hard to the left. "I said: *keep driving!*"

The Firebird slewed, but Mickey got it back under control in a moment, and in another moment they were abaft the ramp, then past it, and speeding away from the nightmarish site beyond and slightly below the superhighway. Gropp stared mesmerized as they swept past. He could see buildings that leaned at obscene angles, the green fog that rolled through the haunted streets, the shadowy forms of misshapen things that skulked at every dark opening.

"That was a real scary-lookin' place, Looten . . . Harold. I don't think I'd of wanted to go down there even for the Grape-Nuts. But maybe if we'd've gone real fast . . ."

Gropp twisted in the seat toward Mickey as much as his muscle-fat body would permit. "Listen to me. There is this tradition, in horror movies, in mysteries, in tv shows, that people are always going into haunted houses, into graveyards, into battle zones, like assholes, like stone idiots! You know what I'm talking about here? Do you?"

Mickey said, "Uh . . ."

"All right, let me give you an example. Remember we went to see that movie *Alien*? Remember how scared you were?"

Mickey bobbled his head rapidly, his eyes widened in frightened memory.

"Okay. So now, you remember that part where the guy who was a mechanic, the guy with the baseball cap, he goes off looking for a cat or some damn thing? Remember? He left everyone else, and he wandered off by himself. And he went into that big cargo hold with the water dripping on him, and all those chains hanging down, and shadows everywhere . . . *do you recall that?*"

Mickey's eyes were chalky potholes. He remembered, oh yes; he remembered clutching Gropp's jacket sleeve till Gropp had been compelled to slap his hand away.

"And you remember what happened in the movie? In the theater? You remember everybody yelling, 'Don't go in there, you asshole! The thing's in there, you moron! Don't go in there!' But, remember, he *did*, and the thing came up behind him, all those teeth, and it bit his stupid head off! Remember that?"

Mickey hunched over the wheel, driving fast.

"Well, that's the way people are. They ain't sensible! They go into places like that, you can see are death places; and they get chewed up or the blood sucked outta their necks or used for kindling . . . but I'm no moron, I'm a sensible guy and I got the brains my mama gave me, and I don't go *near* places like that. So drive like a sonofabitch, and get us outta here, and we'll get your damned Grape-Nuts in Idaho or somewhere . . . if we ever get off this road . . ."

Mickey murmured, "I'm sorry, Lieuten'nt. I took a wrong turn or somethin'."

"Yeah, yeah. Just keep driv—" The car was slowing.

It was a frozen moment. Gropp exultant, no fool he, to avoid the cliché, to stay out of that haunted house, that ominous dark closet, that damned place. Let idiot others venture off the freeway, into the town that contained the basement entrance to Hell, or whatever. Not he, not Gropp!

He'd outsmarted the obvious.

In that frozen moment.

As the car slowed. Slowed, in the poisonous green mist.

And on their right, the obscenely frightening town of Obedience, that they had left in their dust five minutes before, was coming up again on the superhighway.

"Did you take another turnoff?"

"Uh . . . no, I . . . uh, I been just driving fast . . ."

The sign read: **NEXT RIGHT   50 YDS   OBEDIENCE.**

The car was slowing. Gropp craned his neckless neck to get a proper perspective on the fuel gauge. He was a pragmatic kind of a guy, no nonsense, and very practical; but they were out of gas.

The Firebird slowed and slowed and finally rolled to a stop.

In the rearview mirror Gropp saw the green fog rolling up thicker onto the roadway; and emerging over the berm, in a jostling, slavering horde, clacking and drooling, dropping decayed body parts and leaving glistening trails of worm ooze as they dragged their deformed pulpy bodies across the blacktop, their snake-slit eyes gleaming green and yellow in the mist, the residents of Obedience clawed and slithered and crimped toward the car.

It was common sense any Better Business Bureau would have applauded: if the tourist trade won't come to your town, take your town to the tourists. Particularly if the freeway has forced commerce to pass you by. Particularly if your town needs fresh blood to prosper. Particularly if you have the civic need to share.

Green fog shrouded the Pontiac and the peculiar sounds that came from within. Don't go into that dark room is a sensible attitude. Particularly if one is a sensible guy, in a sensible city.

All the Birds of Hell

TANITH LEE

*Tanith Lee is the author of more than three score books for
adults and children, including* The Silver Metal Lover,
Dark Dance, Red as Blood, *and, recently,* Faces Under
Water. *Her fiction is elegant, her prose dreamlike, her vision
is often dazzling . . . as in the story that follows, in which we
see a world trapped in winter's grip.*

1

ONCE THEY LEFT THE CITY, THE DRIVER STARTED TO TALK. HE
went on talking during the two-hour journey, almost without
pause. His name was Argenty, but the dialogue was all about his
wife. She suffered from what had become known as Twilight Sickness. She spent all day in their flat staring at the electric bulbs. At
night she walked out into the streets and he would have to go and
fetch her. She had had frostbite several times. He said she had
been lovely twenty years ago, though she had always hated the
cold.

Henrique Tchaikov listened. He made a few sympathetic
sounds. It was as hopeless to try to communicate with the driver,
Argenty, as to shut him up. Normally Argenty drove important
men from the Bureau, to whom he would not be allowed to speak
a word, probably not even Good-day. But Tchaikov was a minor
bureaucrat. If Argenty had had a better education and more luck,
he might have been where Tchaikov was.

Argenty's voice became like the landscape beyond the cindery
cement blocks of the city, monotonous, inevitably irritating, de-
pressing, useless, sad.

It was the fifteenth year of winter.

Now almost forty, Tchaikov could remember the other seasons of his childhood, even one long hot summer full of liquid colors and now-forgotten smells. By the time he was twelve years old, things were changing forever. In his twenties he saw them go, the palaces of summer, as Eynin called them in his poetry. Tchaikov had been twenty-four when he watched the last natural flower, sprung pale green out of the public lawn, die before him—as Argenty's wife was dying, in another way.

The Industrial Winter, so it was termed. The belching chimneys and the leaking stations with their cylinders of poison. The rotting hulks along the shore like deadly whales.

"The doctor says she'll ruin her eyes, staring at the lights all day," Argenty droned on.

"There's a new drug, isn't there—" Tchaikov tried.

But Argenty took no notice. Probably, when alone, he talked to himself.

Beyond the car, the snowscape spread like heaps of bedclothes, some soiled and some clean. The gray ceiling of the sky bulged low.

Argenty broke off. He said, "There's the wolf factory."

Tchaikov turned his head.

Against the grayness-whiteness, the jagged black of the deserted factory, which had been taken over by wolves, was the only landmark.

"They howl often, sound like the old machinery. You'll hear them from the Dacha."

"Yes, they told me I would."

"Look, some of them running about there."

Tchaikov noted the black forms of the wolves, less black than the factory walls and gates, darting up and over the snow heaps and away around the building. Although things did live out here, it was strange to see something alive.

Then they came down the slope, the chained snow tires grating and punching, and Tchaikov saw the mansion across the plain.

"The river came in here," said Argenty. "Under the ice now."

A plantation of pine trees remained about the house. Possibly they were dead, carved out only in frozen snow. The Dacha had two domed towers, a balustraded verandah above a flight of stairs that gleamed like white glass. When the car drove up, he could see two statues at the foot of the steps that had also been kept clear of snow. They were of a stained brownish marble, a god and goddess, both naked and smiling through the brown stains that spread from their mouths.

There were electric lights on in the Dacha, from top to bottom, three or four floors of them, in long, arched windows.

But as the car growled to a halt, Argenty gave a grunt. "Look," he said again, "look. Up there."

They got out and stood on the snow. The cold broke round them like sheer disbelief, but they knew it by now. They stared up. As happened only very occasionally, a lacuna had opened in the low cloud. A dim pink island of sky appeared, and over it floated a dulled lemon slice, dissolving, half transparent, the sun.

Argenty and Tchaikov waited, transfixed, watching in silence. Presently the cloud folded together again and the sky, the sun, vanished.

"I can't tell her," said Argenty. "My wife. I can't tell her I saw the sun. Once it happened in the street. She began to scream. I had to take her to the hospital. She wasn't the only case."

"I'm sorry," said Tchaikov.

He had said this before, but now for the first time Argenty seemed to hear him. "Thank you."

Argenty insisted on carrying Tchaikov's bag to the top of the slippery, gleaming stair, then he pressed the buzzer. The door was of steel and wood, with a glass panel of octople glazing, almost opaque. Through it, in the bluish yellow light, a vast hall could just be made out, with a floor of black and white marble.

A voice spoke through the door apparatus.

"Give your name."

"Henrique Tchaikov. Number sixteen stroke Y."

"You're late."

Tchaikov stood on the top step, explaining to a door. He was enigmatic. There was always a great deal of this.

"The road from Kroy was blocked by an avalanche. It had to be cleared."

"All right. Come in. Mind the dog, she may be down there."

"Dog," said Argenty. He put his hand into his coat for his gun.

"It's all right," said Tchaikov. "They always keep a dog here."

"Why?" said Argenty blankly.

Tchaikov said, "A guard dog. And for company, I suppose."

Argenty glanced up, toward the domed towers. The walls were reinforced by black cement. The domes were tiled black, mortared by snow. After the glimpse of sun, there was again little color in their world.

"Are they—is it up there?"

"I don't know. Perhaps."

"Take care," said Argenty surprisingly as the door made its unlocking noise.

Argenty was not allowed to loiter. Tchaikov watched him get back into the car, undo the dash panel and take a swig of vodka. The car turned and drove slowly away, back across the plain.

THE PREVIOUS CURATOR did not give Tchaikov his name. He was a tall thin man with slicked, black hair. Tchaikov knew he was known as Ouperin.

Ouperin showed Tchaikov the map of the mansion and the pamphlet of house rules. He only mentioned one, that the solarium must not be used for more than one hour per day; it was expensive. He asked if Tchaikov had any questions, wanted to see anything. Tchaikov said it would be fine.

They met the dog in the corridor outside the ballroom, near where Ouperin located what he called his office.

She was a big dog, perhaps part Cuvahl and part Husky, muscular and well covered, with a thick silken coat like the thick pile carpets, ebony and fawn, with white round her muzzle and on her belly and paws, and two gold eyes that merely slanted at them for a second as she galloped by.

"Dog! Here, dog!" Ouperin called, but she ignored him, prancing on, with balletic shakes of her fringed fur, into the ballroom, where the crystal chandeliers hung down twenty feet on ropes of bronze. "She only comes when she's hungry. There are plenty of steaks for her in the cold room. She goes out a lot," said Ouperin. "Her door's down in the kitchen. Electronic. Nothing else can get in."

They visited the cold room, which was very long, and massively shelved, behind a sort of airlock. The room was frigid; the natural weather was permitted to sustain it. The ice on high windows looked like armor.

Ouperin took two bottles of vodka and a bunch of red grapes, frozen peerless in a wedge of ice.

They sat in his office, along from the ballroom. A fire blazed on the hearth.

"I won't say I've enjoyed it here," said Ouperin. "But there are advantages. There are some—videos and magazines in the suite. You know what I mean. Apart from the library. If you get . . . hot."

Tchaikov nodded politely.

Ouperin said, "The first thing you'll do, when I go. You'll go up and look at them, won't you?"

"Probably," said Tchaikov.

"You know," said Ouperin, "you get bored with them. At first, they remind you of the fairy story, what is it? The princess who sleeps. Then, you just get bored."

Tchaikov said nothing. They drank the vodka, and at seventeen hours, five o'clock, as the white world outside began to turn glowing blue, a helicopter came and landed on the plain. Ouperin took his bags and went out to the front door of the Dacha, and the stair. "Have some fun," he said.

He ran sliding down the steps and up to the helicopter. He scrambled in like a boy on holiday. It rose as it had descended in a storm of displaced snow. When its noise finally faded through the sky, Tchaikov heard the wolves from the wolf factory howling over the slopes. The sky was dark blue now, navy, without a star. If ever the moon appeared, the moon was blue. The pines settled. A few black boughs showed where the helicopter's winds had scoured off the snow. They were alive. But soon the snow began to come down again, to cover them.

Tchaikov returned to the cold room. He selected a chicken and two steaks and vegetables, and took them to the old stone-floored kitchen down the narrow steps. The new kitchen was very small, a little bright cubicle inside the larger one. He put the food into the thawing cabinet and then set the program on the cooker. The dog came in as he was doing this and stood outside the lighted box. Once they had thawed, he put the bloody steaks down for her on a dish and touched her ruffed head as she bent to eat. She was a beautiful dog, but wholly uninterested in him. She might be there in case of trouble, but there never would be trouble. No one stayed longer than six or eight months. The curatorship at the Dacha was a privilege, and an endurance test.

When his meal was ready, Tchaikov carried it to the card room or office, and ate, with the television showing him in color the black and white scenes of the snow and the cities. The card room fire burned on its synthetic logs, the gas cylinder faintly whistling. He drank vodka and red wine. Sometimes, in spaces of sound, he heard the wolves. And once, looking from the ballroom, he saw the dog, lit by all the windows, trotting along the ice below the pines.

AT MIDNIGHT, WHEN the television stations were shut down to conserve power, and most of the lights in the cities, although not here, would be dimmed, Tchaikov got into the manually operated elevator and went up into the second dome, to the top floor.

He had put on again his greatcoat, his hat and gloves.

The elevator stopped at another little airlock. Beyond, only the cold-pressure lights could burn, glacial blue. Sometimes they blinked, flickered. An angled stair led to a corridor, which was wide, and shone as if highly polished. At the end of the corridor, was an annex and the two broad high doors of glass. It was possible to look through the glass, and for a while he stood there, in the winter of the dome, staring in like a child.

It had been and still was a bedroom, about ten meters by eleven. His flat in the city would fit easily inside it.

The bedroom had always been white, the carpets and the silken drapes, even the tassels had been a mottled white, like milk, edged with gilt. And the bed was white. So that now, just as the snow-world outside resembled a white tumbled bed, the bed was like the tumbled snow.

The long windows were black with night, but a black silvered by ice. Ice had formed, too, in the room, in long spears that hung from the ceiling, where once a sky had been painted, a sky-blue sky with rosy clouds, but they had darkened and died, so now the sky was like old gray paint with flecks of rimy plaster showing through.

The mirrors in the room had cracked from the cold and formed strange abstract patterns that seemed to mean something. Even the glass doors had cracked, and were reinforced.

From here you could not properly see the little details of the room, the meal held perfect under ice, the ruined ornaments and paintings. Nor, properly, the couple on the bed.

Tchaikov drew the electronic key from his pocket and placed it in the mechanism of the doors. It took a long time to work, the cold-current not entirely reliable. The lighting blinked again, a whole second of black. Then the doors opened and the lights steadied, and Tchaikov went through.

The carpet, full of ice crystals, crunched under his feet, which left faint marks that would dissipate. His breath was smoke.

On a chest with painted panels, where the paint had scattered out, stood a white statue, about a meter high, that had broken from the cold, and an apple of rouged glass that had also broken, and somehow bled.

The pictures on the walls were done for. Here and there, a half of a face peeped out from the mossy corrosion, like the sun he had seen earlier in the cloud. Hothouse roses in a vase had turned to black coals, petrified, petals not fallen.

Their meal stood on the little mosaic table. It had been a beautiful meal, and neatly served. An amber fish, set with dark jade fruits, a salad that had blackened like the roses but kept its shape of dainty leaves and fronds. A flawless cream round, with two slivers cut from it, reminding him of the quartering of an elegant clock. The champagne was all gone, but for the beads of palest gold left at the bottom of the two goblets rimmed with silver. The bottle of tablets was mostly full. They had taken enough only to sleep, then turned off the heating, leaving the cold to do the rest.

The Last Supper of Love, Eynin had called it, in his poem "This Place."

Tchaikov went over to the bed and looked down at them.

The man, Xander, wore evening dress, a tuxedo, a silk shirt with a tunic collar. On the jacket were pinned two military ribbons and a Knight's Cross. His tawny hair was sleeked back. His face was grave and very strong, a very masculine face, a very clean, calm face. His eyes, apparently, were green, but invisible behind the marble lids.

She, the woman, Tamura, was exquisite, not beautiful but immaculate, and so delicate and slender. She could have danced on air, just as Eynin said, in her sequined pumps. Her long white dress clung to a slight and nearly adolescent body, with the firm full breasts of a young woman. Her brunette hair spread on the pillows with the long stream of pearls from her neck. On the middle finger of her left hand, she wore a burnished ruby the color and size of a cherry.

Like Xander, Tamura was calm, quite serene.

It seemed they had had no second thoughts, eating their last meal, drinking their wine, perhaps making love. Then swallowing the pills and lying back for the sleep of winter, the long cold that encased and preserved them like perfect candy in a globe of ice.

They had been here nine years. It was not so very long.

Tchaikov looked at them. After a few minutes he turned and went back across the room, and again his footmarks temporarily disturbed the carpet. He locked the doors behind him.

IN THE CURATOR'S suite below, he put on the ordinary dimmed yellow lamp and read Eynin's poem again, sipping black tea, while the synthetic fire crackled at the foot of his hard bed.

> *We watched the summer palaces*
> *Sail from this place,*
> *Like liners to the sea*
> *Of yesterday.*

Tchaikov put the book aside and switched off the light and fire. The fire died quite slowly, as if real.

Outside he heard the wolves howling like the old factory machinery.

Behind his closed eyelids, he saw Tamura's ruby, red as the cherries and roses in the elite florist's shops of the city. Her eyes, apparently, were dark.

Above him, as he lay on his back, the lovers slept on in their bubble of loving snow.

2

THE FIRST MONTH WAS NOT EVENTFUL. EACH DAY, HENRIQUE Tchaikov made a tour of the Dacha, noting any discrepancies, a fissure in the plaster, a chipped tile, noises in the pipes of the heating system—conscious, rather, of the fissured plaster and tiles, the thumps of the radiators, in his own apartment building. He replaced fuses and valves. In the library he noted the books which would need renovation. And took a general inventory of the stores the house had accumulated. Every curator did this. Evidently, some items were overlooked. The books, for example, the cornice in the ballroom, while lavatory tissue and oil for the generator were regularly renewed.

He used the hot tub, but only every three or four days. In the city, bathing was rationed. For the same reason he did not go into the solarium, except once a week to check the thermostat and to water the extraordinary black-green plants which rose in storeys of foliage to the roof.

Most of the afternoon he sat reading in the library or listening to the music machine. He heard, for the first time, recordings of Prokofiev and Rachmaninov playing inside their own piano concertos, and Shostakovich conducting his own symphony, and Lirabez singing, in a slightly flat but swarthy baritone, a cycle of his own songs.

For those who liked these things, the Dacha provided wonderful experiences.

Tchaikov also watched films and the recordings of historical events.

Sometimes in the mornings he slept an hour late, letting the coffee-plate prepare a sticky brew, with thick cream from the cold room.

Usually he kept in mind these treats were his only for eight months at the most, less than a year. Then he would have to go back.

The dog became more sociable, though not exactly friendly. He stroked her fur, even brushed her twice a week. He called her Bella, because she was beautiful. Probably this was not the right thing, as again, when he left, some other person would be the curator, who might not even like dogs.

Bella, the dog, each evening lay before the fire in the card room, sometimes even in the suite. But normally she would only stay an hour or two. Then she wanted to go down through the house and out by the electronic dog door.

He began to realize that the wolf howling was often very close to the mansion. At last he saw the indigo form of a wolf on the night snow. The wolf howled on and on, until the dog went out. Then the wolf and the dog played together in the snow.

The first time he saw this, Tchaikov was assailed by a heart-wringing pang of hope.

The house manual told him that the wolves had invaded the factory and remained there, because they lived off the rats which still infested it. The rats in turn lived off the dung of the wolves. It was a disgusting but divinely inspired cycle. Bella and the wolf must have met out upon the frozen ice of the ancient river buried below the Dacha and the pines. Although there would be females of the wolf kind for the wolf to choose from, instead he took to Bella. An individualist. Tchaikov did not see them join in the sexual act, but he accepted that they, too, were lovers. This seemed to symbolize the vigor still clinging in the threatened world, its basic tenacity, its *magic*. But he put such thoughts aside. Magic was illusion. Sex was only that, just like the "hot" magazines Ouperin, or someone, had secreted in the suite, and which Tchaikov did not bother with. For him, sensuality was connected to personality. He preferred memory to invention.

Of course, occasionally he pondered Tamura and Xander, their intrinsic meaning. But never for long. And he did not go up again to look at them.

IN THE FIRST day of the second month, a fax came through from the city computer, informing him a party would be arriving at midday.

He shut the dog Bella in the kitchen, and put on his suit and tie.

At sixteen hours, or four o'clock—they were late, another avalanche—the party drew up in two big buses with leviathan snow tires.

Tchaikov understood he was unreasonably resentful at the stupid intrusion, for which the place was intended. He wanted the Dacha to himself. But he courteously welcomed the party, twenty-three people, who stared about the hall with wide, red-rimmed eyes, their noses running, because the heating in the buses was not very good.

They had their own guide, who led them, following Tchaikov, up the stairs to the manually operated lift. Tchaikov and the guide took them in two groups of eleven and twelve up into the dome.

They seemed frightened on the narrow stair, and in the corridor, as though extreme cold still unsettled—startled—them. They peered through the glass doors, exactly as Tchaikov had. When he and the bossy guide ushered them through, they wandered about the bedroom. Told not to touch anything, they made tactile motions in the air over ornaments and furnishings, with their gloved hands.

One woman, seeing the lovers, Tamura, Xander, on the bed, began to cry. No one took any notice. She pulled quantities of paper handkerchiefs from her pocket; possibly she had come prepared for emotion.

Downstairs in the ballroom, the guide lectured everybody on the Dacha. They stood glassy-eyed and blank. The significance of Tamura and Xander was elusive but overpowering. Tchaikov, too, did not listen. Instead he organized the coffee-plate in the card room and brought the party coffee in relays, laced with vodka, before its return to the city in the two drafty buses.

When they had gone, about six, Bella was whining from the kitchen. He fed her quickly, knowing she wanted to be off to her lover. He gave her that night two extra steaks, in case she should want to take them out as a gift, but she left them on the plate. Oddly, from this, he deduced she would eventually desert the Dacha for her wolf partner. Instinctively she knew not to accustom him to extra food and to prepare herself for future hardship. But doubtless this was fanciful. Besides, she might by now be pregnant with the wolf's children.

BELLA LAY BEFORE the synthetic log fire, her gold eyes burning golden red. Her belly looked more full than it had. It was about twenty-two hours, ten o'clock.

Tchaikov read aloud to her from the poem "This Place."

> *I dreamed once, of this place.*
> *When I was young.*
> *But then I woke—*
> *When I was young.*

It was five nights since the bus party had visited. Once the dog had got up, shaken herself, and padded from the room, Tchaikov went upstairs and stepped into the elevator.

The night was extra cold, minus several more degrees on the gauge, and the great bedroom had a silvery fog in it.

He could look at the couple now quite passively, as if they were only waxworks. A man and a woman who had not wanted to remain inside the sinking winter world. But was it merely that? Was their mystical suicide cowardice—or bravura? Did they think, in dying, that they had somewhere warm to go?

The Bureau had not advanced any records on them, and probably their names were not even those they had gone by in life.

Again, he asked himself what they meant. But it did not really matter. They *were*, that was all.

In the night, about four A.M., an unearthly noise woke him from a deep sleep, where he had been dreaming of swimming in a warm sea jeweled by fish.

The sound had occurred outside, he thought, outside both the dream and the room. He got up and went to the window, and looked out through the triple glazing which was all the suite provided.

The snowscape spread from the pines, along the plain, and in the distance billowed up to the higher land, and the black sky massed with the broken edges of stars. Far away to the right, where the plain was its most level and long, a black mark had appeared in the snow. It must stretch for nearly twenty meters, he thought, a jagged, ink-black *crack* in the terrain.

Tchaikov stared and saw a vapor rising out of the crack, caused by the disparity between the bitter set of the air and some different temperature below.

The sound had *been* a crack. Like a gigantic piece of wood snapped suddenly in half—a bark of breakage.

But new snow was already drifting faintly down from the stars, smoothing and obscuring the black tear in the whiteness. As Tchaikov watched, it began to vanish.

Probably it was nothing. In the city apertures sometimes appeared in the top-snow of streets, where thermolated pipes still ran beneath. Somebody had told Tchaikov there had been a river here, passing below the house. The driver had mentioned it, too. Perhaps the disturbance had to do with that.

Tchaikov went back to bed and lay for a while listening, expectant and tensed. Then he recalled that once, in his early childhood, he had heard such a crack roar out across a frozen lake in the country. Instinctively, hearing it now, he had unconsciously remembered the springs of long-ago, the waxing of the sun, the rains, the melting of the ice. But spring was forever over.

He drifted back down into sleep, numb and calm.

THE NEXT MORNING as he was coming from the solarium, having switched off the sprinklers, he heard the sound of a vehicle on the plain. He went into the ballroom and looked down at the snow, half noticing as he did so that the curious mark of the previous night had completely disappeared. A large black car was now parked by the Dacha's steps, near the statues. After a moment, Tchaikov recognized the car which had brought him here. Puzzled, he waited, and saw the driver, Argenty, get out, and then a smaller figure in a long coat of gray synthetic fur.

They came up the steps, Argenty pausing for the smaller figure, which was that of a woman.

After a minute the house door made a noise.

There had been no communication from the city computer, but sometimes messages were delayed. In any case, you could not leave them standing in the cold.

Tchaikov opened the door without interrogation. Argenty shot him a quick look under his hat.

"It's all right, isn't it?"

"I expect so," said Tchaikov.

He let them come in, and the door shut.

Argenty took off his hat and stood almost to attention. He said, "There aren't visitors due, are there?"

"Not that I know of."

"I thought not. There's been another power failure. I shouldn't think anyone would be going anywhere today."

"Apart from you."

"Yes," said Argenty. He turned and looked at the woman.

She too had taken off her hat, a fake fur shako to match the coat. She had a small pale slender face, without, he thought, any makeup beyond a dusting of powder. Her eyes were dark and smoky, with long lashes of a lighter darkness. Her dark hair seemed recently washed and brushed and fell in soft waves to her shoulders. Just under her right cheekbone had been applied a little diamanté flower. She met his eyes and touched the flower with a gloved fingertip. She said quietly, "A frostbite scar."

"This is my wife," said Argenty. "Tanya."

Then she smiled at Tchaikov, a placating smile, like a child's when it wants to show it is undeserving of punishment. She was like a child, a girl, despite the two thin lines cut under her large eyes and at either side of her soft mouth.

He remembered how Argenty had talked on and on about her, her light-deprived Twilight Sickness, her wanderings in the night and cries. She had been lovely, he said, twenty years ago. In a way she still was.

Unauthorized, they should not be here. It could cost Argenty a serious demotion. What had happened? The power failure? The electricity off in their flat, gloom, and the refrigerator failing, and Argenty saying, Leave all that, I'll take you somewhere nice. As you might, to stop a miserable and frightened child crying.

Tchaikov said, "Come into the card room. There's a fire."

They went through with him, Argenty still stiff and formal, absolutely knowing what he had risked, but she was all smiles now, reassured.

In the warm room, Argenty removed his greatcoat and helped her off with her fur. Tchaikov looked at them, slightly surprised. Argenty wore the uniform of his city service, with an honor ribbon pinned by the collar. While she—she wore a long, old evening gown of faded pastel crimson, which left her shoulders and arms and some of her white back and breast bare. On her left hand, under the woolen glove, was another little glove of lace. She indicated it again at once, laughed and said, "Frostbite. I've been careless, you see."

Tchaikov switched on the coffee-plate. He said, "I usually have lunch in about an hour. I hope you'll join me."

Argenty nodded politely. She began to walk about the room, inspecting the antique oil paintings and the restored damask wall covering. Argenty took out a brand of expensive cigarettes and came to Tchaikov, offering them.

Argenty murmured, very low, "Thank you, for being so good. I can't tell you what it means to her."

"That's all right. You may even get away with it, if the computer's out."

Argenty shrugged. "Perhaps. What does it matter anyway?"

After the coffee, Tchaikov showed them the ballroom, then went to organize a lunch. He selected caviar and pork, the type of vegetables and little side dishes he did not, himself, bother with, fruit, and biscuits, and a chocolate dessert he thought she would like. He took vodka and two bottles of champagne from the liquor compartment. For God's sake, they might as well enjoy the visit.

He opened up the parlor off the ballroom. It, too, had a chandelier dripping prisms. He turned on the fire and lit the tall white candles in the priceless candelabra. He was not supposed to do this. But against Argenty's tremendous gamble it was a small gesture.

Everything sparkled in the room. It was now only like an overcast snowy winter day in the country. Perhaps before some festival. And the lunch was like a celebration.

Argenty ate doggedly, drank quiet sparingly. She ate only a

little, but with interest, excitement. She sparkled up like the room, her personal lights switched on.

In the middle of the meal, the dog, Bella, came padding in, her coat thick with rime and water drops. Tchaikov got up, thinking Tanya would be afraid of the dog. But Tanya only laughed with delight and went straight to Bella, ruffling her fur and drying her inadequately with linen napkins from the table.

As Bella stood before the fire, and the slight woman made a fuss of her, Tchaikov could see the swelling shape of the dog's belly, her extended nipples. She was definitely pregnant from the wolf. And the girl-woman bent shining over her, caressing and stroking, kissing the big animal on the savage velvet of her brow.

Argenty said, "Tanya used to live on a farm. They had dogs, cats, horses, everything."

Tanya said lightly, "I came to the city to sell stockings. Isn't that ridiculous."

When the meal was finished, they drew the large chairs to the fireside. They sat drinking coffee and brandy, and the dog lay between them, glistening gold along her back from the fire.

Outside, the dusk of the afternoon seemed only seasonal through the openings of the heavy drapes.

They were sleepy, muttering little anecdotes of their pasts, quite divorced from their present. In the end, Tanya fell asleep, her head gracefully drooping, a lock of her hair like dark tinsel on her cheek.

"When she wakes up," said Argenty, "we'll be going."

"Why don't you stay tonight?" said Tchaikov. "Leave early in the morning. There's another bedroom in the suite. Quite a good one—I think it's for visiting VIPs. By tomorrow the power failure will be over, probably."

"That's kind . . . you've been kind . . . but we'd better get back."

They looked at the sleeping woman, at the sleeping dog, and the fire.

"Why did this happen?" asked Argenty. His voice was gentle and unemphatic. "Couldn't they have seen—why did they give up all the best things, let them go—they could have—something—surely—"

Tchaikov said nothing, and Argenty fell silent.

And in the silence there came a dense low rumble.

For a moment Tchaikov took it for some fluctuation of the gas jet in the fire, and then, as it grew louder, for the noise of snow dislodged and tumbling from a roof of the mansion.

But then the rumbling became very loud, running in toward them over the plain.

"What is it?" said Argenty. He had gone pale.

"I don't know. An earth tremor, perhaps."

The rumbling was now so vehement he had to raise his voice. On the table the silver and the glasses tinkled and rattled, something fell and broke, and on the walls the pictures trembled and swayed. The floor beneath their chairs was churning.

The dog had woken, sat up, her coat bristling and ears laid flat, a white ring showing round each eye.

Argenty and Tchaikov rose, and in her sleep the woman stretched out one hand, in its lace glove, as if to snatch hold of something.

Then came a thunderclap, a sort of ejection of sound that ripped splintering from earth and sky, hit the barrier of the house, exploded, dropped back in enormous echoing shards.

The windows grated and shook. No doubt some of the external glass had ruptured.

"Is it a bomb?" cried Argenty.

Tanya had started from sleep and the chair, and he caught her in his arms. She was speechless with shock and terror. The dog was growling.

"I don't know. It's stopped now. Not a bomb, I think. There was no light flash." Tchaikov moved to the door. "Stay here."

Outside, he ran across the ballroom, and to the nearer window which looked out to the plain.

What he saw made him hesitate mentally, stumble in his mind, at a loss. He could not decipher what he was looking at. It was a sight theoretically familiar enough. Yet knowing what it was, he stood immobile for several minutes, staring without comprehension at the enormous coal-black dragon which had crashed upward through the dead ice of the frozen river, showering off panes of the marble land, like the black and white concrete blocks of a collapsed building. In the puddle of bubbling iron water, the submarine settled now, tall, motionless, less than thirty-five meters beyond the Dacha, while clouds of stony steam rose in a tumult on the steel sky.

3

THEY MARCHED STEADILY TO THE MANSION, OVER THE SNOW. Henrique Tchaikov watched them come, black shapes on the whiteness.

Reaching the steps, they climbed them and arrived at the door. He could see their uniforms by then, the decorations of rank and authority. They did not seem to feel the cold. They did not bother with the buzzer.

He spoke through the door apparatus.

"You must identify yourselves."

"You'll let us in." The one who spoke then gave a keyword and number. And Tchaikov opened the door.

The cold gushed in with them, in a special way.

"You're the current Bureau man," said the commander to Tchaikov. He was about thirty-six, athletic, tanned by a solarium, his hair cut too short, not a pore·in his face. His teeth were winter white. "We won't give you much trouble. We've come for the couple."

Tchaikov did not answer. His heart kicked, but it was a reflex. He stood very still. He had taken Tanya and Argenty down to the kitchen, with the dog, and shut them all in.

The commander vocalized again. "We don't need any red tape, do we? My men will go straight up. It'll only take the briefest while. The dome, right?"

Tchaikov said slowly, "You mean Tamura and Xander."

"Are those the names? Yes. The pair in the state bedroom. Here's the confirmation disc."

Tchaikov accepted the disc and put it in the analyzer by the door. After ten seconds an affirmative lit up, the key number, and the little message: *Comply with all conditions.* The commander took back his disc. "Where would we be," he said, "without our machines." Then he gave an order, and the four other men ran off and up the stair, like hounds let from a leash, toward the upper floors and the elevator. Obviously they had been primed with the layout of the mansion. Tchaikov saw that two of them carried each a rolled rain-colored thermolated bag. They would have some means of opening the upper doors.

He said, "Why are you taking them away? Where are they going?"

The commander showed all his pristine, repulsive teeth. "Quite a comfortable stint, here, I'd say, yes? Don't worry, they won't recall you until your time's up. Messes up the files. Seven months to go. You can just relax."

Tchaikov grasped it would be useless to question the commander further. He had had his orders, which were to remove the frozen lovers in cold-bags, take them into the submarine, go away with them, somewhere.

Tchaikov said, "It was impressive, the way you surfaced."

"That river," said the commander, "it runs deep. So far down, you know, the water still moves. We came in from the sea, thirteen kilometers. Must have given you a surprise."

"Yes."

"There's nothing like her," said the commander, as though he boasted about a selected woman, or his mother. "The X2M's. Ice-breakers, power-hives. Worlds in themselves. You'd be amazed. We could stay under for a hundred years. We have everything. Clean reusable air, foolproof heating, cuisine prepared by master chefs, games rooms, weaponry. See how brown I am," he added, dancing his narrow eyes, flirting now. "Have you ever tasted eggs?"

"No."

"I have one every day. And fresh meat. Salads. My little boat has everything I'll ever need."

There was a wooden, flat sound, repeated on and on.

The commander frowned.

"It's only the dog," Tchaikov said. "I shut her in, below. In case she annoyed you."

"Dog? Oh, yes. Animals don't interest me, except of course to eat."

Tchaikov thought he heard the lift cranking up the tower, going to the dome.

The commander looked about now, and laughed at the old regal house, the old country Dacha with its sleeping, white-candy dead.

They stood in silence in the hall, until the other four men ran down again, carrying, not particularly cautiously, the two thermolated bags, upright and unpliable. Filled and out of the dome, the material had misted over. Tchaikov could not see Tamura or Xander in these cocoons, although he found himself staring, thinking for a second he caught the scorch of her ruby ring.

"Well done," the commander said to him. "All over." It was like the dentists in childhood. "You can go back to all those cozy duties." He grinned at Tchaikov. But his use of jargon was somehow unwieldy and out of date. Did they speak another tongue on the submarine? "A nice number. Happy days."

The dog had suddenly stopped barking.

The door let the men out. Tchaikov watched them returning over the snow, toward their black dragon-whale. Already the ice was forming round the submarine's casing, but that would not be much of an inconvenience. He wondered where they had been, how far out in jet-black seas, where maybe fish still swam. When the vessel was gone, the ice would swiftly close and tonight's fresh snowfall heal the wound it had made as snow had healed the preface to the wound, last night.

Tamura and Xander, preserved from the submarine's warmth in some refrigerated cubicle. He did not know, could not imagine for what purpose. Although the nagging line from some book— was it a Bible?—began to twitter in his head . . . *And He said: Make thee an ark*—

Above, the dome was void. The great polar room with its stalactites of ice, the footsteps already smoothing from the carpet.

He descended quickly to the kitchen. He had told Argenty where the medicine cabinet was, and suggested that he dial some sedative tablets for his wife. Tchaikov was unsure what he would find.

Yet when he reached the lower floor, there was only quietness. Opening the kitchen door, he found the two of them seated urbanely at the long table.

The dog Bella had gone. But Tanya sat in her red dress, and looking up, she met Tchaikov only with her lambent eyes.

She said to him, reciting from memory from Eynin's poem that he, too, knew so well:

In Hell the birds are made of fire;
If all the birds of Hell flew to this place,
And settled on the snow,
Still darkness would prevail,
And utter cold.

"She knows it by heart," said Argenty.

"So do I, most of it," Tchaikov answered.

"The dog went out," said Argenty. "We thought we heard a wolf."

"Yes. They've mated."

The kitchen was bathed in vague ochre heat, only the light of the new cooking area was raw and too bright.

Tanya's eyes shone. "You were very good, to hide us away."

"It's all right," he said. "The military are shortsighted. They came for something else."

In a while they heard the strange, sluggish hollow suction of the submarine, its motors, diving down again below the ice. The house gave now only a little shudder, and on its shelf one ancient plate turned askew.

Tanya laughed. She lifted her dark springy hair in her hands.

Tchaikov saw that Argenty's hair, under the polishing light, was a rich dull gold.

HE SLEPT A deep leaden sleep and dreamed of the submarine. It was taller than the tallest architecture of the city, the Bureau building. It clove forward, black, ice and steam and boiling water spraying away from it, rending the land with a vicious hull like the blade of some enormous ice-skate. In the dark sky above, red and yellow burning birds wheeled to and fro, cawing and calling, striking sparks from the clouds. The birds of Hell.

When the submarine reached the Dacha, it stopped just outside the wall of the suite, which in the dream was made of glass. The wall shattered and fell down, and looking up the mile of iron, steel and night that was the tower of the submarine, Tchaikov noticed a tiny bluish porthole set abnormally in the side, and there they sat, the lovers, gazing down with cold, closed eyes.

Waking, he got up and made black tea on the plate. From the other bedroom of the suite, across the inner room, came no sound. When he looked out, there was no longer a light beneath their door. If they had switched off the optional lamp, perhaps they slept.

When the afternoon darkened, they had sat on with him in the kitchen, drinking a little, talking idly. There was the subtle ease of remaining; he realized before Argenty asked, that they did after all mean to stay a night at the house.

Later the dog came in again. Tchaikov fed her. She lay by the hot pipes for half an hour before going out once more.

During the interval, Tanya suddenly sang a strange old song in her light girl's voice, "Oh my dog is such a clever dog—"

Bella listened. Her tail wagged slowly. She came to Tanya to be caressed before padding off into the star-spiked night.

They ate cold pork and bread for supper and finished the champagne. Argenty thanked Tchaikov, shaking his hand, throwing his arm around him. The girl-woman did not kiss Tchaikov as he had half expected—hoped?—she would. She only said shyly, "It's been a wonderful day. Better than a birthday."

By the time he concluded his nocturnal check of the Dacha, they had gone up, and just the lamp showed softly under the door.

But they were in full darkness now, so Tchaikov walked almost on tiptoe from the suite. He did not want to wake them if they slept. He wished her not to dream as he had, of the triumphant submarine.

Outside, the ice had superficially closed over again. Snow fell in gentle pitiless flakes.

The elevator seemed particularly sluggish. He had to work at the lever with great firmness.

Above, in the icy corridor, Tchaikov shivered, only his trousers and greatcoat on over his nightshirt. As he walked toward the glass doors, he had a sense of imminence. What was it? Was it loss?

As formerly, he hesitated, and stood at the doors, staring in through the glacial light, the glacial glass, the cracks, the fog of ice.

He experienced a moment of dislocation, pure bewilderment, just as he had with the submarine. He had previously seen the bed clothed by two forms. Now they were removed and the bed was vacant. But there were two forms on the bed.

The bed was clothed.

Tchaikov opened the doors with the electronic key they had so noiselessly replaced on the chest in his room, before going up again. Of course, the key, lying there, had been obvious for what it was. Like the house map in the card room. There would have been no difficulty in deciding.

The bedroom, when he entered it now, did not strike him as so frozen. The breath of the living seemed finally to have stirred it, like the fluid of the deepest coldest pool, stirred by a golden wand.

Tchaikov went across to the bed. Two bottles had fallen on the thick carpet. He looked down, at the couple.

They lay hand in hand, side by side. Their faces were peaceful, almost smiling, the eyes fast shut. Like the faces, the eyes, of Xander and Tamura. Yet these two lovers had needed to be brave. Despite the vodka they had swallowed and the tablets from the medicine cabinet, they had had to face the cold, had had to lie down in the cold. He in his well-brushed uniform with its single honor, and she in her pale red sleeveless gown.

But there had been no struggle. They seemed to have found it very simple, very consoling, if not easy. Perhaps it had been easy, too.

Her somber hair, his gilded hair, both smoked now by the rime. And on the diamanté flower that gemmed her cheek, a single mote of crystal like a tear.

Tchaikov backed slowly and carefully away. It was possible they were not quite dead yet, still in the process of dying. He tiptoed out, not to disturb their death.

BY THE END of the ninth month, when the Bureau at last recalled him, the dog was long gone. He had seen her at first sometimes, out on the snow, playing with the wolf and their three pups. But the wolf was a king wolf, made her queen over the wolf pack, and in the end, she went away to the factory with them.

When he heard the howling in the still night, he thought of her. Once the moon appeared incredibly for a quarter of an hour, sapphire blue, and the wolves' chanting rose to a crescendo. Her children would be very strong, cross-bred from an alpha male and such a well-nourished mother.

His faxed report had been acknowledged, but that was all. Tchaikov never commented upon, thought about the aspects of what had occurred; he detailed and visualized the events only in memorized images.

The night of the blue moon, which was two nights before his return to the city, and to his cramped flat with its thudding radiators, the tepid bath once a week, the rationing, the dark, he wrote in the back of the book of Eynin's poetry, on the blank page which followed the poem called "The Place."

Here, too, he set out the facts sparely, as he had done for the Bureau. Under the facts he wrote a few further lines.

"I have puzzled all this time over what is their meaning, the lovers in the ice, whoever they are, whether right or wrong in their action, and even if they change, their bodies constantly taken and replaced by others. And I think their meaning is this: Love, courage, defiance—the mystery of the human spirit, still blooming, always blooming, like the last flower in the winter world."

We Love Lydia Love

BRADLEY DENTON

Science fiction often mingles with rock and roll. Brad Denton merged the two in his second novel, Buddy Holly Is Alive and Well on Ganymede, *and he does likewise in this short story about how some people fall into the same patterns of behavior repeatedly. Denton plays drums in a Texas band called Ax Nelson when he's not writing such novels as* Blackburn, Lunatics *or his current one, about which he'll reveal nothing. His experiences in the back alleys of the Austin music scene helped inspire "Lydia Love."*

SHE KNOWS ME, AND SHE'S HAPPY, AND SHE'S NOT ASKING HOW or why. She's clutching me so tight that I can't keep my balance, and my shoulder collides with the open door. The door is heavy, dark wood with a circular stained-glass eye set into it. The eye, as blue as the spring sky, is staring at me as if it knows I'm a fraud.

From down the hill comes the sound of the car that brought me, winding its way back through the live oaks and cedars to Texas 27. Daniels didn't even stay long enough to say hello to his number-one recording artist. He said he'd leave the greetings up to me and the Christopher chip.

Stroke her neck. She likes that.

Yes. She's burying her face in my shoulder, biting, crying. Her skin is warm, and she tastes salty. She says something, but her mouth is full of my shirt. Her hair smells of cinnamon.

"Lydia," I say. My voice isn't exactly like Christopher's, but CCA has fixed me so that it's close enough. She shouldn't notice, but if she does, I'm to say that the plane crash injured my throat.

"I tried to get a message to you, but the village was cut off, and I was burned, and my leg was broken—"

Not so much. We're the stoic type.

The whisper sounds like it's coming from my back teeth. I've been listening to it for two weeks, but that wasn't long enough for me to get used to it. I still flinch. I told Daniels that I needed more time, but he said Lydia would be so glad to see me that she wouldn't notice any tics or twitches. And by the time she settles back into a routine life with me—with Christopher—I'll be so used to the chip that it'll be as if it's the voice of my own conscience. So says Daniels. I'm not convinced, but I'll do my best. Not just for my sake, but for Lydia's. She needs to finish her affair with Christopher so she can move on. The world is waiting for her new songs.

And as a bonus, they'll get mine. Willie Todd's, I mean. Not Christopher Jennings'. Christopher Jennings is dead.

You are Christopher.

Right. I know.

She's looking at our eyes. She thinks we're distracted, and she wants our attention. Her lips are moist. Kiss her.

You bet. I'll concentrate on being Christopher.

Being Christopher means that Lydia and I have been apart for ten months. She has thought me dead, but here I am. She kisses me hard enough to make my mouth hurt. Her face is wet from crying, and she breathes in sobs. The videos make her look seven feet tall, but she's no more than five four. Otherwise, she is as she appears on the tube. Her hair is long, thick, and red. Her eyes are green. Her skin is the color of ivory. Her lips are so full that she always seems to be pouting. I would think she was beautiful even if I hadn't admired her for so long.

I meaning me. Willie.

You are Christopher.

To Lydia I'll be Christopher. But to myself I can be Willie.

You are Christopher.

"I didn't believe it when Daniels called," Lydia says. She's still sobbing. "I thought he was mindfucking me like he usually does."

Say "That son of a bitch." We hate Danny Daniels.

"That son of a bitch." It seems ungrateful, considering that Daniels has just now returned us to her.

She's trembling. Hold her tighter.

A moment ago she was crushing me, but now she seems so fragile that I'm afraid I'll hurt her. It's as if she's two different women.

And why not? I'm two different men.

Carry her to the bedroom. When she gets all soft and girly like this, she wants us to take charge. You'll know when she's tired of it.

She weighs nothing. I carry her into the big limestone house, leaving the June heat for cool air that makes me shiver. When I kick the door shut I see that the stained-glass eye is staring at me on this side, too. I turn away from it and go through the tiled foyer into the huge front room with the twenty-foot ceiling, the picture windows, the fireplace, the expensive AV components, and the plush couches.

No. Not in here. When she was a child, she went to her bedroom to feel safe. So take her to the bedroom. It's down the long hall, third door on the right.

I know where it is, and I've already changed direction. But the chip's yammering makes me stumble, and Lydia's head bumps against the wall. She yelps.

"Jesus, I'm sorry," I say, and think of an excuse. "My leg's still not right."

"I know," Lydia says. "I know they hurt you."

Who are "they," I wonder? There was a plane crash, and—in this new version of Christopher's life—a village. A war was being fought in the ice and snow around the village, but all of my injuries were from the crash. The villagers did their best for me, but there was no way to get me out until I'd healed, and no communication with the rest of the world. The soldiers had cut the telecom lines and confiscated the radios but had then become too busy fighting each other to do anything more to the village. So if the soldiers didn't hurt me, and the villagers didn't hurt me, who are "they"?

There is a "they" in Willie's story, but while what they did to me was painful, they did it with my consent. Getting my album recorded and released is worth some pain. It's also worth being Christopher for a while. And it's for damn sure worth having Lydia Love in my arms.

On the bed. Pin her wrists over her head.

That seems a little rough for a tender homecoming, but I

remember that the Christopher chip is my conscience. I let my conscience be my guide.

I still worry that she'll know I'm not him, but it turns out all right. If there's a difference between the new Christopher and the old one, she doesn't seem to be aware of it. The chip tells me a few things that she likes, but most of the time it's silent. I guess that at some point, sex takes control away from its participants— even from Lydia Love and a computer chip—and instructions aren't necessary.

She's sweet.

And here I am deceiving her.

But this pang is undeserved. In any respect that matters to Lydia, I am Christopher. I will live with her, recharge her soul, and give her what she needs before she sends me away. And then, at last, she'll rise again from the ashes of her life to resume her work. Willie can be proud of that.

You are Christopher.

LYDIA AND I have spent most of the past six days in bed. It's been a repeating cycle: tears, sex, a little sleep, more sex, and food. Then back to the tears. According to what Daniels and the Christopher chip have told me, everything with Lydia goes in cycles.

But this particular cycle has to be interrupted, because we've run out of food. Despite her huge house, Lydia has no hired help; and since no one will deliver groceries this far out in the Hill Country, one or both of us will have to make a trip to Kerrville. But Lydia isn't supposed to leave the estate alone without calling CCA-Austin for a bodyguard . . . and if she were to go out with me, the hassle from the videorazzi would be even worse than usual. The headlines would be something like "Lydia Performs Satanic Ritual to Bring Boy-Toy Back from Beyond the Grave." I don't think she can handle that just yet.

But if I slip out by myself, I tell her, I'll be inconspicuous. Christopher Jennings is an ordinary guy. Put him in his old jeans and pickup truck, and no one would suspect that he's the man living with Lydia Love. I have the jeans, and the pickup's still in Lydia's garage. So I can hit the Kerrville H. E. B. supermarket and be back before the sweat from our last round of lovemaking has dried. It makes perfect sense.

But Lydia shoves me away and gets out of bed. She stands over me wild-eyed, her neck and arm muscles popped out hard as marble.

"You just got back, and now you want to leave?" Her voice is like the cry of a hawk. She is enraged, and I'm stunned. This has come on like storm clouds on fast-forward.

She's waiting for an answer, so I listen for a prompt from the Christopher chip. But there isn't one.

"Just for groceries," I say. My voice is limp.

Lydia spins away. She goes to her mahogany dresser, pulls it out from the wall, and shoves it over. The crash makes me jump. Then she flings a crystal vase against the wall. Her hair whips like fire in a tornado. All the while she rants, "I thought you were dead, and you're going out to die again. I thought you were dead, and you're going out to die again. I thought—"

I start up from the bed. I want to grab her and hold her before she hurts herself. She's naked, and there are slivers of crystal sticking up from the thick gray carpet.

Stay put. We never try to stop her.

But she already has a cut on her arm. It's small, but there's some blood—

She always quits before she does serious damage. So let her throw her tantrum. It's a turn-on for her. She expects it to have the same effect on us.

Lydia looks down and sees herself in the dresser mirror on the floor. She screams and stamps her feet on it. The mirror doesn't crack, but she's still stamping, and when it breaks she'll gash her feet. I have to stop her.

No.

This isn't right. But if Christopher would let her rage, then I must do likewise if I want her to believe I'm him. Even now, as she attacks the mirror, she's looking at me with suspicion inside her fury.

She expects arousal.

Having trouble getting aroused in the presence of a naked Lydia Love was not a problem I anticipated.

She stops screaming and stamping as if a switch in her brain has been flipped to OFF. The mirror has cracked, but it hasn't cut her feet. She leaves it and comes toward me, moving with tentative steps, avoiding the broken pieces of crystal. Except for the nick on her arm, she seems to be all right. The rage has drained from her eyes, and what's left is a puzzled fear.

"Christopher?" she says. Her voice quavers. Her ribs strain against her skin as she breathes.

She is looking at my crotch.

What did I tell you?

This was the one area I hoped the surgeons wouldn't touch, and to my relief they decided that it was close enough as it was. Christopher had an average body with average parts, and so do I. So they didn't change much besides my face and voice.

But the surgeons couldn't see me with Lydia's eyes. And now she's looking close for the first time. She's realizing that I'm someone else.

No. She's only confused because we're not excited.

Lydia stops at the foot of the bed and shifts her weight from one hip to the other. Her tangled hair is draped over her left shoulder. Her lips are even more swollen than usual.

"I'm sorry," she whispers.

Oh. Well.

Maybe I'm more like Christopher than I thought.

You are Christopher.

Shut up. I can do this myself now. Whoever I am.

LATER I TAKE Christopher's beat-up white Chevy pickup truck and head for the H. E. B. in Kerrville. Lydia worries over me as I leave the house, but she doesn't pitch another fit. She gives me a cash card with ten thousand bucks on it, kisses me, and tells me to come home safe, goddam it. As I let the truck coast down the switch-backed driveway, I glance into the rearview mirror and see that both Lydia and the stained-glass eye are watching me. Then the trees obscure them, but I know they're still there.

As I reach Texas 27, a guy in a lawn chair under the trees on the far side of the highway points a camcorder at me. He's probably only a tabloid 'razzi, but I wait until the driveway's automatic gate closes behind me before I turn toward Kerrville. After all, Lydia Love has more than her share of obsessive fans. That hasn't changed even though she hasn't recorded and has hardly performed in the three years since Christopher Jennings came into her life. But I guess her fans know as well as I do that the phoenix will rise again.

And it will rise thanks to me. To Willie.

You are Christopher.

Thanks to both of us, then.

The pickup doesn't have air-conditioning, which says something about Christopher's economic situation before he met Lydia. I roll down both windows and let the hot breeze blast me as I follow the twisting highway eastward alongside the Guadalupe River. Kerrville, a small town with a big reputation, is just a few miles away.

Its big reputation is the result of its annual folk-music festival, but I stopped going to the festival two years ago. It seemed as if almost everyone was using amplifiers and distortion, trying to be Lydia Love. She's my favorite singer, too, but some of these kids can't get it through their heads that if Lydia didn't make it big by trying to look and sound like someone else, they shouldn't try to look and sound like someone else, either.

Like I've got room to talk. It's only now that I *do* look and sound like someone else that I have a shot at a future in the music business.

The supermarket's the first thing on my left as I come into town. After parking the truck, I find a pay phone on the store's outside wall, run the cash card through it, and punch up Danny Daniels' number in Dallas. Daniels is an L.A. boy, but he says he'll be working at CCA-Dallas until he can get a new Lydia Love album in the can. If he wants to stay close to her, he'd do better to relocate CCA-Austin—but when I pointed that out, he gave a theatrical shudder and said, "Hippies." I guess Dallas is closer to being his kind of scene.

He comes on the line before it rings. "Yo, Christopher," he says. "Except for that minor bout of impotence this morning, you're doing peachy-keen. Keep it up. And I mean that."

Unlike the original Christopher, I know that I'm being observed while I'm with Lydia. But there ought to be limits.

"You don't have to watch us screw," I say. "Sex is just sex. It's the other stuff that'll break us up."

"But sex is part of 'the other stuff,' Chris," Daniels says. "So just pretend you're alone with her. Besides, if everything continues going peachy-keen, I'm the only one who'll see it. And it's not like I'm enjoying it."

How could anyone not enjoy seeing Lydia Love naked? I wonder. Or is that Christopher?

You are Christopher.

Not when I'm on the phone with Danny Daniels.

You are Christopher.

Let me think.

You are Christopher.

"The chip's talking too much," I tell Daniels. "It's getting in my face, and Lydia's going to notice that something's not right."

Daniels sighs. "We put everything we know about the Christopher–Lydia relationship into that chip, so of course it's gonna have a lot to say. I've already told you, just think of it as your conscience."

"My conscience doesn't speak from my back teeth."

"It does now," Daniels says. "But it won't last long. The shrinks say that Lydia would have given Christopher the heave-ho in another six weeks if he hadn't been killed, and now they tell me that she won't stay with the resurrected version for more than another three months. Then you'll be out on your butt, she'll do her thing, and everybody'll be happy. Including Willie Todd."

What about me?

You'll be happy, too, because I'm you. Isn't that what you keep telling me? Now back off. Daniels sounds like he might be pissed off, and I don't want him pissed off. Not at me, anyway.

Why? You scared of him?

No. But I know where my bread's buttered.

"Thanks, Danny," I say. "We just had a bad morning, that's all. Sorry I griped."

The phone is voice-only, but I can sense his grin. "No problem. You need a pep talk, I'm your guy. And if you feel like chewing my ass, that's cool, too. After all, you're Christopher now, and Christopher once told me that he wanted to rip off my head and shit down my neck."

"Why'd he—I mean why'd I—"

We.

"—do that?"

"Because I told him he was fucking up Lydia's creative process," Daniels says. "Which he was. But I shouldn't have told him so. She was going to dump you anyway."

Or maybe I would have dumped her. Smug asshole never considers that.

I remember Lydia's rage this morning. No matter how beautiful and talented she is that sort of thing can wear a man down. "I think she might be about half crazy," I say.

Daniels laughs. "The bitch is a genius. What do you expect?"

Well, I guess I expect her to dump me, have her usual creative burst, and for the world to be in my debt. And for my first album, *Willie Todd*, to be released on datacard, digital audio tape, and compact disc.

You are Christopher.

Yeah, yeah.

"Guess that's all, Danny," I say. "Just figured I should check in."

Why? He's watching us all the time anyway.

"Glad you did, Chris," Daniels says, and the line goes dead.

I head into the ice-cold store, and now that I'm off the phone, I have a moment in which all of this—my new voice, my new face, my new name, my place in the bed of Lydia Love—seems like a lunatic scam that can't work and can't be justified.

But CCA has the psychological profiles, the gizmos, and the money, so CCA knows best. If it makes sense to them, it makes sense to me, too. And what makes sense to CCA is that Lydia Love's creative process has followed a repeating cycle for the past eleven years:

At seventeen, after graduating from high school in Lubbock, Lydia had a violent breakup with her first serious boyfriend, a skate-punk Nintendo freak. Immediately following that breakup, she went without sleep for six days, writing songs and playing guitar until her fingers bled. Then she slept for three days. When she awoke she drained her mother's savings account, hopped a bus to Austin, and bought twelve hours of studio time. She mailed a digital tape of the results to Creative Communications of America and went to bed with the engineer who'd recorded it.

The recording engineer became her manager, and he lasted in both his personal and professional capacities for a little over a year—long enough for Lydia to start gigging, to land a contract with CCA, and to buy a house in a rich Austin suburb. Then her new neighbors were awakened one night by the sounds of scream-ing and breaking glass, and some of them saw the manager boy-friend running down the street, naked except for a bandanna. The sound of breaking glass stopped then, but the screaming contin-ued, accompanied by electric guitar.

The next day, Lydia's debut album, *First Love*, was released at a party held in the special-events arena on the University of Texas campus. The party was supposed to include a concert, but Lydia didn't show up. She was in the throes of her second creative burst.

The music that emanated from her house over the next three weeks was loud, distorted, disruptive, and Just Not Done in that suburb. The neighbors called the cops every night, and at the end of Lydia's songwriting frenzy, one of the cops moved in with her.

The cop suggested that Lydia take the advance money for her second album and build a home and studio out in the Hill Country west of the city, where she could crank her amplifiers as high as she liked. He supervised the construction while Lydia toured for a year, and when she came home they went inside together and stayed there for a year and a half. Lydia's career might have ended then had it not been for the fact that both her tour and her second album had grossed more money than the rest of CCA's acts com-bined. So between CCA, the tabloid papers and TV shows ("Lydia Love Pregnant with Elvis's Siamese Twins"), and the continuing popularity of her music, Lydia's name and image remained in the public eye even if Lydia didn't.

Then the ex-cop showed up at an emergency room in Kerr-ville with a few pellets of birdshot in his buttocks, and the county sheriff found the alleged shooter making loud noises in her base-ment studio. CCA rejoiced, and the third album sold even better than the first two.

Lydia's next boyfriend lasted almost as long as the ex-cop had. He was your basic Texas bubba (Lydia seems to go for us common-man types), and he and Lydia settled into a happy routine that could have ruined her. But then he went to a rodeo and was seduced by two barrel racers. The photos and videos hit the stands and the tube before the bubba even got out of bed. When he tried to go back to Lydia's, he found the driveway blocked by a pile of his possessions. They were on fire.

Creative Burst Number Four followed, and that resulted in the twenty-three songs of *Love in Flames*, my favorite album by anybody, ever. Lydia followed that with a world tour that took two years of her life and made CCA enough money to buy Canada, if they'd wanted it. And it was while Lydia was on that tour, Daniels says, that CCA bugged her house. The corporation wanted to be sure that they could send help fast if she hurt herself in one of her rages.

When Lydia came home from the tour, she discovered that a hailstorm had beaten up her roof. She hired an Austin company to repair it, and Christopher Jennings, a twenty-four-year-old laborer and semiprofessional guitarist, was on the crew. When the job was finished and the rest of the crew went back to the city, he stayed.

Christopher and Lydia had been together for almost eighteen months when Lydia agreed to do a free concert in India. They went together, but Christopher took a side trip to Nepal. On the way back to New Delhi, his plane detoured to avoid a storm, hit a worse one, and went down in a mountainous wasteland claimed by both India and Pakistan. The mountains, frequent storms, and constant skirmishes between the opposing armies made the area inaccessible, and all aboard the airplane were presumed dead.

Lydia remained in India for two months before coming back to Texas, and then CCA rubbed their collective hands. They figured that with Christopher now a corpse on a mountainside, they'd soon have more Lydia Love songs to sell to the world.

But six more months passed, and the studio in Lydia's basement remained silent. Death and grief couldn't substitute for betrayal and anger. CCA, and the world, had lost her.

Then one night a scruffy day laborer and aspiring singer-songwriter named Willie Todd was playing acoustic guitar for tips in a South Austin bar, and a man wearing a leather necktie approached him.

"Son," the necktied man said, "my name is Danny Daniels, and I sign new artists for CCA. How would you like to record your songs for us?"

To a guy who grew up in a Fort Worth trailer park with six brothers and sisters, no father, and no money, Daniels looked and sounded like Jesus Christ Himself. I'd been trying to break into the money strata of the Austin music scene for five years, and I was still lugging junkyard scrap by day and playing for tips at night. But with just a few words from Danny Daniels, all of that was over. He took me into a studio and paid for my demo, then flew me to Los Angeles to meet some producers.

It was only then that I found out what I'd have to do before CCA would give Willie Todd his shot. And although it sounded weird, I was willing. I still am. As Daniels explained, this thing should have no downside. After the breakup, I get my old face and voice back, Lydia's muse gets busy again, and CCA releases great albums from both of us.

So here I am in the Kerrville H. E. B., buying tortillas and rice for Lydia Love, the biggest Texas rock 'n' roll star since Buddy Holly . . . and for her most recent boyfriend, a dead man named Christopher.

You are Christopher.

But I'm not dead. Dead men don't buy groceries.

Dead men don't sleep with Lydia Love.

IT'S MY SEVENTH week with Lydia, and something I didn't expect is happening. As I've settled back into life with her, I've begun to see her as something other than the singer, the sex symbol, the video goddess: I have begun to see her as a dull pain in the ass.

Her rage before my first grocery run hasn't repeated itself, and I wish that it would. She's gone zombie on me. Sometimes when she's lying on the floor with a bowl of bean dip on her stomach, watching the tube through half-closed eyes, I wonder if she was the one who decided to end her previous relationships. I wonder if maybe one or two of the men made the decision themselves.

Why do you think I took that side trip to Nepal?

She has a gym full of exercise equipment, but she hasn't gone in there since I've come back. So I've been working out by myself to take the edge off my frustration, and I'm heading there now while she watches a tape of a lousy old movie called *A Star Is Born*. A run on the treadmill sounds appropriate.

Even the sex has started going downhill.

We could look elsewhere. I was starting to, before the plane crash.

No. Forget I said anything. Lydia's just moody; that's part of what makes her who she is. It would be stupid of me to mess up a good thing.

Isn't that what you're supposed to be doing?

I don't know. Are we talking about Willie or Christopher? According to CCA, Willie is here to give Lydia someone to break up with, but Christopher ought to be here because he cares about her. So which one am I?

You are Christopher.

All right, then. We can't just let things go on like this, so let's try something. Lydia hasn't picked up a guitar since I came back, and neither have I. Maybe if she and I played together—

She's too critical of other guitar players. We don't like being humiliated.

In front of whom?

Ourselves. And the people behind the walls.

But CCA's already agreed to put out my album. They already know I'm good. What difference will it make if Lydia and I play a few tunes together?

CCA is putting out an album by Willie Todd. You are Christopher.

I don't care.

So I hop off the treadmill, and as I start to leave the gym, Lydia appears in the doorway. She's wearing the same gray sweats she wore yesterday and the day before. Her skin is blotchy, and she looks strung out. It occurs to me that she might be taking drugs.

Of course she is. When things don't go her way, she takes something. Or breaks something.

"I'm going to kill myself," Lydia says. Her voice is a monotone.

Oh, shit.

Don't worry. This is old news. She craves drama, and if she doesn't get it, she invents it. Ignore her.

She's threatening suicide. I'm not going to ignore that.

I would.

Well, Willie wouldn't.

Sure he would. CCA wouldn't pick a new Christopher who didn't have the same basic character traits as the old Christopher.

Shut up. I've got to concentrate on Lydia.

But she's already disappeared from the doorway. I zoned out, and she's gone to kill herself.

No, she's gone to eat or get wasted. Or both.

Fuck off. Just fuck off.

That's no way to talk to yourself.

I run down the hallway, yelling for her. She's not in any of the bedrooms, the kitchen, the dining room, the front room, or the garage. Not out on the deck or in the backyard. But she could be hidden among the trees, hanging herself. She could already be dead, and it would be me that killed her. Just because I wanted a break, just because I made a deal with CCA, just because I flew off and died on a mountainside, leaving her alone and unable to write or sing.

And at that thought I know where she is. She's where her music has lain as if dead all these months. She's gone to join it.

So I find her down in the studio, sitting cross-legged on the floor. She's plinking on a Guild acoustic, but the notes are random. She's staring at the carpet, paying no attention to what she's playing. I sit down facing her.

She looks like a toad.

No, she's beautiful. Look at her fingers. They're slender but strong. Dangerous. Can't you see that?

Sure. But seeing it isn't enough.

She's still alive. That's enough for me.

"I don't think you should kill yourself," I tell her. The gray egg-crate foam on the walls and ceiling makes my voice sound flat and unconvincing.

"Why not?" she asks without looking at me. Her hair is tied back, but some of it has come loose and is hanging against her cheek, curling up to touch her nose. I'm close enough to smell the sweat on her neck, and I want to kiss it away.

If you touch her now, she'll go ballistic.

"Why not?" Lydia asks again.

"Because you wouldn't like being dead," I say. "It's boring."

"So's being alive."

She has a point there.

Quiet. "It doesn't have to be."

Lydia's shoulders hunch, as if she's trying to shrink into herself. "Yes, it does," she says. "Life and death are really the same thing, except that life is more work."

She's still plinking on the Guild, but I notice that the notes aren't random anymore. They're starting to punctuate and echo her words. They sound familiar.

It's the progression for "Love in Flames," but she's playing it a lot bluesier than on the album.

It sounds good, though. It gives me an idea.

"I think you should do some gigs," I say.

Lydia looks up at me now. Her eyes are like stones. "I don't have anything new."

And except for the India concert, she's always refused to perform unless she has new material.

Well, there's a first time for everything. "So play your old stuff," I say, "only do something different with it, like you are now. Play it like it was the blues. See if it gets your juices flowing—"

I'm just able to duck out of the way as she swings the Guild at my head. Then she stands up and smashes the guitar against the floor over and over again.

I could have told you that she doesn't like being given advice.

So why didn't you?

Because I thought it was good advice.

Thanks, Christopher.

You are Christopher.

Whatever.

When the guitar is little more than splinters and strings, Lydia flings the neck away and glares down at me.

"I'll call Danny Daniels and have him schedule some dates," she says. "Small clubs, I think. And then I'm going to bed. See you there." She goes out, and the studio's padded steel door swings shut behind her with a solid click.

Now you've done it. When this doesn't work out, it'll be our fault. She likes it when it's our fault.

I thought you said it was good advice.
But good advice isn't enough. Nothing is. Not for Lydia Love.
Apparently not for you, either, Christopher.
You are Christopher.

WE'RE AT A blues club on Guadalupe Street in Austin on a Wednesday night, and it's jam-packed even though there's been no advertising. Word spreads fast. I'm in the backstage lounge with Lydia, and it's jam-packed back here, too. The cigarette smoke is thick. We're sitting on the old vinyl couch under the Muddy Waters poster, and I'm trying not to be afraid of being crushed by the mob. CCA has sent a dozen beefy dudes to provide security, and I can tell that they're itching for someone to try something.

But Lydia, dressed in faded jeans and a black T-shirt, doesn't seem to be aware that anyone else is in the room. She's picking away on a pale green Telecaster, eyes focused on the frets. The guitar isn't plugged in, so in all of this cacophony she can't possibly hear what she's playing. But she plays anyway. She hears it in her head.

A spot between my eyes gets hot, as if a laser-beam gunsight has focused on me, and I look across the room and see Danny Daniels in the doorway. He's giving me a glare like the Wicked Witch gave Dorothy. When he jerks his head backward, I know it's a signal to me to get over there.

He's got our career in his pocket. Better see what he wants.
Why? You scared of him?
Up yours.
That's no way to talk to yourself.

I lean close to Lydia and yell that I'm going to the john. She nods but doesn't look up. Her music matters to her again, so screw CCA and their shrinks.

I squeeze through the throng to Daniels, and he yanks me toward the fire exit. My new black-and-white cowboy hat gets knocked askew.

Out in the alley behind the club, I pull away and straighten my hat. "You grab some guys like that," I say, "and you'd get your ass kicked."

Daniels' face is pale in the white glow of the mercury lamp

on the back wall. "You haven't been doing your job," he says.

I take a deep breath of the humid night air. "How do you figure?"

As if we didn't know.

I'll handle this. "I'm supposed to be Lydia Love's boyfriend, right? Well, that's what I'm doing."

Daniels tugs at his leather necktie. "You're supposed to behave as Christopher would behave so that she'll go berserk and kick you out. But you're obviously ignoring the Christopher chip's instructions."

I can't help chuckling. "The chip hasn't been handing out many instructions lately. It's been making comments, but not giving orders. So I must be behaving as Christopher would. After all, I'm him, right?"

Daniels shakes his balding head. "Not according to CCA's psychs. Christopher wouldn't reason with Lydia when she goes wacko. He gave up on reasoning with her a long time ago."

Never really tried.

Guess you should have.

Guess so.

"If the chip's lying down on the job," I say, "that's not my fault. I'm holding up my end of the contract."

Daniels grins.

Watch out when the sonofabitch does that.

"Our contract," Daniels says, "is with Willie Todd. But if you were Willie, you'd be behaving more like Christopher even without the chip. That's why we picked Willie in the first place. You, however, seem to be a third party with whom CCA has no arrangement whatsoever." He sighs. "And if Willie has disappeared, there's no point in releasing his album."

This is bullshit.

"This is bullshit."

Daniels shrugs. "Maybe so, Willie-Chris, Chris-Willie, or whoever you are. But it's legal bullshit, the most potent kind."

My back teeth are aching. "So if I have to be Willie for you to honor his contract," I say, "how can I be Christopher?"

You can beat his ugly face into sausage, that's how.

"Chris and Willie are interchangeable," Daniels says. "Both are working-class dullards who think they deserve better because

they know a few chords. Any superficial differences can be wiped
out by the chip. So I say again: Listen to the chips as if it were
your conscience."

If I listened to the chip, Danny, you'd have blood running out
your nose.

If he was lucky.

"I know you're getting attached to Lydia," Daniels continues,
his tone now one of false sympathy, "but sooner or later she'll
dump you. That's just what she does. It wasn't until Christopher's
death that we realized she trashes her boyfriends for inspiration,
but then it became obvious. So we brought Christopher back to
life so she could get on with it. The only variable is how long it
takes, and that's up to you. If you drag things out until CCA loses
patience, Willie's songs will never be heard. And he won't get his
own face back, either, because we won't throw good money after
bad. He might not even be able to regain his legal identity. He'll
have lost his very existence."

There are worse things.

"Willie's existence wasn't much to begin with," I say.

Daniels puts a hand on my shoulder, and I resist the urge to
break his fingers. "Something is always better than nothing, Christopher. And if you go on the way you've been going, nothing is
what you'll be."

Big deal.

"So what do you want me to do?" I ask.

"Only what the chip and I tell you," Daniels says. "If you
don't like my conscience metaphor, then think of CCA, me, and
the chip as the Father, Son, and Holy Ghost. Mess with any one
of us, and you get slapped down with heavenly wrath. Mess with
all of us, and you go straight to hell." He gestures at the club's
back wall. "See, this kind of crap can't continue. Neither Lydia
nor CCA makes real money from a gig like this. So your current
directive from the Son of God is as follows: Go and spend thee
the night in a motel. You still have that cash card?"

"Yeah, but—"

Daniels gives me a shove. "You, whoever you are, talked her
into doing this gig. So she'll expect you to be here for it. But you
won't be. So saith the Son."

No. We can't leave now. Not with Lydia about to go on stage for the first time since India. She'd hate me. Us.

Yeah. But that might be what she wants. She thrives on being treated like dirt. That's why she goes for guys like us. But we've been too nice lately, and it's screwed her up.

That's sick.

That's Lydia.

"All right," I tell Daniels. "I'm going. But I don't like it."

Daniels grins again. "Shit, neither do I. But it's for her own good, and yours, too. If you weren't fucked in the head right now, you'd know that."

Come on. Let's get out of here.

I turn away from Daniels and walk off down the dark alley, abandoning Lydia to herself. My boots crunch on the broken asphalt. A bat flies past my—our—face, coming so close that we feel a puff of air from its wings.

Is Daniels right? Am I fucked in the head?

In the soul, Christopher. In the soul.

THE STAINED-GLASS EYE has become an open mouth surrounded by jagged teeth. Blue shards cover the front step, and they make snapping sounds as I come up to the door. I smell something burning. The stereo in the front room is blaring an old thrash-metal number about a murder-suicide. My back teeth begin to ache again.

As I cross the foyer into the front room, I see what Lydia has done. The picture windows have been broken, and the walls are pockmarked with holes. Some of the holes seem to be the results of shotgun blasts, and some have been punched with free-weight bars from the gym. The bars are still sticking out of some of these.

All of the furniture has been torn to pieces. The only things left intact are the AV components, which are stacked on the floor in front of the fireplace. But the cabinet that housed them is with everything else from the room—with everything else from the entire house, I think. Everything has been broken, shredded, crumpled, melted, or twisted, and then piled in the center of the room. A misshapen pyramid reaches three-quarters of the way up to the ceiling.

Lydia, wearing the jeans and T-shirt from last night's gig, is sitting atop the pyramid and using a fireplace-lighter to burn holes into white cloth that used to be drapes. She doesn't notice me until I cross the room and turn off the stereo.

"Christopher," she says, glancing at me with a distracted expression "You're back." Her voice is thick. I wonder if she's taken pills.

No. Her eyes are clear. She knows what she's doing. If the shotgun's handy, she might kill us now.

"I'm sorry I left last night," I say, trying to think of a lie to explain myself. "Daniels told me it was my fault that you were playing a joint instead of an arena, and I was afraid that if I stuck around I was gonna pop him. So I went for a walk, but when I got back, you and the truck were gone. I tried to call, but my card wouldn't work. And I couldn't find a cab that would bring me out here at night. So I stayed in a motel."

Too much. She won't buy it.

"I thought your card didn't work," Lydia says.

We're meat.

Not if you back off and let me deal with this.

"It didn't work in the phone," I say. "But the motel took it."

"So why didn't you call from the motel?"

Told you.

Piss on it, then. I'm going to tell her the truth, including who I am.

Who's that?

"Don't answer," Lydia says. "Just turn on the VCR and watch the monitor."

So I do as she says. The monitor flashes on as the tape starts, and there I am, doing it with a brown-haired girl I've never seen before.

Yee-oww. Where was I when this was going on?

This never went on. I know that's the motel room we stayed in last night, because I recognize the bent corner on the picture frame over the bed. But I don't know that girl. So that can't be me.

Looks like us.

So it must be you. It's Christopher before the crash.

You are Christopher.

Yeah, but I'm Christopher after the crash.

Check out the hat on the floor. We were wearing it last night. We're wearing it right now. And it didn't belong to Christopher before the crash. It's brand new.

But I don't have a chance to figure out what that means, because Lydia has succeeded in setting the white drapery on fire. She waves it like a flag, bringing its flames close to her hair, so I move to yank it away from her. But she tosses it away before I can reach for it, and it snags on a chair leg sticking out of the pyramid. To my relief, the flames start to die down.

Lydia is staring at me now. "Tell me what happened last night," she says. "Tell me where you found that girl while I was sweating in front of all those people. Tell me whether you started with her while I was singing, or whether you waited until you knew I'd be on my way home. Tell me whether she can suck the chrome off a trailer hitch." She points the fireplace lighter at me. "Tell me the truth, Christopher."

I look at the video monitor. The brown-haired girl and I are still going at it. The clothes on the floor are the ones I'm wearing now. The stamp on my left hand is the one that was put on at the club last night, the one that's still here on my skin. But that man is not me. I didn't do those things. We're watching an imaginary past with false faces and artificial voices.

Whoa. Sounds familiar.

Danny Daniels. CCA.

"Where'd the tape come from?" I ask, turning back toward Lydia. But if there's an answer I don't hear it, because the fire, instead of dying, has jumped to some paper and plastic in the pyramid. I can still smother it with the drapery if I hurry.

But Lydia jumps down partway and jabs her lighter at my face, stopping me. The yellow flame at the end of the barrel is two inches from my nose. The brim of my hat scorches.

"Tell me the truth," Lydia says.

A wisp of black smoke rises to the ceiling.

All right, then. The truth. Or as close as I can get.

"I've never seen that girl before," I say. "Daniels faked that tape to split us up."

Just doing his job.

Right. This is the way things are supposed to be, and I'm supposed to help them along.

But I don't want to anymore, and I don't care if it costs me my album or my face or my name. Looking at her now, I realize that I only care about one thing: I love Lydia Love.

I know. So do I. But loving her isn't enough.

Lydia's upper lip pulls back from her teeth. "Why should Danny care who I'm with? He doesn't have a thing for me." The flame waves before my eyes.

"No," I say, "but CCA does."

"What—" Lydia begins, and then a deafening buzz buries her words.

It's the smoke alarm. The pyramid shudders with the sound, and Lydia loses her balance and pitches forward. My hat gets knocked off, and Lydia's flame burns across my cheek as I catch her and fall backward. We hit the floor as pieces of the pyramid crash down around us.

The video monitor is right before our eyes. The brown-haired girl's lips are forming a name over and over again.

Christopher, she says. Christopher, Christopher.

But that's not my name.

No. You are Willie.

But we are Christopher.

Sprinkler nozzles pop out of the ceiling hissing and begin drenching us. The fireplace lighter sputters out, and Lydia drops it. Then she pushes away from us, snatches up a pump shotgun from behind the AV components, and runs from the room. The fire in the pyramid dies, but the alarm keeps buzzing and the sprinklers keep spraying.

We struggle up and go after her. The door to the studio slams shut as we come down the stairs. A glimpse before it closes shows us that the sprinklers aren't on in there. We try the door but it won't open, so we pound on it and try to shout through the noise of the alarm. The door isn't padded on the inside, and the steel is cold and hard. We tell Lydia our names and the truth of why we put on this face and came back to her. We tell her about CCA wanting to get its money's worth, about the surgery and the chip, about everything we can think of. The burn on our cheek stings as the water hits it.

She wouldn't believe anything we said now. Even if she could hear us.

But we have to try. She has the shotgun. And last week she said she was going to kill herself—

The alarm stops, and we shout Lydia's name as loud as we can.

There are two quick explosions, and circular patterns of bumps appear in the door's metal skin. From the other side, Lydia's muffled voice tells us to go back to the dead where we belong.

Then comes the sound of an electric guitar and of a scream fueled by betrayal and anger.

Lydia Love is writing songs again.

And we know what that means. It means that our name, or whether we even have a name, doesn't matter anymore.

We are—

Shut up. It doesn't matter.

No. We guess not.

We sit down to soak in the artificial rain.

ON THE DAY after our return to Austin, Danny Daniels called us at the motel and asked when we wanted to have the surgery to remove the chip and to return Willie's face and voice to their pre-Christopher states. We'd had a night to calm down, so we didn't accuse him of using the sex video to give our relationship with Lydia a shove over a cliff. Of course he had done it. But his job, and ours, was to get Lydia Love to start producing again. We had a contract, and all he did was help it along.

And he lived up to his end of the bargain. We got Willie's face and voice back, more or less, and the chip was removed from our jaw. The doctors made a point of showing it to us after the operation.

As if a conscience could be removed so easily.

Quiet. Willie can't shake hands, think, and listen to Christopher all at the same time.

So let Christopher take over the social duties. Crush a few knuckle-bones.

Deal.

Today our album, *Willie Todd,* has been released on datacard, DAT, and compact disc. Just in time for Christmas. And thanks to Daniels, three of its tracks are already in heavy rotation on the audio and video networks. He even arranged for this release party at the Austin Hyatt Regency with a whole shitload of CCA bigshots and performers in attendance.

We asked Daniels if one performer in particular would be here, and he winked. But we don't see her anywhere.

The sonofabitch can lie without opening his mouth.

Daniels has done a lot for us, but we still don't like him.

Wait. There she is, by the waterfall, talking to a couple of CCA execs.

She might not want to see us.

Sure she will. We don't look like Christopher anymore.

There's a touch on our arm. It's Daniels. Our well-wishers melt away until we're alone with him beside the fake creek burbling through the atrium.

"Your hat's crooked, Willie," he says, giving us that alligator grin of his. "You want to make a good impression on her, don't you?"

"It's all right if I meet her?" we ask.

Daniels raises his eyebrows. "None of my business."

What a load. It's exactly his business.

"You've finished her sessions?" we ask.

He straightens his necktie. "Yup. Got the last four tracks in the can yesterday. She wants to call the album *Go Back to the Dead,* but we're trying to talk her into something more upbeat. My co-producers like *Once More With Love,* but I'm partial to *What Goes Around Comes Around.* We've gotta decide soon, because it has to be out by Valentine's Day."

"Valentine's Day?"

Cute.

"Yeah, her tour kicks off in New York on February 14," Daniels says. He nudges our shoulder. "How'd you like to be the opening act?"

Opening act. Right. You know what kind of act he wants us to be. Should we refuse?

Like we could.

We turn away from Daniels and start toward her.

"Attaboy," Daniels says behind us.

The CCA honchos move away from her as we approach. Her hair is even longer now, and her skin is smooth and healthy. Her eyes are a bright green, like sunlight shining through emeralds.

"You're Willie Todd," she says, extending her right hand. "I'm Lydia Love. Congratulations on the album. It's good work."

Our fingers touch hers with a snap of electricity. We jump, then laugh.

"Danny Daniels played me some songs from your own new album," we say. "They sound okay, too."

She smiles at the understatement. "Gee, thanks." She tilts her head, and her hair falls over one eye. "Did he mention that I'd like you to open for me on the tour? Your music makes you sound like a guy I could get along with."

For a while, maybe.

But a while is better than never. A while is all anyone ever has.

"Maybe we could talk about it after the party," we say.

"Maybe we could," Lydia says.

And so the cycle comes back to its beginning. But now Lydia isn't the only one who can play the phoenix game.

Across the atrium, Daniels raises his glass to us.

Like the man said: What goes around comes around.

Or "Once more with Love."

So we might as well plan ahead. What name shall we go under next time?

One we can use for both of us. It'll avoid confusion.

If you want to avoid confusion, you're in love with the wrong woman, Christopher.

My name is Willie.

Whatever. She's looking at our eyes. Her lips are moist. Kiss her.

We let our conscience be our guide.

Paul and Me

MICHAEL BLUMLEIN

*Michael Blumlein is a practicing doctor who has never shied
away from difficult themes in his fiction. His novels* X, Y *and*
The Movement of Mountains *have both taken on
challenging premises and treated them with surprising results.
His short stories—many of which are collected in* The Brains
of Rats—*are often as sharp as scalpels. "Paul and Me" was
one of our more controversial stories when it first appeared;
this poignant fantasy got through to many readers, and some
of them found the experience discomfiting. Others found it
very affecting, this editor among them.*

For Terry

I FIRST MET PAUL IN '71, THE YEAR I GOT OUT OF COLLEGE. I WAS
bumming around the country, crashing in city parks and church
basements, cadging food and companionship, avoiding the future.
In keeping with the spirit of the times, I considered my carefree
and unfettered existence both highly evolved and intrinsically
righteous, when in truth I had no fucking idea. It didn't matter.
My girlfriend was in New York City, living in a commune and
doing guerrilla theater. My ex-girlfriend was in Vancouver, B.C.,
with her boyfriend, who'd fled the U.S. because of the draft. Those
two women were ballast for me. In my imagination anyway, they
were fixed points and gave me the security to do what I wanted in
between.

I'd been in Bozeman a few days when I was busted for stealing a sandwich. After a night in jail, the judge threw me out of town. The first ride I got was headed to Seattle, but I wasn't ready for another city quite yet. I got out in Wenatchee, caught a ride to Carlton and two days later, a pack on my back and enough brown rice to last a week, was in the high country north of Lake Chelan.

There is nothing like the mountains to make a person feel simultaneously large and small. Incomparably large, I should say, and insignificantly small. Distances are vast, and yet life, because conditions are so exacting, is condensed. At the higher elevations the trees and wildflowers, the voles that skitter in and out of rocks, even the mosquitoes seem lilliputian. Which made Paul, at first glance, all the more striking.

He was kneeling by the edge of a stream, taking a drink of water. He had on those trademark jeans of his, the navy blue suspenders, the plaid shirt. From a distance he looked as big as a house, up close even bigger. Because of his size I expected him to be oafish, but he was nothing of the kind. He moved with remarkable grace, dipping his cupped hand delicately into the water then sipping from it with the poise of a lady sipping tea.

I was alone. It was July, and I had camped by a lake in a high meadow two valleys over. That morning I had gone exploring, following the drainage creek down as it fell through a boulder-strewn slope of fir and pine. An hour of walking brought me to the confluence of another, similar-sized creek, at which point the water picked up force. The trail leveled off for about a hundred yards, then dropped precipitously. This was the site of a magnificent waterfall, sixty, seventy feet high. Paul was at the far end of a deep pool carved by the water. His hair was dark and short, his beard trim, his lips as red as berries. Waves of reflected sunlight lit his face. He had the eyes of a dreamer.

The trail zigzagged down a granite cliff, coming out near the base of the waterfall. The noise was deafening and masked my approach. By the time he noticed me, I wasn't more than a stone's throw away. He stopped drinking, and a frown crossed his face. Quickly, this gave way to a stiff kind of courtesy, a seemliness and a handsome, though remote, civility. His public persona. I apologized for intruding and was about to continue on my way when he motioned me over.

Standing, he was thirty feet tall; kneeling, nearly half that height. His thighs when I first met him were as wide as tree trunks; his biceps, like mountains. As I drew near, he stood up and stretched, momentarily blotting out the sky. Then, as though conscious of having dwarfed me and wanting to put me at ease, he sat down and leaned back against a pine, which, though venerable, bent beneath him like rubber.

It was he who spoke first. His voice was deep and surprisingly gentle.

"Hello."

"Hello," I answered.

"Nice day."

"Incredible."

He looked at the sky, which was cloudless. Sunlight streamed down. "Doesn't get any better."

"Can't," I replied insipidly.

An awkward silence followed, then he asked if I came here often. I said it was my first time.

"You?" I asked.

"Every few months. It's a little hot for me this time of year. In the summer I tend to stay farther north."

I was wearing a T-shirt and shorts. He was in long pants and a flannel shirt with the sleeves rolled up partway. I suggested that he might be more comfortable in other clothes.

"I like to stay covered," he replied, which nowadays would mean he wanted to keep out of the sun but then was more ambiguous. I searched for something else to keep the conversation alive.

"So what made you come?" I asked. "South, I mean."

He shrugged. "I don't know. I had an urge."

I nodded. Urges I knew about. My whole last year of college had been one urge after another. Sex, drugs, sit-ins. As a life, it was dizzying. And now, having hiked into the high country with the lofty purpose of getting away from it all, of finding a little perspective, here I was talking to a man as tall as a tower. I was no less dizzy than before, and beyond that, I was humbled by the realization that the very impulsiveness I was running from was what had gotten me into the mountains to begin with. I had to steady myself against a rock, and even then my head spun. Thinking the light-headedness might in part be a product of hunger, I took out a bag of peanuts. I offered him some, but he shook his head.

"I'm allergic to nuts. I blow up like a blimp."

This was news to me. Of everything I'd read or heard about him, nothing ever mentioned his being sick. I didn't know he could be.

"You don't want to be around," he said. "When you're used to pulling up trees like toothpicks and knocking off mountaintops like cream puffs, it's no fun being weak as a kitten. I'm a lousy invalid. Worse if I'm really sick. I had a fever once that started a fire and chills that fanned the flames so hot that half the camp burned down before the boys finally got it out. Then they had to truck in three days of snow to cool me off."

I could picture it. "One time I had a fever like that. It made me hallucinate. I was reading a book and the characters started appearing in my room. It was freaky."

"This was no hallucination," he said indignantly.

In those days, theories of the mind were undergoing a radical transformation. The word psychotic was being used in some circles interchangeably with the word visionary, and people who hallucinated without drugs were held, at least theoretically, in high esteem. Obviously, Paul didn't see it that way, and I apologized if I'd offended him. At the same time it surprised me that he'd care.

"I have a reputation to uphold," he said.

It turned out he'd been getting bits and pieces of news from the lower forty-eight and knew, for example, about the Vietnam War, the protests, the race riots, women's liberation, and the like. Institutions were toppling everywhere. Traditions were in a state of upheaval. The whole thing had him worried, and I tried to reassure him.

"As far as I know, your reputation's intact."

"For now."

"Don't worry about it."

"No? How about what's happening to your President Nixon? He was loved once. Now look at him."

Loved seemed a strong word for what the President was, and even then, it was hard to believe Paul considered himself in the same category as a man on his ignominious way out of the White House.

"People are fickle," he said. "Times change, you don't, and what happens? All of a sudden you're a villain."

"Fame's a bitch," I said without much sympathy.

He gave me a look, and for an instant I thought I had gone too far. What did I know of impetuosity? He could squash me like an ant. But then he laughed, and the Earth, god bless her, trembled, too.

"I'm not famous, little man. I'm a legend."

WE ENDED UP spending a week together. He took me north to his logging camp, which lay in a valley between two wooded ridges. He kept Babe in a pen at the foot of the valley beside the river that drained it, and every afternoon for an hour or two the ox would dutifully lie on his side and dam up the churning water, creating a lake for the loggers' recreation. They bathed and fished, and the few who knew how swam. In winter, when the waters froze, they played hockey and curling.

Each morning we had hotcakes for breakfast. It was a ritual the men adored. Half a dozen of them would strap bacon fat to their feet and skate around the skillet, careful to avoid the batter, which was coming out of full-size concrete mixers with stainless steel flumes ten feet above their heads. I heard stories of skaters who'd fallen and been cooked up with the batter, dark-skinned men who'd been mistaken for raisins, light-skinned ones, for blanched almonds. Nothing like that happened while I was there. Paul was sensitive to the reports of cannibalism and kept careful track of the skaters. If one fell, he'd quickly pluck him up, and if there'd been a skillet burn, he'd rub it with that same bacon fat they had on their feet. And that man would be offered the day off, though none of them ever took it for fear of being accused a sissy.

After we had our fill of hotcakes, Babe would be led in and allowed to eat what was left. One morning I saw him sweep up ten stacks with a single swipe of his tongue, each stack the size of a silo. It took him less than a minute to stuff it all in his mouth, swallow it down, and bellow for more. It was a bone-shattering sound. When it came to hotcakes, the Babe was not to be denied.

"They'll be the death of him," said Paul. "But I don't have the heart to say no."

"I'm not sure he'd listen."

"He's quite reasonable about everything else. Works straight through from dawn to dusk. As many days as I ask. Never complains. Which makes it hard to deny him his one weakness. I feel caught. Too lenient if I let him eat, too strict if I don't."

"It's nice you care," I said. "But look. It's his choice. You're not responsible for what he does."

Paul looked at me as if I were crazy, and maybe I was. On the other hand, maybe I was just ahead of my time.

"Don't let him victimize you," I said.

His incredulity increased, then all at once he leaned over and cupped his hand over his mouth.

"He can't," he whispered, as though letting me in on a big secret. "He's an ox."

THE MEN IN THE CAMP worked in shifts around the clock, but as a rule Paul didn't get started until after breakfast. But once he did, he was unstoppable. I saw him log the entire side of a mountain in a single morning, strip the trees, dress them, and have them staged to be hauled out by lunch. He carried a double-bladed ax that allowed him to chop two trees at once, and when he got going, he could fell a whole stand in the time it took for the first tree to hit the ground. He was a furious worker, with a wild spirit and a love for people. In response, people loved Paul, and they came from all over to work for him.

But he had a quiet side, too, and a need for solitude. One evening the two of us took a walk over the ridge above camp and down into the next valley. The meadows were lush with lupine and Indian paintbrush. There was aspen and spruce and a lazy stream that flowed without a sound. We built a fire and gazed at the sky, which that far north dimmed but never completely darkened, so that only the brightest stars were visible. We shared our dreams. Being twenty-one, mine was to taste life. Paul's was more specific.

"I want to fall in love," he said.

I laughed, but he was serious. And wistful. And uncertain that he ever could.

To my mind he already had. "You have a vision," I told him.

"To tame nature, but with a spirit that refuses to be tamed. You do love. You love freedom. You love life."

"I want to love a man."

Timidly, his eyes sought mine. I could see how desperately his heart wanted to open. I was twenty-one and eager for experience. To put it another way, I was a rebel even against myself.

IT WAS THE first time I ever had sex with a man. Obviously, some things were beyond my capability. Afterward, we joked about it. He called me little tiger and revealed how much he had always liked little people. His parents were small, as was his older sister. At first they thought Paul had a glandular condition and took him to prominent doctors and specialists who prescribed various nostrums, all to no avail. They tried a Penobscot medicine man, who diagnosed possession by a powerful spirit and performed a daylong ceremony designed either to rid or to honor this spirit, they were never quite sure which. After that they gave up and just let the boy grow, which he did with a vengeance. By six months he required a cradle the size of a ship; by twelve he was plucking up full-grown trees and tossing them in the air like matchsticks. His parents did their best to keep him out of trouble, but he had a spirit that couldn't be harnessed. They had to move frequently, and by the time Paul reached adolescence, they'd had enough. Unwilling and unable to control him any longer, his parents abandoned him in the forests of the Upper Peninsula, a deprivation to which he attributed his craving to love and be loved. There were four Great Lakes at that time. Paul's tears made the fifth.

OUR MEETING ONE another was one of those rare instances of two people's paths happening to cross at just the right time. We came together with equal passion, equal need, and an equal degree of commitment. It was intense, satisfying, and brief. Paul told me his deepest secrets and I told him mine. Three days later we parted company, promising to see each other again as soon as possible. Twenty years passed before we did.

.   .   .

AGAIN IT WAS summer. I had recently separated from my wife. This was not my college sweetheart, the one who'd gone to New York to fight the beast and topple the patriarchy, although we had been married briefly. This was the woman I had met after law school. She was coming out of a bad relationship at the time, a burn-and-destroy affair with another woman, and was ready to try something new. I was new, and we did famously for eight years, therapy for five, and now we were trying separation. It was her idea, and I was having a lot of trouble adjusting. A friend suggested I get away, and the first place I thought of, or the first person, was Paul.

I took a plane to Wenatchee, picked up supplies and a car, then drove to Carlton. The town had grown. With the opening of the North Cascades Highway there were all sorts of new development. I saw no sign and heard no mention of Paul, and it crossed my mind that, despite his fondness for little people, this influx of commerce would not be to his liking. But I had a premonition that he'd be at that waterfall where we first met, a vague and vain idea that our lives were somehow running in parallel, that I would be on his mind as much as he was now on mine. It was a Sixties' kind of notion. Unfortunately, this was the Nineties. He was not there, and he didn't come. I waited three days, then left.

I drove back to Wenatchee, turned in the car, and took a plane to Seattle. From there I headed north, on successively smaller planes, ultimately commandeering a four-seater Piper Cherokee that dropped me in the town of Ross River, a few hundred miles south of the Arctic Circle in the Yukon. This was the vicinity of Paul's old camp, up in the Selwyn Range to the east, and here I heard mention of him, a whisper really, not much more. But a whisper was all I needed. The next day I was on my way.

It was August, and this was north. The days stretched on forever. I wandered in twilight, caught glimpses of moose and bear, fox on the run, geese in migration. I saw mountains decked in snow and a sky that shimmered with magnetism and light. But no Paul. His camp was empty and by the looks of it had been for years. The skillet that had cost old man Carnegie a year's output of steel was warped and covered with debris. The pen where Babe had slept was down, the field now overgrown with trees. I pitched my camp beside the creek he used to dam for the men and cooked myself meals of desiccated sausage and freeze-dried eggs, all the while dreaming of hotcakes swimming in maple syrup. I took day hikes, resigning myself to the fact that this past, like my marriage, was over.

Then one day in a snowfield I saw footprints. Boot shaped, waist-deep, as long and wide as a wagon. That evening I found him.

He was sitting by a lake in a talus-sloped basin above tree line, absently tossing stones the size of tires into the water. The evening chill that had me in parka and mittens didn't seem to be affecting him. He was wearing what he always wore, though not in the way he always wore it. He was unkempt, his shirttails out, his boots untied. One of the legs of his pants was torn, and his beard, which I remembered as being neatly trimmed, was scraggly and matted.

The trail passed through scree, and the sound of shifting rock announced my arrival while I was still high above the lake. He looked up and frowned, as though unhappy at being disturbed. When he recognized who it was, the frown turned to a kind of puzzlement. He could have helped me down, but instead, he waited while I descended on my own.

It was a thrill to see him again. He said the same about me. But after the first flush of excitement our conversation lapsed. He seemed listless and preoccupied. I mentioned I'd been by the old camp.

"I saw you," he said.

"You saw me? When?"

"A couple of days ago."

My blood rose. "I've been looking for you nearly two weeks."

If this bothered him, he gave no indication of it. "I haven't been in the mood for people."

"What does that mean?"

"I'm depressed."

"You? C'mon. You're a mover. A shaker. You're a dreamer. You're the opposite of depressed."

"The world is leaving me. Everything I've ever loved is gone."

Gradually it came out. The logging industry had been in a prolonged slump. Demand for timber was a fraction of what it had been. And most of the first-growth forests were gone and the livable land cleared. Paul couldn't support a camp, and one by one the boys had left. Ole the Blacksmith, Slim Mullins, Blue-Nose Parker, Batiste Joe—all the old gang were gone. And then one day Babe had died. It was the hotcakes, just as Paul had always feared.

"He had an eating disorder. That's what the vet said. And I said all right, an eating disorder, so tell me what to do. But he didn't know, he'd never seen an ox like that.

"It got to be harder and harder to control him. The smell of me mixing the batter was enough to drive him crazy. One day he broke out of his pen and rushed the kitchen. The hotcakes were still in the oven, and he swallowed the whole thing at once, oven, burners, smokestack. Everything. Stupid ox. He burned to death, from the inside out."

"That's awful."

"Saddest day of my life," said Paul.

"When did this happen?"

"A year ago. Maybe two."

"Did you have someone to talk to? Someone to help you through?"

He looked at me with woebegotten eyes. "Did. Then he died, too."

Randy was his name. They were lovers, and Paul nursed him to his dying day. Buried him deep and built a mountain on top for a gravestone. It was less than a year since he'd passed away.

"Seems like yesterday," said Paul.

"I'm so sorry."

He sighed. "I keep wondering who's going to bury me."

"You planning on dying?"

"I dream of it sometimes. Is dreaming planning? You tell me."

A couple of years before, I'd had a bout of depression that responded nicely to a short course of Prozac. Fleetingly I wondered how many truckloads of pills it would take to help Paul. I could hear the outcry from all those deprived by him of their precious drug, which made me weigh in my mind the good of the one against the good of the many, a quandary made all the more difficult by the one in this case having dedicated his whole life to the many. My brain was too weak to solve that riddle, and fortunately, Paul interrupted my attempt.

"I don't grow old the same as you," he said. "It may be a thousand years before I die. It may be never."

"Everyone dies."

"I'm as good as dead now. That's how I feel. The rivers are cut. The forests are logged. My friends are gone. Who needs me now?"

"I do," I said. "I need you."

He gave me a skeptical look. "You're being nice."

"I'm being honest. My wife left me. I know what it's like to feel unwanted and unloved."

Granted, my loss paled beside his own, but misery is misery and I needed to talk. It was all he could do to listen. His attention kept wandering, drawn inward by a self-absorption that, frankly, offended me. Talking to Paul was like talking to a pit, and finally, I gave up.

The silence of the high country took over, normally a vast and soul-inspiring event. But neither of us was getting much inspiration. Paul was hopelessly withdrawn, and I felt angry at being cheated of my fair share of attention. I suggested, in lieu of conversation, a walk. Reluctantly he agreed.

I had in mind a short stroll, something to stretch the legs and stir the blood, a constitutional. We ended up on a three-day trek to the Arctic Circle and back. Most of the time I rode on his shoulders, which he said made him feel useful. The scenery was magnificent, the land utterly uninhabited. We had snow and wind and skies the color of gemstones. I thought frequently of my wife and the early years of our relationship. I missed her. The vast and untrammeled beauty in that deserted land made my heart ache to have her back.

Paul seemed happy enough to be on the move, but when we returned, his spirits again plummeted. I stayed with him a day or two more, listening to his troubles, stifling my own, growing resentful while trying to appear otherwise. Eventually I couldn't stand it anymore.

"I have to get back," I told him.

He nodded morosely, then gave me a penetrating look. "Why did you come?"

It was the first genuine interest he had shown in me since I arrived.

"To see you," I answered.

"Why?"

I thought about it. "I had an urge," I said at length, flashing a smile. "Remember urges?"

"I do. Yes. Vividly."

He gave me a look, beseeching maybe, and then fell silent. As the silence grew, I began to feel defensive.

"I didn't come to replay the past, if that's what you're asking." I hesitated. "I'm not gay, Paul."

"Is that why you came? To tell me that?"

This irritated me. "I came because I needed a friend."

He seemed to find this amusing. "And have I been?"

"It's been a rough time for you. I understand. Yes. Of course you've been a friend."

"Of course." He made a parody of the words. "Just so you know, you haven't. Not at all. You're patronizing and self-serving. You breeze in at your whim, then you breeze out. You don't care." He made a motion with his hand of sweeping me away. "Go away, little man. Enjoy your little life and your little troubles. Your little country. Go away and do me the pleasure of not coming back."

THAT WAS '91. It was the culmination of a bad stretch of time. Two years before, I had turned forty and Sheila, my wife, forty-one. We had put off having a family because that's what our generation did, put off certain commitments in order to indulge others. We traveled. We became enlightened. We fought injustice. We didn't have children because we were children, children of the new age. And then when we were ready, we couldn't. The equipment just wasn't up to snuff. Sperm without heads, ovaries without eggs. It was pathetic. We'd grown old before we'd even grown up.

We went to doctors. Took tests, hormones, injections. Tried the turkey baster, the baking soda douche, the upside-down post-coital maneuver. We charted temperature and checked mucus, fucked on schedule and the rest of the time not at all. Were we having fun? Sure we were. And just to emphasize the point, we upped our therapy to three times a week.

And those, believe it or not, were the good times. The bad started after we visited the baby broker. Met her in an unfurnished tract home on an empty street in a white-bread suburb of Sacramento. Our hopes were high, but one look told us it was all wrong.

She was a right-to-lifer, smug and self-possessed. She marched
outside abortion clinics and hurled insults while on the side she
gave Christian guidance to unwed mothers. She had a photo album
of all the children she had placed and showed it to us like a lady
selling Tupperware. Beautiful babies with angelic faces, flawless
parents with milky complexions and award-winning smiles. She
advised up to print up a thousand leaflets and pass them out in
parking lots. Stand on street corners with placards announcing our
need. Beg for babies.

She told us, in essence, that we were to blame for our child-
lessness and if the Lord willed us to be parents, then and only then
would we be.

It just wasn't our thing.

We paid her her two hundred dollars, then went home and
puked. Two months later, Sheila moved out.

The shock of it sent me reeling, as though gravity had suddenly ceased. I cried on and off for weeks, couldn't get a purchase
on things, felt disoriented and wracked by a sense of guilt, failure,
and self-doubt. In retrospect, that had been my purpose in visiting
Paul, to restore some degree of proportion and balance to my life.
He was, if nothing else, a man with his head on his shoulders and
his feet on the ground. Mr. Dependable, the quintessential prag-
matist. Or so I thought. When he turned out to be such a downer,
when he gave me nothing, when in the end he accused me of being
a fraud, I felt betrayed.

On my return from that ill-conceived trip, I threw myself into
work, which at the time was malpractice litigation. Perhaps in re-
action to being hurt myself, first by Sheila, then Paul, I went after
those hospitals and doctors who had hurt others. That most of
these injuries were unintentional was beside the point. Errors are
errors, and in matters of law it makes no difference that all of us
are guilty. I sued on behalf of a woman who'd lost her baby at
birth, a man who'd lost an eye, a teenager with brain damage after
being struck in the head by the plaintiff, his father. We got a huge
settlement for that one, and a few months later we got a fat check
in a sexual impropriety verdict against a surgeon who'd been fon-
dling his anesthetized patients. That case made the newspapers,
and my wife, who at the time was teaching a course on sexual
harassment at the local community college, called to offer her con-

gratulations. It was a little more than a year since we had separated, an anniversary that we had diligently failed to observe. That date now safely past, we felt capable of meeting for dinner. Sheila, I have to say, was ravishing. Evidently she thought the same of me. We couldn't keep our hands to ourselves, nor our laughter, nor delight. One thing led to another, and we ended up spending the night together. Three weeks later she called to say she was pregnant.

Now we have a two-year old son. He's got the build of an ox and the temperament, alternately, of a rabbit and a mule. Lately he's been constructing tall and elaborate towers of blocks that he subsequently reduces to rubble with a kick. In other games he is equally omnipotent, digging a hole in the sandbox, for example, which he then fills with water and proclaims an ocean, before draining it completely a minute later and naming it, triumphantly, a desert.

Paul was once like that, making lakes with his footsteps, straightening rivers with a tug of his massive arms, causing tidal waves when he sneezed. A creator and a destroyer. I've been thinking of him a lot lately.

The anger and hurt I felt after that last visit lessened with time, and as sometimes happens, my feelings actually reversed themselves, so that I started to blame myself and not him for being insensitive and unsympathetic. Now, with a good marriage, a happy child, a successful job—in short, with everything going my way, I felt I could brave whatever resentment he might still harbor toward me. I wanted to make peace.

This time I called first. Got the phone number of the Ross River post office and asked the postmaster, who'd lived there his whole life, if he'd had wind of Paul. He hadn't, not in a year or two. He told me to try farther north, up around Mayo, but instead I called Carlton, where, after getting nowhere with one lackey after another, I ended up talking to the head of the Chamber of Commerce. He knew nothing of Paul, although he had heard reports, strictly off the record, of some sort of creature on the loose. A Bigfoot, the locals were saying, which he discounted as a hopelessly crass ploy by the environmentalist cabal to keep the latest ski resort from being built. Bigfoot, he explained, had been listed by some joker in the state senate as an endangered species. It was a pretext to stymie development. What had happened could have been the result of almost anything.

I asked what he was talking about.

"Oh," he said offhandedly. "A thirty-foot anchoring tower disappeared from the top of one of our mountains the other day. Reappeared the next day in the same spot, but upside down."

That sounded promising. I asked if he had any theories.

"It's been a heavy winter." There was a pause on the line. "You one of those ecology nuts?"

"I'm looking for my friend," I assured him. "It's strictly personal."

There was another pause, as if he were calculating whether my actually finding this person would be to the Chamber's benefit or not. Apparently he decided it would be, because he told me by all means to come up and have a look.

That was in May. In July I took a week off work, promising Sheila to be careful and my son Jonah to bring back a present, and headed to the mountains west of Carlton and north of Lake Chelan.

It had, indeed, been a heavy winter. There was still snow across many of the trails, and the streams and rivers were running full. Penstemon and buttercup bloomed in the meadows, and the young trees looked plump and green. I made camp the first night near the base of a burnt-out pine and the next day hiked to the waterfall. There was a level spot about fifty feet from the water's edge where I pitched my tent, laid out my bedroll, and promptly fell asleep.

When I woke, Paul was standing in the pool. He was facing upstream, so that I saw him in profile. It was truly a shock.

His arms, once so massive, were the size of twigs; his legs, barely as big as saplings. His beard was motheaten; his skin, blotchy and pale. He splashed some water on his naked chest and neck, then cupped his hands to get a drink from the waterfall itself. But he lacked the strength, so that the force of the water kept pushing his arms away. He tried again and again, and then for a minute he seemed to forget what he was doing. When he remembered, he sank to his knees and drank directly from the pool. Then he crawled onto the shore, at which point he caught sight of me.

His eyes narrowed, then he quickly tried to cover his naked

body with his hands. Just as quickly, I turned away to give him his privacy.

When he had dressed, he told me I could turn around. I apologized for taking him by surprise.

He gave a little shrug. "It's all right. I expect I'm quite a sight."

I found myself nodding. "What's happened to you?"

"Clothes don't fit too well, do they?" Grinning, he hitched up his suspenders. "Good thing I don't wear a belt. My pants would be down by my ankles. Then where would I be?"

It was a feeble attempt at humor and took more breath than he had. Several seconds passed before he got it back.

"What was I saying?"

"Your pants . . ."

He glanced at them and brushed away some dirt. Then he looked at me. "I'm dying."

"That's ridiculous. You can't die."

He pointed to a purple lump on his arm as big as a grapefruit. And another under his beard. "They're all over. It's how my lover died. Now I will, too."

This was unacceptable to me. "Have you been to doctors? Have you seen anyone for this?"

"What would they do? Give me medicine? I know about that. It's in short supply as it is. And besides, I don't mind dying. I've been alive long enough. Longer than I care to be."

"Legends don't die," I said, the words catching in my throat.

He smiled, a look less of the sun as it used to be and more now of the moon. A reflective smile. A sad, sweet one.

"It's too cold for me up north. That's why I'm here. Stay with me. Will you?"

I couldn't refuse. And am forever glad that I didn't. I stayed with him more than a week, almost two, sending word to Sheila through a passing hiker that I'd be delayed. After a few days, we moved to the high country, which was deserted. Paul was forgetful but otherwise remarkably cheerful, an effect, I suppose, of the illness, although I couldn't ignore the other truth, which was that he had lived his life and now was ready, even eager, to die. He was also weak as a kitten, and one morning he fell while we were traversing a snowfield and ended up sliding down the icy slope into a glacial lake at the bottom. He laughed at his ineptitude, but the next day he developed a cough. The following morning it was worse, and by that evening he could barely breathe.

We were in the drainage of a semicircle of tall peaks, at the foot of which was a meadow fed by snowmelt. He dragged himself there, then collapsed, faceup, eyes closed. Between labored breaths, he asked to be cremated, his ashes scattered. He whispered something else I didn't hear, then fell silent.

I made a pallet by his head and to pass the time told him stories, tales of Paul Bunyan and Babe, the Blue Ox, how they plowed the land into valleys and rivers, moved the mountains and logged the forests. I told him the story of the Blue Winter, and the popcorn blizzard that froze the cattle. And the one about the killer bees, and the carving of Puget Sound. Some time later he opened his eyes.

"I *have* loved," he said, with emphasis on the have, as though he were debating some point, or answering a question. And then he died.

It took me two days to gather enough wood for the pyre. The blaze lit the sky. And his ashes, when they cooled, made such a pile that to scatter them took two days and a wind out of Heaven, and as far away as Spokane the sky turned dark and people spoke of a new volcano, though no one ever found a trace.

PLUMAGE FROM PEGASUS:
Have Gun, Will Edit

PAUL DI FILIPPO

"He writes like I used to. . . . I should have him assassinated before it's too late."
—Larry Niven, blurbing Stephen Baxter's Raft

"Do I sound a little envious? Well, let's say that if I was fifty years younger I might have considered terminating Mr. Savage with extreme prejudice."
—Arthur C. Clarke, introducing Marshall Savage's
The Millennial Project

I STUDIED THE ADDRESS ON THE BUSINESS CARD ONCE AGAIN, then compared it to the polished brass numbers and letters on the heavy oak door. They matched. I was impressed. The door belonged to a mansion worth at least a cool three million, or my name wasn't—well; you don't really need to know my name. Anonymity is a survival trait in my line of work.

The mansion was surrounded by two acres of manicured lawn and gardens straight out of *Architectural Digest*. A circular gravel drive carved out a grassy island, where a chrome fountain in the shape of a retro 'Forties' rocket burbled gently. The whole estate was set in a fenced neighborhood where the security guards earned more than your average Silicon Valley programmer, and made the agents of Mossad look like Greenpeace wimps. After I had flashed my guy's business card back at the gates and claimed an appointment, I had been expertly frisked. I wasn't carrying a piece, since I didn't need one—yet. But a call to my prospective client had still been necessary to let me pass. (And you don't need to know his name, either.)

But he had done all right for himself, my client-to-be. Not a
bad place to end up in his senior years, especially for a guy who
had started out writing for the pulps at a penny a word fifty years
ago. He was the biggest customer I had landed so far, after two
years in this new racket. I guessed maybe my reputation for delivering the goods was really starting to spread. The fact that my
handiwork had indirectly garnered two Hugos, six Nebulas, a Tip-
tree, a Sturgeon, and a Campbell award for my various clients
didn't hurt either.

Hell, maybe if this kept up, I'd spend my own retirement days
in a place like this.

I had a better chance at it than my victims anyhow. Their
estates measured six feet by two by one and were deep underground, with grass doormats and granite nameplates.

Now I rang the bell. It took only ten seconds for the door to
be opened by the maid.

"Your boss is expecting me. . . ."

She nodded and led me through the antique-laden house.

My client's study was paneled in lumber that had once
sprouted out of the soil of the rain forest. Now the shelves of
exotic woods that had formerly supported monkeys and macaws
held arrays of the writer's awards and published volumes. It looked
like a comfortable bulwark against death and eternity, and would
have fooled anyone but me. I knew how easy it was to render such
shoddy defenses meaningless.

The writer himself was nothing much to look at: a scrawny,
self-important, balding schlump dressed in a Hermès-patterned
silk robe—at two o'clock in the afternoon, for Christ's sake! He
sat behind a big desk whose top bore a neat stack of papers and a
lot of computer hardware. A single unmarked manila envelope
caught my eye.

I figured the setup was supposed to make me go all wiggly
and deferential, like. But any respect and awe I had once held for
writers had been wiped out by my very first client. At our first
meeting, I had caught the jerk unawares while he was masturbating
as he reread his best reviews. Then it turned out he wanted me to
frag some pitiful *fan* who was bugging him.

This one must have picked up my cynical vibes, because he
got real nervous. He tried to cover it up by turning his back to

me, moving to a wet bar and offering me a drink.

"What will you have, Mister, uh—"

"Just some Perrier with lime," I said coolly. "I don't drink hard stuff while I'm working. Unlike some types I could name."

He decided to take offense at this, focusing a weak glare on me. "Listen here, Mister, what do you know about the stresses and rigors of a writing lifestyle? So what if I keep a bar in my study? I still turn out the pages. Two solo novels and a collaboration last year alone."

I took my drink from him and sipped it before replying, to keep him nervous. "I know plenty. Believe me, I've seen it all. And as for turning out the pages—well, it doesn't seem to be quite enough nowadays, does it? Otherwise, you wouldn't have called on me."

He sank despondently into an overstuffed leather chair next to his desk and wiped a clammy hand across his brow. "It's true. The competition is too fierce these days. I just can't come up with ideas fast enough. Not like I used to in my prime. It's bad enough worrying about the other survivors of my generation pushing me aside. But now there's all these young kids moving up through the ranks, nipping at my heels, invading my niche. I can't take anything for granted anymore. Why, even the critics are against me! I used to have them all on my side. But now some of them are even calling me a die—die—die—"

He couldn't say the D-word, but I could. "Dinosaur?"

He collapsed like a neophyte's shoddy plot. "Yes. That's it."

Now that I had put him in his place, I felt a little sorry for the poor little guy. It wasn't easy living past your prime, no matter what your line of work. How would I feel when I was finally outgunned? And he *was* the client, after all, the one footing the bill. So I decided to toss him a bone.

"Well, you shouldn't feel so bad, you know. It's not just you old guys who employ me. A lot of the young turks have hired me too. At least the ones who've gotten big enough advances to afford me. Usually they've got to sell at least a trilogy before I'll consider them. But it's even more savage down on their level. They're just getting started, right, and they don't care what it takes. They'd knife their own grannies just for a short-story slot in one of the prozines. Anyhow, I'm sorry if I was a little rough on you. But you can't go treating me like your agent or editor. I'm an independent contractor, a freelancer. Just like you."

In a pig's eye, I thought to myself. But what the hell, a little flattery never hurt.

Hearing this, he perked up a little. "A freelancer. Why, of course. Quite understandable. Why, I suppose you people even have your own trade organization something like the Ess-Eff-Double-You-Ay?"

"Not quite so vicious. But yes, we do."

Now he was positively beaming, as if we were peers. "Very good. Let's discuss terms then. Here's the, ah, competition I would like to see, ah, removed from the marketplace."

He handed me a glossy black-and-white publicity photo.

It showed a woman.

I recognized her face from last month's *Locus*. Seven-figure advance for her next two books. Twenty-city tour for her current novel, which sat smack dab in the middle of all the bestseller lists. A lot of hype about Spielberg being interested in the movie rights, with Schwarzenegger to star.

A little butterfly of queasiness fluttered in my gut. I hadn't known the victim was going to be a woman. If I accepted this assignment, she'd be the first female writer I had taken out.

But then the butterfly drowned in my stomach acids. A job was a job. I couldn't afford to have any scruples in this line of work. It was a mean, nasty arena, and I had chosen it. If only the Feds hadn't legalized drug sales, I'd still be shaking down cheating pushers for the Mob. That was sweet and easy, compared to this writing business.

I felt cold and disgusted and rotten all at once. The least I could do to make myself feel better was to force my client to share it, rub his nose in reality a little, rattle his cage and shake his comfortable tree.

"So," I pretended to misunderstand, "you figure breaking her hands will take her out of action long enough for you to catch up?"

He squirmed. "Well, I had something more permanent in mind . . ."

"Oh, I get it. You want me to whack her, ice her, cut her off at the knees. A little simple wetwork. No problem. You want it to

look like an accident, a suicide, or random violence? 1
extra, I can even burn her house down after I do it, or
suffer a little beforehand."

He tossed up his hands in a warding-off motion. I thi   was
the part about burning the house down that got to him more than
the torture stuff.

"No details!" he shouted. "No details! I just want it done!"

"Funny. I thought details were kinda your stock-in-trade . . ."

He didn't reply but just grabbed the envelope off the desk and
shoved it at me. I could tell by the thickness that it was something
a lot more valuable than a manuscript inside. I didn't bother to
count it. If it wasn't the amount I had stipulated, the job just
wouldn't get done.

I turned to leave, but couldn't resist one more parting dig.

"Hey, you know what the Golden Age of Ess Eff is nowadays,
right?"

The writer's face was the color of acid-free bond. I foresaw
some heavy drinking after I left. He forced his attention away from
his thoughts and back to me.

"No. What?"

"Dead."

Forget Luck

KATE WILHELM

For more than thirty years, Kate Wilhelm has been one of the guiding forces in science fiction, both through her own stories and by virtue of the many writing workshops she leads (including the famous Clarion workshop in Michigan, which she helped found). For the past decade or so, most of her fiction has been mysteries and suspense novels, including the popular Barbara Holloway courtroom thrillers and her acclaimed novel The Good Children. *Fortunately, she still turns out an occasional SF story, as you can see.*

TONY MANETTI HAD NOT BEEN ASSIGNED TO COVER THE COLLO-quium at Michigan State, but the day before it was to start, his editor had a family crisis. Tony would have to go. A suite was already reserved in the magazine's name at the Holiday Inn; a rental car would be waiting at the Lansing airport.

Tony had called Georgina twice, leaving the message that meant she was to return the call when her husband was not around, but she had not called back. Already on her way from Berkeley, he decided. Of course, she thought Harry would be covering the conference, and accordingly had not been in touch with Tony. Five nights, he kept thinking, five nights, and days, of course.

When he checked in at the motel, Georgina had not yet registered. He paid scant attention to the academic papers the desk clerk handed him; the speakers would all make certain *Academic Currents* received a copy of their papers. He checked the schedule. That evening, Saturday, there would be opening ceremonies, then people would drift away to eat and drink. On Sunday there would be a brunch, several luncheons, teas, more eating and drinking, and on Monday the attendees would start lecturing one another. He planned to miss it all. He could read the papers any time, and if anything interesting happened, someone would tell him all about it. He planned to be in upper Michigan with the gorgeous Georgina.

She had not checked in yet when he came back down, after leaving his gear in his suite. He went to the bar, crowded with academics, ordered a gin and tonic, and looked for a place to sit where he could keep an eye on the lobby.

Someone said, "Ah, Peter, good to see you again." A heavyset bald man was beckoning to him.

"Dr. Bressler," Tony said. "How are you?" He looked past him toward the front desk where people were checking in in a continuous flow.

"Very well, Peter. Here, take a seat."

"It's Tony. Tony Manetti." Bressler had been his teacher for a term at Columbia; Tony had seen him twice, once in the hall and once in class, and every time they met at a conference, Bressler called him Peter.

"Yes, of course. You're the FBI fellow."

"No sir. I work for *Academic Currents*, the magazine." A new group had replaced the old; she was not among them.

"Of course. Of course. Peter, you're just the sort of fellow I've been looking for, someone with your training."

Bressler was in his sixties, a contender for the Nobel any year now for his past work in genetics, and he was more than a little crazy, Tony had decided six years ago in his class. A redhead appeared. He strained to see. Wrong redhead.

". . . a bit of a problem getting blood . . ."

He thought of her legs, a dancer's long legs.

". . . can't seem to get even a drop. One can't very well simply ask for it, you see."

He had been to the upper peninsula once in late summer; it had been misty and cool, romantic, with a lot of shadowy forest.

". . . have to think they're onto me. I simply can't account for it in any other way. Four accidents in the last two years, and some of my finest graduate students . . ."

Admit it, he would say, your marriage is a sham. I can move

out to the West Coast, he would say. I don't have to stay in Chicago; I can work out of anywhere.

". . . really substantiates my theory, you see, but it also poses a severe problem."

Tony had hardly touched his gin and tonic; it was simply something to do while he waited. He tasted it and put it down again. Bressler was gazing off into space, frowning.

And then she appeared, clinging to the arm of Melvin Witcome, smiling up at him the same way she sometimes had smiled up at Tony. Melvin Witcome was some kind of special course coordinator for the Big Ten, a man of power and influence; not yet forty, independently wealthy, handsome, suave, Phi Beta Kappa, with a doctorate in charm or something, he was everything Tony was not. He watched Witcome sign the registration, watched him and Georgina take their computer keys, watched them point out their bags to a bellboy, then board the elevator together. He was not aware that he had stood up until he heard Bressler's voice.

"I don't mean to imply there's any immediate danger. Sit down, Peter."

He sat down and gulped some of his drink. It was a mistake; they simply happened to arrive at the same time; they were old friends; she had not expected Tony to be there. He finished his drink. She had not expected him to be there.

"You're not going to the beastly opening ceremony, are you?" Bressler placed his hand on Tony's arm. "Let's go have some dinner instead. I want to pick your brain. You're a godsend, Peter. I was desperate for guidance, and you appeared. A godsend."

He had talked to the class about angels, Tony remembered then. Something about angels. Tony had tuned out. He had tuned out most of that year, in fact.

Bressler's voice had grown a bit shrill. "No one knows how humiliating it is to be considered a weirdo. A weirdo," he repeated with bitter satisfaction. "Simply because you have come upon a truth that others are not yet willing to accept or even to see."

"Angels," Tony said.

"Excellent, Peter! Ten years or more and you remember. But, of course, they prefer to see angels. Come on, let's go have some dinner."

Tony stood up. It had been six years ago; he didn't bother to make the correction. When they emerged from the dim bar, a mirage of pine forest danced in the street before him. A taxi drove through the dripping trees, and Bressler waved it over.

They had flaming cheese, and retsina with lamb kebabs, and ouzo with honey-doused walnut cakes. Bressler talked without letup throughout. Tony listened sporadically, brooding about the gorgeous Georgina.

"Of course, we all knew you were very special," Bressler said, then sipped his Greek coffee. "Your job is proof enough. I know people who would kill for your job. Rumor was you saved Bush's life or something, wounded in the line of duty, permanently disabled and quite justly rewarded, all that."

What really had happened was that when he was twenty-two, with a bachelor of science degree, he had applied to the FBI, along with his best friend, Doug Hastings, and to their surprise, they both had been accepted. A year later, his first real assignment had taken him and a senior agent out to do a routine background security check. A nothing assignment, until a fourteen-year-old boy with no hair had used him for target practice. Tony would have been quite seriously wounded, even shot dead, if he had not bent over at precisely the right moment to free his pants leg from the top of his sock. As it was he had been shot in the upper arm. Then, two weeks after being declared fit to resume a life of fighting evil, he had been shot again. The second time had been from the rear, and the only people behind him that day had been two other special agents and their supervisor, a unit chief.

He rather liked the version Bressler was voicing, and, as he had been enjoined never to reveal the truth of the matter, he remained silent, impassive, inscrutable. And, he was afraid, ridiculous. The second time he had been approaching a Buick in a crouch, and when he realized it was empty, he had stood up and started to turn to say the coast was clear. The bullet had gone through his arm instead of his head. The other arm this time.

"Must be like being a priest, once a priest always a priest. One doesn't forget training like that. Once FBI, always FBI; isn't that right?"

Tony finished his ouzo. The last time he had seen his former best friend Doug Hastings, Doug had said, "Keep away from me, jinx. Orders. Okay? No hard feelings?"

"Well, no one expects you to talk about it," Bressler said. He waved his tiny cup for more Greek coffee. "But you have had the training. Put your mind to it, Peter. How can I get blood samples from those people?"

Cautiously Tony said, "I need to think about it."

"Of course, of course. When we go back to the hotel I'll hand you the reports, my notes, everything. It was providence that sent you to me, Peter. I had a feeling. Are you ready?"

What he would do, Tony had declared, was gather up the papers already in hand, check out in the morning, and beat it.

BACK IN HIS suite, he gazed morosely at the stack of papers; the desk clerk had handed him another pile, and Bressler had added his own bulging package. His head was aching with a dull distant surflike monotony; he had had more to drink that evening than he generally consumed in a year, and he was not at all ready for sleep. When he found himself wondering if Georgina and Witcome were in a suite like his, with a couch like his, the same coffee table, the same king-sized bed, he began to shuffle papers. Not Bressler's— he put them aside and looked over a few others. But bits and pieces of what Bressler had said floated back to his mind, not in any rational coherent way, in phrases. He suspected that Bressler had talked in disconnected phrases.

Then, because it was his job to condense ten, fifteen, twenty pages of academic papers to a paragraph that would make sense to a reader, even if only temporarily, he found he was doing the same thing to this evening with Bressler.

Genes were the secret masters of the universe. Tony blinked, but he was certain Bressler had said that. Right. Genes ruled the body they inhabited, communicated with it; they ordered black hair, or red. And silky skin, and eyes like the deepest ocean . . . He shook himself. Genes were immortal, unless the carries died without progeny. They decided issues like intelligence, allergies, homosexuality . . .

He closed his eyes, trying to remember where the angels came in. Sixty-eight percent of those polled believed in angels; 45 percent believed in their own personal guardian angel. That was it. For guardian angel read genes.

Everyone knew someone or about someone who had had a miraculous escape from certain death or terrible injury. The sole survivor of an airplane crash; the infant who didn't freeze when abandoned in zero temperature; a highway accident that should have been fatal . . .

"Forget angels, forget a sixth sense, an intuitive avoidance of danger. Think alleles, the right combination of alleles. Genes are the secret masters and a particular combination of alleles, a particular gene, or more than one possibly, comes into being occasionally to rule all the others, for what purpose we can only guess. These very special genes can cause other genes to do their bidding, cause a change in metabolism that keeps a freezing infant from dying, regulate heart and lung functions to allow a drowned boy to be revived, alter every tissue in the human body and permit it to walk away from an impact that should have killed it outright . . ."

Tony yawned. There had been more, three hours' worth more, but he had condensed, combined, edited, and had made it coherent. He wished he had some aspirin. What he had done was compact a yard of garbage into a small neat package, but it was still the same garbage. He took a shower and went to bed, and felt lost in an acre of hard, cold, polyester loneliness.

HE WAS UP and dressed by seven-thirty, determined to be gone before West Coast people, Berkeley people, before Georgina was awake. He ordered breakfast, and while waiting for it he stuffed papers into his briefcase, leaving Bressler's stack to be turned in at the front desk, to be put in the man's message box, or thrown away, or whatever. When those were the only reading material remaining, he glanced at them.

The subject reports were on top. Everett Simes, at eleven, had been found in a snowdrift, body temperature sixty-three. He had survived with no ill effects. At nineteen he had fallen off a two-hundred-foot cliff and had walked away from the accident, no ill effects. Vera Tanger had survived an explosion in a restaurant that had killed everyone else there; she had survived having her stalled car totaled by a train. Carl Waley, two miraculous survivals. Beverly Wang, two. Stanley R. Griggs, two.

He replaced the papers in the folder when there was a knock on his door. His breakfast had arrived, and looming over the cart was Dr. Bressler, nearly pushing it himself in his eagerness to gain entrance.

"Peter, I'm so glad you're up and about already. Did you read my material?"

Tony motioned to the waiter to unload the cart by the window, signed the charge, and waved him away without speaking.

"Do you have another cup lurking under there?" Bressler asked. The waiter produced another cup and saucer. "And you might bring another pot of coffee," Bressler said. He settled down at the window table and began to lift lids off dishes.

They shared the breakfast; Bressler ate only the finger food since he had no silverware. Sausage was finger food. He talked constantly.

"The subjects I'm after all had at least two escapes," he said. "Often three or even four. But two is sufficient. I excluded those with only one reported escape. One could be considered coincidence, but two, three, four? Forget coincidence. No one knows how many possible subjects are out there; not all accidents get reported, of course. I settled for five who live close enough to New York to make it possible, I thought, to extract a sample from them. Hair follicles, saliva, blood, skin scrapings. You know, you're a scientist. But four times in the past two years the graduate students I sent out had accidents of their own. One lost the hair brush he had stolen when he was mugged. Another was chased away by a ferocious dog; he fell and broke his leg trying to elude the beast. One never could get near the subject; she was as wary as a Mata Hari." He smiled at his little rhyme. "My students are showing some reluctance concerning further attempts."

Tony emptied the coffee pot into his cup.

Bressler looked at it in disappointment. "Have you come up with an idea?" he asked then.

"Ask outright for a sample," Tony said. "Offer to pay five bucks a spit. Align yourself with a doctor, a clinic or something like that, and offer free checkups. Find their dentists and pay him to collect a sample. Hire a mugger and have him do a scraping before he snatches the loot. Hire a flock of guys in white coats to swarm over an apartment building, or an office, or wherever the hell the subject is, and say you're checking for an outbreak of plague. Hire some prostitutes, male and female, to seduce them one and all." There was a tap on the door; he went to open it. "There must be a thousand ways you can get what you're after." He admitted the waiter with another pot of coffee.

When they were alone again, Bressler was beaming. "See, that's what I meant. A man with certain training. I tried some of those ideas, of course, but some are quite ingenious. I couldn't do anything that even suggested harm, naturally. Heaven alone knows what the repercussions would be if the genes thought they were under attack. It's bad enough that they know they have been discovered." He poured coffee for them both.

Tony gazed at him in disbelief. "The genes know you're after them," he said after a moment. "The genes are taking defensive measures."

"No doubt about it. They know." He put one finger in his coffee, then used the moistened tip to pick up toast crumbs, which he ate.

"What will you do with the data if you get it?" Tony asked.

Bressler looked very blank. "Do? You mean like the agriculture bioengineers? Breeding potatoes with enough poison to kill off the potato bugs? Strawberries that grow and bear fruits in subfreezing temperature? I don't plan to *do* anything except publish, of course. Those genes have absolutely nothing to fear from me, Peter."

"I understand," Tony said. He looked at his watch and stood up. "Gosh, I've got to run." He picked up Bressler's papers to hand back to the man.

"Keep them, Peter. Keep them. I have copies. I know you haven't had time to think this through. Read them, then get back to me. Will you do that?"

"Sure," Tony said. "I'll get back to you."

BY THE TIME he had checked out and was on the road, he was grinning broadly. Bressler wouldn't get in touch with him, he thought. He wouldn't know who to get in touch with, just Peter somebody. His grin faded as he realized he had no destination. Not the upper peninsula, those cool misty dark romantic forests.

Not alone. He had no one he had to go back home to; no one expected him in the office ever. He drifted in, drifted out; eventually he would lug in the ton of scholarly papers he had collected, turn in his column on the symposium, and be free until the next one. He remembered Bressler's words: people would kill for his job.

He was exactly what the job description stated: special assistant editor responsible for a column devoted to academic symposia, colloquia, conferences, meetings of all sorts that involved two or more university-level representatives of two or more universities, wherever such a meeting was being held—Paris, Hong Kong, Boston, Rio . . .

Sometimes he wondered how high the supervisor who had shot him had risen, or if he had been tossed overboard. Tony had never doubted that it was an accident, but a trigger-happy unit chief was not a good idea. He knew it had been the supervisor if only because neither of the other two agents had been even chided for carelessness. Sometimes he wondered how the agency had managed to get him, Tony, into Columbia on such short notice, and see that he got a master's, and then this plum of a job. It was understood that the job required at least a master's degree.

Sometimes, more ominously, he wondered if one day they would reel him in and demand . . . He never could finish the thought. Demand what?

Signs had been warning him that if he wanted to go to Detroit, to get in the right lane. He eased into the left lane.

THAT NIGHT HE sat in a screened porch on a pseudorustic cabin and watched the sun set across Lake Michigan. Mosquitoes worked on the screens with chainsaws trying to get in. He had spent all day driving aimlessly, talking himself out of the notion of Georgina. She was too old for him, at least forty to his thirty-one. He had been flattered that an older woman had found him attractive. She had been grateful when he mentioned her various papers at various conferences, and had in fact helped him write her notices. Her return rate for his calls had been no more than one out of six, but, she had explained, her husband was so jealous, and always there.

Then, to escape the reality of love lost, he had turned to the fantasy of master genes ruling the universe. Pretend, he had told himself, pretend it's true, that life-saving intuition, coincidence, messages from the collective unconscious, good luck, guardian angels can all be attributed to a single source, and that source is genetic. Then what? He knew, from the various conferences he had attended, that the genotyping success rate was accelerating at a pace that astounded even those participating in it. So, he had continued, pretend they find such a master gene, isolate it, then what? The answer had come with surprising swiftness. Breed a master race, supermen.

He grinned at the idea, as he watched the last cerise band in the sky darken. When it merged into inky black, he went inside his cabin and regarded with some fondness the bulky pile of Bressler papers. He began to read through them.

Bressler had a list of thirty or forty possible subjects, each one with an impressively complete dossier. He had done his homework. They were scattered throughout the states; the five he had targeted were all within a hundred miles of Manhattan. Every subject had escaped death at least twice; all the escapes had been reported in various newspapers, which were referenced in footnotes.

Tony scanned the dossiers briefly, then went to the summaries. Bressler had anticipated the few questions Tony had: none of the parents showed any of the survival traits of their offspring. A higher than normal percentage of the subjects were single children of their biological parents, although there were stepbrothers and sisters. Few of the subjects showed any other unusual traits; they were a good cross-section of the population, some very bright, some dim, laborers, professionals, technicians . . . The one thing they all had in common, it appeared, was the ability to survive situations that should have killed them. And five of them, at least, were too elusive to catch and sample.

He felt almost sad when he closed the folder. Poor old guy, spending the past six years or more on this. He remembered something Bressler had said in the restaurant: "How many more do you suppose there are? We'll never know because no one keeps track of those who don't board the airplane that crashes into the ocean. The ones who stay home the day the mad bomber wipes out the office building. The ones who take a different route and miss the twenty-car pile-up and fireball. The ones who . . . But you get my point. We can't know about any of them."

The ones who bend down to straighten out a pants leg and don't get shot through the heart, Tony thought suddenly. *The ones who stand up and turn around and don't get shot in the head,*

Oh, boy! he thought then. *Folie à deux!* He went out on the porch and gazed at the lake where uneasy moonlight shimmered. After a moment he stripped, wrapped a towel around his waist, and went out for a swim. The water was shockingly cold. He could demonstrate to Bressler just how nutty his theory was, he thought, swimming; all he had to do was keep going toward Wisconsin until cold and fatigue sank him like a stone. Another time, he decided, turning back to shore.

In bed, every muscle relaxed to a puddinglike consistency, he wondered what he would have done if Bressler had asked for a sample of his blood. His entire body twitched and he plummeted into sleep.

The next morning, he found himself driving back to East Lansing. He listened to talk radio for a while, then sang harmony with Siegfried on tape and tried to ignore the question: Why? He didn't know why he was going back.

There was no vacancy at the Holiday Inn. The desk clerk kindly advised him to go to the Kellogg Center where someone would see that he got housing.

He never had driven through the campus before; it appeared to have been designed as a maze, with every turn taking him back and forth across the same brown river again and again. The grounds, the broad walks, the streets, the expanses of manicured lawn were almost entirely deserted and eerily silent. When he approached the botanical gardens for the third time, luck intervened in his wanderings; he spotted Dr. Bressler strolling with another man, both facing away from him. He parked, opened his door to go after Bressler, hand back the package, be done with it. Then he came to a stop, half crouched in his movement to leave the car. The men had turned toward him briefly, and the second man was his old long-lost pal, Doug Hastings. They walked to a greenhouse, away from him. He drew back inside the car.

He drove again, this time to Grand River, the main street in East Lansing. He turned toward Lansing. Without considering why he was doing this, he stopped at a shopping complex that covered acres and acres, miles maybe, and took the Bressler papers into an office supply warehouse store where he used a self-service copy machine and made copies of everything. He bought a big padded envelope and addressed it to himself, in care of his mother in Stroudsburg, Pennsylvania, put his copies inside, and mailed it at a post office in the sprawling mall. Then, finished, he returned to the Michigan State campus, and this time he found the Kellogg Center building on the first try.

Kellogg Center was the heart of the conference; here the academics met and talked, ate lunch, many of them had rooms, and the conference staff people manned a table with receptionist, programs, name tags, and general information. In the lobby Tony chatted with several people, was asked to wait a second while someone dashed off to get him a copy of a presentation paper; someone else handed him another folder. He was waiting for either Doug Hastings or Dr. Bressler, whoever came first.

Someone thrust another folder at him. He took it and let a woman draw him toward a small alcove; then he saw Bressler enter, followed seconds later by Doug. He turned his attention to the woman whose hand was heavy on his arm. "Will you attend our session this afternoon?" she was asking. "It's at three."

"Oh, Peter!" Bressler called out, and came lumbering across the hallway toward him. Doug Hastings turned to the reception table and began to examine the schedule.

The woman looked bewildered as Bressler reached them and took Tony's other arm, dragged him away. "Peter, do you still have my material? I thought you left already. They said you checked out."

Tony was carrying several folders by then, and a manila envelope, as well as his bulging briefcase. "Sure, it's in here somewhere," he said. He opened his briefcase on a small table, added the new papers to the others, and drew out Bressler's package. "I'll get to it in the next couple of weeks."

"No, no," Bressler said hastily, snatching the package, which he held against his chest with both hands. "That's all right, Peter. All that material to read. You don't need to add to it." He backed up a step or two, turned, and hurried away.

Tony was closing his briefcase again when he heard Doug's

voice very close to his ear. "Well, I'll be damned if it isn't Tony Manetti!"

Doug grasped his shoulders and swung him around, examined his face, then wrapped him in a bear hug. "My God, how long's it been? Eight, nine years? Hey, how you been doing? What's going on? Looks like you're collecting bets or something." Talking, he drew Tony toward the front entrance, away from the others milling about. "How about a cup of java? Some place less crowded. Hey, remember when we used to duck out of class for a beer? Those were the days, weren't they?"

They never had gone out for a beer together; Tony hadn't been a drinker then any more than he was now. "You an academic?" he asked on the sidewalk.

"No way. Assignment. Listened to a bunch of guys and gals explain the economic importance of joint space exploration. Whew! Heavy going."

For the next hour, in a coffee shop, Doug talked about his life, and asked questions; talked about the past, and asked questions; talked about traveling, and asked questions.

"You mean you get their papers and don't go to the talks? What a racket! Let's see what you've got."

Tony handed over his briefcase, and watched Doug go through the contents.

"You're really going to read all that stuff? Read it here?"

"Not a word. They'd want to talk to me about it if they thought I'd read the material. I save it for home."

"You know, I thought that was you the other night, going out with a big bald guy?"

Tony laughed. "Old Bressler. He's into angels. Spent too much time looking in an electron microscope or something, I guess." He added sadly, "He gave me some stuff to take home and then grabbed it back. Around the bend, poor old guy."

Later, answering another question slipped into a monologue, he told Doug that he had had a heavy date Sunday and Sunday night, and talked dreamily about a moonlight swim.

Doug leered. "Girl on every campus, I bet." Soon afterward he glanced at his watch and groaned. "This job ain't what I thought it'd be," he said. "You going back?"

"Just to pick up my car. I've got what I need."

They walked back to the Kellogg Center, where Tony got into the rental car, waved to Doug, and took off. He worked at putting the pieces together on the way to Lansing Airport. They must not want Bressler to publish a word about what he was up to. And Doug would report that there was no reason to reel in Tony, who didn't suspect a thing.

At the airport, he turned in the car, went to the ticket desk to change his reservation, and sat down to wait for his flight back to Chicago.

They probably didn't believe a word of it, he mused, and yet, what if? They would watch and wait, let the genius work it out if he could. But they would be there if he did. Right.

He was remembering incidents from his nearly forgotten childhood. At seven he and his stepbrother had played in the barn loft, and he had fallen out the highest window, gotten up, and walked away. Neither ever mentioned it to anyone; they had been forbidden to play up there. At twelve he and two other kids had been in a canoe on the Delaware River when a storm roared in like a rocket ship. The canoe had been hit by lightning, two kids had died, but he had swum to shore; he had not told anyone he had been there, since no one would have believed him anyway.

Now what? he wondered. Visit his mother, of course, and read all the Bressler material. After that was a blank, but that was all right. When the time came he would know what to do. He felt curiously free and happy, considering that he was simply following orders, was little more than a slave.

Quinn's Way

DALE BAILEY

One of the most lyrical—and most prolific—new voices in the field, Dale Bailey has contributed two or three new stories to our pages in each of the past half-dozen years. He lives in Tennessee, where he teaches at the University of Tennessee, but he hails from West Virginia and notes that he drew inspiration for this story from the tales his father told of life in the town of Princeton during the depression.

JEMMY E. USED TO SAY THAT SAULS RUN WAS SO SMALL THAT IF you farted on the east side of town, they'd be talking about it on the west side before the stink even died. By the time I was twelve years old, I knew this to be a lie.

These days it has become fashionable for folks to claim they have been abused: physically, mentally, sexually, you name it, I've seen it all and litigated most of it. But in those days—the good old days, a few of the treasured relics I call friends like to term them—no one claimed anything of the sort, under any circumstances. Ever. Which is not to say that it didn't exist—or that most people weren't aware of it, either. Such atrocities have always been more common than most folks like to think about, and good people everywhere have mastered the art of not seeing what's plain before their eyes, and maybe that's okay too. In my bleaker moments, I've often thought that our illusions alone—our cherished, beloved illusions—enable us to wake up each morning without stuffing the barrel of a revolver in our collective mouths.

But such philosophical abstractions don't help much when you're twelve years old and in almost constant pain—physical or mental, or both—more often than you want to think about. By the time I was twelve, I knew that the town of Sauls Run stank, literally (of the coal slag forever smoldering in the hills above town) and figuratively (we'll get to that). I knew also that the stink was a miasma more oppressive than any mere intestinal gas. And I had begun dimly and with horror to perceive that it just might not be limited to Sauls Run; it might be present everywhere. But one thing I knew and knew for certain: Jemmy E. had it wrong when he said that Sauls Run was so small that everybody in town was sure to gossip about the latest stink. The truth was that nobody in town would say a word about the things that really stank in Sauls Run, West Virginia.

But we both knew that everyone could smell them.

IN FORTY YEARS as a lawyer, I have learned one true thing about stories, real stories as opposed to fictional ones. They have no true beginnings. There is an irony in this, I suppose, for if I have learned even one other true thing, it is that more than anything else, people want their stories to be shapely as the stories of fiction are shapely. Clear beginnings, problematic middles, sensible resolutions.

This accounts for the fascination most folks have with the law, for a court of law is designed to create beginnings where none are visible, to force problems to unnatural resolutions. The law tells us a lie we want to believe: that past history is inadmissible. It does not matter if the thief who stole your wallet only wanted to feed his hungry children. It does not matter if the drunk driver who killed your daughter had no control over the disease coded into his genes. Beginnings lead to moral distinctions; and moral distinctions . . . well, we'll come to them, too, I guess.

Thousands of facts are relevant, of course, and past history always counts, but I'm enough of a lawyer to know that still we must begin. So. This story starts in the bright, hopeful summer of a long-ago year when a good war had ended in victory, when a famine of want had drawn to a prosperous conclusion, when the nation turned its face to a future unblemished by presentiment of disaster. It begins in an age of innocence, in a day when children—

even twelve-year-old boys—could still believe in magic. It begins here, with the sound of a train whistle.

Listen:

DARKNESS SHROUDED THE town of Sauls Run, West Virginia, and everyone was sleeping. Nothing stirred but the wind, which chased ragged scraps of newspaper through streets of dew-settled dust. The dew had been early and generous; it glinted from every surface, from every blade of grass and leaf; it hung like jewels in the silken webs of fat and drowsy spiders. Here and there, electric night-lights shone dimly in the windows of the shuttered houses, but many homes still depended on gas and kerosene for heat and light. The great war was over, and mushroom clouds over Hiroshima and Nagasaki had ushered in an age of anxiety, but Sauls Run lingered still, only three years short of the middle of the century, in the innocent moment between the agrarian past and the industrial future. If anyone had been awake to observe it (no one was), he could have noted the juxtaposition of these worlds: in the hills above town, the mines had long since been mechanized. Great machines gnawed coal out of the earth and sometimes gnawed the arms and legs of miners, too. Here, alone of all the places near the town, men were awake and the night jostled with the noise of trucks and chain-driven cars. Elsewhere, it might have been 1897 instead of 1947. Hitching posts still stood outside most public buildings; many homes still had an outhouse in the backyard; and at three-thirty in the morning, everyone in town still slept. Cats dozed in open windows, dreaming of mice; chained up in the vacant lot by the Grand Hotel, a monkey slumbered atop a locust post, dreaming of the moist verdant jungle he used to know; even the presses of the *Daily Telegraph* were still, dreaming their unfathomable dreams—that quiet, that hushed, that peaceful.

In a ground-floor bedroom of a rambling structure near the courthouse lay a dark, fragile-looking boy named Henry Sleep—ironic, this name, for of all the people in the town, Henry Sleep alone hovered in that dreamful state between sleep and wakefulness. He alone thrashed in his bedclothes, his ears pricked to detect the slightest noise at the open window.

Listen:

The howling siren song of a locomotive broke across the sleeping town, suddenly and clear. Henry's eyelids sprang up like window shades. In the moment before he came fully awake, he dreamily recalled the poster he had first seen three endless weeks ago, half hidden among the sun-bleached war-bond placards and faded ads for patent medicines that thronged the Grand Hotel bulletin board: a tiger, a flaming hoop, these bright proclaiming words:

Bitterroot & Crabbe's World Famous
Circus and Menagerie!
Direct from a Command Performance
Before the Crowned Heads of Europe for
a SPECIAL LIMITED ENGAGEMENT!!
3 DAYS ONLY: JUNE 7–10!!!

The train roared again, shredding the poster into streams of vivid colors. *Wake up!* it screamed. *Wake up!* Henry sat up in bed, his heart thundering. Again the whistle shouted, and this time it blew open all the closed doors in his heart. Who cared if the whole damn town was sleeping?

Henry kicked the bedclothes aside and reached for his trousers. He slid his shoes on and lifted the window sash. Night air flooded the room, freighted with the scent of lilac. Every cell in his body screamed itself awake as he slid his leg over the window sill and into the blackness.

Just then, just there, he experienced a single twinge of doubt. If his father found out—

Away over the folded hills and sleeping houses of Sauls Run, the whistle bellowed again. Hell with it, he thought. Ducking through the window, he dropped to the ground and headed off through the dark to find Jemmy E. The whistle blasted again as the circus train came roaring into town.

THROUGH THE DESERTED streets they ran: Henry Sleep and the black cowlick his mother couldn't tame, dark eyes and furtive, fearful smile; Jemmy E., wild-eyed and pale, his spiky hair ashimmer with a jack-o' lantern glow. Breathless through the dirty streets—past the monkey, scolding from his post; past the Stull house, broken window shards like jagged hungry teeth; past the Bluehole, depthless in the moonlight, lair of serpents carnivorous and dread.

To Cinder Bottom they raced, row after row of burnished rails strewn with cast-off spikes and coal. Their leather shoes pounded the ties. Smells of dirt and diesel and oiled iron hovered in the air. The train whistle shattered the stillness and harried them across the tracks to a switchplate above the yards. Here a single track on a mounded hillock curved away to the county fairgrounds.

"Let's go!" Henry shouted. "Hurry! It's coming!"

He glanced over his shoulder. Jemmy E. had dropped to the tracks behind him. Henry paused, his breath burning in his lungs.

"What are you *doing?*"

Jemmy E. lifted his hand for silence. Henry fidgeted impatiently. The Stone Bridge loomed over the yards, black against the graying sky. Here and there a light blazed in a lonely window. Along the ridge to the west, the milkman's headlights made fitful progress from house to house. Henry's stomach growled.

"Come on!" he hollered.

"Quiet, you dope," said Jemmy E. "Listen."

Henry dropped to his knees beside the tracks. Cinders ground into the knees of his trousers; too late he regretted his carelessness. A shadow like a summer cloud slid across his heart. Then he pressed his ear to the dew-chilled rail and all shadows were forgotten. The iron bucked with tidings of the onrushing locomotive. *Bitterroot and Crabbe!* the rail screamed. *Circus! Menagerie! Coming! Coming!*

He had almost forgotten the trousers when he felt a hand at his shoulder. He twisted around, his heart rattling in its cage of ribs. Jemmy E. stood limned against the pale sky. He grinned like Old Nick himself: a grin crooked and charming, and just a little dangerous.

"Let's go!" he said.

He went, a pale blur, a wraith against the lifting dark. Henry trailed his fingers along the rail—it sang with greetings—and watched the soles of Jemmy's shoes flashing in the murk. Jemmy E.'s voice floated back to him—gently mocking—and took substance in the air. "Can't catch me!"

Henry, shouting laughter, leapt forward, his feet scrabbling for purchase in the cinders. Off like a rocket, like a bullet from a gun, sucking in lungfuls of the sweet, sweet morning air, until the other boy appeared before him. The tracks curved still farther from the Cinder Bottom railyards, dove through a crepuscular stand of birch—white trunks like sentinels in the gloom—and emerged into the open fields that bordered the fair grounds.

Bitterroot and Crabbe! sang the locomotive in a voice that filled the world. *Menagerie! Circus! Bitterroot and Crabbe!*

Out of nowhere, it bore down upon them. Henry felt its hot breath upon his shoulder; its iron wheels screamed like banshees. He lowered his head. His legs pumped furiously. His feet found the ties as if by magic. He risked a glance behind him, and the train—train?—the monster—the fury—the dragon—encompassed his entire field of vision. Still Jemmy E. fled on, an arm's length before him, his legs rising and falling as if all the demons of hell had been loosed upon his heels. The locomotive screamed like some terrible beast from the prehistoric past.

"Jemmy!" Henry screamed. "Jemmy!"

But the clangor, the din, the sheer preposterous world-shattering pandemonium of the monster sweeping down upon them, drowned out his little cry.

His feet flashed over the ties. He willed them to move faster, faster. A deadly vision hovered before him: a badly placed foot, a moment of vertigo, and then the train, the train, hungry wheels gnawing at his flesh. Henry risked another backward glance. The locomotive roared and surged after him. He screamed in exhilaration and ran as he had never run before. A little wind touched him, tugged at him. He reached out for Jemmy in the last moment before the train devoured them; together, shrieking gales of joyous laughter, they leapt from the tracks. He seemed to fall forever, and then the soft, sweet-smelling grass reached up for him with a thousand eager hands. He skidded into the marshy soil at the base of the declivity and opened one eye as the train blurred by above him in a rage of sparks and thunder.

"Damn! Did you see that? Did you? *Did you?*" Jemmy E. popped out of the weeds beside him, pounding his chest and chortling with delight. He pounced on Henry, braying demented laughter, and they wrestled with the simple joy and exhilaration of survival. At last, exhausted, they parted.

Henry plucked a long blade of grass and sucked on it meditatively as he watched the train slow, disgorging billows of steam. An elephant trumpeted; roustabouts leapt from open cars in groups of two and three. Jemmy E. turned his face to the sky and let loose a wordless shout of delight. As if in answer, the elephant trumpeted again.

"God," said Jemmy E. "Don't you wish it could be like this forever?"

The sheer absurdity of the idea set them off again. By the time the laughter ceased, a fat crescent of orange had appeared over the eastern ridges. Henry studied his pants—so soiled with cinders and grass stains that he could only surmise their original color—and, once again, that shadow passed over his heart. He glanced at Jemmy E. Now, visible in the spreading light, he saw the puffy bruise that discolored the other boy's cheek. He thought of Jemmy E.'s father, sullen drunk and down with the black lung. Not too long ago—no more than a year—Jemmy's dad had smashed him with a whiskey bottle. It took seven stitches to close that wound.

If only it didn't have to be this way, he thought. If only it could be like Jemmy E. had said: *Don't you wish it could be like this forever?* And he did, he did. Henry tilted his head against the slope and chewed thoughtfully at the blade of grass. He closed his eyes. An inexpressible longing to extend this moment endlessly possessed him. He could not say why tears trembled at the corners of his eyes.

THE HEARSE SLID UP behind Henry three blocks from home—no longer technically a hearse, but forbidding nonetheless; long and low, forever stamped with the imprimatur of death. The county had picked it up cheap and pressed it into service as a police car, but the insignia on the door—*Sheriff*—could not wholly dispel the vehicle's macabre associations.

Once a vehicle for the dead, now the car itself was dying. The engine ran with a halting chop, and the tailpipes choked out clouds of malodorous blue smoke. But Henry trudged along the dusty street unawares, his head down, preoccupied with his thoughts.

They continued thus—Henry first, the hearse lumbering after him like a cancerous mutt—for a block before the car abruptly sped up and passed him. A sooty cloud of smoke and dust engulfed Henry as the driver angled the hearse into a driveway, blocking his path.

"Henry!"

Henry licked his lips. He swallowed.

"Henry!"

"Yes, sir."

His father didn't answer. The hearse idled raggedly in the driveway, and Henry stood before it like a sinner called to judgment, his pants soiled and his suspenders dangling at his knees.

"Hello, Sheriff," someone called from down the street.

His father turned. Sunlight flashed off the badge pinned to his cap.

"Morning, Mrs. Vellner," his father hollered in that voice he had—Henry's mother called it his "people voice," mellifluous and charming. "Charlie doing okay?" He used the smile that went with the voice. Without looking at Henry, he said, "Get in the car, son."

Henry climbed in, swinging the door closed on its rusty hinges. It latched with a fatal *thunk*. His father backed the hearse into the street. The car sputtered, coughing smoke as they started slowly home.

"You weren't in your room this morning, son."

"No, sir."

"Circus train come in this morning. A fellow down the fairgrounds told me it near killed a couple kids on the track out there. You know anything about that?"

Henry didn't answer.

"I drove down t'other side of town. Seems Jemmy E. wasn't in his room this morning, either."

Henry stared out the window and did not speak. The air felt cool against his face. At the intersection near the courthouse, ten or twelve cattle milled. Three boys with switches hustled about, urging them on. His father cut left to avoid the backup.

"You know what I think of that boy."

"Yes, sir."

"Well, what then?"

Henry blinked twice. "He's no account. Him nor his family."

His father didn't answer. They made another cut and the house came into view, a sprawling clapboard structure built by three generations of Sleeps of uncertain architectural competence. It stood at the corner, bordered on the east by a brick house belonging to the Millers and on the west by fields that climbed to the rim of the valley and the ridge beyond. Last summer, Henry and his father had painted the house, or Henry had painted it while his father limped along behind him, offering advice.

The limp was what the Germans had done to him, that and something more: for the man who came back from the war could be grim and cruel in a way that the man who left never had been. Henry still remembered the first time he had seen the archipelago of scars rising from the dense hair on his father's calf—like the humped spine of a serpent breaking the surface of a black, black sea. Even now, when his father wasn't home, he occasionally sneaked upstairs to gaze at his father's medals, arrayed as casually as a pocketful of change atop the dresser. His father had served in the war and he was a hero, Henry's mother liked to say. But he had seen some awful things, and now he was a little broken inside and they had to love him anyway. Henry tried to imagine what it was like to be broken inside—he had an image of sharp little pieces of glass poking into everything—but his father had started to speak again:

"That ain't all is it, Henry?"

"No, sir."

"Well, go on, then."

Henry swallowed. "He ain't no account and you don't want me running around with him. They ain't—they aren't—" That was his mother's voice, that correction. "They aren't our kind of folks."

His father braked in front of the house. He turned the car off. "Your mother ain't going to be happy when she sees those trousers."

"No, sir."

"Go on in the house and get them off. Maybe your mom can wash them before the stains set."

"Yes, sir." Henry opened the door and started toward the house.

His father said: "I'll be along directly, Henry. We got some business together."

"Yes, sir."

"Go on, then. I'll be along."

Henry's mother waited in the kitchen. When she saw him, she said, "Oh, Henry," but he sped by without speaking, through the living room, past the kitchen and dining room, and down the hall to his bedroom. He stripped off the soiled pants and left them in the hall for his mother. He could hear her out there, saying. "Asa, please—"

"Leave me alone, Lil," his father said. "The boy has to learn."

"He doesn't have to learn. He's a child. He'll learn soon enou—"

A quick sharp sound like a handclap stilled her, and Henry didn't have to be there to see the expression on her face. He had seen it before, her lips in a narrow whitened line, her large eyes swimming as she turned away. Henry clenched his fists and stared out the window. The sun stood straight overhead and the world looked hard-edged and sharp, without shadow. The full heat of the day had begun to bear down and a stillness had settled over the town. Dust from the streets gathered on the windowsill and on the stone walk to the disused privy; it coated even the grass and leaves, so that everything seemed less alive and green than it had that morning, as if all the magic had drained out of the world.

From the doorway, his father said, "Henry."

He still wore his uniform, blue slacks, gray shirt, gun-laden belt. He had taken off his cap. Henry could see tiny beads of sweat on his forehead. His scalp was chafed pink by his hat band where his hair had started to thin. He carried a willow switch, green where he had cut it.

"Now, then," his father said, without raising his voice. He came into the room and closed the door. He moved with an awkward gait, lunging with his good leg and sweeping the other one along behind it, so you could hear it and know he was coming— a thump and a long sweep, like somebody dragging a body across a wooden floor.

Henry lowered his underwear. He braced himself against the mattress and dragged a pillow close so he could bite down on it if he had to. He had learned not to cry out.

"This hurts me more than it does you, son."

Henry clenched his jaws as the willow switch descended with a hiss, but you could not prepare yourself for the pain. Fire raced along his bottom. His father grunted with the effort of it. Again. Again. Again. Each blow so painful that it seemed you could not experience such hurt and live.

Henry squeezed his eyes shut so hard that tears streamed down his face. His father was a good man. *He was!* He was a hero. Henry tried to picture the medals arrayed across the dresser and tried to remember his mother's words: *It was the war that had made him this way. It was the war, it was—*

But then he couldn't think that anymore. He couldn't think anything. It was all he could do not to scream—

His father paused, breathing hard. "Okay, son."

Henry collapsed against the bed. A moment passed, and when he thought he could stand without falling, he eased the under-shorts over the welts. The brassy clamor of the circus band drifted through the open window; they were tuning up in the square by the courthouse.

"Parade's fixing to get under way," his father said. He shook his head. "You're grounded, son. You got to learn."

HIS FATHER DRAGGED him from the sprawling circus tent, saying over and over in his gentle voice "You got to learn. You got to learn." The voice had a bizarre, sinister quality that puzzled Henry until he realized that it wasn't his father speaking at all. It was a clown, a capering, grinning harlequin with hair that jutted out in three comical tufts; he wore gigantic, floppy pantaloons and shoes six sizes too big. The clown seized his collar and dragged him through the muck. Henry thrashed in desperation, but the clown just clutched him tighter. At last it paused, moonlight like teeth in those unruly tufts of hair. It leaned into his face. If the voice—

—his father's voice—

—had been unsettling, this was worse. Shadows slid like oil over the thing's face, and in this oleaginous play of dark and light, Henry saw that the bulbous rubber nose had come askew and the colorful greasepaint had started to run. Underneath, he thought he saw another face, lupine and cruel, but in the mercurial light, he couldn't be sure. The clown moved closer, his breath a contagion in the air. He lifted Henry higher, and only then, dangling helpless above the ground, did Henry see the willow switch. The clown whipped it around in vicious, whispering circles. Henry could feel the wind of its passage. "You got to learn," the clown chanted. "You got to learn, you—"

"—dope! Come on ! *Wake up!*"

Henry opened his eyes. Twilight shimmered among the trees, insubstantial as gauze. Jemmy E. stood at the window, his hair wildly aspike. He had a fresh bruise on his cheek and a light in his eyes like Henry had never seen before.

"Come *on,*" he said. "It'll be starting soon."

Henry rubbed at his eyes. Mocking rags of dream—

—*got to learn!*—

—drifted in the still air. "What?" he said. He sat up too fast, and sharp little barbs sizzled along his back and rear. Then he remembered. The circus had come to town at last. "I can't. My dad."

"The hell with your dad," said Jemmy E. "The hell with him and his whole damn town. Come on!"

"I can't."

But there it was, clear and beckoning through the evening air, the voice of the circus: the honeyed charm of cotton candy and magicians, the monstrous chortle of the freaks. There it was: the joyous shout of the calliope, the basso trumpet of the elephant, the brassy jig of the band, the snap of canvas in a summer breeze. The voice of all wild, untamed things, calling out to his boy's heart. He would not let this be taken from him. He could not.

Out then, out through the window to the welcoming dark, to streets lit fitfully by fireflies and moonlight. Out and away, his father's house eclipsed by night. To Cinder Bottom and the fairgrounds beyond, to the midway thronged with townsfolk in their grays and browns. You could see the coal in the lines of their tired faces and their knotty, bruise-knuckled hands, in their clothes and hair and in their eyes, hungry for wonder. The circus folk flitted like spirits among them—hucksters and acrobats, dwarves and clowns, their faces burnished and shiny beneath the electric lights strung hastily overhead. Alleys and alleys full of such people— jugglers, vendors, freaks, and fortune-tellers—talking and yelling and selling all at once in glorious pandemonium. And such smells! Hot dogs and cotton candy and good old-fashioned sweat, and over all, the wild, earthy exhalation of the animals, caged and tawny in their alley beyond the tent.

A trumpet sounded, and a barker cried out in the dark. "This way," said Jemmy E. He grabbed Henry's hand, and led him through the twisting crowds that shuffled toward the tent, their faces slack and eager, like the faces of pilgrims or of children. They ducked through the slow-crawling line to the ticket booth; ran along a track of garishly painted boxcars, shuttered now and dim; and emerged into the lane where the animal cages had been parked. Smells hung heavy in the air here—smells of wet fur and old straw and rotting meat; and the unfettered stink of the animals themselves, tigers astalk in their cages, goats huddled in their pen, elephants all in line, hooked trunk to tail as they waited with sad, patient eyes for the show to get under way. Just ahead, in the pool of radiance beneath an electric bulb, three roustabouts struggled to control a balky horse. Jemmy E. clutched at Henry.

"Now," he whispered fiercely, and for the second time that night, Henry saw a light in his eyes that he'd never seen before. A crazed shine of joy or fear or maybe both.

They ducked into a narrow space between two cages. A heavy paw swiped the air over their heads, and Jemmy chuckled fearlessly. Beyond the cages, the crawlspace ended at a wall of taut canvas.

"Here," said Jemmy E., tugging at the base of the tent. He lifted it a foot while Henry crawled beneath it, and then he followed. The vast space within was garishly illuminated. Henry saw towering many-peopled stands, three vacant rings in the center of the earthen floor, and everywhere troupes of ebullient clowns. Then the lights went out, plunging them into impenetrable dark. There was a sound as of a thousand in-drawn breaths.

The circus had begun.

THE LIGHTS BLAZED up with a flourish of trumpets. In marched the circus folk, led by a tall, cadaverous ringmaster clad in tails, his gray hair in a fan across his collar. Acrobats tumbled, clowns capered, elephants marched in lockstep with exotic women astride their broad heads. Around the tent they went, big cats roaring in their cages, horses prancing, jugglers juggling.

A flame of joy sprang alight in the heart of Henry Sleep. He flipped a hank of hair from his eyes and watched hungrily, needfully. Around and around the circus people marched while the crowd cheered them on . . . and then the show began. The ringmaster appeared and disappeared as if by magic, in the darkness of the first ring or in the brilliance of the third or in the towering reaches of the tent itself, on a platform high atop the center post. Act after act he introduced in a rich-timbred voice that filled the airy reaches of the big top: Knife Throwing! Frank Buck and the Lions of Darkest Africa! The Soaring Marconi Brothers and the Never-Before-Attempted Triple Somersault!

On and on it went, act after fabulous act, a seizure of delight that Henry hoped would never end. But at last the tent fell dark. With a flourish, the ringmaster appeared in a spotlight. He bowed deeply and wished them a good night.

Jemmy E. tugged at Henry's sleeve. Out they went, under the canvas into the space between the cages, down the reeking alley to the lane of shuttered boxcars. As they merged into the crowd, Henry's heart jumped into his throat. He had seen his father.

"RUN!" SCREAMED JEMMY E.

But it was too late. Jemmy's face had gone slack; the bruises stood out lividly against his pale flesh. "We have to run, Henry," he whispered. "We have to!" Emotion seized his features. "Come on," he said. Henry took half a step toward him.

"Henry," his father said.

"*Please*," said Jemmy E.

Henry swallowed. "Let's go," he said.

They fled. People milled across the grounds, gathering in clusters to chat or smoke. Long lines wound from the concession and souvenir stands. Jemmy E. dodged through them recklessly, Henry close behind him.

He didn't see what arrested his flight, but it felt like running full-tilt into a down mattress. Something big and soft and smelling of lavender soap gathered him up. "Why, Henry Sleep!" it said, and his heart fell.

"Evening, Miss Wickasham," he said. He tried to move past her, but her wrinkled fingers clamped like talons over his shoulders.

"I haven't seen you in ages—look how you've grown!" Miss Wickasham said. "How is your dear father? Such a shame about his leg, and him such a brave man. I haven't seen him in ages, but I voted for him in the—" She blushed. "Why Sheriff Sleep, I was just asking about you!"

Henry subsided.

"Miss Wickasham." His father doffed his cap. "The boy and I were just having a bit of quarrel, I'm afraid."

"Henry?"

"That's right, ma'am."

She drew Henry close and pinched his cheeks. "Have you been bad? You know what happens to boys who misbehave."

He knew all right. He'd seen the fresh and livid bruise on Jemmy's cheek. Every time he moved, he felt thin stripes of agony erupt across his back and buttocks. Oh, yes, he knew—but he didn't know what he intended to say until the words were out, fatal and irrevocable: "I don't give a damn." He tore himself away, but his father clutched him and spun him around. Henry looked up just in time to catch the slap full across the face.

"You apologize to Miss Wicka—" his father began, but he didn't finish for a flat stone whizzed past Henry's shoulder and caught his father square in the forehead. He staggered. Henry wrenched loose, sending Miss Wickasham sprawling. She rolled on her back like an upended turtle, lunging after him as he passed.

"Murder!" she shrieked.

Heads turned as Henry sprinted by.

"Murder! Murder!" shrieked Miss Wickasham. She jabbed a claw after Henry. "Get that child!"

"What did she say?" someone asked.

"Murder," said someone else.

The crowd picked it up. "Murder, murder, murder." A torrent of accusations flooded the throng. Someone grabbed for Henry, but he slipped away. He followed the arc of the tent at a dead run and collided head-on with Jemmy E. They went down in a tangle of limbs, struggled up, and dashed off into the maze of cages and boxcars beyond the midway. Henry risked a glance back at the mob as they flew down the line of cages behind the tent.

"You didn't have to throw the rock," he gasped.

"You didn't have to push the fat lady down."

They ducked between the cages opposite the tent, into a lane of garish boxcars.

"Here!" someone shouted. "There they go!"

"He's going to beat us within an inch of our lives," Henry said. "He's going to kill us."

"That's what I'm afraid of."

"Why'd you throw that rock?"

They turned a corner into another line of cars. Back here, far behind the main concourse, few lights had been strung. Minatory shadows loomed up, and for a moment Henry wasn't certain what was worse: getting lost in the maze of circus vehicles or facing the pursuing crowd.

"I'm just sick of it," said Jemmy E. He started to say something else and then stopped abruptly, panting. They had reached a dead end. Boxcars crowded in on three sides. A single light gleamed at the far end of the lane, but here the night pressed down thick and unyielding. Henry thought he heard things moving— slithering maybe—in the tenebrous depths under the cars.

"We've got to do something," Jemmy said. "If they catch us they'll hang me."

"Hang you? Are you crazy?" Henry stared, but he could see only a shadowed wedge of Jemmy's face.

Jemmy turned away. "I threw the rock because I wanted a chance to say good-bye."

"Good-bye?"

"I'm leaving. I'm running away."

"What happened?"

Jemmy was silent for a long moment. Henry could hear the pursuing mob, drawing closer. He could hear something moving under the boxcars. He was so afraid that he hardly dared to draw breath. Jemmy E. said:

"I think I killed my old man."

"Killed him? What are you talking about?"

"When I got home, he'd been drinking all morning. He said your dad had been hassling him." Jemmy laughed bitterly. "He beat the hell out of me. You think my face looks bad, you should see my ribs." He paused, and Henry thought of the red welts on his back and bottom. While they had been running, he had felt them cracking, breaking open.

Jemmy said: "After a while, he passed out and I . . . I was so mad, Henry. I've never been that mad. The whiskey bottle was still half full, but I didn't care. That's how mad I was. I just smashed it over his head without even thinking. There was so much blood."

Henry didn't speak. The crowd had drawn nearer. He could hear them shouting, "Murder! Murder!" If only they knew, he thought, and fine hairs prickled at the back of his neck.

"I hid out all day. I didn't know what to do. I just wanted to say good-bye. I didn't mean to get you in trouble."

"It's okay."

"You don't think less of me, do you? Do you?"

"No."

The crowd sounded very close indeed.

"You've got to get away," Henry said. A sickening image had come into his mind: Jemmy E., his face blue and puffy, his black tongue extruding from his mouth. Jemmy E. swinging at the end of a hangman's rope. He didn't know if they hanged kids, but he didn't want to chance it.

"What are we going to do?" said Jemmy E., and it was the first time in all the years they had known each other that *he* had asked that question instead of Henry Sleep.

Henry thought he heard a moist slithering sound in the dark spaces beneath the cars. But it didn't matter. He *knew* he heard the crowd, shouting angrily. Any minute they would appear at the end of the lane.

"The boxcars," Henry said. "We'll go under them."

Just then a door opened in a nearby car and a wedge of light fell out, shattering the gloom. Henry swallowed as a long, bony arm clad all in black extended from within. A single gaunt finger with a yellow nail curled itself into an inviting crook. A calm, mellifluous voice said, "Why don't you boys step inside?"

LIKE DRINKING WITH Livingstone from the fabled well-springs of the Nile, or opening a long-dead pharaoh's tomb, mouth agape at

the wonders there but fitfully revealed. That was what stepping
into that car was like. A suit of armor glimmered dully in one dim
corner. In another, the calcified tusks of some prehistoric monster
had been propped as carelessly as tent-posts. Amid the clutter piled
atop the table along the far wall stood an abacus, a crystal ball, a
shrunken head. Jemmy E. gasped. Henry executed an awe stricken
revolution, choking back a cry as a rattlesnake struck down at him
from a shelf. He stumbled back and saw that the snake had been
expertly stuffed—stilled forever in midstrike, its eyes glassy and
blind.

The door slammed shut behind them.

"Now then," said the ringmaster. He sat at the far end of the
car in a chair as ornately carven as a throne. At the circus he had
seemed vibrant, youthful. Close up, he looked like a man past
death and into the first stages of decay. His long fingers steepled
before his gaunt and bony face; his iron-gray hair swept back from
a pronounced widow's peak and fell loose about his shoulders. He
regarded them with obsidian eyes. After a moment, he reached out
to the table beside his chair and adjusted a kerosene lantern. Skel-
etal shadows capered around the room.

Henry swallowed audibly. Paper rustled near his foot; a dun-
colored rat the size of a loaf of bread emerged from a stack of
disintegrating magazines and began to nose around the cluttered
perimeter of the room. Henry saw that the abacus hadn't moved
in days or weeks. A layer of dust clung like dandruff to the
shrunken head. The ringmaster's tuxedo was frayed about the
sleeves and shoulders; it had the threadbare sheen of clothes too
often worn.

"Let's see," said the ringmaster. "You—" He leveled a gnarled
finger at Jemmy E. "—must be Jemmy—Jemmy E., the locals call
you, your name defies them. And you—" He nodded at Henry.
"—must be Henry Sleep."

"How did you—" said Jemmy E.

"I spoke with your father this morning," the ringmaster said
to Henry. "Charming man." He picked up a snifter of greenish
fluid. Steam curled from it in wisps as he passed it under his
hooked nose and sniffed delicately.

No one said a word. After a while, the tramp of heavy feet
and voices raised in anger broke the silence. The sounds continued

for a few moments—"I swear they went this way," "Murderous little wretches"—and then faded back the way they had come.

"I fear you are in dreadful trouble."

"What's going on here?" said Jemmy E. "Who are you?"

"I am Quinn. This is my circus. This is my car."

"What about Bitterroot?" said Jemmy E. "What about Crabbe?"

"Bitterroot and Crabbe are pompous little ledger-keepers and number-toters. Mere conveniences. This is Quinn's circus, Quinn's place, Quinn's way. Quinn is master here."

"Lots of neat stuff you've got," said Henry.

"Trinkets," said the ringmaster. "Rubbish, trinkets, and junk." He leaned forward. "I want to talk about you."

Henry looked up. Jemmy E. stepped forward, his face half in shadow, that crazed gleam of fear or anger in his eyes.

"We have to get back," Henry said.

"Get back where, my young friend? Your father will hide you when you return. *His* father—" He nodded at Jemmy E. "—lies dead in a shack with blood drying on his face. Stay awhile. The circus has only just begun."

Quinn stood. He towered over them in the flickering light, clad all in black with his crimson bow tie like a daub of blood at the base of his neck. He drained the snifter of vile fluid, and it seemed to Henry that the deep furrows in his face softened just a touch, that his gray hair had grown almost imperceptibly darker.

Then, with something like shock, he felt the impact of the ringmaster's words: *Dead, dead in a shack*. Then it was true. He saw the bone-weary shack where Jemmy E. lived with his father, desolate above a stream that ran black with coal dust. It seemed then that he stepped forward, stepped somehow through a doorway into the shack itself, and there he saw it for himself: Jemmy E.'s father, cheek to splintered table, his arms dangling, a froth of blood and snot caked on his chin.

He screamed and stumbled back. Wrenching his gaze from the crystal ball—

—how did I come to look in there?—

—he saw that he was in the ringmaster's cluttered car. "Dad?" Jemmy E. said, and Henry saw that he too had been in the broken shack, that still he lingered there, that maybe he would never leave. A spark of hatred tumbled into the dry kindling of his heart— hatred that Jemmy E. had been driven to this, hatred that such men existed. The stripes on his back burned. His mind churned with incoherent thoughts—*he's a good man, he's a good*—

"Dad?" Jemmy E. sobbed. "I'm sorry, Dad." He sank to his knees, his yearning hands uplifted. "I'm sorry."

"Stop it," Henry said. "Stop it! You're killing him!" He snatched the crystal from the table. It threw off crazed, maniacal reflections as he hurled it away. The rat squealed and burrowed into the debris. Jemmy E. fell forward on his face, his thin shoulders heaving.

"I can take this pain from you," Quinn said into the silence. "I can make it go away."

Jemmy E. looked up.

They watched as Quinn knelt and threw back the lid of an oaken casket that alone of all the mysterious rubbish in the room lay free of dust. Hinges glided noiselessly in their sleeves as the lid fell open, revealing half a hundred glittering vials cradled in velvet collars. Quinn turned to look at them. The light flickered in the hollows around his eyes. It danced along the polished edge of the casket and fired the many-faceted vials with dancing luminescent beauty.

"Come to me," Quinn said, and they came. In fear and voiceless longing, they came. In eight willing steps apiece, they crossed that room.

Quinn retrieved a vial and held it aloft, its contents splashing motes of ruby light around the car. He loosened its little cork and tipped a droplet into each of two tiny snifters, which he then held out to them. "Here is the essence of the thing," he said, though what thing he meant Henry could not say. He did not pause to wonder. He brought the snifter to his nostrils, inhaled the smell rising from within, like garlic and blood, and tilted it to his dry lips.

It lifted him out of himself, it swirled him away. He found himself at a window he had not seen before, gazing at a stricken desert landscape. The sun had fallen behind the distant mountains and evening scrabbled at the rocks with shadowy fingers. He was filled with terrible knowing: this day had been exactly as empty as the last and tomorrow would be the same. This is what it is to be old, Henry thought.

"Abalone, Arizona," Quinn said. "She sought me out when she saw that the world had died for her, that never again in her little span of days would she know passion."

Quinn said, "Here, now." Henry turned as the ringmaster tipped into his snifter a droplet of bitter yellow bile. "Selma, Alabama," Quinn was saying. "He sought me out—"

But Henry was not listening. He lifted the snifter to his lips and tasted almonds and bitter coffee. He stood in a rain-swept street beneath a flickering neon sign. There was an ashen flavor in his mouth that Henry could not know, but which he somehow recognized as the aftertaste of cigarettes and bourbon. I will never see her again, he thought—

Quinn was saying "An old man from Hannibal, Missouri, left me this," and he let fall into the outstretched snifter a single droplet of clear blue river water.

Henry tipped it to his lips. Tears sprang to his eyes, for this pain he knew, though he had not known he knew it. He knew it in his heart or in his bones. Time held him green and dying; nothing gold could stay.

The snifter slipped from his nerveless fingers. Again Henry seemed to hear the long, low whistle of the locomotive break across the town where he alone lay sleepless; and now its voice was mournful, full of grief for all things past and passing. No more the joy of circus trains. No more the joy of sunlit, drowsy afternoons. Just the endless toil of life in these hard mountains. He thought of his mother, the gentle way she had, and how she would not meet your eyes; he thought of his father, who had gone to war a whole man and come back with the shards of his broken self sawing at his heart. All of them—his parents; Jemmy E.'s sad father, alone in his shack with his black lungs and his whiskey; the weary folk who had thronged the midway, their faces gray with coal that would not wash away and their eyes hollow with a hunger for some transitory wonder—all of them somehow lost and broken. Young, he thought desperately, to be young and hopeful in spite of everything. *Don't you wish it could be like this forever?* Jemmy E. had said. And he did. He did.

Jemmy E. said, "Who are you? What are you?" His voice was dim with fear or wonder. Henry turned to look at him and saw him, really *saw* him for the first time ever—helpless and afraid. It was as if a fog had been lifted from his eyes, or as if he had for all these years been gazing through a film of waxen paper, perceiving the larger shapes of the world, but blind to the details that made the vision whole and true. *I do not want truth*, he thought, and a hollow pain went through his belly, a kind of longing for a state forever lost to him.

Jemmy E. stood looking up at Quinn, the little snifter empty in his veined and ragged hands. His clothes hung too large about his frame—old castoffs Henry saw—and his hair stood blond and spiky about his head. He thought of Jemmy's father, slack and lifeless against the beat-up table where he had done his drinking. His heart was like a coal, white-hot with hatred.

Quinn sighed as he closed the oaken chest; he shuffled to his thronelike chair, neither as tall nor as looming as Henry had thought. "I am just an old, old man," he said, and the way he said it you knew that it was true. "But I can take this pain from you. I can leave you as you are or were. Young, free, hopeful." He waved a hand. "A boy's will is the wind's will," he said, and he seemed almost to envy them.

"How?" said Henry.

Quinn stroked the sinewy flesh between his finger and thumb. When he spoke, he seemed almost to be talking to himself. "Old," he said, "older than old, not seventy years or a hundred and seventy, but older still. Decades now I've feasted on the pain of others but found no one to relieve me of my own." He chuckled under his breath and shook his head.

What fear had shackled Henry's heart now fell away, for it was true, he saw: Quinn had no power over them unless they surrendered it themselves. And if they did? He thought of the anticipation that had seized him when the circus train bellowed out across the sleeping town. A child alone could feel such joy. If Quinn could give them that—childhood everlasting, forever free of pain—was that so bad? Why not?

"And then?" said Jemmy E.

"You join the circus. Or you go off on your own, a boy that will not grow. 'Then' is up to you."

Jemmy E. stepped forward. When he spoke there was a hopeful and defiant note that Henry had never heard in his voice before. As if he feared this chance would somehow get away. "Please." His voice broke, and so Henry knew what was in his mind and heart: the dilapidated shack where lay his father's corpse. He could never leave that room, Henry knew, not unless Quinn could make him whole again.

"And you, Henry Sleep?" said Quinn, surprising him.

Across the stillness in the room, Henry's eyes sought Jemmy's face. *Don't you wish it could be like this forever?* Jemmy E. had said. And it could be. It could be.

The welts along his back flared red with agony. It did not have to be that way anymore, he thought. Hope surged up within him as he thought of himself and Jemmy E., how he had always envied the other boy—his quick, sardonic wit and the daring that was nothing more than the freedom of nothing left to lose. I can be like him, Henry thought, I can be like him. And another thought occurred to him, an image from his dream: the clown who was not a clown but his father, and the father who was not his father but a creature wolfish and cruel. That was true, he knew—except . . . except that his father never raised his voice. Except that he could be kind. Except that he was a hero—and if he was broken inside, that wasn't really his fault, was it? Henry knew this to be true, as well. His mother had told him it was so.

And now he saw his mother as he knew she would be: her face lined with worry for him, and with grief. He thought of the way she slicked his cowlick down on Sunday mornings, of the way she looked away when she spoke and would not meet your eyes. He thought: *I cannot leave her to him.*

"I am not evil, Henry Sleep," Quinn said kindly. "I can make you whole again."

But he had never been broken, or if he had been he would mend himself. He would be strong at the broken places.

"I have to get home," he said. Again he met Jemmy E.'s eyes, and because they were boys and didn't know how to say good-bye, they did not hug or shake hands. But Henry could feel the loss of it; he knew that Jemmy E. could feel it, too.

"See you around," he said.

"You know it, you dope," said Jemmy E.

Without another word, he slipped out of the car and off into the night. The town slept—the cats in their windows, the monkey chained atop his post, the presses in their gloomy subterranean chamber. It had grown chill, and as he hurried through the desolate streets a million million stars gazed down from watchful skies, and could not be troubled to care that never in all the years of his life would Henry Sleep see his one true friend again.

BY THE TIME Henry reached home, the moon had fallen and the long front porch lay in shadow under its shingled canopy. From the fragrant darkness by the lilacs, he heard the steady rhythm of the rocker against the porch's slatted floor and he knew that his father had waited up for him. For a moment, he thought of turning, fleeing back through the sleeping streets to Quinn and Jemmy E. and the solace that they offered.

And then he resolved himself. He walked across the yard and mounted the stairs to the porch, deliberately treading on the creaking step. A lamp glowed thinly inside the house, and dim light fell through the window by which his father rocked, his face ascending into light and retreating into darkness with chill regularity. They waited like that for a time. Light gleamed against his father's badge and along the edge of the gun-belt, which he had removed and placed beside his chair. He rocked and rocked, and Henry warmed himself at the white-hot coal that was his heart and watched the light steal across his father's features and retreat before the encroaching mask of darkness.

"I don't want you to run away from me like that, Henry."

"Yes, sir."

Silence then, and more waiting. A shadow passed in the living room, occluding the light, and Henry knew that his mother, too, was awake. He could picture her clearly, sitting on the sofa, her hands twisting in her lap until nerves got the better of her and she had to stand and pace.

"I need to know where he is."

Henry didn't speak.

His father rocked awhile and Sauls Run slept around them and did not acknowledge them.

His father said: "You got to grow up, son. You got to grow up and see what it's all about."

"I know," Henry said.

"I only want what's best for you."

"I know you do, Dad."

An owl called softly in the darkness, and then there was only the sound of the rocker; his father's face loomed out of the shadows and retreated.

"I want to tell you a story," his father said. "This happened to me in the war. I was in a German POW camp. It was pretty bad there. The Germans were too busy trying to keep the war going on two fronts to care much what happened to us. We were so hungry that we ate the leather from our shoes. When they would let us into the yard for exercise—maybe once a day for fifteen minutes—we would spend the whole time looking for something to eat. Grass . . . worms . . . bugs. Just anything, you understand?"

Henry nodded, and then he thought: *He can't see me*, so he said aloud, "Yes, sir."

"A lot of men were very sick. From hunger, exposure, whatever. They would die pretty frequently, and the Germans would drag them out of the barracks where they kept us and bury them somewhere. I saw lots of dead men, and a lot of them were men I called friends."

His father fell silent then, for a very long time, and Henry waited. He could sense that his mother was listening through the screen, and he didn't think she had heard this story, either, though he didn't know. His father didn't talk much, and one of the things he didn't talk about most was the war and what happened to him in it.

When he began to speak again, his voice was pitched low and without emotion. "One night, a man I knew woke me up—an American, another prisoner of war. He woke me up, and I could see that his face was covered with blood. That blood was smeared around his face and around his mouth especially. And he said, 'Rabkin's dead.' He said, 'Come on, you have to eat if you're going to survive. Rabkin wouldn't mind,' he told me. So I got up, but I couldn't do it. I couldn't do it. I went back to bed and early in the morning, it was just starting to get light, German soldiers woke us up and marched us into the yard. They had built a gallows and five men I knew were hanging dead there, and one of them was the man who had woken me up. They had painted on the gallows in English, 'Here are five brave American cannibals,' and they let those bodies hang there until they had rotted almost to skeletons. As a reminder, they said."

"I'm sorry," Henry said, and then he didn't say anything because when the light slid across his father's face he saw the tears that glinted there. What could he say? What could anyone?

"Don't be. You have to understand. The Germans were awful, they were often evil. But they were right in what they did that night, because those men, they had broken a taboo that should not ever be broken. And they had to be punished because unless you punish the people who do wrong, society falls apart. You can understand why those men did what they did, but people have to be punished or we'll have chaos."

"Okay," Henry said. But he wasn't sure it was okay. He didn't think he understood at all.

His father said, "That's why you have to tell me where he is, Henry. Even if you understand why he did it. You have to tell me where he is."

Henry said nothing. He felt as if the world had slipped from beneath his feet, as if gravity had been reversed, unshackling him from the earth and all things earthly he had known. Everything had changed so swiftly, so completely. He reached out and took the rail that ran along the edge of the porch, as if by gripping it he could reestablish contact with the world he had lost: a world where creatures like Quinn could not exist, where fathers were fathers and not clowns or wolves or shattered and unhappy men.

"You have to tell me where he is."

Far, far away from here, Henry thought. He thought: I don't know where he's gone or how he's getting there. And a fierce longing seized him. *I should not have chosen this path. I should have chosen Quinn's way, I should have stayed with Jemmy E.*

"Henry." His father stood, dark against the light from the living room. He moved toward Henry.

Henry backed away. "He's gone. You won't find him."

From the screen door, his mother said, "Let the boy be, Asa. He hasn't done anything."

"This is between me and Henry. You stay out of it."

"I won't."

She opened the screen and stepped onto the porch. The wooden screen whined closed on its spring, striking the door frame with a bang. Henry stood there, caught between them.

"Don't you understand?" his father said. His voice had begun to rise. "A man has been murdered. Murdered, Lil. Beat to death with a whiskey bottle. Henry has to tell me."

His mother took a second hesitant step onto the porch. When she spoke, her voice quavered. She would not look up, and Henry saw then how it was for her and knew something of her courage.

"Asa, I'm sorry that happened to you. I'm sorry you had to experience that. But you're home now, and Henry and I—we love you, and we want you to be better. Just let him be."

"Goddammit, Lil, don't you see! A man died!"

Henry saw lights come on at the Millers'. A face appeared at a window, but his parents didn't seem to care.

"—not a good man," his mother was saying. "He had it coming. He beat that boy constantly and the whole town knew it, Asa!"

"That don't matter, Lil! It ain't our place to judge. You can't just go around killing people you don't approve of! Now Henry is going to tell me where that boy is!"

"I can't," Henry said. "I'm sorry, but I can't." He moved away, but he wasn't quick enough. He never saw the blow, but all at once the left side of his face went entirely numb, and a thousand bells began to peal in his head. He staggered against the rail. Half the world had gone dim and blurry. The light shifted and distorted in his left eye.

Through the incessant clangor of the bells, Henry heard his mother scream. He tried to reach out for her to tell her it was okay—his daddy was broken inside and he couldn't help being this way—but he couldn't seem to get his legs to move. He realized he had slumped over somehow. His legs stuck out in front of him like broken sticks.

He was crying, and his mother was crying. He watched the two of them struggle in the half-light there before him, his father trying to get at him, saying "He's got to tell me," and his mother sobbing and screaming through her sobs "You're no better than he is, you son of a bitch, you're no better than he is!"

His head hurt so he closed his eyes, and when he opened them again, he saw that his mother had curled herself into a knot on the porch. She held her hands cupped over her face. Her legs kicked helplessly beneath her. A dark animal shape crouched over her, massive fist upraised. Henry heard the dull thud of flesh on flesh as it descended. He blinked. He felt like he was underwater. In the wavering light he seemed to confuse this moment with his dream—the clown drew back its fist for yet another blow, and Henry saw that the rubber nose had come askew. The greasepaint had started to run. He caught a glimpse of something thin and lupine, unremitting in its hatred and despair.

"No, please—" he said through thick lips. He tried to push himself to his feet and sagged back against the rail.

His mother had stopped kicking. He could hear nothing but the sound of the wolf-thing, panting over her. He began to crawl toward the rocker. He heard the thumps of two more heavy blows before he made it there, and the detonation of a third as he fumbled at the gun-belt. At last, he dragged the revolver free. He pulled himself erect, using the rocker as a crutch. He almost dropped the pistol. It was unbelievably heavy, the heaviest thing he had ever touched. He staggered toward them—his unmoving mother and the wolfish thing that hunkered over her—and dragged back the hammer. Using both hands, he leveled the gun and pressed the icy barrel to the wolf-thing's temple.

"Stop," he said, as the thing drew back its fist for yet another blow. "Stop or I'll kill you."

The fist dropped to the porch. It became a hand. His mother drew a weak breath and began to cry. The wolf-thing looked up to meet his eyes, and in the light from the living room its face was pale and drawn, blanched by grief and fear. It was a human face and the tears it shed were human tears. It was his father's face. In that moment, Henry Sleep did not know whom he pitied most: the broken man or the huddled woman or the little boy with the gun who stood over them and wept. In the long run, he supposed, it didn't matter.

He said: "If you ever lay another hand on her, I'll kill you."

He said: "If you ever touch me again, I'll kill you."

He said: "The Germans were wrong to hang those men. They were wrong because they drove those men to do what they did."

Very softly, then, he lowered the hammer on the revolver and heaved it with every ounce of his strength into the dark yard. He glanced at the Miller house and saw that the lights were on and that there were faces in the window. He looked back along the broad, dirty street and in every house as far as he could see, lights gleamed and faces peered out the windows. No one had come to help them. No one had cared.

Henry turned and went through the door into the house. He turned off the light in the living room and walked through the familiar dark, past the kitchen and dining room and down the long hall to his bedroom. He slept soundly that night, and without dreams. He slept that way for many nights, and if he dreamed he could not remember what dreams they were. But sometimes, waking in darkness, he would hear across the valley and the sleeping houses of the town the lonesome, mournful exhalation of a locomotive, and on those nights he thought of Quinn and Jemmy E. He could not say whether the path he had chosen was right or wrong. But these things he knew: He had been broken. And he was strong at the broken places.

THE PAST IS TREACHEROUS, memory deceitful. But I do not lie when I say that this story is a true one.

I am Henry Sleep.

I recall these events at such length not out of some misguided nostalgia but because of the boy who showed up in my office the other day: a slim redheaded child with eyes the size of saucers and a ragged bear he clutched white-knuckled, like a talisman. No more than seven, he had the wide prominent bone structure of the woman who accompanied him, and a touch of her frail beauty, too: his mother, of course, also a redhead. She wore that expression you sometimes see on the faces of broken women: a wide-eyed look I've glimpsed in the eyes of headlight-dazzled deer. It was especially distressing on her, not only because of the lucid intelligence in her eyes, but because she reminded me of my mother. The furtive way she had of moving, maybe, like a dog that's been too often kicked; or the way she wouldn't meet my eyes when she talked.

"Redhead, deadhead, five cents a cabbage head," I told the

boy, and I leaned forward to pluck a quarter from behind his ear.

I've picked up a few such tricks. They're helpful in this line of work. My hands are age-spotted now, not as swift as they used to be. But I still believe in magic.

This boy, this Eric—he was having nothing of it. He flinched when I extended my hand, and he would not take the coin when I proffered it. So I placed the quarter on the edge of my desk, where he could get it if he wanted it, and I listened to the story his mother had to tell.

I'd heard the story a thousand times or so—you have, too, though maybe you didn't listen like you should have—but I listened anyway and it moved me, like it always does. When she finished, I made a phone call or two; I found her a place to stay in the shelter over in Princeton, and I promised her that Jesse wouldn't find her, though that's probably a lie.

When they stood to leave, I leaned over the desk once more. "Hey, carrot-top," I said. "What's that bear's name? If I'm going to be your lawyer, see, I got to know the names of all the folks with an interest in your case."

They paused by the door, looking back at me. I turned my head so I could see them better—out of the good eye, the right one.

"Go ahead, Eric," his mother said.

But still the boy didn't answer me. We just looked at one another until we came to an understanding. He had eyes like bright gems, I remember thinking. Eyes like bright gems in dark settings.

"That bear's name is Fred Howard," he said. He took a step forward when he said it. His features had taken on a set, defiant quality I thought I'd seen before.

"Fred Howard, huh?"

"That's right."

"Well, you and Fred Howard come back and see me, okay?"

The boy gazed at me fixedly for another moment, and then his mother twitched his hand. They turned and saw themselves out, and that's when I noticed: the boy had hooked the coin off my desk, all right. He'd done it slicker than owl shit.

But his eyes—those eyes like bright gems—they lingered after him and seemed to illuminate my shabby office. I thought again of that look in his face, that look I knew I'd seen before. I didn't remember where at the time, but that night it came to me. It was the look in Jemmy E.'s face the last time I saw him: a look of defiance and hope and just a touch of desperation. It was the look of an opportunist who thinks that maybe, just maybe, he's found the way out. But mostly it was the look of fear.

JEMMY E. WAS RIGHT about one thing: talk travels fast in a place as small as Sauls Run. But he was wrong, as well. My father served as sheriff of our county until he was sixty-three years old; he was reelected to that office four times, an unprecedented run. To this day, he remains fondly remembered in these parts. A brass plaque in the courthouse commemorates him: *war hero, sheriff, beloved husband and father.* I stop to look at the plaque almost every day—my duties take me there—and every day I cannot help but wonder: How could they reelect him year after year? How could they reelect him when they knew?

Jemmy E. was wrong. Talk travels quickly in a town the size of Sauls Run—but only sometimes. People never talk about the things that really matter, about the things that really stink. They cling to their illusions—that the child fell from the swing set, that the mother hit herself with the corner of a kitchen cabinet. Without their illusions, they cannot survive.

A LIST OF the guilty:

Miss Wickasham, my fifth-grade teacher, who saw bruises and never said a word. The Millers, who lived next door. Casey Burroughs, my father's deputy. Reverend Wells, our church's pastor. Merrick Kennedy, who ran the pharmacy. Bill Honaker, my pediatrician. All the fellows who used to sit out front of the Grand Hotel, whittling and chewing the fat: J. C. Cade, Ed Goode, Tosack Burdette, Tillo, Luke Harvey, Wimpy Holland, Mack Asbury, Jack Catarussa. Slick the shoeshine man, who called me "Mistah Henry." The Widow Baumgarten, who taught piano. Deke Burton. Lucy James. Fanny Anderson. Lyle Nottingham. Francis Welland. All of them. All of them are guilty.

I am guilty.
You are.

A FEW YEARS ago I decided to track down the circus that came to our town in that long-distant summer. I checked every reference book I could think to look at. I talked to every two-bit carny and circus roustabout I could find. I called a professor who knows about such matters at West Virginia University. Nothing. Bitterroot and Crabbe never existed according to any official register. No one has ever heard of a man named Quinn who was something more than a man.

The past is treacherous, memory deceitful. But I know that it is true.

Whenever a circus or a carnival comes to Sauls Run—whenever one comes near—I haunt the place. I seek it out. It's become known about town as an eccentricity of mine, on the order of the peculiar law practice I have built, if perhaps not quite as odd or inexplicable. My law practice caters almost exclusively to victims of abuse, women and children who rarely have a dime to meet my fees, who have left me impoverished and wealthy beyond my wildest dreams of riches. Such a practice is entirely inexplicable to the people of this town; my penchant for haunting freak shows and circuses and carnivals and other such disreputable places is somewhat less so, but it, too, has been noted, and held as a mark against me.

But that's okay. I love the midway. I love the smell of exotic animals borne on a summer wind. I love the clowns and the jugglers and the bears on unicycles. I love them all. But that's not the reason I haunt such places. This is the reason:

I'm looking for a certain blond child. I'm looking for Jemmy E. I have something I want to tell him.

Are you out there Jemmy E.?

Listen:

I didn't run away, Jemmy E. I didn't take Quinn's way. I stayed when it was hardest. I stayed and fought. And it has made all the difference to me.

Partial People

TERRY BISSON

Terry Bisson is the author of five novels, including Talking
Man *and* Pirates of the Universe. *In honor of his mastery
of one of literature's most difficult forms, we'll keep this
introduction short-short.*

QUESTIONS ARE BEING RAISED ABOUT PEOPLE ONLY INCOMPLETELY
seen, or found in boxes, perhaps under benches. Lips and eyes
stuck under benches. Lips and eyes stuck under theater seats like
gum. Feet in shoes in rude doorways.

Whatever mystery may have surrounded them can be cleared
up at once. These are partial people.

Partial people are not entire in themselves. They do not merit
your consideration though they may vie for it.

Partial people may seem to need medical attention, because of
lacking a leg, a side, an essential attribute, etc. Their partial quality
[sic] is not however indication of a genuine medical condition.
They do not need medical treatment, and if so, only a little.

THEY MAY (THEY WILL!) claim to be dying, but how can that be?
As a wise man once said, how can they truly die, who have only
partially lived.

Read my lips: These are partial people.

There has been speculation that they are from another or a
parallel Universe. Science however has confirmed that this is not
so; or that if they are from another Universe, it is not an important
one.

The question of food is bound to come up. In general, it is best to pretend that partial people have already eaten.

Appearance is an issue. The grotesque and often unpresentable appearance of partial people may provoke discussion. Particularly among those looking for something ugly to talk about. Such discussion should be kept to a minimum.

Traffic. It is rarely that they undertake to drive. Automotive controls, even with automatic transmissions (most cars these days!), may prove daunting. Not to mention rentals.

Partial people can cause traffic delays, however. As Leslie R— drove toward a box in his/her lane on G—— Ave. in M——, he/she was surprised to find an arm sticking out of it. He/she was able to judge from the size of the rest of the box, however, that it was not large enough to contain an entire person, and therefore was able to maintain speed and direction, thus avoiding lane changing with its potential for accidents.

To make a long story short, Leslie was not distracted by frantic hand waving. Crushing the box.

Partial people may try to pass themselves off as entire people. Sometimes all, or almost all, the customary visual aspects may be present. It may be an internal organ or aspect that is missing, not apparent to the eye (or eyes, among the entire). For this reason, it is best to assume that importunate strangers are partial people.

Travel. Partial people must pay full fare but may not go the whole way. This limits their travel.

Police experience with partial people is inconclusive. In general, they are worth a beating but not worth an arrest.

In crowds, they stand cunningly so that three or four together may look like an entire person, or even two embracing. This marks the limit of their ability to cooperate.

Neither "p" is capitalized in partial people.

When they insist on having children, their children are also partial people (partial children). They hardly play.

They may claim to be veterans, especially those which are dis- or un-figured.

They may have trouble counting (being less than one to begin with). Their ideas may appear in contradiction to the ones you hold. Their speech is riddled with sentence fragments and futile attempts at dogma. Even a hello can lead to a loud harangue.

Frantic hand waving is not a friendly greeting with partial people. It is a blatant attempt to gain attention.

Do yourself and society a favor. Don't be taken in. Just say "no" to partial people.

Thank you.

The Lincoln Train

MAUREEN F. MCHUGH

*Maureen McHugh electrified the SF field in 1992 with her
first novel,* China Mountain Zhang, *and she has followed up
with two more well-received books,* Half the Day Is Night
and Mission Child. *Her short fiction is just as astute and as
well crafted as are her books, and frequently as powerful.
"The Lincoln Train" visits one of the most common subjects of
alternate history stories—the Civil War—and spins it in a
new and refreshing (not to mention poignant) way.*

SOLDIERS OF THE G.A.R. STAND ALONGSIDE THE TRACKS. THEY
are General Dodge's soldiers, keeping the tracks maintained for
the Lincoln Train. If I stand right, the edges of my bonnet are
like blinders and I can't see the soldiers at all. It is a spring evening.
At the house the lilacs are blooming. My mother wears a sprig
pinned to her dress under her cameo. I can smell it, even in the
crush of these people all waiting for the train. I can smell the lilac,
and the smell of too many people crowded together, and a faint
taste of cinders on the air. I want to go home but that house is
not ours anymore. I smooth my black dress. On the train platform
we are all in mourning.

The train will take us to St. Louis, from whence we will leave
for the Oklahoma territories. They say we will walk, but I don't
know how my mother will do that. She has been poorly since the
winter of '62. I check my bag with our water and provisions.

"Julia Adelaide," my mother says, "I think we should go
home."

"We've come to catch the train," I say, very sharp.

I'm Clara, my sister Julia is eleven years older than me. Julia is married and living in Tennessee. My mother blinks and touches her sprig of lilac uncertainly. If I am not sharp with her, she will keep on it.

I wait. When I was younger I used to try to school my unruly self in Christian charity. God sends us nothing we cannot bear. Now I only try to keep it from my face, try to keep my outer self disciplined. There is a feeling inside me, an anger, that I can't even speak. Something is being bent, like a bow, bending and bending and bending—

"When are we going home?" my mother says.

"Soon," I say because it is easy.

But she won't remember and in a moment she'll ask again. And again and again, through this long long train ride to St. Louis. I am trying to be a Christian daughter, and I remind myself that it is not her fault that the war turned her into an old woman, or that her mind is full of holes and everything new drains out. But it's not my fault, either. I don't even try to curb my feelings and I know that they rise up to my face. The only way to be true is to be true from the inside and I am not. I am full of unchristian feelings. My mother's infirmity is her trial, and it is also mine.

I wish I were someone else.

The train comes down the track, chuffing, coming slow. It is an old, badly used thing, but I can see that once it was a model of chaste and beautiful workmanship. Under the dust it is a dark claret in color. It is said that the engine was built to be used by President Lincoln, but since the assassination attempt he is too infirm to travel. People begin to push to the edge of the platform, hauling their bags and worldly goods. I don't know how I will get our valise on. If Zeke could have come I could have at least insured that it was loaded on, but the Negroes are free now and they are not to help. The notice said no family Negroes could come to the station, although I see their faces here and there through the crowd.

The train stops outside the station to take on water.

"Is it your father?" my mother says diffidently. "Do you see him on the train?"

"No, Mother," I say. "We are taking the train."

"Are we going to see your father?" she asks.

It doesn't matter what I say to her, she'll forget it in a few minutes, but I cannot say yes to her. I cannot say that we will see my father even to give her a few moments of joy.

"Are we going to see your father?" she asks again.

"No," I say.

"Where are we going?"

I have carefully explained it all to her and she cried, every time I did. People are pushing down the platform toward the train, and I am trying to decide if I should move my valise toward the front of the platform. Why are they in such a hurry to get on the train? It is taking us all away.

"Where are we going? Julia Adelaide, you will answer me this moment," my mother says, her voice too full of quaver to quite sound like her own.

"I'm Clara," I say. "We're going to St. Louis."

"St. Louis," she says. "We don't need to go to St. Louis. We can't get through the lines, Julia, and I . . . I am quite indisposed. Let's go back home now, this is foolish."

We cannot go back home. General Dodge has made it clear that if we did not show up at the train platform this morning and get our names checked off the list, he would arrest every man in town, and then he would shoot every tenth man. The town knows to believe him. General Dodge was put in charge of the trains into Washington, and he did the same thing then. He arrested men and held them and every time the train was fired upon he hanged a man.

There is a shout and I can only see the crowd moving like a wave, pouring off the edge of the platform. Everyone is afraid there will not be room. I grab the valise and I grab my mother's arm and pull them both. The valise is so heavy that my fingers hurt, and the weight of our water and food is heavy on my arm. My mother is small and when I put her in bed at night she is all tiny like a child, but now she refuses to move, pulling against me and opening her mouth wide, her mouth pink inside and wet and open in a wail I can just barely hear over the shouting crowd. I don't know if I should let go of the valise to pull her, or for a moment I think of letting go of her, letting someone else get her on the train and finding her later.

A man in the crowd shoves her hard from behind. His face is

twisted in wrath. What is he so angry at? My mother falls into me, and the crowd pushes us. I am trying to hold on to the valise, but my gloves are slippery, and I can only hold with my right hand, with my left I am trying to hold up my mother. The crowd is pushing all around us, trying to push us toward the edge of the platform.

The train toots as if it were moving. There is shouting all around us. My mother is fallen against me, her face pressed against my bosom, turned up toward me. She is so frightened. Her face is pressed against me in improper intimacy, as if she were my child. My mother as my child. I am filled with revulsion and horror. The pressure against us begins to lessen. I still have a hold of the valise. We'll be all right. Let the others push around, I'll wait and get the valise on somehow. They won't leave us to travel without anything.

My mother's eyes close. Her wrinkled face looks up, the skin under her eyes making little pouches, as if it were a second blind eyelid. Everything is so grotesque. I am having a spell. I wish I could be somewhere where I could get away and close the windows. I have had these spells since they told us that my father was dead, where everything is full of horror and strangeness.

The person behind me is crowding into my back and I want to tell them to give way, but I cannot. People around us are crying out. I cannot see anything but the people pushed against me. People are still pushing, but now they are not pushing toward the side of the platform but toward the front, where the train will be when we are allowed to board.

Wait, I call out, but there's no way for me to tell if I've really called out or not. I can't hear anything until the train whistles. The train has moved? They brought the train into the station? I can't tell, not without letting go of my mother and the valise. My mother is being pulled down into this mass. I feel her sliding against me. Her eyes are closed. She is a huge doll, limp in my arms. She is not even trying to hold herself up. She has given up to this moment.

I can't hold on to my mother and the valise. So I let go of the valise.

O merciful God.

I do not know how I will get through this moment.

The crowd around me is a thing that presses me and pushes me up, pulls me down. I cannot breathe for the pressure. I see specks in front of my eyes, white sparks, too bright, like metal and like light. My feet aren't under me. I am buoyed by the crowd and my feet are behind me. I am unable to stand, unable to fall. I think my mother is against me, but I can't tell, and in this mass I don't know how she can breathe.

I think I am going to die.

All the noise around me does not seem like noise anymore. It is something else, some element, like water or something, surrounding me and overpowering me.

It is like that for a long time, until finally I have my feet under me, and I'm leaning against people. I feel myself sink, but I can't stop myself. The platform is solid. My whole body feels bruised and roughly used.

My mother is not with me. My mother is a bundle of black on the ground, and I crawl to her. I wish I could say that as I crawl to her I feel concern for her condition, but at this moment I am no more than base animal nature and I crawl to her because she is mine and there is nothing else in the world I can identify as mine. Her skirt is rucked up so that her ankles and calves are showing. Her face is black. At first I think it something about her clothes, but it is her face, so full of blood that it is black.

People are still getting on the train, but there are people on the platform around us, left behind. And other things. A surprising number of shoes, all badly used. Wraps, too. Bags. Bundles and people.

I try raising her arms above her head, to force breath into her lungs. Her arms are thin, but they don't go the way I want them to. I read in the newspaper that when President Lincoln was shot, he stopped breathing, and his personal physician started him breathing again. But maybe the newspaper was wrong, or maybe it is more complicated than I understand, or maybe it doesn't always work. She doesn't breathe.

I sit on the platform and try to think of what to do next. My head is empty of useful thoughts. Empty of prayers.

"Ma'am?"

It's a soldier of the G.A.R.

"Yes sir?" I say. It is difficult to look up at him, to look up into the sun.

He hunkers down but does not touch her. At least he doesn't touch her. "Do you have anyone staying behind?"

Like cousins or something? Someone who is not "reluctant" in their handling of their Negroes? "Not in town," I say.

"Did she worship?" he asks, in his northern way.

"Yes sir," I say, "she did. She was a Methodist, and you should contact the preacher. The Reverend Robert Ewald, sir."

"I'll see to it, ma'am. Now you'll have to get on the train."

"And leave her?" I say.

"Yes ma'am, the train will be leaving. I'm sorry, ma'am."

"But I can't," I say.

He takes my elbow and helps me stand. And I let him.

"We are not really recalcitrant," I say. "Where were Zeke and Rachel supposed to go? Were we supposed to throw them out?"

He helps me climb onto the train. People stare at me as I get on, and I realize I must be all in disarray. I stand under all their gazes, trying to get my bonnet on straight and smoothing my dress. I do not know what to do with my eyes or hands.

There are no seats. Will I have to stand until St. Louis? I grab a seat back to hold myself up. It is suddenly warm and everything is distant and I think I am about to faint. My stomach turns. I breathe through my mouth, not even sure that I am holding on to the seat back.

But I don't fall, thank Jesus.

"It's not Lincoln," someone is saying, a man's voice, rich and baritone, and I fasten on the words as a lifeline, drawing myself back to the train car, to the world. "It's Seward. Lincoln no longer has the capacity to govern."

The train smells of bodies and warm sweaty wool. It is a smell that threatens to undo me, so I must concentrate on breathing through my mouth. I breathe in little pants, like a dog. The heat lies against my skin. It is airless.

"Of course Lincoln can no longer govern, but that damned actor made him a saint when he shot him," says a second voice, "And now no one dare oppose him. It doesn't matter if his policies make sense or not."

"You're wrong," says the first. "Seward is governing through him. Lincoln is an imbecile. He can't govern, look at the way he handled the war."

The second snorts. "He won."

"No," says the first, "we *lost*, there is a difference, sir. We lost even though the North never could find a competent general." I know the type of the first one. He's the one who thinks he is brilliant, who always knew what President Davis should have done. If they are looking for a recalcitrant southerner, they have found one.

"Grant was competent. Just not brilliant. Any military man who is not Alexander the Great is going to look inadequate in comparison with General Lee."

"Grant was a drinker," the first one says. "It was his subordinates. They'd been through years of war. They knew what to do."

It is so hot on the train. I wonder how long until the train leaves.

I wonder if the Reverend will write my sister in Tennessee and tell her about our mother. I wish the train were going east toward Tennessee instead of north and west toward St. Louis.

My valise. All I have. It is on the platform. I turn and go to the door. It is closed and I try the handle, but it is too stiff for me. I look around for help.

"It's locked," says a woman in gray. She doesn't look unkind.

"My things, I left them on the platform," I say.

"Oh, honey," she says. "they aren't going to let you back out there. They don't let anyone off the train."

I look out the window but I can't see the valise. I can see some of the soldiers, so I beat on the window. One of them glances up at me, frowning, but then he ignores me.

The train blows that it is going to leave, and I beat harder on the glass. If I could shatter that glass. They don't understand, they would help me if they understood. The train lurches and I stagger. It is out there, somewhere, on that platform. Clothes for my mother and me, blankets, things we will need. Things I will need.

The train pulls out of the station and I feel so terrible I sit down on the floor in all the dirt from people's feet and sob.

The train creeps slowly at first, but then picks up speed. The *clack-clack-clack-clack* rocks me. It is improper, but I allow it to rock me. I am in others' hands now and there is nothing to do but be patient. I am good at that. So it has been all my life. I have tried to be dutiful, but something in me has not bent right, and I have never been able to maintain a Christian frame of mind, but like a chicken in a yard, I have always kept my eyes on the small things. I have tended to what was in front of me, first the house, then my mother. When we could not get sugar, I learned to cook with molasses and honey. Now I sit and let my mind go empty and let the train rock me.

"Child," someone says. "Child."

The woman in gray has been trying to get my attention for a while, but I have been sitting and letting myself be rocked.

"Child," she says again, "would you like some water?"

Yes, I realize, I would. She has a jar and she gives it to me to sip out of. "Thank you," I say. "We brought water, but we lost it in the crush on the platform."

"You have someone with you?" she asks.

"My mother," I say, and start crying again. "She is old, and there was such a press on the platform, and she fell and was trampled."

"What's your name?" the woman says.

"Clara Corbett," I say.

"I'm Elizabeth Loudon," the woman says. "And you are welcome to travel with me." There is something about her, a simple pleasantness, that makes me trust her. She is a small woman, with a small nose and eyes as gray as her dress. She is younger than I first thought, maybe only in her thirties? "How old are you? Do you have family?" she asks.

"I am seventeen. I have a sister, Julia. But she doesn't live in Mississippi anymore."

"Where does she live?" the woman asks.

"In Beech Bluff, near Jackson, Tennessee."

She shakes her head. "I don't know it. Is it good country?"

"I think so," I say. "In her letters it sounds like good country. But I haven't seen her for seven years." Of course no one could travel during the war. She has three children in Tennessee. My sister is twenty-eight, almost as old as this woman. It is hard to imagine.

"Were you close?" she asks.

I don't know that we were close. But she is my sister. She is all I have now. I hope that the Reverend will write her about my mother, but I don't know that he knows where she is. I will have to write her. She will think I should have taken better care.

"Are you traveling alone?"

"My companion is a few seats farther in front. He and I could not find seats together."

Her companion is a man? Not her husband, maybe her brother? But she would say her brother if that's who she meant. A woman traveling with a man. An adventuress, I think. There are stories of women traveling, hoping to find unattached girls like myself. They befriend the young girls and then deliver them to the brothels of New Orleans.

For a moment Elizabeth takes on a sinister cast. But this is a train full of recalcitrant southerners, there is no opportunity to kidnap anyone. Elizabeth is like me, a woman who has lost her home.

It takes the rest of the day and a night to get to St. Louis, and Elizabeth and I talk. It's as if we talk in ciphers, instead of talking about home we talk about gardening, and I can see the garden at home, lazy with bees. She is a quilter. I don't quilt, but I used to do petit pointe, so we can talk sewing and about how hard it has been to get colors. And we talk about mending and making do, we have all been making do for so long.

When it gets dark, since I have no seat, I stay where I am sitting by the door of the train. I am so tired, but in the darkness all I can think of is my mother's face in the crowd and her hopeless open mouth. I don't want to think of my mother, but I am in a delirium of fatigue, surrounded by the dark and the rumble of the train and the distant murmur of voices. I sleep sitting by the door of the train, fitful and rocked. I have dreams like fever dreams. In my dream I am in a strange house, but it is supposed to be my own house, but nothing is where it should be, and I begin to believe that I have actually entered a stranger's house, and that they'll return and find me here. When I wake up and go back to sleep, I am back in this strange house, looking through things.

I wake before dawn, only a little rested. My shoulders and hips and back all ache from the way I am leaning, but I have no energy

to get up. I have no energy to do anything but endure. Elizabeth
nods, sometimes awake, sometimes asleep, but neither of us speak.

Finally the train slows. We come in through a town, but the
town seems to go on and on. It must be St. Louis. We stop and
sit. The sun comes up and heats the car like an oven. There is no
movement of the air. There are so many buildings in St. Louis,
and so many of them are tall, two stories, that I wonder if they
cut off the wind and that is why it's so still. But finally the train
lurches and we crawl into the station.

I am one of the first off the train by virtue of my position near
the door. A soldier unlocks it and shouts for all of us to disembark,
but he need not have bothered for there is a rush. I am borne
ahead at its beginning but I can stop at the back of the platform.
I am afraid that I have lost Elizabeth, but I see her in the crowd.
She is on the arm of a younger man in a bowler. There is something about his air that marks him as different—he is sprightly and
apparently fresh even after the long ride.

I almost let them pass, but the prospect of being alone makes
me reach out and touch her shoulder.

"There you are," she says.

We join a queue of people waiting to use a trench. The smell
is appalling, ammonia acrid and eye-watering. There is a wall to
separate the men from the women, but the women are all together.
I crouch, trying not to notice anyone and trying to keep my skirts
out of the filth. It is so awful. It's worse than anything. I feel so
awful.

What if my mother were here? What would I do? I think
maybe it was better, maybe it was God's hand. But that is an awful
thought, too.

"Child," Elizabeth says when I come out, "what's the matter?"

"It's so awful," I say. I shouldn't cry, but I just want to be
home and clean. I want to go to bed and sleep.

She offers me a biscuit.

"You should save your food," I say.

"Don't worry," Elizabeth says, "We have enough."

I shouldn't accept it, but I am so hungry. And when I have a
little to eat, I feel a little better.

I try to imagine what the fort will be like where we will be
going. Will we have a place to sleep, or will it be barracks? Or

worse yet, tents? Although after the night I spent on the train I can't imagine anything that could be worse. I imagine if I have to stay awhile in a tent then I'll make the best of it.

"I think this being in limbo is perhaps worse than anything we can expect at the end," I say to Elizabeth. She smiles.

She introduces her companion, Michael. He is enough like her to be her brother, but I don't think that they are. I am resolved not to ask, if they want to tell me they can.

We are standing together, not saying anything, when there is some commotion farther up the platform. It is a woman, her black dress is like smoke. She is running down the platform, coming toward us. There are all of these people and yet it is as if there is no obstacle for her. "NO NO NO NO, DON'T TOUCH ME! FILTHY HANDS! DON'T LET THEM TOUCH YOU! DON'T GET ON THE TRAINS!"

People are getting out of her way. Where are the soldiers? The fabric of her dress is so threadbare it is rotten and torn at the seams. Her skirt is greasy black and matted and stained. Her face is so thin. "ANIMALS! THERE IS NOTHING OUT THERE! PEOPLE DON'T HAVE FOOD! THERE IS NOTHING THERE BUT INDIANS! THEY SENT US OUT TO SETTLE BUT THERE WAS NOTHING THERE!"

I expect she will run past me but she grabs my arm and stops and looks into my face. She has light eyes, pale eyes in her dark face. She is mad.

"WE WERE ALL STARVING, SO WE WENT TO THE FORT BUT THE FORT HAD NOTHING. YOU WILL ALL STARVE, THE WAY THEY ARE STARVING THE INDIANS! THEY WILL LET US ALL DIE! THEY DON'T CARE!" She is screaming in my face, and her spittle sprays me, warm as her breath. Her hand is all tendons and twigs, but she's so strong I can't escape.

The soldiers grab her and yank her away from me. My arm aches where she was holding it. I can't stand up.

Elizabeth pulls me upright. "Stay close to me," she says and starts to walk the other way down the platform. People are looking up following the screaming woman.

She pulls me along with her. I keep thinking of the woman's hand and wrist turned black with grime. I remember my mother's face was black when she lay on the platform. Black like something rotted.

"Here," Elizabeth says at an old door, painted green but now weathered. The door opens and we pass inside.

"What?" I say. My eyes are accustomed to the morning brightness and I can't see.

"Her name is Clara," Elizabeth says. "She has people in Tennessee."

"Come with me," says another woman. She sounds older. "Step this way. Where are her things?"

I am being kidnapped. O merciful God, I'll die. I let out a moan.

"Her things were lost, her mother was killed in a crush on the platform."

The woman in the dark clucks sympathetically. "Poor dear. Does Michael have his passenger yet?"

"In a moment," Elizabeth says. "We were lucky for the commotion."

I am beginning to be able to see. It is a storage room, full of abandoned things. The woman holding my arm is older. There are some broken chairs and a stool. She sits me in the chair. Is Elizabeth some kind of adventuress?

"Who are you?" I ask.

"We are friends," Elizabeth says. "We will help you get to your sister."

I don't believe them. I will end up in New Orleans. Elizabeth is some kind of adventuress.

After a moment the door opens and this time it is Michael with a young man. "This is Andrew," he says.

A man? What do they want with a man? That is what stops me from saying "Run!" Andrew is blinded by the change in light, and I can see the astonishment working on his face, the way it must be working on mine. "What is this?" he asks.

"You are with Friends," Michael says, and maybe he has said it differently than Elizabeth, or maybe it is just that this time I have had the wit to hear it.

"Quakers?" Andrew says. "Abolitionists?"

Michael smiles, I can see his teeth white in the darkness. "Just Friends," he says.

Abolitionists. Crazy people who steal slaves to set them free. Have they come to kidnap us? We are recalcitrant southerners, I have never heard of Quakers seeking revenge, but everyone knows the Abolitionists are crazy and they are liable to do anything.

"We'll have to wait here until they begin to move people out, it will be evening before we can leave," says the older woman.

I am so frightened, I just want to be home. Maybe I should try to break free and run out to the platform, there are northern soldiers out there. Would they protect me? And then what, go to a fort in Oklahoma?

The older woman asks Michael how they could get past the guards so early and he tells her about the madwoman. A "refugee," he calls her.

"They'll just take her back," Elizabeth says, sighing.

Take her back, do they mean that she really came from Oklahoma? They talk about how bad it will be this winter. Michael says there are Wisconsin Indians resettled down there, but they've got no food, and they've been starving on government handouts for a couple of years. Now there will be more people. They're not prepared for winter.

There can't have been much handout during the war. It was hard enough to feed the armies.

They explain to Andrew and to me that we will sneak out of the train station this evening, after dark. We will spend a day with a Quaker family in St. Louis, and then they will send us on to the next family. And so we will be passed hand to hand, like a bucket in a brigade, until we get to our families.

They call it the underground railroad.

But we are slave owners.

"Wrong is wrong," says Elizabeth. "Some of us can't stand and watch people starve."

"But only two out of the whole train," Andrew says.

Michael sighs.

The old woman nods. "It isn't right."

Elizabeth picked me because my mother died. If my mother had not died, I would be out there, on my way to starve with the rest of them.

I can't help it but I start to cry. I should not profit from my mother's death. I should have kept her safe.

"Hush, now," says Elizabeth. "Hush, you'll be okay."

"It's not right," I whisper. I'm trying not to be loud, we mustn't be discovered.

"What, child?"

"You shouldn't have picked me," I say. But I am crying so hard I don't think they can understand me. Elizabeth strokes my hair and wipes my face. It may be the last time someone will do these things for me. My sister has three children of her own, and she won't need another child. I'll have to work hard to make up my keep.

There are blankets there and we lie down on the hard floor, all except Michael, who sits in a chair and sleeps. I sleep this time with fewer dreams. But when I wake up, although I can't remember what they were, I have the feeling that I have been dreaming restless dreams.

The stars are bright when we finally creep out of the station. A night full of stars. The stars will be the same in Tennessee. The platform is empty, the train and the people are gone. The Lincoln Train has gone back south while we slept, to take more people out of Mississippi.

"Will you come back and save more people?" I ask Elizabeth.

The stars are a banner behind her quiet head. "We will save what we can," she says.

It isn't fair that I was picked. "I want to help," I tell her.

She is silent for a moment. "We only work with our own," she says. There is something in her voice that has not been there before. A sharpness.

"What do you mean?" I ask.

"There are no slavers in our ranks," she says, and her voice is cold.

I feel as if I have had a fever: tired, but clear of mind. I have never walked so far and not walked beyond a town. The streets of St. Louis are empty. There are few lights. Far off a woman is singing, and her voice is clear and carries easily in the night. A beautiful voice.

"Elizabeth," Michael says, "she is just a girl."

"She needs to know," Elizabeth says.

"Why did you save me then?" I ask.
"One does not fight evil with evil," Elizabeth says.
"I'm not evil!" I say.
But no one answers.

Another Fine Mess

RAY BRADBURY

Here is one writer who needs no introduction—how many people don't know that Ray Bradbury is the author of Dandelion Wine, The October Country, Fahrenheit 451, *and* The Martian Chronicles? *But some readers may be unaware of his recent burst of energy in the realm of short fiction: During the past few years, he has written several dozen new stories, most of which are collected in* Driving Blind *and in* Quicker Than the Eye. *This gentle homage to old Hollywood is a wonderful reminder of why Mr. Bradbury remains one of our most beloved writers.*

THE SOUNDS BEGAN IN THE MIDDLE OF SUMMER IN THE MIDDLE of the night.

Bella Winters sat up in bed about three A.M. and listened and then lay back down. Ten minutes later she heard the sounds again, out in the night, down the hill.

Bella Winters lived in a floor apartment on top of Vendome Heights, near Effie Street in Los Angeles, and had lived there now for only a few days, so it was all new to her, this old house on an old street with an old staircase, made of concrete, climbing steeply straight up from the lowlands below, one hundred and twenty steps, count them. And right now . . .

"Someone's on the steps," said Bella, to herself.

"What?" said her husband Sam in his sleep.

"There are some men out on the steps," said Bella. "Talking, yelling, not fighting, but almost. I heard them last night, too, and the night before, but . . ."

"What?" Sam muttered.

"Sh, go to sleep, I'll look."

She got out of bed in the dark and went to the window, and yes, two men were indeed talking out there, grunting, groaning, now loud, now soft. And there was another noise, a kind of bumping, sliding, thumping like a huge object being carted up the hill.

"No one could be moving in at this hour of the night, could they?" asked Bella of the darkness, the window, and herself.

"No," murmured Sam.

"It sounds like . . ."

"Like what?" asked Sam fully awake now.

"Like two men moving—"

"Moving what, for God's sake?"

"Moving a piano. Up those steps."

"At three in the *morning!?*"

"A piano and two men. Just listen."

The husband sat up, blinking, alert.

Far off, in the middle of the hill, there was a kind of harping strum, the noise a piano makes when suddenly thumped and its harp strings hum.

"There, did you *hear?*"

"Jesus, you're right. But why would anyone steal—"

"They're not stealing, they're delivering."

"A *piano?*"

"I didn't make the rules, Sam. Go out and ask. No, don't, I will."

And she wrapped herself in her robe and was out the door and on the sidewalk.

"Bella," Sam whispered fiercely, behind the porch screen. "Crazy."

"So what can happen to a woman fifty-five, fat and ugly at night?" she wondered.

Sam did not answer.

She moved quietly to the rim of the hill. Somewhere down there she could hear the two men wrestling with a huge object. The piano on occasion gave a strumming hum and fell silent. Occasionally one of the men yelled or gave orders.

"The voices," said Bella. "I know them from somewhere," she

whispered, and moved in utter dark on stairs that were only a long pale ribbon going down, as a voice echoed:

"Here's *another* fine mess you've got us in."

Bella froze. Where have I heard that voice, she wondered, a million *times!*

"Hello," she called.

She moved, counting the steps, and stopped.

And there was no one there.

Suddenly she was very cold. There was nowhere for the strangers to have gone. The hill was steep and a long way down and a long way up, and they had been burdened with an upright piano, *hadn't* they?

How come I know *upright?* she thought. I only *heard.* But— yes, *upright!* Not only that, but inside a box!

She turned slowly and as she went back up the steps, one by one, slowly, slowly the voices began to sound again, below, as if, disturbed, they had waited for her to go away.

"What *are* you doing?" demanded one voice.

"I was just—" said the other.

"*Give* me that!" cried the first voice.

That *other* voice, though Bella, I know that, *too.* And I know what's going to be said next!

"Now," said the echo far down the hill in the night, "just don't stand there, *help* me!"

"Yes!" Bella closed her eyes and swallowed hard and half fell to sit on the steps, getting her breath back as black-and-white pictures flashed in her head. Suddenly it was 1929 and she was very small, in a theater with dark and light pictures looming above the first row where she sat, transfixed, and then laughing, and then transfixed and laughing again.

She opened her eyes. The two voices were still down there, a faint wrestle and echo in the night, despairing and thumping each other with their hard derby hats.

Zelda, thought Bella Winters. I'll call Zelda. She knows everything. She'll tell me what this is. Zelda, yes!

Inside she dialed Z and E and L and D and A before she saw what she had done and started over. The phone rang a long while until Zelda's voice, angry with sleep, spoke halfway across L.A.

"Zelda, this is Bella!"

"Sam just *died?*"

"No, no, I'm sorry—"

"*You're* sorry?"

"Zelda, I know you're going to think I'm crazy, but . . ."

"Go ahead, be crazy."

"Zelda, in the old days, when they made films around L.A. they used lots of places, right? Like Venice, Ocean Park . . ."

"Chaplin did, Langdon did, Harold Lloyd, sure."

"Laurel and Hardy?"

"What?"

"Laurel and Hardy, did *they* use lots of locations."

"Palms, they used Palms lots, Culver City Main Street, Effie Street."

"*Effie* Street!"

"Don't yell, Bella."

"Did you say *Effie* Street?"

"Sure, and God, it's three in the morning!"

"Right at the *top* of Effie Street!?"

"Hey, yeah, the stairs. Everyone knows them. That's where the music box chased Hardy down hill and ran over him."

"Sure, Zelda, *sure!* Oh, God, Zelda, if you could *see*, hear, what *I* hear!"

Zelda was suddenly wide awake on the line. "What's going *on?* You *serious?*"

"Oh, God, yes. On the steps just now, and last night and the night before maybe, I heard, I hear—two men hauling a—a piano up the hill."

"Someone's pulling your leg!"

"No, no, they're there. I go out and there's nothing. But the steps are haunted, Zelda! One voice says: 'Here's another fine mess you got us in.' You got to *hear* that man's voice!"

"You're drunk and doing this because you know I'm a nut for them."

"No, no. Come, Zelda. Listen. Tell!"

Maybe half an hour later, Bella heard the old tin lizzie rattle up the alley behind the apartments. It was a car Zelda, in her joy at visiting silent movie theaters, had bought to lug herself around in while she wrote about the past, always the past, and steaming into Cecil B. DeMille's old place or circling Harold Lloyd's nation-state, or cranking and banging around the Universal back-lot, paying her respects to the Phantom's opera stage, or sitting on Ma and Pa Kettle's porch chewing a sandwich lunch. That was Zelda, who once wrote in a silent country in a silent time for *Silver Screen*.

Zelda lumbered across the front porch a huge body with legs as big as the Bemini columns out front of St. Peter's in Rome, and a face like a harvest moon.

On that round face now was suspicion, cynicism, skepticism, in equal pie-parts. But when she saw Bella's pale stare she cried:

"Bella!"

"You *see*, I'm *not* lying!" said Bella.

"I *see!*"

"Keep your voice down, Zelda. Oh, it's scary and strange, terrible and nice. So come on."

And the two women edged along the walk to the rim of the old hill near the old steps in old Hollywood and suddenly as they moved they felt time take a half turn around them and it was another year, because nothing had changed, all the buildings were the way they were in 1928 and the hills beyond like they were in 1926 and the steps, just the way they were when the cement was poured in 1921.

"Listen, Zelda. *There!*"

And Zelda listened and at first there was only a creaking of wheels down in the dark, like crickets, and then a moan of wood and a hum of piano strings, and then one voice lamenting about this job, and the other voice claiming he had nothing to do with it, and then the thumps as two derby hats fell, and an exasperated voice announced:

"Here's *another* fine mess you've got us in."

Zelda, stunned, almost toppled off the hill. She held tight to Bella's arm as tears brimmed in her eyes.

"It's a trick. Someone's got a tape recorder or—"

"No, I checked. Nothing but the steps, Zelda, the steps!"

Tears rolled down Zelda's plump cheeks.

"Oh, God, that *is* his voice! I'm the expert, I'm the mad fanatic, Bella. That's Ollie. And that other voice, Stan! And you're not nuts after all!"

The voices below rose and fell and one cried: "Why don't you do something to *help* me?"

Zelda moaned. "Oh, God, it's so *beautiful*."

"What does it mean?" asked Bella. "Why are they here? Are they really ghosts, and why would ghosts climb this hill every night, pushing that music box, night on night, tell me, Zelda, why?"

Zelda peered down the hill and shut her eyes a moment to think. "Why do *any* ghosts go anywhere? Retribution? Revenge? No, not *those* two. Love maybe's the reason, lost loves or something. *Yes?*"

Bella let her heart pound once or twice and then said, "Maybe nobody *told* them."

"Told them *what?*"

"Or maybe they were told a lot but still didn't believe because maybe in their old years things got bad, I mean they were sick, and sometimes when you're sick you forget."

"Forget *what!?*"

"How much we loved them."

"They *knew!*"

"*Did* they? Sure, we told each other, but maybe not enough of us ever wrote or waved when they passed and just yelled 'love!' you think?"

"Hell, Bella, they're on TV every *night!*"

"Yeah, but that don't count. Has anyone, since they left us, come here to these steps and *said?* Maybe those voices down there, ghosts or whatever, have been here every night for years, pushing that music box, and nobody thought, or tried, to just whisper or yell all the love we had all the years. Why not?"

"Why not?" Zelda stared down into the long darkness where perhaps shadows moved and maybe a piano lurched clumsily between the shadows. "You're right."

"If I'm right," said Bella, "and you say so, there's only one thing to do—"

"You mean you and *me?*"

"Who else? Quiet. Come on."

They moved down a step. In the same instant lights came on around them, in a window here, another there. A screen door opened somewhere and angry words shot out in the night:

"Hey, what's going *on?*"

"Pipe down!"

"You know what *time* it is?"

"My God," Bella whispered, "everyone *else* hears now!"

"No, no," Zelda looked around, wildly. "They'll spoil every-thing!"

"I'm calling the cops!" A window slammed.

"God," said Bella, "if the cops come—"

"What?"

"It'll be all wrong. If anyone's going to tell them to take it easy, pipe down, it's gotta be us. We *care*, don't we?"

"God, yes, but—"

"No buts. Grab on. Here we go."

The two voices murmured below and the piano tuned itself with hiccoughs of sound as they edged down another step and another, their mouths dry, hearts hammering and the night so dark they could only see the faint street light at the stair bottom, the single street illumination so far away it was sad being there all by itself, waiting for shadows to move.

More windows slammed up, more screen doors opened. At any moment there would be an avalanche of protest, incredible outcries, perhaps shots fired, and all this gone forever.

Thinking this, the women trembled and held tight, as if to pummel each other to speak against the rage.

"Say something, Zelda, quick."

"*What?*"

"Anything! They'll get hurt if we don't—"

"*They?*"

"You know what I mean. Save them."

"Okay. Jesus!" Zelda froze, clamped her eyes shut to find the words then opened her eyes and said, "Hello."

"Louder."

"Hello," Zelda called softly, then loudly.

Shapes rustled in the dark below. One of the voices rose while the other fell and the piano strummed its hidden harpstrings.

"Don't be afraid," Zelda called.

"That's good. Go on."

"Don't be afraid," Zelda called, braver now. "Don't listen to those others yelling. We won't hurt you. It's just us. I'm Zelda, you wouldn't remember, and this here is Bella, and we've known you forever, or since we were kids, and we love you. It's late, but we thought you should know. We've loved you ever since you were in the desert or on that boat with ghosts or trying to sell Christmas trees door to door or in that traffic where you tore the headlights off cars, and we still love you, right, Bella?"

The night below was darkness, waiting.

Zelda punched Bella's arm.

"Yes!" Bella cried, "what she *said*. We love you."

"We can't think of anything else to say."

"But it's enough, yes?" Bella leaned forward, anxiously. "It's *enough*?"

A night wind stirred the leaves and grass around the stairs and the shadows below that had stopped moving with the music box suspended between them as they looked up and up at the two women who suddenly began to cry. First tears fell from Bella's cheeks and when Zelda sensed them, let fall her own.

"So now, said Zelda, amazed that she could form words but managed to speak anyway," we want you to know, you don't have to come back anymore. You don't have to climb the hill every night, waiting. For what we said just now is it, isn't it? I mean you wanted to hear it here on this hill, with those steps, and that piano, yes, that's the whole thing, it had to be that, didn't it? So now here we are and there you are and it's said. So rest, dear friends."

"Oh there, Ollie," added Bella, in a sad sad whisper. "Oh Stan, Stanley."

The piano, hidden in the dark, softly hummed its wires and creaked its ancient wood.

And then the most incredible thing happened. There was a series of shouts and then a huge banging crash as the music box, in the dark, rocketed down the hill skittering on the steps, playing chords where it hit, swerving, rushing and ahead of it, running, the two shapes pursued by the musical beast, yelling, tripping, shouting, warning the Fates, crying out to the gods, down and down, forty, sixty, eighty, one hundred steps.

And half down the steps, hearing, feeling, shouting, crying themselves, and now laughing and holding to each other, the two women alone in the night wildly clutching, grasping, trying to see, almost sure that they *did* see, the three things ricocheting off and away, the two shadows rushing, one fat, one thin, and the piano blundering after, discordant and mindless, until they reached the street where, instantly, the one overhead street lamp died as if struck, and the shadows floundered on, pursued by the musical beast.

And the two women, abandoned, looked down, exhausted with laughing until they wept and weeping until they laughed, until suddenly Zelda got a terrible look on her face as if shot.

"My God!" she shouted in panic, reaching out. "Wait. We didn't mean, we don't want—don't go *forever!* Sure, go, so the neighbors here sleep. But once a year, you *hear?* Once a year, one night a year from tonight, and every year after that, come back. It shouldn't bother anyone so much. But we got to tell you all over again, huh? Come back and bring the box with you, and we'll be here waiting, won't we, Bella?"

"Waiting, yes."

There was a long silence from the steps leading down into an old black-and-white silent Los Angeles.

"You think they *heard?*"

They listened.

And from somewhere far off and down there was the faintest explosion like the engine of an old jalopy knocking itself to life, and then the merest whisper of a lunatic music from a dark theater when they were very young. It faded.

After a long while they climbed back up the steps, dabbing at their eyes with wet Kleenex. Then they turned for a final time to stare down into the night.

"You know something?" said Zelda. "I think they *heard.*"

Solitude

URSULA K. LE GUIN

*One of America's most prominent storytellers, Ursula Le
Guin has been honored with numerous Hugo and Nebula
awards (including one of the latter for this story), and she was
recently given the World Fantasy Award for Life
Achievement. Among her many books are* The Dispossessed,
The Left Hand of Darkness, A Wizard of Earthsea, *and
recent collections include* Four Ways to Forgiveness *and* A
Fisherman of the Inland Sea. *It's no secret that her parents
were prominent anthropologists (in fact, her mother's book*
Ishi *is considered a classic). "Solitude" seems to draw on some
experiences of growing up exposed to other cultures, and the
results are wonderful.*

*An addition to "POVERTY: The Second Report on Eleven-Soro" by
Mobile Entselenne'temharyonoterregwis Leaf, by her daughter, Serenity.*

MY MOTHER, A FIELD ETHNOLOGIST, TOOK THE DIFFICULTY OF
learning anything about the people of Eleven-Soro as a personal
challenge. The fact that she used her children to meet that challenge might be seen as selfishness or as selflessness. Now that I
have read her report I know that she finally thought she had done
wrong. Knowing what it cost her, I wish she knew my gratitude
to her for allowing me to grow up as a person.

Shortly after a robot probe reported people of the Hainish
Descent on the eleventh planet of the Soro system, she joined the
orbital crew as backup for the three First Observers down onplanet. She had spent four years in the tree-cities of nearby Huthu.

My brother In Joy Born was eight years old and I was five; she wanted a year or two of ship duty so we could spend some time in a Hainish-style school. My brother had enjoyed the rain forests of Huthu very much, but though he could brachiate he could barely read, and we were all bright blue with skin-fungus. While Borny learned to read and I learned to wear clothes and we all had antifungus treatments, my mother became as intrigued by Eleven-Soro as the Observers were frustrated by it.

All this is in her report, but I will say it as I learned it from her, which helps me remember and understand. The language had been recorded by the probe and the Observers had spent a year learning it. The many dialectical variations excused their accents and errors, and they reported that language was not a problem. Yet there was a communication problem. The two men found themselves isolated, faced with suspicion or hostility, unable to form any connection with the native men, all of whom lived in solitary houses as hermits or in pairs. Finding communities of adolescent males, they tried to make contact with them, but when they entered the territory of such a group the boys either fled or rushed desperately at them trying to kill them. The women, who lived in what they called "dispersed villages," drove them away with volleys of stones as soon as they came anywhere near the houses. "I believe," one of them reported, "that the only community activity of the Sorovians is throwing rocks at men."

Neither of them succeeded in having a conversation of more than three exchanges with a man. One of them mated with a woman who came by his camp; he reported that though she made unmistakable and insistent advances, she seemed disturbed by his attempts to converse, refused to answer his questions, and left him, he said, "as soon as she got what she came for."

The woman Observer was allowed to settle in an unused house in a "village" (auntring) of seven houses. She made excellent observations of daily life, insofar as she could see any of it, and had several conversations with adult women and many with children; but she found that she was never asked into another woman's house, nor expected to help or ask for help in any work. Conversation concerning normal activities was unwelcome to the other women; the children, her only informants, called her Aunt Crazy-Jabber. Her aberrant behavior caused increasing distrust and dislike among the women, and they began to keep their children away from her. She left. "There's no way," she told my mother, "for an adult to learn anything. They don't ask questions, they don't answer questions. Whatever they learn, they learn when they're children."

Aha! said my mother to herself, looking at Borny and me. And she requested a family transfer to Eleven-Soro with Observer status. The Stabiles interviewed her extensively by ansible, and talked with Borny and even with me—I don't remember it, but she told me I told the Stabiles all about my new stockings—and agreed to her request. The ship was to stay in close orbit, with the previous Observers in the crew, and she was to keep radio contact with it, daily if possible.

I have a dim memory of the tree-city, and of playing with what must have been a kitten or a ghole-kit on the ship; but my first clear memories are of our house in the auntring. It is half underground, half aboveground, with wattle-and-daub walls. Mother and I are standing outside it in the warm sunshine. Between us is a big mudpuddle, into which Borny pours water from a basket; then he runs off to the creek to get more water. I muddle the mud with my hands, deliciously, till it is thick and smooth. I pick up a big double handful and slap it onto the walls where the sticks show through. Mother says, "That's good! That's right!" in our new language, and I realize that this is work, and I am doing it. I am repairing the house. I am making it right, doing it right. I am a competent person.

I have never doubted that, so long as I lived there.

We are inside the house at night, and Borny is talking to the ship on the radio, because he misses talking the old language, and anyway he is supposed to tell them stuff. Mother is making a basket and swearing at the split reeds. I am singing a song to drown out Borny so nobody in the auntring hears him talking funny, and anyway I like singing. I learned this song this afternoon in Hyuru's house. I play every day with Hyuru. "Be aware, listen, listen, be aware," I sing. When Mother stops swearing she listens, and then she turns on the recorder. There is a little fire still left from cooking dinner, which was lovely pigi root; I never get tired of pigi. It is dark and warm and smells of pigi and of burning duhur, which is a strong, sacred smell to drive out magic and bad feelings, and as I sing "Listen, be aware," I get sleepier and sleepier and lean against Mother, who is dark and warm and smells like Mother, strong and sacred, full of good feelings.

Our daily life in the auntring was repetitive. On the ship, later, I learned that people who live in artificially complicated situations call such a life "simple." I never knew anybody, anywhere I have been, who found life simple. I think a life or a time looks simple when you leave out the details, the way a planet looks smooth, from orbit.

Certainly our life in the auntring was easy, in the sense that our needs came easily to hand. There was plenty of food to be gathered or grown and prepared and cooked, plenty of temas to pick and rett and spin and weave for clothes and bedding, plenty of reeds to make baskets and thatch with; we children had other children to play with, mothers to look after us, and a great deal to learn. None of this is simple, though it's all easy enough, when you know how to do it, when you are aware of the details.

It was not easy for my mother. It was hard for her, and complicated. She had to pretend she knew the details while she was learning them, and had to think how to report and explain this way of living to people in another place who didn't understand it. For Borny it was easy until it got hard because he was a boy. For me it was all easy. I learned the work and played with the children and listened to the mothers sing.

The First Observer had been quite right: there was no way for a grown woman to learn how to make her soul. Mother couldn't go listen to another mother sing, it would have been too strange. The aunts all knew she hadn't been brought up well, and some of them taught her a good deal without her realizing it. They had decided her mother must have been irresponsible and had gone on scouting instead of settling in an auntring, so that her daughter didn't get educated properly. That's why even the most aloof of the aunts always let me listen with their children, so that I could become an educated person. But of course they couldn't ask another adult into their houses. Borny and I had to tell her all the songs and stories we learned, and then she would tell them to the radio, or we told them to the radio while she listened to us. But she never got it right, not really. How could she, trying to learn it after she'd grown up, and after she'd always lived with magicians?

"Be aware!" she would imitate my solemn and probably irritating imitation of the aunts and the big girls. "Be aware! How many times a day do they say that? Be aware of *what?* They aren't aware of what the ruins are, their own history—they aren't aware of each other! They don't even talk to each other! Be aware, indeed!"

When I told her the stories of the Before Time that Aunt Sadne and Aunt Noyit told their daughters and me, she often heard the wrong things in them. I told her about the People, and she said, "Those are the ancestors of the people here now." When I said, "There aren't any people here now," she didn't understand. "There are persons here now," I said, but she still didn't understand.

Borny liked the story about the Man Who Lived with Women, how he kept some women in a pen, the way some persons keep rats in a pen for eating, and all of them got pregnant, and they each had a hundred babies, and the babies grew up as horrible monsters and ate the man and the mothers and each other. Mother explained to us that that was a parable of the human over-population of this planet thousands of years ago. "No, it's not," I said, "it's a moral story."—"Well, yes," Mother said. "The moral is, don't have too many babies."—"No, it's not," I said. "Who could have a hundred babies even if they wanted to? The man was a sorcerer. He did magic. The women did it with him. So of course their children were monsters."

The key, of course, is the word "tekell," which translates so nicely into the Hainish word "magic," an art or power that violates natural law. It was hard for Mother to understand that some persons truly consider most human relationships unnatural; that marriage, for instance, or government, can be seen as an evil spell woven by sorcerers. It is hard for her people to believe magic.

The ship kept asking if we were all right, and every now and then a Stabile would hook up the ansible to our radio and grill Mother and us. She always convinced them that she wanted to stay, for despite her frustrations, she was doing the work the First Observers had not been able to do, and Borny and I were happy as mudfish, all those first years. I think Mother was happy, too, once she got used to the slow pace and the indirect way she had to learn things. She was lonely, missing other grown-ups to talk to, and told us that she would have gone crazy without us. If she missed sex she never showed it. I think, though, that her Report is not very complete about sexual matters, perhaps because she was troubled by them. I know that when we first lived in the auntring, two of the aunts, Hedimi and Behyu, used to meet to make love, and Behyu courted my mother; but Mother didn't understand, because Behyu wouldn't talk the way Mother wanted to talk. She couldn't understand having sex with a person whose house you wouldn't enter.

Once when I was nine or so, and had been listening to some of the older girls, I asked her why didn't she go out scouting. "Aunt Sadne would look after us," I said hopefully. I was tired of being the uneducated woman's daughter. I wanted to live in Aunt Sadne's house and be just like the other children.

"Mothers don't scout," she said scornfully, like an aunt.

"Yes, they do, sometimes," I insisted. "They have to, or how could they have more than one baby?"

"They go to settled men near the auntring. Behyu went back to the Red Knob Hill Man when she wanted a second child. Sadne goes and sees Downriver Lame Man when she wants to have sex. They know the men around here. None of the mothers scout."

I realized that in this case she was right and I was wrong, but I stuck to my point. "Well, why don't you go see Downriver Lame Man? Don't you ever want sex? Migi says she wants it all the time."

"Migi is seventeen," Mother said drily. "Mind your own nose." She sounded exactly like all the other mothers.

Men, during my childhood, were a kind of uninteresting mystery to me. They turned up a lot in the Before Time stories, and the singing-circle girls talked about them; but I seldom saw any of them. Sometimes I'd glimpse one when I was foraging, but they never came near the auntring. In summer the Downriver Lame Man would get lonesome waiting for Aunt Sadne and would come lurking around, not very far from the auntring—not in the bush or down by the river, of course, where he might be mistaken for a rogue and stoned—but out in the open, on the hillsides, where we could all see who he was. Hyuru and Didsu, Aunt Sadne's daughters, said she had sex with him when she went out scouting the first time, and always had sex with him and never tried any of the other men of the settlement.

She had told them, too, that the first child she bore was a boy, and she drowned it, because she didn't want to bring up a boy and send him away. They felt queer about that and so did I, but it wasn't an uncommon thing. One of the stories we learned was about a drowned boy who grew up underwater, and seized his mother when she came to bathe, and tried to hold her under till she too drowned; but she escaped.

At any rate, after the Downriver Lame Man had sat around for several days on the hillsides, singing long songs and braiding and unbraiding his hair, which was long, too, and shone black in the sun, Aunt Sadne always went off for a night or two with him, and came back looking cross and self-conscious.

Aunt Noyit explained to me that Downriver Lame Man's songs were magic; not the usual bad magic, but what she called the great good spells. Aunt Sadne never could resist his spells. "But he hasn't half the charm of some men I've known," said Aunt Noyit, smiling reminiscently.

Our diet, though excellent, was very low in fat, which Mother thought might explain the rather late onset of puberty; girls seldom menstruated before they were fifteen, and boys often weren't mature till they were considerably older than that. But the women began looking askance at boys as soon as they showed any signs at all of adolescence. First Aunt Hedimi, who was always grim, then Aunt Noyit, then even Aunt Sadne began to turn away from Borny, to leave him out, not answering when he spoke. "What are you doing playing with the children?" old Aunt Dnemi asked him so fiercely that he came home in tears. He was not quite fourteen.

Sadne's younger daughter Hyuru was my soulmate, my best friend, you would say. Her elder sister Didsu, who was in the singing circle now, came and talked to me one day, looking serious. "Borny is very handsome," she said. I agreed proudly.

"Very big, very strong," she said, "stronger than I am."

I agreed proudly again, and then I began to back away from her.

"I'm not doing magic, Ren," she said.

"Yes you are," I said. "I'll tell your mother!"

Didsu shook her head. "I'm trying to speak truly. If my fear causes your fear, I can't help it. It has to be so. We talked about it in the singing circle. I don't like it," she said, and I knew she meant it; she had a soft face, soft eyes, she had always been the gentlest of us children. "I wish he could be a child," she said. "I wish I could. But we can't."

"Go be a stupid old woman, then," I said, and ran away from her. I went to my secret place down by the river and cried. I took the holies out of my soulbag and arranged them. One holy—it doesn't matter if I tell you—was a crystal that Borny had given me, clear at the top, cloudy purple at the base. I held it a long time and then I gave it back. I dug a hole under a boulder, and wrapped the holy in duhur leaves inside a square of cloth I tore out of my kilt, beautiful, fine cloth Hyuru had woven and sewn for me. I tore the square right from the front, where it would show. I gave the crystal back, and then sat a long time there near it. When I went home I said nothing of what Didsu had said. But Borny was very silent, and my mother had a worried look. "What have you done to your kilt, Ren?" she asked. I raised my head a little and did not answer; she started to speak again, and then did not. She had finally learned not to talk to a person who chose to be silent.

Borny didn't have a soulmate, but he had been playing more and more often with the two boys nearest his age, Ednede who was a year or two older, a slight, quiet boy, and Bit who was only eleven, but boisterous and reckless. The three of them went off somewhere all the time. I hadn't paid much attention, partly because I was glad to be rid of Bit. Hyuru and I had been practicing being aware, and it was tiresome to always have to be aware of Bit yelling and jumping around. He never could leave anyone quiet, as if their quietness took something from him. His mother, Hedimi, had educated him, but she wasn't a good singer or storyteller like Sadne and Noyit, and Bit was too restless to listen even to them. Whenever he saw me and Hyuru trying to slow-walk or sitting being aware, he hung around making noise till we got mad and told him to go, and then he jeered, "Dumb girls!"

I asked Borny what he and Bit and Ednede did, and he said, "Boy stuff."

"Like what?"

"Practicing."

"Being aware?"

After a while he said, "No."

"Practicing what, then?"

"Wrestling. Getting strong. For the boygroup." He looked gloomy, but after a while he said, "Look," and showed me a knife he had hidden under his mattress. "Ednede says you have to have a knife, then nobody will challenge you. Isn't it a beauty?" It was metal, old metal from the People, shaped like a reed, pounded out and sharpened down both edges, with a sharp point. A piece of polished flintshrub wood had been bored and fitted on the handle to protect the hand. "I found it in an empty man's-house," he said. "I made the wooden part." He brooded over it lovingly. Yet he did not keep it in his soulbag.

"What do you *do* with it?" I asked, wondering why both edges were sharp, so you'd cut your hand if you used it.

"Keep off attackers," he said.

"Where was the empty man's-house?"

"Way over across Rocky Top."

"Can I go with you if you go back?"

"No," he said, not unkindly, but absolutely.

"What happened to the man? Did he die?"

"There was a skull in the creek. We think he slipped and drowned."

He didn't sound quite like Borny. There was something in his voice like a grown-up; melancholy; reserved. I had gone to him for reassurance, but came away more deeply anxious. I went to Mother and asked her, "What do they do in the boygroups?"

"Perform natural selection," she said, not in my language but in hers, in a strained tone. I didn't always understand Hainish anymore and had no idea what she meant, but the tone of her voice upset me; and to my horror I saw she had begun to cry silently. "We have to move, Serenity," she said—she was still talking Hainish without realizing it. "There isn't any reason why a family can't move, is there? Women just move in and move out as they please. Nobody cares what anybody does. Nothing is anybody's business. Except hounding the boys out of town!"

I understood most of what she said, but got her to say it in my language; and then I said, "But anywhere we went, Borny would be the same age, and size, and everything."

"Then we'll leave," she said fiercely. "Go back to the ship."

I drew away from her. I had never been afraid of her before: she had never used magic on me. A mother has great power, but there is nothing unnatural in it, unless it is used against the child's soul.

Borny had no fear of her. He had his own magic. When she told him she intended leaving, he persuaded her out of it. He wanted to go join the boygroup, he said; he'd been wanting to for a year now. He didn't belong in the auntring anymore, all women and girls and little kids. He wanted to go live with other boys. Bit's older brother Yit was a member of the boygroup in the Four Rivers Territory, and would look after a boy from his auntring. And Ednede was getting ready to go. And Borny and Ednede and Bit had been talking to some men recently. Men weren't all ignorant and crazy, the way Mother thought. They didn't talk much, but they knew a lot.

"What do they know?" Mother asked grimly

"They know how to be men," Borny said. "It's what I'm going to be."

"Not that kind of man—not if I can help it! In Joy Born, you must remember the men on the ship, real men—nothing like these poor, filthy hermits. I can't let you grow up thinking that that's what you have to be!"

"They're not like that," Borny said. "You ought to go talk to some of them, Mother."

"Don't be naive," she said with an edgy laugh. "You know perfectly well that women don't go to men to *talk*."

I knew she was wrong; all the women in the auntring knew all the settled men for three days' walk around. They did talk with them, when they were out foraging. They only kept away from the ones they didn't trust; and usually those men disappeared before long. Noyit had told me, "Their magic turns on them." She meant the other men drove them away or killed them. But I didn't say any of this, and Borny said only, "Well, Cave Cliff Man is really nice. And he took us to the place where I found those People things"—some ancient artifacts that Mother had been excited about. "The men know things the women don't," Borny went on. "At least I could go to the boygroup for a while, maybe. I ought to. I could learn a lot! We don't have any solid information on them at all. All we know anything about is this auntring. I'll go and stay long enough to get material for our report. I can't ever come back to either the auntring or the boygroup once I leave them. I'll have to go to the ship, or else try to be a man. So let me have a real go at it, please, Mother?"

"I don't know why you think you have to learn how to be a man," she said after a while. "You know how already."

He really smiled then, and she put her arm around him.

What about me? I thought. I don't even know what the ship is. I want to be here, where my soul is. I want to go on learning to be in the world.

But I was afraid of Mother and Borny, who were both working magic, and so I said nothing and was still, as I had been taught.

Ednede and Borny went off together. Noyit, Ednede's mother, was as glad as Mother was about their keeping company, though she said nothing. The evening before they left, the two boys went to every house in the auntring. It took a long time. The houses were each just within sight or hearing of one or two of the others, with bush and gardens and irrigation ditches and paths in between. In each house the mother and the children were waiting to say good-bye, only they didn't say it; my language has no word for hello or good-bye. They asked the boys in and gave them something to eat, something they could take with them on the way to the Territory. When the boys went to the door everybody in the household came and touched their hand or cheek. I remembered when Yit had gone around the auntring that way. I had cried then, because even though I didn't much like Yit, it seemed so strange for somebody to leave forever, like they were dying. This time I didn't cry; but I kept waking and waking again, until I heard Borny get up before the first light and pick up his things and leave quietly. I know Mother was awake, too, but we did as we should do, and lay still while he left, and for a long time after.

I have read her description of what she calls "An adolescent male leaves the Auntring: a vestigial survival of ceremony."

She had wanted him to put a radio in his soulbag and get in

touch with her at least occasionally. He had been unwilling. "I want to do it right, Mother. There's no use doing it if I don't do it right."

"I simply can't handle not hearing from you at all, Borny," she had said in Hainish.

"But if the radio got broken or taken or something, you'd worry a lot more, maybe with no reason at all."

She finally agreed to wait half a year, till the first rain; then she would go to a landmark, a huge ruin near the river that marked the southern end of the Territory, and he would try and come to her there. "But only wait ten days," he said. "If I can't come, I can't." She agreed. She was like a mother with a little baby, I thought, saying yes to everything. That seemed wrong to me; but I thought Borny was right. Nobody ever came back to their mother from boygroup.

But Borny did.

Summer was long, clear, beautiful. I was learning to starwatch; that is when you lie down outside on the open hills in the dry season at night, and find a certain star in the eastern sky, and watch it cross the sky till it sets. You can look away, of course, to rest your eyes, and doze, but you try to keep looking back at the star and the stars around it, until you feel the earth turning, until you become aware of how the stars and the world and the soul move together. After the certain star sets you sleep until dawn wakes you. Then as always you greet the sunrise with aware silence. I was very happy on the hills those warm great nights, those clear dawns. The first time or two Hyuru and I starwatched together, but after that we went alone, and it was better alone.

I was coming back from such a night, along the narrow valley between Rocky Top and Over Home Hill in the first sunlight, when a man came crashing through the bush down onto the path and stood in front of me. "Don't be afraid," he said. "Listen!" He was heavyset, half naked; he stank. I stood still as a stick. He had said "Listen!" just as the aunts did, and I listened. "Your brother and his friend are all right. Your mother shouldn't go there. Some of the boys are in a gang. They'd rape her. I and some others are killing the leaders. It takes a while. Your brother is with the other gang. He's all right. Tell her. Tell me what I said."

I repeated it word for word, as I had learned to do when I listened.

"Right. Good," he said, and took off up the steep slope on his short, powerful legs, and was gone.

Mother would have gone to the Territory right then, but I told the man's message to Noyit, too, and she came to the porch of our house to speak to Mother. I listened to her, because she was telling things I didn't know well and Mother didn't know at all. Noyit was a small, mild woman, very like her son Ednede; she liked teaching and singing, so the children were always around her place. She saw Mother was getting ready for a journey. She said, "House on the Skyline Man says the boys are all right." When she saw Mother wasn't listening, she went on; she pretended to be talking to me, because women don't teach women: "He says some of the men are breaking up the gang. They do that, when the boygroups get wicked. Sometimes there are magicians among them, leaders, older boys, even men who want to make a gang. The settled men will kill the magicians and make sure none of the boys gets hurt. When gangs come out of the Territories, nobody is safe. The settled men don't like that. They see to it that the auntring is safe. So your brother will be all right."

My mother went on packing pigi-roots into her net.

"A rape is a very, very bad thing for the settled men," said Noyit to me. "It means the women won't come to them. If the boys raped some woman, probably the men would kill *all* the boys."

My mother was finally listening.

She did not go to the rendezvous with Borny, but all through the rainy season she was utterly miserable. She got sick, and old Dnemi sent Didsu over to dose her with gagberry syrup. She made notes while she was sick, lying on her mattress, about illnesses and medicines and how the older girls had to look after sick women, since grown women did not enter one another's houses. She never stopped working and never stopped worrying about Borny.

Late in the rainy season, when the warm wind had come and the yellow honey-flowers were in bloom on all the hills, the Golden World time, Noyit came by while Mother was working in the garden. "House on the Skyline Man says things are all right in the boygroup," she said, and went on.

Mother began to realize then that although no adult ever entered another's house, and adults seldom spoke to one another, and men and women had only brief, often casual relationships, and men lived all their lives in real solitude, still there was a kind of community, a wide, thin, fine network of delicate and certain intention and restraint: a social order. Her reports to the ship were filled with this new understanding. But she still found Sorovian life impoverished, seeing these persons as mere survivors, poor fragments of the wreck of something great.

"My dear," she said—in Hainish; there is no way to say "my dear" in my language. She was speaking Hainish with me in the house so that I wouldn't forget it entirely.—"My dear, the explanation of an uncomprehended technology as magic *is* primitivism. It's not a criticism, merely a description."

"But technology isn't magic," I said.

"Yes, it is, in their minds; look at the story you just recorded. Before-Time sorcerers who could fly in the air and undersea and underground in magic boxes!"

"In *metal* boxes," I corrected.

"In other words, airplanes, tunnels, submarines; a lost technology explained as supernatural."

"The *boxes* weren't magic," I said. "The *people* were. They were sorcerers. They used their power to get power over other persons. To live rightly a person has to keep away from magic."

"That's a cultural imperative, because a few thousand years ago uncontrolled technological expansion led to disaster. Exactly. There's a perfectly rational reason for the irrational taboo."

I did not know what "rational" and "irrational" meant in my language; I could not find words for them. "Taboo" was the same as "poisonous." I listened to my mother because a daughter must learn from her mother, and my mother knew many, many things no other person knew; but my education was very difficult, sometimes. If only there were more stories and songs in her teaching, and not so many words, words that slipped away from me like water through a net!

The Golden Time passed, and the beautiful summer; the Silver Time returned, when the mists lie in the valleys between the hills, before the rains begin; and the rains began, and fell long and slow and warm, day after day after day. We had heard nothing of

Borny and Ednede for over a year. Then in the night the soft thrum of rain on the reed roof turned into a scratching at the door and a whisper, "Shh—it's all right—it's all right."

We wakened the fire and crouched at it in the dark to talk. Borny had got tall and very thin, like a skeleton with the skin dried on it. A cut across his upper lip had drawn it up into a kind of snarl that bared his teeth, and he could not say p, b, or m. His voice was a man's voice. He huddled at the fire trying to get warmth into his bones. His clothes were wet rags. The knife hung on a cord around his neck. "It was all right," he kept saying. "I don't want to go on there, though."

He would not tell us much about the year and a half in the boygroup, insisting that he would record a full description when he got to the ship. He did tell us what he would have to do if he stayed on Soro. He would have to go back to the Territory and hold his own among the older boys, by fear and sorcery, always proving his strength, until he was old enough to walk away—that is, to leave the Territory and wander alone till he found a place where the men would let him settle. Ednede and another boy had paired, and were going to walk away together when the rains stopped. It was easier for a pair, he said, if their bond was sexual; so long as they offered no competition for women, settled men wouldn't challenge them. But a new man in the region anywhere within three days' walk of an auntring had to prove himself against the settled men there. "It would 'e three or four years of the same thing," he said, "challenging, fighting, always watching the others, on guard, showing how strong you are, staying alert all night, all day. To end up living alone your whole life. I can't do it." He looked at me. "I'ne not a 'erson," he said. "I want to go ho'e."

"I'll radio the ship now," Mother said quietly, with infinite relief.

"No," I said.

Borny was watching Mother, and raised his hand when she turned to speak to me.

"I'll go," he said. "She doesn't have to. Why should she?" Like me, he had learned not to use names without some reason to.

Mother looked from him to me and finally gave a kind of laugh. "I can't leave her here, Borny!"

"Why should you go?"

"Because I want to," she said. "I've had enough. More than enough. We've got a tremendous amount of material on the women, over seven years of it, and now you can fill the information gaps on the men's side. That's enough. It's time, past time, that we all got back to our own people. All of us."

"I have no people," I said. "I don't belong to people. I am trying to be a person. Why do you want to take me away from my soul? You want me to do magic! I won't. I won't do magic. I won't speak your language. I won't go with you!"

My mother was still not listening; she started to answer angrily. Borny put up his hand again, the way a woman does when she is going to sing, and she looked at him.

"We can talk later," he said. "We can decide. I need to sleep."

He hid in our house for two days while we decided what to do and how to do it. That was a miserable time. I stayed home as if I were sick so that I would not lie to the other persons, and Borny and Mother and I talked and talked. Borny asked Mother to stay with me; I asked her to leave me with Sadne or Noyit, either of whom would certainly take me into their household. She refused. She was the mother and I the child and her power was sacred. She radioed the ship and arranged for a lander to pick us up in a barren area two days' walk from the auntring. We left at night, sneaking away. I carried nothing but my soulbag. We walked all next day, slept a little when it stopped raining, walked on and came to the desert. The ground was all lumps and hollows and caves, Before-Time ruins; the soil was tiny bits of glass and hard grains and fragments, the way it is in the deserts. Nothing grew there. We waited there.

The sky broke open and a shining thing fell down and stood before us on the rocks, bigger than any house, though not as big as the ruins of the Before Time. My mother looked at me with a queer, vengeful smile. "Is it magic?" she said. And it was very hard for me not to think that it was. Yet I knew it was only a thing, and there is no magic in things, only in minds. I said nothing. I had not spoken since we left my home.

. . .

I HAD RESOLVED never to speak to anybody until I got home again; but I was still a child, used to listen and obey. In the ship, that utterly strange new world, I held out only for a few hours, and then began to cry and ask to go home. Please, please, can I go home now.

Everyone on the ship was very kind to me.

Even then I thought about what Borny had been through and what I was going through, comparing our ordeals. The difference seemed total. He had been alone, without food, without shelter, a frightened boy trying to survive among equally frightened rivals against the brutality of older youths intent on having and keeping power, which they saw as manhood. I was cared for, clothed, fed so richly I got sick, kept so warm I felt feverish, guided, reasoned with, praised, befriended by citizens of a very great city, offered a share in their power, which they saw as humanity. He and I had both fallen among sorcerers. Both he and I could see the good in the people we were among, but neither he nor I could live with them.

Borny told me he had spent many desolate nights in the Territory crouched in a fireless shelter, telling over the stories he had learned from the aunts, singing the songs in his head. I did the same thing every night on the ship. But I refused to tell the stories or sing to the people there. I would not speak my language there. It was the only way I had to be silent.

My mother was enraged, and for a long time unforgiving. "You owe your knowledge to our people," she said. I did not answer, because all I had to say was that they were not my people, that I had no people. I was a person. I had a language that I did not speak. I had my silence. I had nothing else.

I went to school; there were children of different ages on the ship, like an auntring, and many of the adults taught us. I learned Ekumenical history and geography, mostly, and Mother gave me a report to learn about the history of Eleven-Soro, what my language calls the Before Time. I read that the cities of my world had been the greatest cities ever built on any world, covering two of the continents entirely, with small areas set aside for farming; there had been 120 billion people living in the cities, while the animals and the sea and the air and the dirt died, until the people began dying, too. It was a hideous story. I was ashamed of it and wished nobody else on the ship or in the Ekumen knew about it. And yet, I thought, if they knew the stories I knew about the Before Time, they would understand how magic turns on itself, and that it must be so.

After less than a year, Mother told us we were going to Hain. The ship's doctor and his clever machines had repaired Borny's lip; he and Mother had put all the information they had into the records; he was old enough to begin training for the Ekumenical Schools, as he wanted to do. I was not flourishing, and the doctor's machines were not able to repair me. I kept losing weight, I slept badly, I had terrible headaches. Almost as soon as we came aboard the ship, I had begun to menstruate; each time the cramps were agonizing. "This is no good, this ship life," she said. "You need to be outdoors. On a planet. On a civilized planet."

"If I went to Hain," I said, "when I came back, the persons I know would all be dead hundreds of years ago."

"Serenity," she said, "you must stop thinking in terms of Soro. We have left Soro. You must stop deluding and tormenting yourself, and look forward, not back. You whole life is ahead of you. Hain is where you will learn to live it."

I summoned up my courage and spoke in my own language: "I am not a child now. You have no power over me. I will not go. Go without me. You have no power over me!"

Those are the words I had been taught to say to a magician, a sorcerer. I don't know if my mother fully understood them, but she did understand that I was deathly afraid of her, and it struck her into silence.

After a long time she said in Hainish, "I agree. I have no power over you. But I have certain rights: the right of loyalty; of love."

"Nothing is right that puts me in your power," I said, still in my language.

She stared at me. "You are like one of them," she said. "You are one of them. You don't know what love is. You're closed into yourself like a rock. I should never have taken you there. People crouching in the ruins of a society—brutal, rigid, ignorant, superstitious—each one in a terrible solitude—And I let them make you into one of them!"

"You educated me," I said, and my voice began to tremble and my mouth to shake around the words, "and so does the school here, but my aunts educated me, and I want to finish my education." I was weeping, but I kept standing with my hands clenched. "I'm not a woman yet. I want to be a woman."

"But, Ren, you will be!—ten times the woman you could ever be on Soro—you must try to understand, to believe me—"

"You have no power over me," I said, shutting my eyes and putting my hands over my ears. She came to me then and held me, but I stood stiff, enduring her touch, until she let me go.

The ship's crew had changed entirely while we were onplanet. The First Observers had gone on to other worlds; our backup was now a Gethenian archeologist named Arrem, a mild, watchful person, not young. Arrem had gone down onplanet only on the two desert continents, and welcomed the chance to talk with us, who had "lived with the living," as heshe said. I felt easy when I was with Arrem, who was so unlike anybody else. Arrem was not a man—I could not get used to having men around all the time—yet not a woman; and so not exactly an adult, yet not a child: a person, alone, like me. Heshe did not know my language well, but always tried to talk it with me. When this crisis came, Arrem came to my mother and took counsel with her, suggesting that she let me go back down onplanet. Borny was in on some of these talks, and told me about them.

"Arrem says if you go to Hain you'll probably die," he said. "Your soul will. Heshe says some of what we learned is like what they learn on Gethen, in their religion. That kind of stopped Mother from ranting about primitive superstition. . . . And Arrem says you could be useful to the Ekumen, if you stay and finish your education on Soro. You'll be an invaluable resource." Borny sniggered, and after a minute I did, too. "They'll mine you like an asteroid," he said. Then he said, "You know, if you stay and I go, we'll be dead."

That was how the young people of the ships said it, when one was going to cross the light-years and the other was going to stay. Good-bye, we're dead. It was the truth.

"I know," I said. I felt my throat get tight, and was afraid. I had never seen an adult at home cry, except when Sut's baby died. Sut howled all night. Howled like a dog, Mother said, but I had never seen or heard a dog; I heard a woman terribly crying. I was afraid of sounding like that. "If I can go home, when, I finish making my soul, who knows, I might come to Hain for a while," I said, in Hainish.

"Scouting?" Borny said in my language, and laughed, and made me laugh again.

Nobody gets to keep a brother. I knew that. But Borny had come back from being dead to me, so I might come back from being dead to him; at least I could pretend I might.

My mother came to a decision. She and I would stay on the ship for another year while Borny went to Hain. I would keep going to school; if at the end of the year I was still determined to go back onplanet, I could do so. With me or without me, she would go on to Hain then and join Borny. If I ever wanted to see them again, I could follow them. It was a compromise that satisfied no one, but it was the best we could do, and we all consented.

When he left, Borny gave me his knife.

After he left, I tried not to be sick. I worked hard at learning everything they taught me in the ship school, and I tried to teach Arrem how to be aware and how to avoid witchcraft. We did slow walking together in the ship's garden, and the first hour of the untrance movements from the Handdara of Karhide on Gethen. We agreed that they were alike.

The ship was staying in the Soro system not only because of my family, but because the crew was now mostly zoologists who had come to study a sea animal on Eleven-Soro, a kind of cephalopod that had mutated toward high intelligence, or maybe it already was highly intelligent; but there was a communication problem. "Almost as bad as with the local humans," said Steadiness, the zoologist who taught and teased us mercilessly. She took us down twice by lander to the uninhabited islands in the Northern Hemisphere where her station was. It was very strange to go down to my world and yet be a world away from my aunts and sisters and my soulmate; but I said nothing.

I saw the great, pale, shy creature come slowly up out of the deep waters with a running ripple of colors along its long coiling tentacles and a ringing shimmer of sound, all so quick it was over before you could follow the colors or hear the tune. The zoologist's machine produced a pink glow and a mechanically speeded-

up twitter, tinny and feeble in the immensity of the sea. The cephalopod patiently responded in its beautiful silvery shadowy language. "CP," Steadiness said to us, ironic—Communication
Problem. "We don't know what we're talking about."

I said, "I learned something in my education here. In one of
the songs, it says," and I hesitated, trying to translate it into Hainish, "it says, thinking is one way of doing, and words are one way
of thinking."

Steadiness stared at me, in disapproval I thought, but probably
only because I had never said anything to her before except "Yes."
Finally she said, "Are you suggesting that it doesn't speak in
words?"

"Maybe it's not speaking at all. Maybe it's thinking."

Steadiness stared at me some more and then said, "Thank
you." She looked as if she too might be thinking. I wished I could
sink into the water, the way the cephalopod was doing.

The other young people on the ship were friendly and man-
nerly. Those are words that have no translation in my language. I
was unfriendly and unmannerly, and they let me be. I was grateful.
But there was no place to be alone on the ship. Of course we each
had a room; though small, the *Heyho* was a Hainish-built explorer,
designed to give its people room and privacy and comfort and
variety and beauty while they hung around in a solar system for
years on end. But it was designed. It was all human-made—everything was human. I had much more privacy than I had ever had
at home in our one-room house; yet there I had been free and
here I was in a trap. I felt the pressure of people all around me,
all the time. People around me, people with me, people pressing
on me, pressing me to be one of them, to be one of them, one of
the people. How could I make my soul? I could barely cling to it.
I was in terror that I would lose it altogether.

One of the rocks in my soulbag, a little ugly gray rock that I
had picked up on a certain day in a certain place in the hills above
the river in the Silver Time, a little piece of my world, that became
my world. Every night I took it out and held it in my hand while
I lay in bed waiting to sleep, thinking of the sunlight on the hills
above the river, listening to the soft hushing of the ship's systems,
like a mechanical sea.

The doctor hopefully fed me various tonics. Mother and I ate breakfast together every morning. She kept at work, making our notes from all the years on Eleven-Soro into her report to the Ekumen, but I knew the work did not go well. Her soul was in as much danger as mine was.

"You will never give in, will you, Ren?" she said to me one morning out of the silence of our breakfast. I had not intended the silence as a message. I had only rested in it.

"Mother, I want to go home and you want to go home," I said. "Can't we?"

Her expression was strange for a moment, while she misunderstood me; then it cleared to grief, defeat, relief.

"Will we be dead?" she asked me, her mouth twisting.

"I don't know. I have to make my soul. Then I can know if I can come."

"You know I can't come back. It's up to you."

"I know. Go see Borny," I said. "Go home. Here we're both dying." Then noises began to come out of me, sobbing, howling. Mother was crying. She came to me and held me, and I could hold my mother, cling to her and cry with her, because her spell was broken.

FROM THE LANDER approaching I saw the oceans of Eleven-Soro, and in the greatness of my joy I thought that when I was grown and went out alone I would go to the seashore and watch the seabeasts shimmering their colors and tunes till I knew what they were thinking. I would listen, I would learn, till my soul was as large as the shining world. The scarred barrens whirled beneath us, ruins as wide as the continent, endless desolations. We touched down. I had my soulbag, and Borny's knife around my neck on its string, a communicator implant behind my right earlobe, and a medicine kit Mother had made for me. "No use dying of an infected finger, after all," she had said. The people on the lander said good-bye, but I forgot to. I set off out of the desert, home.

It was summer; the night was short and warm; I walked most of it. I got to the auntring about the middle of the second day. I went to my house cautiously, in case somebody had moved in while I was gone; but it was just as we had left it. The mattresses were moldy, and I put them and the bedding out in the sun, and started going over the garden to see what had kept growing by itself. The pigi had got small and seedy, but there were some good roots. A little boy came by and stared; he had to be Migi's baby. After a while Hyuru came by. She squatted down near me in the garden in the sunshine. I smiled when I saw her, and she smiled, but it took us a while to find something to say.

"Your mother didn't come back," she said.

"She's dead," I said.

"I'm sorry," Hyuru said.

She watched me dig up another root.

"Will you come to the singing circle?" she asked.

I nodded.

She smiled again. With her rosebrown skin and wide-set eyes, Hyuru had become very beautiful, but her smile was exactly the same as when we were little girls. "Hi, ya!" she sighed in deep contentment, lying down on the dirt with her chin on her arms. "This is good!"

I went on blissfully digging.

That year and the next two, I was in the singing circle with Hyuru and two other girls. Didsu still came to it often, and Han, a woman who settled in our auntring to have her first baby, joined it, too. In the singing circle the older girls pass around the stories, songs, knowledge they learned from their own mother, and young women who have lived in other auntrings teach what they learned there; so women make each other's souls, learning how to make their children's souls.

Han lived in the house where old Dnemi had died. Nobody in the auntring except Sut's baby had died while my family lived there. My mother had complained that she didn't have any data on death and burial. Sut had gone away with her dead baby and never came back, and nobody talked about it. I think that turned my mother against the others more than anything else. She was angry and ashamed that she could not go and try to comfort Sut and that nobody else did. "It is not human," she said. "It is pure animal behavior. Nothing could be clearer evidence that this is a broken culture—not a society, but the remains of one. A terrible, an appalling poverty."

I don't know if Dnemi's death would have changed her mind. Dnemi was dying for a long time, of kidney failure I think; she turned a kind of dark orange color, jaundice. While she could get around, nobody helped her. When she didn't come out of her house for a day or two, the women would send the children in with water and a little food and firewood. It went on so through the winter; then one morning little Rashi told his mother Aunt Dnemi was "staring." Several of the women went to Dnemi's house, and entered it for the first and last time. They sent for all the girls in the singing circle, so that we could learn what to do. We took turns sitting by the body or in the porch of the house, singing soft songs, child-songs, giving the soul a day and a night to leave the body and the house; then the older women wrapped the body in the bedding, strapped it on a kind of litter, and set off with it toward the barren lands. There it would be given back, under a rock cairn or inside one of the ruins of the ancient city. "Those are the lands of the dead," Sadne said. "What dies stays there."

Han settled down in that house a year later. When her baby began to be born she asked Didsu to help her, and Hyuru and I stayed in the porch and watched, so that we could learn. It was a wonderful thing to see, and quite altered the course of my thinking, and Hyuru's, too. Hyuru said, "I'd like to do that!" I said nothing, but thought, So do I, but not for a long time, because once you have a child you're never alone.

And though it is of the others, of relationships, that I write, the heart of my life has been my being alone.

I think there is no way to write about being alone. To write is to tell something to somebody, to communicate to others. CP, as Steadiness would say. Solitude is non-communication, the absence of others, the presence of a self sufficient to itself.

A woman's solitude in the auntring is, of course, based firmly on the presence of others at a little distance. It is a contingent, and therefore human, solitude. The settled men are connected as stringently to the women, though not to one another; the settlement is an integral though distant element of the auntring. Even a scouting woman is part of the society—a moving part, connecting the settled parts. Only the isolation of a woman or man who chooses to live outside the settlements is absolute. They are outside the network altogether. There are worlds where such persons are called saints, holy people. Since isolation is a sure way to prevent magic, on my world the assumption is that they are sorcerers, outcast by others or by their own will, their conscience.

I knew I was strong with magic, how could I help it? and I began to long to get away. It would be so much easier and safer to be alone. But at the same time, and increasingly, I wanted to know something about the great harmless magic, the spells cast between men and women.

I preferred foraging to gardening, and was out on the hills a good deal; and these days, instead of keeping away from the man's-houses, I wandered by them, and looked at them, and looked at the men if they were outside. The men looked back. Downriver Lame Man's long, shining hair was getting a little white in it now, but when he sat singing his long, long songs I found myself sitting down and listening, as if my legs had lost their bones. He was very handsome. So was the man I remembered as a boy named Tret in the auntring, when I was little, Behyu's son. He had come back from the boygroup and from wandering, and had built a house and made a fine garden in the valley of Red Stone Creek. He had a big nose and big eyes, long arms and legs, long hands; he moved very quietly, almost like Arrem doing the untrance. I went often to pick lowberries in Red Stone Creek valley.

He came along the path and spoke. "You were Borny's sister," he said. He had a low voice, quiet.

"He's dead," I said.

Red Stone Man nodded. "That's his knife."

In my world, I had never talked with a man. I felt extremely strange. I kept picking berries.

"You're picking green ones," Red Stone Man said.

His soft, smiling voice made my legs lose their bones again.

"I think nobody's touched you," he said. "I'd touch you gently. I think about it, about you, ever since you came by here early in the summer. Look, here's a bush full of ripe ones. Those are green. Come over here."

I came closer to him, to the bush of ripe berries.

When I was on the ship, Arrem told me that many languages have a single word for sexual desire and the bond between mother and child and the bond between soulmates and the feeling for one's home and worship of the sacred; they are all called love. There is no word that great in my language. Maybe my mother is right, and human greatness perished in my world with the people of the Before Time, leaving only small, poor, broken things and thoughts. In my language, love is many different words. I learned one of them with Red Stone Man. We sang it together to each other.

We made a brush house on a little cove of the creek, and neglected our gardens, but gathered many, many sweet berries.

Mother had put a lifetime's worth of nonconceptives in the little medicine kit. She had no faith in Sorovian herbals. I did, and they worked.

But when a year or so later, in the Golden Time, I decided to go out scouting, I thought I might go places where the right herbs were scarce; and so I stuck the little noncon jewel on the back of my left earlobe. Then I wished I hadn't, because it seemed like witchcraft. Then I told myself I was being superstitious; the noncon wasn't any more witchcraft than the herbs were, it just worked longer. I had promised my mother in my soul that I would never be superstitious. The skin grew over the noncon, and I took my soulbag and Borny's knife and the medicine kit, and set off across the world.

I had told Hyuru and Red Stone Man I would be leaving. Hyuru and I sang and talked together all one night down by the river. Red Stone Man said in his soft voice, "Why do you want to go?" and I said, "To get away from your magic, sorcerer," which was true in part. If I kept going to him I might always go to him. I wanted to give my soul and body a larger world to be in.

Now to tell of my scouting years is more difficult than ever. CP! A woman scouting is entirely alone, unless she chooses to ask a settled man for sex, or camps in an auntring for a while to sing and listen with the singing circle. If she goes anywhere near the territory of a boygroup, she is in danger; and if she comes on a rogue she is in danger; and if she hurts herself or gets into polluted country, she is in danger. She has no responsibility except to herself, and so much freedom is very dangerous.

In my right earlobe was the tiny communicator; every forty days, as I had promised, I sent a signal to the ship that meant "all well." If I wanted to leave, I would send another signal. I could have called for the lander to rescue me from a bad situation, but though I was in bad situations a couple of times I never thought of using it. My signal was the mere fulfillment of a promise to my mother and her people, the network I was no longer part of, a meaningless communication.

Life in the auntring, or for a settled man, is repetitive, as I said; and so it can be dull. Nothing new happens. The mind always wants new happenings. So for the young soul there is wandering and scouting, travel, danger, change. But of course travel and danger and change have their own dullness. It is finally always the same otherness over again; another hill, another river, another man, another day. The feet begin to turn in a long, long circle. The body begins to think of what it learned back home, when it learned to be still. To be aware. To be aware of the grain of dust beneath the sole of the foot, and the skin of the sole of the foot, and the touch and scent of the air on the cheek, and the fall and motion of the light across the air, and the color of the grass on the high hill across the river, and the thoughts of the body, of the soul, the shimmer and ripple of colors and sounds in the clear darkness of the depths, endlessly moving, endlessly changing, endlessly new.

So at last I came back home. I had been gone about four years.

Hyuru had moved into my old house when she left her mother's house. She had not gone scouting, but had taken to going to Red Stone Creek Valley; and she was pregnant. I was glad to see her living there. The only house empty was an old half ruined one too close to Hedimi's. I decided to make a new house. I dug out the circle as deep as my chest; the digging took most of the summer. I cut the sticks, braced and wove them, and then daubed the framework solidly with mud inside and out. I remembered when I had done that with my mother long, long ago, and how she had said, "That's right. That's good." I left the roof open, and the hot sun of late summer baked the mud into clay. Before the rains came, I thatched the house with reeds, a triple thatching, for I'd had enough of being wet all winter.

My auntring was more a string than a ring, stretching along the north bank of the river for about three kilos; my house lengthened the string a good bit, upstream from all the others. I could just see the smoke from Hyuru's fireplace. I dug it into a sunny slope with good drainage. It is still a good house.

I settled down. Some of my time went to gathering and gar-

dening and mending and all the dull, repetitive actions of primitive
life, and some went to singing and thinking the songs and stories
I had learned here at home and while scouting, and the things I
had learned on the ship, also. Soon enough I found why women
are glad to have children come to listen to them, for songs and
stories are meant to be heard, listened to. "Listen!" I would say
to the children. The children of the auntring came and went, like
the little fish in the river, one or two or five of them, little ones,
big ones. When they came, I sang or told stories to them. When
they left, I went on in silence. Sometimes I joined the singing circle
to give what I had learned traveling to the older girls. And that
was all I did; except that I worked, always, to be aware of all I did.

By solitude the soul escapes from doing or suffering magic; it
escapes from dullness, from boredom, by being aware. Nothing is
boring if you are aware of it. It may be irritating, but it is not
boring. If it is pleasant the pleasure will not fail so long as you are
aware of it. Being aware is the hardest work the soul can do, I
think.

I helped Hyuru have her baby, a girl, and played with the
baby. Then after a couple of years I took the noncon out of my
left earlobe. Since it left a little hole, I made the hole go all the
way through with a burnt needle, and when it healed I hung in it
a tiny jewel I had found in a ruin when I was scouting. I had seen
a man on the ship with a jewel hung in his ear that way. I wore it
when I went out foraging. I kept clear of Red Stone Valley. The
man there behaved as if he had a claim on me, a right to me. I
liked him still, but I did not like that smell of magic about him,
his imagination of power over me. I went up into the hills, north-
ward.

A pair of young men had settled in old North House about
the time I came home. Often boys got through boygroup by pair-
ing, and often they stayed paired when they left the Territory. It
helped their chances of survival. Some of them were sexually
paired, others weren't; some stayed paired, others didn't. One of
this pair had gone off with another man last summer. The one
that stayed wasn't a handsome man, but I had noticed him. He
had a kind of solidness I liked. His body and hands were short and
strong. I had courted him a little, but he was very shy. This day,
a day in the Silver Time when the mist lay on the river, he saw

the jewel swinging in my ear, and his eyes widened.

"It's pretty, isn't it?" I said.

He nodded.

"I wore it to make you look at me," I said.

He was so shy that I finally said, "If you only like sex with men, you know, just tell me." I really was not sure.

"Oh, no," he said, "no. No." He stammered and then bolted back down the path. But he looked back; and I followed him slowly, still not certain whether he wanted me or wanted to be rid of me.

He waited for me in front of a little house in a grove of red-root, a lovely little bower, all leaves outside, so that you would walk within arm's length of it and not see it. Inside he had laid sweet grass, deep and dry and soft, smelling of summer. I went in, crawling because the door was very low, and sat in the summer-smelling grass. He stood outside. "Come in," I said, and he came in very slowly.

"I made it for you," he said.

"Now make a child for me," I said.

And we did that; maybe that day, maybe another.

Now I will tell you why after all these years I called the ship, not knowing even if it was still there in the space between the planets, asking for the lander to meet me in the barren land.

When my daughter was born, that was my heart's desire and the fulfillment of my soul. When my son was born, last year, I knew there is no fulfillment. He will grow toward manhood, and go, and fight and endure, and live or die as a man must. My daughter, whose name is Yedneke, Leaf, like my mother, will grow to womanhood and go or stay as she chooses. I will live alone. This is as it should be, and my desire. But I am of two worlds; I am a person of this world, and a woman of my mother's people. I owe my knowledge to the children of her people. So I asked the lander to come, and spoke to the people on it. They gave me my mother's report to read, and I have written my story in their machine, making a record for those who want to learn one of the ways to make a soul. To them, to the children I say: Listen! Avoid magic! Be aware!